VILLAIN

CARO SAVAGE

Boldwood

First published in Great Britain in 2020 by Boldwood Books Ltd.

A CIP catalogue record for this book is available from the British Library.

Paperback ISBN 978-1-83889-287-6

Large Print ISBN 978-1-83889-792-5

Ebook ISBN 978-1-83889-289-0

Kindle ISBN 978-1-83889-288-3

Audio CD ISBN 978-1-83889-285-2

MP3 CD ISBN 978-1-83889-789-5

Digital audio download ISBN 978-1-83889-286-9

Boldwood Books Ltd
23 Bowerdean Street
London SW6 3TN
www.boldwoodbooks.com

For CPC

1

It was an exceptionally cold winter's evening in Chiswick in West London. Cold enough to freeze the balls off a brass monkey. Colder than the hinges of hell. Colder than a witch's tit. Colder than a bucket of snowman's piss. Colder than...

The homeless man lying in the doorway tried to recall yet some further expression for the cold weather. He was playing this little game in an attempt to distract himself from the icy chill that was biting through to the very marrow of his bones.

Shivering, he huddled deeper into his sleeping bag, which he had additionally cocooned with sheets of newspaper and bits of cardboard boxes. With his fingerless mittens, he reached for the small bottle of cheap brandy he'd purchased earlier that day from a nearby off-licence. He held it up to the light and examined it with a glum expression on his face. Empty.

Illuminated Christmas decorations hung from the lamp posts all along the affluent street in which he'd chosen to bunk down on this particular evening, their glittering lights projecting a wholly illusory warmth. He didn't know the exact date, but he knew Christmas wasn't far off, although it was kind of hard to get into the festive spirit when you were homeless.

If anyone had asked his name, if anyone had cared, he would have told them it was Dave Boakes. He came from Bristol originally but had ended up here on the streets of London by dint of a long chain of unfortunate occurrences the nature of which he didn't like to dwell on too much.

These days, Dave just concentrated on getting through life day by day, hour by hour, minute by minute, and not for the first time he wished he owned a watch so that he could mark each of those seconds passing by. The only problem was that time seemed to pass so much more slowly when you were cold.

Dave had positioned himself strategically near the entrance to an expensive restaurant in the hope that the passing patrons would feel sorry for him and give him some money. In front of him was a metal mug in which he'd placed a few coins in order to stimulate people's generosity, but he hadn't had much luck so far this evening.

He looked over at the restaurant. What he wouldn't give to be in there right now, sitting in the warm, tucking into a nice juicy steak accompanied by a big glass of red wine. He felt his mouth begin to water.

He blinked the fantasy away. No point in tormenting oneself. He turned his head away from the restaurant and as he did so a movement caught his eye a little way down the road. Squinting, he tried to make out what it was.

At first, in the dimness of the shadows, everything was indistinct, but then he saw it again, a twitch of motion there, low down, by the back of a smart-looking S-Type Jaguar, one of several very nice cars parked along this road. If he wasn't mistaken, there was a figure clad in black kneeling down doing... something.

Intrigued, Dave squinted harder, but it was difficult to make out details for the figure was operating just beyond the pool of light cast by the nearest street lamp, and they were wearing some kind of hat pulled down low over their face which obscured their features. However, some instinct told him that whoever they were and what-ever they were doing, they were up to no good. So he stayed completely still as he watched, figuring it was probably in his best interests not to draw too much attention to his presence. At times like this the relative invisibility of being a homeless man conferred a distinct advantage.

After a short while, the figure stood up, fluidly detached itself from the car and melted away into the shadows.

Dave blinked and looked again but it had vanished completely, like some spectral presence that had never really been there in the first place. Much as he'd recently polished off a bottle of brandy, he was pretty certain he hadn't been imagining what he'd just seen.

At that point, the door of the restaurant swung open, letting out a gust of noise which made him turn his head sharply, all thoughts of the mysterious figure dropping from his mind. He saw that a couple had emerged into the chilly night and it looked like they were heading in his direction. A bolt of anticipation shot through him. Here was his opportunity, the chance to earn some money.

The man ambled along in a self-assured swagger, his black leather jacket flapping open despite the freezing weather. The woman was wrapped in a figure-hugging fur coat, below which a pair of slender long legs ended in towering stiletto heels. The woman, in particular, looked quite glamorous, like some kind of model or actress, and both of them looked considerably well-off.

The couple were laughing, the man saying something indiscernible in a low rumble, the woman tittering in response, their puffs of breath frosting in the night air. It sounded like they were tipsy, bathing in the high of a good evening.

They were drawing closer, the woman's heels clacking sharply on the pavement as she tottered along a little unsteadily, her arm hooked into the man's elbow, their conversation becoming more clearly audible the nearer they got.

'Now remember you promised me,' the man was saying in a rough, gravelly voice.

'When we get back to the car,' the woman replied, with a coy twinkle in her eye.

'I've been waiting for it all evening,' he said with a leering grin. 'And I can't wait any longer.'

'You won't be disappointed,' she purred seductively.

Dave readied himself for their imminent approach. They were only a few metres away now. He projected the appropriate air of two parts dejected to one part cheerful and one part humble, a recipe he'd spent some time refining.

'Spare some change?' he said as they passed, making sure not to sound too whiny.

The man stopped abruptly, pulling the woman to a halt beside him. He peered down at Dave, the smile dropping off his face. Up close, Dave absorbed his appearance – a large diamond stud in his left ear, his loud shirt open at the collar revealing a heavy gold chain around his neck, a chunky, expensive-looking watch on his left wrist and one of those rings with a gold sovereign in it on the little finger of his right hand. He certainly didn't look short of cash, that was for sure. And he appeared to be coked up, if the wide twitching eyes and the clenching jaw were anything to go by.

Dave suddenly felt uneasy. Just beneath the surface, he could detect the whiff of violence, as if this was the kind of bloke who thought nothing of doling out a beating to anyone who looked at him the wrong way. Maybe he should have kept his mouth shut. He wondered if the man was going to assault him. It wouldn't be the first time someone had done so. He felt a faint quake of fear. He gulped and braced himself for a possible kicking.

'Taters, innit?' growled the man.

Dave had no idea what the man was talking about. He could have been talking Mongolian for all Dave knew.

The man tutted and shook his head in mock scorn at Dave's ignorance.

'Taters-in-the-mould,' he said slowly, enunciating each word.

Now Dave understood.

It was Cockney rhyming slang.

Potatoes in the mould. Cold.

It was a London thing. It also meant the bloke wasn't posh. Even if he was well-off.

Dave nodded slowly, mentally adding it to his list of idioms. 'Yeah,' he said. 'It's bloody cold.'

The man eyed him for a few moments, then fished inside his leather jacket and pulled out a diamond-encrusted gold money clip containing a fat wad of notes. Dave eyed it hungrily and licked his lips.

The man ostentatiously plucked out a note. It was red in colour.

Surely not...

Dave swallowed and wondered if he was seeing things. His heart began to beat a little harder.

The man bent down and dropped the note in Dave's metal cup, alongside the ten- and twenty-pence pieces. 'Merry Christmas,' he said.

Dave stared at it, speechless. It was indeed a fifty-pound note. He picked it up. It was real. Crisp and firm. He wasn't dreaming. Rarely, if ever, did he get to handle one of these. It was miracle enough when he got given a fiver but this was something else. Merry Christmas indeed.

He looked up, stunned with gratitude, but the couple were now walking away, sauntering across the street. He hadn't even had the opportunity to say thank you.

He looked back down at the note. What sort of person carried around that kind of cash? The bloke must be properly loaded to give away fifty quid just like that.

Fifty quid. His mind swam with the possibilities. This was a game changer. Now he could pay for a warm bed to sleep in tonight. Or he could buy something decent to drink at last. Maybe a nice whisky like Talisker or Highland Park. Or get himself a big slap-up meal. Hell, he could even go into that restaurant right now and order a big juicy steak.

Fingering the note lovingly, he looked up in teary-eyed gratitude at the couple. They were now immersed once more in conversation. Dave suddenly glanced around vigilantly. Best put the money out of sight before some street person or mugger noticed it and tried to take it from him. He quickly tucked the note inside his grubby coat.

Regarding the couple again, he saw that they had now crossed the road and had come to a halt by a parked car about a hundred metres away. It was an S-Type Jaguar. The classiest one out of all the cars parked there.

At that point, a recollection tugged at Dave's memory. Something about that particular car, that S-Type Jaguar... But then it passed. What with the cold and the residual alcohol in his system, the neurons in his head were moving too sluggishly to be able to do their job properly.

The couple got into the car. The doors slammed shut.

BANG.

The S-Type Jaguar exploded in a huge fireball.

Dave felt a wave of heat scorch his face.

He blinked in shock as pieces of twisted burning wreckage crashed down on the pavement around him. A lump of smoking flesh landed, plop, right in front of him. It was a human arm attached to a piece of torso. Still fastened to the wrist of the severed body part was the big pricey-looking watch he'd noticed the man wearing just moments earlier.

Dave looked on in horror, his ears ringing in the aftermath of the blast.

At least it wasn't so cold any more. Quite the opposite.

2

Detective Constable Bailey Morgan unfurled the piece of paper that had just fallen out of the end of the Christmas cracker.

Both of her parents looked at her expectantly across the dinner table. The three of them were wearing paper party hats at her father's insistence. They had finished the main course and were now taking a breather before dessert.

'Well?' said her mother, an expectant smile lighting up her small wrinkled face.

Bailey scanned the slip of paper with her ash-grey eyes. She sighed and dutifully read what it said. 'What do lions sing at Christmas?'

Her parents both frowned as they tried to think of the answer.

'I give up,' said her father, scratching his thinning grey hair.

'So do I,' said her mother.

'Jungle Bells.'

Her parents laughed. Bailey didn't. She crumpled the piece of paper and dropped it onto the table.

It was Christmas Day. It also happened to be her birthday. She had just turned thirty.

Her mother put on her half-moon reading glasses and squinted down at her own cracker joke. Her eyes widened.

'Ooh, you'll like this one, Bailey. It's right up your street.'

Somehow Bailey doubted that but she didn't say anything.

Her mother took a deep breath. 'What happened to the man who stole an advent calendar?'

Bailey paused for thought. As was her habit when she was thinking, she fiddled with the lock of hair that she wore loose down the left side of her face to cover the thin white scar that ran from the top of her cheek down to the bottom of her jaw. The scar had been inflicted upon her during the course of her job, the grim handiwork of a vicious perpetrator who still haunted her nightmares.

She curled the hair around her fingers and let it uncurl.

'He got twenty-five days,' she said.

Her mother looked a little crestfallen. 'You've heard it before!'

Bailey shook her head.

Thirty. It had come so suddenly. Weren't you supposed to do something special on your thirtieth? She hadn't really had the chance to give it much thought as she'd been too busy working. Her last police operation had come to a close only recently and she was still getting over it; she'd been undercover in a women's prison and had come perilously close to never making it out of there alive.

Now, here she was, thirty, single, at her parents' suburban pebble-dashed house in Bromley, reading crummy cracker jokes. Not one to normally feel sorry for herself, she was finding it hard to shake the feeling of existential despondency that had settled upon her all of a sudden.

She realised she should probably try and make the effort to meet up with some friends. That'd put an end to the navel-gazing. But it had been a while since she'd done so. Immersed in undercover work, she'd let a lot of her friendships fall by the wayside. Although in truth there wasn't much she could do about that; on her last case, posing as a prison inmate, inviting her friends to drop by for a visit at Her Majesty's Pleasure just wouldn't have been a viable option, not least because she'd been pretending to be someone completely different to who she actually was.

Still, a birthday was always a good excuse for a celebration with friends... but when your birthday fell on Christmas Day, friends tended to be with their own families, and these days most of her friends from school and university were married with kids, which made it all the more difficult to catch up. So, for the time being, it was just her and her parents...

And to that end, Christmas dinner had been much like all the previous ones that she could remember: the turkey had been too dry – her mother never got it quite right – but her dad's stuffing had been excellent as usual; it was the only dish he knew how to make.

Although there were three of them sitting at the table, four places had actually been set. It had been the same every Christmas for the past twenty-four years or so, ever since Bailey's older sister Jennifer had gone missing at the age of eight years old, abducted off the street without a trace. Her father insisted on laying a place for Jennifer, resolute in his belief that she was still out there somewhere alive, vainly convinced that his efforts to find her would one day bear fruit. Bailey's mother had long ago lost the will to argue with him, and Bailey herself knew that raising any objection to his delusions would only result in a big row, and no one wanted that at Christmas. So no one said anything.

Bailey noticed her mother frowning at her.

'You know, you don't look very happy, Bailey.' Her face broke into a beaming smile. 'Today is a day of joyous celebration.'

'I'm fine,' lied Bailey.

'Today is the day that our Lord Jesus Christ came into the world. You should feel privileged to share your birthday with Him.'

Her mother had become increasingly religious as she'd grown older and her social life now almost exclusively revolved around her church. For Bailey's combined Christmas and birthday present, she'd bought her a silver hairgrip in the shape of a fish.

'It's an ancient Christian symbol,' her mother had explained. 'It's a fish.'

'Yeah I can see that,' Bailey had replied, turning it over in her hands. The minimalist design consisted of little more than two intersecting arcs of thin flat silver, the tips joining at one end to form the nose, and crossing at the other end to form a tail.

'In ancient times, during the darkest days of Roman oppression, when those brave few who followed the Christian faith—'

'Thanks, Mum,' Bailey had said, cutting her off. 'I'm sure it'll come in very handy.' Once her mum got started on Christian matters she never shut up and sometimes Bailey just couldn't stomach it; she didn't possess any religious convictions whatsoever, having confronted far too many acts of senseless evil in her line of work to trust in any form of divine goodness or justice.

Her father had bought her *The Bumper Book of Cryptic Crosswords*, knowing how fond she was of them.

Now, sitting at the dinner table, she idly flicked though it while her mother took their dirty dinner plates out into the kitchen and went to get dessert.

Her father tilted his head and fixed Bailey with a serious look. She felt a pre-emptive surge of unease. She recognised that expression only too well.

'Bailey, I want to talk to you about Mister Snigiss,' he said, arching one eyebrow gravely.

Bailey rolled her eyes. 'Not again,' she muttered.

At the time that Jennifer had gone missing, she, like many children her age, had possessed an invisible friend. The name of this invisible friend had been Mister Snigiss. Mister Snigiss had been present throughout many of their childhood games, leading both sisters on an array of imaginary adventures. Bailey remembered how hard she'd always strained to see Mister Snigiss, but only Jennifer had been able to see him, and Bailey had just taken it on faith from her older sister that Mister Snigiss existed.

In the wake of Jennifer's disappearance, Bailey's father had seized upon every aspect of her childhood in an effort to try and work out what had happened to her and Mister Snigiss was no exception.

'I want you to help me find Mister Snigiss,' he said, without an ounce of irony.

Bailey sighed. 'Mister Snigiss was nothing more than a figment of Jennifer's imagination, Dad.'

Her father shook his head. 'Mister Snigiss was real.' His eyes bore that all-too-familiar glaze of conviction and Bailey knew he was deaf to anything other than his own dogmatic beliefs.

'As I recall,' she said, 'Mister Snigiss wore a funny hat and had a pet cobra called Sid. Kids make up all kinds of stupid stuff.'

Her father was shaking his head vehemently. He was building up to one of his rants.

'No! The more I think about it, the more I'm convinced that Mister Snigiss was a real person. An adult. A man who secretly wormed his way into Jennifer's life. He was grooming her. That's what he was doing. He told her not to tell anyone about him, told her to make out like he was her invisible friend so we wouldn't get suspicious. If only I'd paid more attention to her! If I'd known he was real, I could have saved her from him. He was the one who took her. It was Mister Snigiss who abducted her.'

'Dad, you're beating yourself up over something that doesn't exist and never existed.'

But her father wasn't listening. He was in full flow now.

'That pet snake of his was probably just a way to lure her to meet him. You remember how much Jennifer wanted a pet snake and we never let her have one. Well, Mister Snigiss told her exactly what she wanted to hear.'

Bailey was starting to run out of patience. It wasn't that she was uncaring. It was more that because, as a police officer, she'd encountered enough similar cases to know that there was little point in her father holding out hope in this way. After twenty-four years it was time for him to face up to the fact that Jennifer was gone for good, one way or another.

'Get a grip Dad. Listen to yourself. Mister Snigiss wasn't real.'

'You can't be sure.' He pointed a finger at her. 'You could find out.'

She rolled her eyes. She knew what was coming next.

'You're in the police!' he said. 'You can find these things out. You can find out the truth about Mister Snigiss. If we find Mister Snigiss, we can find out what happened to Jennifer.'

Bailey resisted the urge to lean across the table and try and shake some sense into him. Instead she took a deep breath and attempted to rein in her emotions.

'I already looked into Jennifer's case. I told you before. I've told you a thousand times before.'

'But you haven't looked into it properly, have you? Not in any detail.'

Not long after joining the police, Bailey had indeed examined the old case files pertaining to Jennifer's disappearance and she'd even checked the Police National Database for evidence of Mister Snigiss, but, much as she'd expected, there had been no evidence of anyone with that name or alias. And she'd told her father as much, but he still wouldn't give up, and they still always ended up having this argument, like clockwork, especially on Christmas Day even though it was her birthday and supposedly a day of joy and celebration as her mother always pointed out.

'Well, I've got a new theory about Mister Snigiss,' he whispered excitedly. 'About who he is.'

'Not another one,' she said, rolling her eyes.

'Just listen to me, Bailey! We know he must be at least fifty years old by now. But what if his name wasn't really Mister Snigiss? What if—'

Bailey slammed her hand down on the table. Her father recoiled slightly.

'That's enough, Dad! Can't you get it through your head? Jennifer is gone! She's dead! She's been dead for over twenty years!'

At the mention of the word 'dead', her father lapsed into a stony silence. Her mother, who'd just re-entered the living room holding a Christmas pudding, stopped and looked at Bailey in shock. Even she knew better than to say the 'd' word in the house.

'Don't you ever say that Jennifer is dead,' said her father in a low, injured tone.

'I'm going upstairs,' said Bailey, thinking how yet again, despite whatever she might have hoped for, this birthday and Christmas had gone south in much the same way as all the previous ones had.

'Don't you want any Christmas pudding?' said her mother.

'Nah, I'm stuffed.'

Bailey stood up, left the table and walked upstairs, laden with the customary mixture of frustration and sadness.

Why couldn't her father just accept the brutal truth? Bailey had. And her way to deal with it had been to join the police. If justice wasn't going to materialise for Jennifer, then at least Bailey could try and do something about all the other bad things happening in the world.

Standing by the window on the landing, she gazed out through the net curtains at the dull expanse of suburbia under the grey washed-out sky.

Bromley.

She couldn't think of anything worse than ending up living here in one of these drab pebble-dashed houses, trapped in a nine-to-five existence, slowly dying inside from the sheer monotony of it.

She tried to shake off the depressing thoughts. Maybe it had been a mistake coming to her parents' house for Christmas. Maybe she should have just stayed at home in her flat in Crystal Palace.

The sound of the song 'The Power of Love' by Huey Lewis and the News suddenly blared from her trouser pocket, breaking the stillness of the upstairs landing. A committed fan of eighties power ballads, Bailey had changed the ringtone of her mobile phone to that of the 1985 number one hit in a moment of idle boredom the previous day.

Pulling her phone from her pocket, she saw that the name flashing on the screen was that of Detective Superintendent Frank Grinham, her sometime boss who she'd worked for on numerous undercover operations in the past.

Knowing him as she did, she couldn't imagine he was calling to wish her either Merry Christmas or Happy Birthday.

There was only one reason he'd be contacting her, and that would be to present her with the opportunity of fresh undercover work. A way out. And with that tempting possibility in mind, she answered the phone.

'Don't you ever take the day off?' she said.

'Christmas is just a day like any other.'

'You're at the office, aren't you?'

There was a sheepish silence. She could visualise him right now, dressed in his grey suit, yellow tie and buffed black Oxfords, sitting in front of a computer, tapping away as they spoke.

She was glad to hear his voice though. It had already started to lift her out of her gloomy introspection.

'I know it's a bit soon since the last one finished, but I've got a new job for you,' he said.

She hesitated for a few moments. It had been around five and a half months since the operation in the prison had come to an end, and following a little time off recuperating from that experience, she'd been back in the office working in her regular role as a normal detective constable.

'I've been concentrating on trying to pass my sergeant's exams,' she said. 'So I don't think I'll be able to do any more undercover jobs for the time being.'

Working undercover for as long as she had meant that she'd let her career stagnate and she'd reluctantly realised that advancing up the ladder would probably be beneficial in the long term. Although there was no denying that she missed the rush that came with undercover work, she'd talked herself out of taking on any more undercover jobs until she'd sorted out her career. However, if she was to be honest with herself, her heart wasn't really in it – the slow diligent slog up the greasy pole. It all seemed a bit too much like normal life, just the kind of thing she was trying to avoid.

In the faint hiss of static over the phone, she sensed that Frank detected the lacklustre tone in her voice. After all, he knew her well.

'It's a job that requires a woman's touch,' he said.

'Come on, Frank, you know I'm not that much of a pushover. Don't try to flatter me.' But secretly she knew she'd be climbing the walls if she spent much longer cooped up inside studying. Being on a new undercover job would provide a welcome break from the books and, after all, it was the only thing that really got her adrenaline going. She took a deep breath. 'Okay,' she said. 'I'm listening...'

'I can't talk about it over the phone. When can you come in?'

3

'I don't think the cleaners have got back from holiday yet,' said Frank by way of apology as he and Bailey passed by a half-eaten chocolate Yule log lying at the end of a bank of desks.

It was Boxing Day and the office was more or less deserted. A few sad-looking Christmas decorations hung from the ceiling and some bits of stringy tinsel were draped along the top of a few of the computers, a meagre counterpoint to the gallery of criminals staring back at her sullenly from the numerous mugshots pinned to the walls.

'Have you cleared this job with my CID detective sergeant?' she asked.

'I left a message on his answerphone but he hasn't got back to me yet. I can't imagine there'll be any problems though.'

Undercover work was something Bailey did alongside her routine job as a detective constable, and whenever Frank wanted her to participate in one of his undercover operations he had to obtain approval from her superiors.

'I did manage to get through to the psychologist though,' he said. 'The normal checks. Y'know. Just as a matter of course.'

'Oh yeah?' murmured Bailey apprehensively. 'What did she say?'

Frank glanced over his shoulder at her. 'She told me you passed your most recent psychological evaluation. She said you were fit for work.'

'That's reassuring.'

'Unless you've been deceiving her somehow?' he said, with an enquiring glint in his eye.

Bailey evaded his gaze slightly. 'I'm glad you called me. I'm looking forward to starting a new job.'

'You've already agreed to do it and you haven't even heard what it is yet.'

She followed him through to a small meeting room off to the side of the main office. He opened the door and bade her enter. She'd been expecting the meeting to be just her and Frank, but to her surprise there was someone else in the room.

Lounging back in a chair with one leg crossed over his knee was a face she recognised from the distant past. He was tall, athletic, with a square jaw, blonde hair, blonde eyebrows and striking blue eyes which now observed her intently with a cool, measured calm. At the sight of him, Bailey felt her breath momentarily catch in her throat and her knees go a little weak.

'Bailey, I believe you already know DI Dale Bleudore,' said Frank.

'I believe I do,' replied Bailey. Eight years earlier, she and Dale had both formed part of the new intake going through training at Hendon Police College.

Dale stood up and held out his hand.

Bailey sheathed her hand in his firm cool grip, and her heart skipped a beat as she thought to herself that he was even more handsome than she remembered.

'Although I don't think we ever spoke more than two words to each other,' he said, with a disarming smile.

Back at Hendon, Bailey had got the impression that Dale was a bit arrogant, but looking back now, she wondered if her reticence to talk to him had partially been out of shyness because she'd been a little intimidated by his good looks.

She brushed an imaginary speck of dust from the lapel of her

Donna Karan trouser suit, suddenly glad she'd made the effort to dress smartly for this meeting.

So Dale was a detective inspector, she thought with interest. He was the same rank as Frank. While she'd been working undercover, Dale had taken the time to get promoted and move up the police hierarchy. He'd clearly done well for himself.

'So what brings you here?' she said, genuinely curious.

Dale raised one eyebrow and made an 'over to you' gesture to Frank.

Frank rubbed his greying red hair and fixed Bailey with his dead watery eyes. 'You know that car bomb in West London a few days before Christmas?'

Of course Bailey knew about it. It had been all over the news. A nice posh street in Chiswick had been totally wrecked, all the windows blown out, including those of a restaurant belonging to some celebrity chef. Initial reports had speculated that it was a terrorist incident, but unofficial opinions were now leaning in a different direction.

'Yeah, they reckon it was a gangland hit, right?'

Frank nodded slowly. 'The victim's name was Adrian Molloy. A member of the Molloy crime family.'

'The notorious Molloys, eh?' murmured Bailey.

'Yeah,' said Frank, with a knowing raise of the eyebrow. 'He was one of them. He got blown up, along with some poor floozy who happened to be in the wrong place at the wrong time. They found bits of them everywhere. They found her head in a tree a hundred and fifty metres away... and they're still finding bits.'

'Urgh!' said Bailey as she visualised the macabre scene.

'Initial feedback from the murder investigation team indicates that the bomb was clamped magnetically to the underside of the car, probably to the petrol tank at the rear. A small device, likely an RDX charge, set off remotely, probably via mobile phone.'

'Any information as to the culprits?'

Frank shook his head. 'CCTV in the street got us a brief glimpse of someone moving through the shadows, but visibility was very poor, and then they disappeared down a side alley which wasn't covered by any public surveillance systems. Whoever it was, they were very good at evading CCTV coverage. They just seemed to disappear completely.'

'Sounds like a professional,' said Bailey. She paused and frowned. 'So what does this have to do with me? Why the need for undercover?'

Frank swapped glances briefly with Dale and then turned his attention back to Bailey. 'Do you know much about the Molloy crime family?'

'Well, apart from their general bad reputation, I know they're a pretty heavyweight OCG.'

OCG stood for organised crime group.

Frank nodded. 'You're definitely right about that. The best way to think of them is as a multinational corporation whose business portfolio includes extortion, gun-running, drug trafficking, prostitution, hijacking, kidnapping, money laundering, bribery, fraud, counterfeiting, armed robbery, large-scale car theft and contract killing... amongst other things.'

Bailey smiled as she watched Frank run out of fingers as he counted off their crimes.

'Their assets are rumoured to run into the hundreds of millions,' he continued, 'and they use every trick in the book to launder their illicit cash. In order to conceal their criminal enterprises, they operate a whole host of front companies, as well as a variety of legitimate businesses. They have hundreds, if not thousands, of people working for them, and most of those people probably have no idea that they're actually really working for the Molloys.'

'Impressive,' said Bailey. 'Where exactly are they based?'

'Well, they're headquartered mainly in the East London–Essex area, legacy of the previous generation, but they're not territorial in the traditional sense, and they don't control a "manor" as such. Like I said, they're multinational in nature and they run a sophisticated global operation with links to organised crime groups on just about every continent to facilitate their illicit activities.'

'They sound like major players,' Bailey acknowledged. She tilted her head pensively. 'Molloy's an Irish name, isn't it?'

Frank nodded. 'That's right. The Molloy family are of Irish origin, although they've been living here in London for several generations.' He paused thoughtfully. 'Molloy means "proud chieftain" in Gaelic apparently.'

Bailey smiled. 'Didn't know you had an interest in etymology, Frank.' She paused. 'Talking of chieftains, remind me again who runs this outfit.'

'A very pertinent question,' he said. 'These days, the Molloy crime empire is run by Rick Molloy. He's Adrian's younger brother. He's a premier-league gangster, although he tells people he's just an innocent property developer. Takes the business side of things very seriously apparently, which probably goes some way to explaining the success of their organisation. But although he may act like the proverbial businessman, he's a ruthless thug and a villain at the end of the day, who maintains his position, and that of his organisation, just like any other gangster – by the calculated use of violence. The Molloys have been linked to at least twenty-one murders, and that's just in the UK, and those are just the ones we know about.'

'Sounds like a dangerous character,' said Bailey. She paused. 'You said this job needed a woman's touch. Why? In fact, come to think of it, you haven't told me what the job is yet.'

Frank again glanced at Dale, who'd been sitting back listening with his leg resting on his knee. Dale uncrossed his legs and leaned forward to speak.

'It'll help first if you know a bit of background about the family themselves. The Molloy organisation was founded by Arthur Molloy back in the mid-eighties. He was an armed robber who used his ill-gotten gains to invest in the drugs trade and he did well enough out of that to be able to branch out into other criminal activities and make even more money.'

Bailey watched him talk, getting a better impression of him as he did so. He exuded an undeniable aura of confidence and an authority in his subject, and she found he commanded her attention with ease.

'But then, in 1994, Arthur was murdered in Spain, shot dead in the back garden of his luxury hacienda in Marbella. At this point, his wife, Nancy, took over the operation. She's a formidable character in her own right, but more about her later.'

A smile crinkled the corners of his eyes as he spoke to her, indicating to Bailey that he enjoyed being in the spotlight like this.

'Eventually, because she was getting older, I guess, Nancy decided she wanted to step back a bit and put one of her sons in charge. After all, they were more than old enough by then. Adrian, being the eldest, was logically the one to step up and take charge, but he was too much of a playboy and a cokehead. He liked to trade off his dad's reputation, but he lacked that inner steel and ice-cold intelligence that's crucial for staying on top within the underworld. So Nancy skipped Adrian and put Rick in charge instead.

'Rick's a much cooler customer, and the smarter of the two by a long way. He's got an extremely short record sheet and he's never once been to prison. He's very good at keeping his hands clean and he's beaten almost every charge that's been thrown at him. Witnesses tend to have a habit of dropping their testimony at the last minute, or in some cases, meeting with unfortunate accidents.'

Dale paused for a moment, his face taking on a weighty expression. She sensed he was about to reveal something important.

'It's common knowledge that Adrian Molloy was a gangster,' he said. 'And we won't be shedding too many tears now that he's gone. One less villain for us to worry about. But what's less well known... in fact, what has been kept top-secret, and remains so even now, is that he was a registered informant.'

4

Bailey raised her eyebrows in surprise.

'Adrian was a snout?' she murmured. A snout was police slang for an informant.

'That's the reason Dale's here,' said Frank.

Dale nodded. 'My job is working with confidential informants. I was Adrian's handler.'

Bailey regarded him with an added layer of respect. Working with informants was highly sensitive work. You definitely had to be a cut above the average plod to be entrusted with CIs. But it didn't surprise her that Dale had graduated into this type of work. Even back at Hendon, it had been apparent that he'd possessed that special kind of drive, and as for that slight taint of arrogance he had, she'd witnessed the same thing in other individuals she'd encountered in elite units, and they'd been among some of the best police officers she'd met; it was a form of self-belief that was often crucial to success in the high-stakes world in which both he and she operated.

'Did he get caught for something?' she asked, seeking to establish how a member of one of the city's top crime families had crossed to the side of the law.

Dale shook his head. 'Unusually, he was a walk-in.'

Criminals most often turned informant after being caught as a way to get out of being charged for their offence or to lessen the sentence that they ultimately received. However, some of them volunteered their services for motives of their own, as appeared to be the case here.

'And that's why I wanted to give you a bit of background on the family,' he said. 'Because that's who Adrian was stitching up. His own family. His own brother, to be precise.'

Bailey shook her head in wonderment. But then perhaps she shouldn't have been too surprised. After all, she herself was only too well acquainted with how illogical and dysfunctional families could be, but at least hers weren't criminals.

Dale continued. 'He'd developed a real chip on his shoulder about Rick being put in control of the family. Adrian thought he was the one who should have been boss, being older, and he really resented the fact that he wasn't. And this was his way of getting back at his younger brother.'

'And that suited us very well,' said Frank with a wry smirk. 'We've been trying to crack the Molloys for years. I've got a huge file on them, which I'll let you have a look at, and you'll be able to see the scale of the things they get away with.'

Dale nodded in agreement. 'That's why Adrian was graded as one of our highest-level informants. Because of the information he was able to provide. We're not talking dinky little street corner busts here. We're talking about transactions of a very significant nature, the kind of thing the Molloys specialise in.'

'Like what?' Bailey asked.

'Well, for example, just before he got blown up, he told us the Molloys are planning to smuggle a load of ecstasy pills into an airstrip in Essex on the third of February. We passed that information to Essex police and Customs and they're now in the process of putting together an operation to swoop on the drugs as soon as they arrive.'

'But the drugs aren't why you're here,' Frank intervened. 'You're here for something that I personally regard as much more serious.'

Bailey felt a prickle of anticipation and leaned forward in her chair.

Dale spoke up. 'Adrian told me that Rick had secured a large quantity of firearms. Automatic and semi-automatic weapons. And that he was looking for a buyer. As you well know, this type of scenario presents the ideal opportunity for infiltration by an undercover police officer to catch him in a bust. As soon as I heard about it, I knew we had to act.'

Frank nodded gravely. 'The quantities are significant. A hundred and twenty CZ 805 BREN assault rifles, and a hundred and forty K100 pistols, along with seventy silencers and a hundred and thirty thousand rounds of assorted ammunition. That's five hundred bullets for each weapon. And did I mention, it's all brand new. Totally clean. This is one major arsenal we're talking about.'

Bailey absorbed the details while Frank continued.

'Although the UK has traditionally had low levels of gun crime, firearms offences have increased significantly in recent years and most of the victims are young – under thirty-five, and often they're just teenagers. We're seeing more firearms than ever on the streets of the UK, and that trend, worryingly, is growing. Seizures of guns by the likes of the National Crime Agency have gone up by more than three hundred per cent, but still the weapons are flooding in, and it's people like Rick who are responsible.

'Weapons like his ones, which are new and clean, are all the more appealing to criminals because they don't have any associations with past crimes. He's got a load of military-grade weaponry in his possession and it could inflict untold damage in the wrong hands. It won't just be hard-core criminals who'll be looking to buy these guns, it could also be terrorists.'

Bailey nodded. 'So you want me to pose as a buyer for these guns and set up Rick for a bust.'

'That's right,' said Dale. 'After discussing it with me, Adrian agreed to vouch for an undercover police officer who would pose as a buyer for the guns. He went back to Rick, and hinted that he might have found a potential buyer, but at that point he didn't give Rick a name or anything because we hadn't yet found a police officer to play the role.

Rick turned out to be keen though, wanted to know more, and wanted to hear from this potential buyer. So I went to Frank and we thought about possible undercover candidates to fill this role.'

'And we came up with your name, Bailey,' said Frank with a wan smile.

Bailey frowned and shook her head. 'But Adrian's dead now. How can he vouch for me?'

'Well, that's the thing,' Frank replied. 'I was about to approach you for this job just before Christmas, but then Adrian got blown up and we thought the whole thing was off.'

Dale spoke up. 'But then we realised that this doesn't change the fact that Rick has still got those guns and he's still probably looking for a buyer.'

'And we cannot just sit back and allow this quantity of firearms to hit the streets of the UK,' said Frank. 'We knew we had to stop him. So we've decided to try and go ahead with it all the same, before he finds another buyer. And that's why I called you, on Christmas Day.'

'As far as Rick's concerned,' Dale added, 'this potential buyer that Adrian suggested is still out there somewhere wanting to buy a load of guns. It's just a case of that person getting in contact with him.'

'But how will Rick know that I'm the one Adrian suggested?' asked Bailey.

'Good question,' said Dale. 'Well, Rick provided Adrian with a special code word for this buyer to use in relation to this transaction. When you call Rick, if you use the code word, he'll know that you're the buyer that Adrian was going to vouch for and he'll trust you. Hopefully.'

'So Adrian gave you Rick's personal telephone number as well?'

'Yes, you'll call him on that number,' said Dale. 'But you should know that Rick is paranoid about police surveillance. He doesn't like talking business over the phone in case anyone's listening in. Hence the use of a code word.'

'What is this code word?'

'"Furniture".'

'Furniture?' Bailey asked, bemused.

'You ask about buying the "furniture". He'll ask what sort. You say "Victorian oak dining set". And he'll know you're the one.'

'And that's it?' said Bailey.

Dale nodded. 'When you meet him to discuss the deal, he'll expect you to be aware of the quantities and the types of guns involved because Adrian will supposedly have told you all about it. Your knowledge of that in itself will demonstrate that you're the bona-fide buyer that Adrian was talking about. The only thing you'll need to do is negotiate a price.'

'It doesn't mean he won't be suspicious, of course,' said Frank. 'That's just how he operates. And, of course, without Adrian there to corroborate you, he'll be extra careful and want to know all about you and how you met Adrian and so on and so forth. But I reckon he's really keen to shift these guns, and I think, with a bit of luck, you should be able to pull it off.'

Bailey frowned. Something was niggling at her. 'Adrian got blown up. Did it occur to you that maybe his own family blew him up because they found out he was a snout? And if that's the case, then surely they'll be expecting anyone who approaches them via Adrian to be a potential undercover cop? Everyone knows that the police use informants in just this way to infiltrate criminal groups.'

'That's a very good point,' said Frank, 'And it's one that we've already thought about. It's very simple really. Rick is extremely suspicious by nature. If you call him and use the code word he gave Adrian, and he thinks you're a cop because Adrian was an informant, he'll just hang up on you and that'll be that. He won't want to have anything to do with you and he certainly won't want to meet up with you as that would be way too risky for him, not to mention a complete waste of his time. The operation will be over before it's even started.' He paused. 'However... if he doesn't hang up on you, then that means in all likelihood that he didn't know that Adrian was an informant, which means he didn't blow up Adrian, and it means that he won't immediately suspect that you're a cop.'

'It sounds like a bit of a gamble,' said Bailey.

'It is,' Frank agreed. 'But it's the only card we've got left to play, and we have to try and play it if we want to stop these guns from hitting the streets. It's either that or let him sell them to someone who'll use them to inflict real harm.'

'Are you still up for it?' asked Dale, looking concerned.

Bailey nodded. 'I'll just have to think of a good cover story.'

Her mind was already humming with potential options. It was the responsibility of the undercover police officer to think up their own cover story and she always relished the opportunity to put her imagination to use in this way.

'I think my best bet is to pose as a mid-level player looking to move up the food chain,' she said. 'I'll need an apartment, a car and the appropriate credentials.'

The kind of street player she was aiming to emulate always had a number of schemes running at any given time. Stolen vehicles, fur coats, gold bullion. Potential burglaries. Drugs. Weapons. Buying and selling. Wheeling and dealing. She knew the type well.

'You just have to think of a good reason why you'd need to acquire so many guns,' said Frank.

Bailey let her mind work on it for a few moments.

'How about guns for right-wing contacts?' she said. 'There are plenty of fringe groups that have sprung up in recent years, what with the global shift to the right.'

Frank and Dale looked at each other and nodded in approval.

Bailey knew that with a little bit of research she could be vague enough to spin it into something plausible.

'With a transaction of this importance,' said Dale, 'it's likely that you'll be dealing directly with Rick himself at all stages of the process. Like I said, he's paranoid about police surveillance, so he generally prefers to meet up face-to-face when he wants to communicate anything important.

'Those ecstasy pills I mentioned are pretty run-of-the-mill, and the Molloys will probably just send some lower-level subordinates to pick up the drugs, and those are the people the Essex police will end up arresting. But these guns are something else and we reckon they give us the opportunity to capture Rick himself. It's all too easy for us to arrest the minor players. But to make a real impact, we need to catch the guys at the top, guys like Rick. He's been operating with virtual impunity for so long, but hopefully we'll get him this time. With your help.'

'So who's running this operation?' said Bailey.

'With a large quantity of guns like this, the National Crime Agency would normally be the ones to run such an operation,' Frank explained. 'However, due to the particular circumstances and sensitive nature of this infiltration, I've convinced them to let us run it as a Metropolitan Police operation. However, I'll be feeding back directly to them, and the NCA will be instrumental in the final bust. Having laid much of the groundwork already, in terms of his work with Adrian, Dale will be part and parcel of this operation, and you and he will be working together very closely throughout the course of the whole thing.'

She shot Dale a thin smile. He smiled back and she felt a little twist of butterflies in her stomach.

'Your identity will remain secret of course,' Frank continued. 'Only Dale and I will be aware of your true identity. We'll keep this operation very tightly insulated in order to minimise any potential breach of security or accidental leaks. And we'll set up the usual operational emergency security protocols, including a fake company you can call should anything go seriously amiss; your call will be patched through directly to me.'

Getting her head around everything she'd just been told, Bailey looked up at Frank with a frown as she suddenly remembered something.

'Frank, I thought the reason I was here was because this job required a feminine touch. Buying a large amount of guns isn't the kind of thing you'd normally associate with a woman. Quite the opposite in fact.'

'Remember I mentioned Nancy Molloy?' said Dale.

Bailey turned her attention to him. 'You said she was a formidable character.'

Dale nodded. 'Although it's Rick who officially runs things, the real power behind the throne is Nancy, the matriarch. According to Adrian, Rick defers to her completely. If he's the CEO, then you can think of her as the Non-Executive Director.

'As a matter of course, he runs all new business past her first, to let her sound it out. A lot of people fall at that first hurdle, some of them permanently, if you know what I'm saying. She's one reason why we've never really managed to penetrate their organisation. She has an uncanny knack of being able to sniff out cops. It must be the criminal blood running through her veins – her father was an old-school blagger back in the sixties, so she's got a criminal pedigree of her very own, and that includes an inbuilt aversion to the police.

'The thing is, though, Adrian told me that Nancy always regretted not having a daughter. Two sons but no daughter. And he also said that she respects strong women, being one herself – remember, she ran the Molloy organisation all on her own for a good few years after Arthur's death.'

Bailey saw the pieces falling into place now. 'So even though Adrian's vouching for me from beyond the grave, they're still going to stick me in front of Nancy to see if I make the cut. But you think the fact that I'm a woman playing a man's role will work in my favour. And you think there's also scope to play up the daughter angle at some point.'

'You've got it in one, Bailey,' said Frank with an approving smile.

'This operation will require a certain amount of psychological finesse,' Dale added. 'The stakes are very high and the deeper you go, and the further you gain their trust, the riskier it'll become as they'll have more to lose. Only someone at the very top of their game will be able to manage a job like this.'

Bailey realised it was a veiled compliment. She wouldn't be here if they'd thought she wouldn't be able to handle it. She blushed a little.

Dale's expression suddenly turned grave. 'But whatever you do, don't underestimate Nancy Molloy. She's a very dangerous person indeed. She possesses a rather traditional view of the world. For her, it's all about family, blood ties... and revenge.

'Down in Spain, the Guardia Civil never got to the bottom of Arthur's murder, but Nancy never gave up. She eventually managed to track down his killers. Apparently it was a rival firm who claimed Arthur had stiffed them on a drugs deal some years earlier. Rumour has it that once they'd been captured, she insisted on personally dispatching them one by one... by putting a masonry drill through their skulls. She's a vengeful and vindictive person. And if she finds out you've crossed her, she'll never forgive and she'll never forget.'

Bailey felt a chill shudder go through her. What a family. And she thought hers was bad.

5

Bailey pushed open the double doors to enter the lift area. She pressed the button and waited for the lift to come.

As she stood there, she reflected on the job she had just decided to undertake, once again savouring the bite of a new challenge.

The double doors swung open as someone else entered the lift area.

'Hold up. Bailey.'

She turned around. It was Dale. He looked a little out of breath, like he'd been running to catch up with her.

Seeing him standing there, she noted how, with his blonde hair and blue eyes, he bore more than a passing resemblance to Mark, the detective sergeant she'd dated for two years before ending the relationship due to a stark difference in outlook on the matter of starting a family. She just seemed to have a thing for men who looked like that – the 'Teutonic' type, as someone she'd once known had referred to them.

'I forgot to mention,' he said. 'There's a murder investigation team working on Adrian's car bomb. So any information you encounter in the course of the operation that could help them out, you can feed back to me and I'll relay it to them.' He paused. 'But, like Frank was saying, your main focus should be the guns.'

Bailey nodded as she registered the piece of information, getting the impression Dale had just used it as an excuse to come out and talk to her.

There was a slightly awkward pause. She swallowed nervously and felt her heart flutter a little.

'You female undercovers are a rare commodity,' he said. 'You must be in high demand.'

He was right about that. There was a definite imbalance in the ratio of female to male undercover police officers. But, in some ways, women had the advantage as they were less likely to be suspected of being police because they weren't deployed as often as men.

She shrugged, attempting to remain casual. 'Well, I guess it keeps me busy. Anyhow, revising for my sergeant's exams was getting kind of boring. Working undercover is the ideal form of procrastination.'

Dale raised his eyebrows and shook his head. 'I don't think I could do what you do. I just haven't got the bottle. I guess you've got the natural instinct for it though.'

She felt pride in her abilities well up inside her, vindicating her choice of career. The kudos from colleagues was one of the main reasons people worked undercover.

'Frank told me you got a commendation for the last job,' he continued. 'Where was that?'

'In a women's prison.'

'Well, I'm glad to hear it turned out well.'

'If only they all did,' she muttered, rubbing reflexively at the scar on her face.

She saw him register her movements with a tiny probing twitch of his eyes. She self-consciously brushed her loose lock of hair back down over her scar.

'Anyhow,' he said. 'What I also wanted to say was, seeing as we'll be working closely together on this job, why don't we catch up for a drink soon? Get to know each other a little better.'

He suddenly looked a little uncertain as he awaited her response, almost shy, and it occurred to her that perhaps he wasn't quite as arrogant and self-assured as she'd first assumed.

'Sure,' she said. 'Why not.'

There was a 'ping' as the lift arrived. She stepped inside and turned around to wave goodbye to his smiling face as the doors closed on him.

As the lift descended to the ground floor, Bailey realised with some surprise that he'd just asked her out on a date. Or had he? It had been so long since she'd been on one that she'd forgotten what it felt like to be asked.

No. Surely not. Not with her scars. Why would he want to do that?

6

Two days into January and Bailey found herself on the tenth floor of a tower block looking out over the cluttered sprawl of East London beneath the grey chill of an overcast sky.

She turned away from the floor-to-ceiling window to face back into the apartment she'd just entered.

It was a new-build flat in Stratford, situated on one of the upper floors of a shiny tower block that had been thrown up in the wake of the 2012 Olympics when the whole area had undergone a regeneration of sorts. Fairly spacious for a one-bedroom apartment, it possessed generous windows and questionable taste in interior design, and it was reserved especially for the use of undercover police officers, but it also occasionally functioned as a safe house when the need arose.

With the more lightweight undercover jobs, Bailey would just return to her own flat at the end of the day, but for an operation like this it would be necessary for her to live a deep-cover lifestyle twenty-four hours a day. An organisation like the Molloys was likely to have good surveillance and it would be too risky for her to go back to her own place with the possibility that someone might be following her.

'I have to say, I prefer South London,' she said to Frank, who'd just let her in and was showing her around. 'But this flat does have a good view though.'

Her own place in Crystal Palace was a basement flat and the view from her living room consisted of a moss-coated metal slab covering a storm drain which had an annoying tendency to back up when it rained a lot.

'It's not *Miami Vice* or anything,' said Frank. 'But it's not bad for taxpayers' money. And it should do the job of convincing anyone who decides to check you out. And Stratford is kind of in the Molloys' neck of the woods.'

She glanced around the rest of the flat, seeing that the kitchen was open-plan with a breakfast bar separating it from the living room area. She'd always wanted an open-plan kitchen – her own kitchen was a rather cramped galley affair. She wandered over to have a closer look.

Meanwhile, Frank took a thick chunky envelope out of the bag he was carrying and dropped it onto the living room table.

'These are your credentials. Passport, driver's licence, and so on. Even a gym membership for the gym on the ground floor. All under the name of Bailey Sharpe. Just as you requested.'

She nodded absently as she peered inside various cupboards. 'Thanks. I'll go through them later.'

He placed a laptop on the table next to the envelope. 'And here's a laptop.'

Bailey turned the tap on in the kitchen. The water dribbled out in a feeble trickle. 'The water pressure's a bit low,' she said.

Frank looked up and shrugged apologetically. 'I can get someone to look at it if you want.'

'And I'm really not sure about this decor,' she said, casting her gaze around the inside of the apartment. There was something fundamentally kitsch and tasteless about the way the place had been decked out. In the centre of the living room was a round nautical-themed coffee table constructed out of a ship's wheel. On the wall by the entrance hallway there was a large garish mirror with a gold bevelled frame. And standing beneath the mantelpiece was a life-sized porcelain model of a jaguar. Bailey's eyes rested on the porcelain jaguar, her fore-head wrinkling in puzzlement. 'Who on earth thought that was a good idea? I've never seen anything so tacky in all my life.'

'I'm sure you'll make the place your own. But don't make it too cosy. Remember to stay in character.' Frank paused. 'Talking of which. Here. A moving-in present.' He opened a carrier bag and took out a handful of DVDs, which he placed on the table. 'I picked up a load of films this morning. Any self-respecting gangster would own these movies.'

'DVDs, Frank?' she said, shaking her head. 'You're so old-school. I do have Netflix, you know.'

'Yeah, but these'll look cooler on your bookshelf. And this place does come with a DVD player.'

She gave a concessionary nod and went over to the table to have a look through them.

'*Scarface*...' she murmured. It was one of those films she'd never got round to watching.

'With Al Pacino,' he said. 'All aspiring gangsters seem to be obsessed with that film. They can't get enough of it. Especially that bit at the end where he shoots everybody.'

She continued to leaf through them. '*The Godfather*... *Carlito's Way*... *Goodfellas*...' She frowned and held up a DVD. She raised one eyebrow. '*Frozen*?'

Frank looked perplexed. Then his face broke into a sheepish smile. 'Oh whoops! I bought that for when my daughter comes round. Must have got mixed up with the others.'

Looking a little embarrassed, he took it back from her. Frank had a five-year-old daughter called Isabel who he rarely saw, legacy of a marriage wrecked by his extreme dedication to his job.

He suddenly clicked his fingers. 'Oh yeah, I almost forgot. This place does have a special feature. Follow me.'

He walked into the bathroom. Intrigued, she followed him. He stood by the sink and turned to face her. He raised his eyebrows expectantly.

'Yes?' she said, feeling like he was playing games with her.

'Notice anything?'

So he was testing her observation skills. She looked around. Up, down. Left, right. Nothing special, so it seemed. She shook her head.

'Good,' he said, seemingly pleased.

He nodded at the bathroom cabinet which was affixed to the wall just above the sink. 'There's a secret compartment in a cavity in the wall behind the cabinet. If you need to hide anything, you can put it in there.'

Grasping the top and bottom of the bathroom cabinet, he gave it a hard pull, and with a small click, the entire thing came away from the wall, opening up like a door, with a hinge on one side. Behind it was a small square recess in the wall.

'I guess there wasn't quite enough room to stick a safe in there. But I suppose there's no need if it's supposed to be hidden.'

'I'd only have forgotten the combination,' said Bailey. 'Still, it's a pretty neat feature. I'm sure I'll find a use for it.'

He nodded with a satisfied smile and pushed the cabinet back into place with a click.

They both returned to the living room.

'Well, I guess I'll be going now,' he said, surreptitiously picking up the DVD of *Frozen*. 'I'll let you get settled in. We'll be in touch soon about the next stage of the operation. Oh... and Happy New Year by the way.'

On the subject of his final point, Bailey decided she'd wait and see how the next few weeks panned out before making a judgement about whether that was the case or not.

After he'd gone, she stood there for a few moments looking down at the two large bags she'd brought with her. They represented the sum total of her existence from this point onwards. She had to admit, they looked a bit pathetic.

She sighed and knelt down and began to unpack. Along with a few outfits she'd deemed suitable for this particular role, she'd also brought several books of cryptic crosswords, including the one her father had given her for Christmas, as well as a portable Bluetooth speaker so she could listen to her Spotify lists of her favourite eighties power ballads.

She'd left her jiu-jitsu kit back at her Crystal Palace flat. Much as she loved going to her jiu-jitsu club and honing her martial arts skills, she'd decided to put that on hold for the time being. She didn't want to keep her jiu-jitsu gear in her undercover flat in case someone hostile ended up poking around in there and found it; when it came to undercover work, she thought it more advantageous to keep her self-defence capabilities concealed from the criminals she was working with.

As she unpacked her stuff, she reflected on the transience of undercover life and wondered if she'd ever properly settle down. She couldn't imagine living a conventional domestic life, and she wasn't sure she wanted one anyhow.

She took out a large tub of Quality Street that her mother had given her for Christmas. In a small concession to homeliness, she pulled off the lid and upended the whole tub of sweets into a large ceramic bowl that had been standing empty on the sideboard next to the front door. She immediately picked out one of the red ones, unwrapped it and popped it in her mouth. Fudge. Yum. Her favourite.

Throwing herself down on the sofa, Bailey began to go through the identity documents Frank had provided, chewing on the fudge as she did so. She flicked through the passport, the driver's licence, the credit card, the gym membership and the other various bits of identification that supported her cover identity as one Bailey Sharpe. As well as the credentials, she had the laptop, and of course she also had her second mobile phone which she used purely for undercover operations.

She briefly contemplated changing the ringtone on her undercover phone to one of her favourite eighties pop classics but then thought better of it, figuring it was a safer bet to remain with the boring default ringtone instead. On an undercover job you never knew what kind of delicate situation you might be in when your phone rang and the wrong type of person just might get offended by your taste in ringtone, with potentially detrimental consequences.

She examined the photo on the driving licence. She was wearing a particularly sullen and shifty expression, which, combined with the scar on her face, made her look appropriately villainous. She smiled to herself, pleased with the result. She ran the tips of her fingers over the embossed letters of her new name. Bailey Sharpe. Yet another new identity to immerse herself in. There had been so many by now that she'd lost count.

New Year, New You, she thought.

7

'Spyros!'

Bailey jerked awake. Breathing hard. Her heart beating furiously. The sheets soaked in sweat. Her nostrils filled with the smell of her own burning flesh fused with the sickly aroma of clove smoke. That name on her lips...

With the agony of the torture still uppermost in her mind, she instinctively ran her hands over her body to check her injuries. But there was no blood now, no raw wounds. Not any more. Just the hard raised ridges of the scars made by the straight razor and the rough patches of the burn marks made by the glowing tip of a clove cigarette.

With a start, Bailey realised she didn't recognise where she was. The bed felt odd. The shape of the room was different. Then, as her disorientation began to evaporate, she remembered she was in her new apartment. Her undercover apartment. Her tension started to subside a little.

It was dark outside beyond the blinds. She leaned over and pressed the button on her phone on the bedside table. The illuminated screen told her it was three thirty in the morning.

It had just been a dream. A nightmare. But it had seemed so real. It always did. She'd had it so many times, but it never got stale. The horror was always as fresh and visceral as it had been the first time. She might have a new identity, but she still couldn't get rid of the nightmares from the old ones. Still she awoke in the middle of the night skewered by the savage memory of that botched job that had gone so terribly wrong, leaving her scarred for life both inside and out.

She'd been working undercover to catch a gang of professional car thieves when her cover had been blown. They'd left her to the mercies of a gangland torturer who'd taken his sweet time and enjoyment to make her give up the name of the informant who'd infiltrated her into their group.

Spyros.

But she hadn't given up the name. Despite the razor slicing her face, neck, breasts, belly. Despite the red-hot cigarette burning its way through the layers of her skin. Despite the sexual violations that had been inflicted upon her.

Her torturer's face was etched into her memory, leering as he desecrated her flesh in every way. She would catch up with him one day. She would punish him for what he'd done to her. But her attempts to track him down had so far proved fruitless. She didn't know his name and had failed to dig out even the smallest piece of information about him – he was too professional, too anonymous, and probably long gone now, vanished back into the darkness from whence he'd emerged.

Now she just screamed the name of the informant every night in her dreams to try and make them stop. To give her torturer what he wanted. But it didn't work. It never worked.

She'd known for a while now that she suffered from post-traumatic stress disorder. On the last undercover job, when she'd been incarcerated at HMP Foxbrook, the prison psychologist, Doctor Bodie, had diagnosed her as such. He might not have known who she was in terms of her true identity, but he definitely knew what she was – a woman with severe emotional damage.

When she wasn't on an undercover job, she was required to attend periodic appointments with the police psychologist. Bailey hadn't found her to be of much help however. She just found it too hard to open up. But she knew if she didn't turn up to the meetings, or if the psychologist found her to be mentally unfit, then she would be withdrawn from doing undercover work and Bailey couldn't afford to let that happen because undercover was what she lived for. So she exercised her skills in deception to maintain a convincing appearance of good mental health.

For Bailey, undercover work was a necessity rather than a choice. Her adrenaline threshold had been pushed so high by that life of constant peril that normal existence seemed pallid and flat by comparison. The irony was that although undercover work was responsible for her PTSD, it was also the one thing that mitigated its impact. The nightmares, the trouble focusing, the panic attacks – all of those things receded when she was fully engaged in that role, mainlining on the danger she craved so profoundly.

She pulled herself out of bed. Once she was awake, Bailey found it near impossible to get back to sleep and she knew that rather than lie there ruminating in the darkness, letting negative thoughts overwhelm her, the best thing she could do right now was to get up and find other things to occupy her mind.

Entering the bathroom, she flicked on the light and looked at herself in the mirror, confronted once again by that familiar ghostly complexion of ashen skin and dark rings around the eyes. Frequent lack of sleep left her with a constant residual background fatigue which threatened to take the edge off her capabilities. She'd have to push it back with an energy drink or two later in the day.

Opening the bathroom cabinet, she took out a box of beta blockers, popped two from the blister pack and knocked them back with a mouthful of water straight from the tap.

She went into the living room and sat down on the sofa. Switching on the TV, she flicked aimlessly from channel to channel, as usual finding little at this hour that grabbed her interest.

She paused on the news to watch that for a bit. It was going on about some of the candidates who were running for Mayor of London in the upcoming mayoral elections in May. It seemed the favourite to win was the Conservative candidate, Lewis Ballantyne. His manifesto was strong on law and order, with pledges to significantly increase both the size and the power of the Metropolitan Police. Bailey knew he was supremely popular with the Met's top brass for this very reason. On the TV right now, talking in a pre-recorded segment, she watched him speaking in his Home Counties accent as he smoothly reiterated his election agenda. Probably in his late forties, he was immaculately groomed, with one of those healthy tans you got from going on plenty of expensive holidays abroad. But like so many politicians, he emanated a faint air of sleaze and Bailey wondered just how far he'd actually keep to his pledges if he did end up getting elected.

After a short while, she switched over, eventually settling on a vapid reality TV show about people who'd had terrible tattoos and now wanted something done about them. Bailey herself still had the tattoo on her lower back that she'd acquired during the prison job as part of her infiltration into a prison gang. But unlike the people on the TV show, Bailey was actually very fond of her tattoo and had no plans to get it removed. It was just too good a piece of artwork.

The thought of that job and the circumstances under which she'd acquired the tattoo triggered a tumult of emotions, some good... some bad. It seemed that with every job she did, she seemed to pick up some form of physical memento. The tattoo from the prison job... The scars from the car theft job...

One thing she definitely seemed to gain with every job were enemies. She was slowly and steadily amassing them. They were people who she'd had locked up, as well as people who she'd tried and failed to have locked up. They were all out there, somewhere, her face in their heads and vengeance in their hearts. But she refused to let herself think about them too much. If she did that, then she'd never feel safe...

8

The police property storeroom was an Aladdin's cave filled to the brim with things that had been seized in the course of various operations – designer clothing, drugs, weapons, antiques, jewellery, state-of-the-art electronics... It was a resource that undercover police officers drew on a lot. They were allowed to use just about any object in there as a prop in an operation, so long as it wasn't some vital piece of evidence that needed to be exhibited in court, and so long as they followed due procedure in signing it out and signing it back in again when they'd finished with it.

The place was located down in the basement, and in fitting with the sensitive character and often high-value nature of its contents, it was well secured behind a heavy metal grille door.

Bailey had used her swipe card to gain access and was now gazing around in awe at the metal shelving units packed with plastic bags and boxes all labelled up with details of the various operations to which they pertained.

'I love this place,' she murmured. 'It's like some kind of crazy junk shop.'

'How can I be of assistance?' said the man working there, taking his feet off the desk and putting down the comic book he'd been reading.

Bailey glanced at the cover. It looked like a vintage edition.

'Superman issue one,' he said informatively. 'Proceeds of a burglary. Can't be that many in existence, so I'm sure we'll find the owner soon enough.'

His name was Keith and he was somewhat on the podgy side, his belly straining at his T-shirt, and he was kind of pasty, like he didn't get enough vitamin D being cooped up down here all day long in the basement.

'What have you got in the way of designer clothing?' Bailey asked.

She wanted to look the part and the kind of player she was intending to transform herself into for this role would wear expensive clothing. However, her detective constable salary only stretched so far, so she thought she'd save herself a bit of cash and come down to the police property storeroom to see what they had.

'Hmm... designer clothing eh?' He frowned and scratched his crew cut. 'We've usually got plenty of that down here. Let me have a look.'

With a grunt, he pulled himself to his feet and began to root around in various boxes, pulling them out and peering inside and mumbling to himself, breaking into a slight sweat with the exertion.

'Not that one... How about this one... No... Let's have a look up here...'

While he did so, Bailey poked around curiously. The police property storeroom always fascinated her. You never knew quite what you would find in here.

She picked up a plastic bag containing a metallic ball-shaped object. It was heavy, olive green in colour, and about the size of a large kiwi fruit. She held it up with a puzzled frown. 'What's this?'

Keith glanced over his shoulder. 'I believe that is an M67 fragmentation grenade.'

Bailey's eyes widened. 'It's a bomb?!'

'Basically. Confiscated from some outlaw biker who was on his way to chuck it into the clubhouse of a rival motorcycle gang. Those fellas don't do things by halves.'

She peered through the bag at it. It had yellow military writing stencilled on it. 'Are you sure it's safe to keep it in here?'

'Yeah, it's perfectly safe... so long as you don't pull the pin out.'

'If you say so,' she said, gingerly placing the grenade back into its evidence box on the shelf.

Rummaging around in a cardboard box, Keith pulled out a black leather coat and held it up for her inspection. 'How about Hugo Boss?'

She gave it an appraising gaze. 'I like it.'

He tossed it to her. She pulled it on. It was a fraction too large. But it felt right. It felt like it fitted this particular cover identity.

'I think it's genuine and everything,' said Keith. 'Fell off the back of a lorry, apparently.'

Stolen goods recovered from criminals made up a good proportion of the stuff in here. Bailey knew that anything that couldn't be returned to its original owners would eventually be disposed of at auction.

On a shelf next to her, she noticed a box full of black Oakley Holbrook sunglasses. She pulled out a pair and tried them on. She knew that criminals often wore sunglasses in order to conceal what they were thinking, even if the weather didn't particularly warrant them, and that was the kind of vibe she wanted to project.

Keith looked at her and nodded in approval. 'Very stylish.'

She went over to the desk with him and filled out the necessary forms to sign the items out.

He smiled at her when she'd finished. 'Now these are just a loan, remember?'

9

Sitting opposite Dale in the noisy cocktail bar, sipping her vodka black-currant, Bailey frowned as she tried to work out what was different about him since Hendon. There'd been some subtle physical change, but she couldn't determine exactly what it was. Maybe he'd just grown older.

He was perched on a stool with his elbow resting on the bar sipping a whisky sour. Dressed casually now it was the evening, he was clad in black Levi's and a slim-fit white shirt which showed off his muscular physique to good effect.

Misinterpreting the frown on her face, he smiled and said, 'Don't worry, the drinks are on me. I know this place isn't cheap.'

She blinked away her preoccupations. 'It's fine. I don't mind paying my way.'

Whether or not this was actually a date or just an informal work catch-up, both of them had clearly made the effort to look good. Not normally a fan of make-up, Bailey had stretched to a dash of lip gloss and a bit of eyeliner, and she'd decided to forego the baseball cap she normally liked to wear when she dressed casually.

Dale's striking blue eyes flickered curiously over the scars on her face and neck, his interest more overt now that he'd had a drink to lessen his inhibitions. He didn't appear to be repulsed by them, however, much to her relief, and she felt flattered for that reason, but at the same time she also still felt deeply insecure about her disfigurement, particularly because she found herself attracted to him.

She brushed her loose lock of hair down further over the scar on her face and tried to divert his attention onto something else.

'So how did you get into working with informants?' she asked.

He pursed his lips as he thought about it. 'Well, working as a detective, I found I had quite a knack for getting confessions out of people. And from there it was a logical progression into recruiting informants.'

'It must be quite challenging work.'

'It can be. Yes. As I'm sure you probably know from your own experience, informants can be pretty unreliable people and they've almost always got some self-serving agenda of their own.'

'You mean they don't do it because they care about justice?' said Bailey sarcastically.

Dale smiled. 'Adrian was no different to the rest of them, although perhaps his motives were a little more personal. He was quite a flamboyant and reckless person. Liked to flash wads of cash around, liked to race high-performance cars, talked himself up endlessly, had a gigantic ego, and took a lot of cocaine. All in all, not a great recipe for a reliable source of information. But you've got to work with what you've got.'

'Sounds like he's delivered the goods though,' she said, thinking about the information Adrian had provided on the ecstasy and the guns.

'Yeah,' conceded Dale, 'although I found I had to turn a bit of a blind eye now and then.'

'He had other schemes running?'

'These people always do, and sometimes they really take the piss. I was very clear with him at the beginning on the rules. The deal was that he could only participate in a crime if his role was minor and he didn't engage in any of the planning or committing of it; and I told him he had to keep me, as his handler, fully informed about everything he was doing. I said if I found out he was involved in any crimes he wasn't telling me about, then he'd be liable for arrest and prosecution.

'Even so, I had the very strong feeling he was still engaged in various bits of skullduggery behind my back. But I didn't probe too hard. Because at the end of the day you've got to see the bigger picture, and that's to take down the Molloys, for good.'

'How did you feel when he got blown up?' asked Bailey, curious to understand more about Dale's line of work. She herself hadn't worked anywhere near as closely with informants as he had.

Dale sighed. 'Well, technically, as his handler, I was responsible for his well-being as a confidential source. But I can't say I was all that cut up about it. He wasn't a great human being or anything. I'm just glad no innocent people were hurt in the blast.'

'Apart from that girl who was with him.'

'Who? Tiffany?'

'Was that her name?'

'Yes. It was a shame that she died of course. I suppose she was innocent. But then, if you're going to hang around with a villain like Adrian...'

'She probably didn't know any better. Probably just thought he was a bloke with a fancy car and lots of money.'

They lapsed into momentary silence. Bailey took a sip of her drink and found that she'd finished it.

Once more she caught Dale scrutinising her scars and she had the feeling he wanted to raise the subject in some way. Again she attempted to deflect his interest.

'So... are you in a relationship at the moment?' she said, guessing that he probably wasn't.

He fixed her with a gaze for a few long moments and she wondered if she'd asked too personal a question, then he smiled. 'Not at the moment. Haven't been for a while. I was engaged... a long time ago. But she broke it off. She wanted kids and all that, but I wasn't ready.'

Bailey raised her eyebrows at the similarities to her own situation. 'Same thing with me,' she said. 'I dated a guy called Mark for two years.

He's a detective sergeant. We were also engaged. He wanted to have kids... and that basically meant me having the kids, and having to give up the work I loved, whilst nothing essentially changed for him.'

'So you ended it?'

'I just didn't see myself as a stay-at-home mum of two.'

'Are you seeing anyone currently?' he asked.

Bailey shook her head. She'd been more or less single ever since she'd acquired the scars. The torture had left a vicious legacy: on one level, she was riddled with insecurities about her physical appearance, and on a deeper level, the violations she'd suffered had crippled her ability to form intimate relationships. Sitting here now, on what might be a date, she felt somewhat awkward and out of practice with the whole idea of getting to know someone. But despite all that, she knew inside herself that it was good for her to be going out like this. It was a step towards overcoming her negative experiences. Anyhow, she found she was enjoying Dale's company.

He eyed her empty glass. 'Would you like another drink?'

She nodded.

He got them both the same again, insisting on buying this second round also. She didn't protest.

'You know,' he said carefully. 'I'm kind of surprised you're still working undercover.'

She silently contemplated him. 'What do you mean?'

But she knew exactly what he was referring to. He had, finally, got around to asking.

He swallowed uncomfortably. 'I mean... Everyone knows you did an amazing job with that car theft ring. They all went down for years, right?' He took a deep breath. 'But I also heard you were lucky to escape with your life.'

She tried to give an offhand shrug. 'Not all operations go to plan.'

'What went wrong?' he asked.

'My cover got blown.'

The sweet cloying smell of clove smoke suddenly filled her nostrils. A wave of nausea hit her. She flashed back to that bare concrete room.

Hanging chained up from the meat hook. The blood running in hot rivulets down her body. The incessant excruciating pain. Her heart palpitated and the cocktail bar began to spin around her and she felt as if she might fall off her bar stool. Maybe she'd had too much to drink already.

She gulped hard and placed her hand on the edge of the bar to steady herself.

Dale leaned in with concern, placing a gentle hand on her forearm.

'Bailey, are you okay?'

She blinked and took a deep breath and nodded.

He gave her arm a soft squeeze, then withdrew his hand.

'I'm sorry,' he said. 'I shouldn't have brought it up.'

'No, it's okay.' She forced a smile. 'But do you mind if we change the subject?'

They chatted a short while longer, just inane small talk, until they'd both finished their drinks. And then they left the bar.

Standing outside, they prepared to go their separate ways. There was a pregnant pause, then Dale said, 'You know, I always had a bit of a soft spot for you, Bailey. Back at Hendon.'

Bailey swallowed as a little spasm of warm butterflies went through her.

'You could have fooled me,' she laughed nervously. 'I never even thought you noticed me. Mr Hotshot Dale Bleudore.'

'Oh, I certainly noticed you,' he said.

He suddenly looked embarrassed and dropped his gaze, shifting bashfully from one foot to the other. Then he looked up again, putting on a businesslike face.

'Anyway, better get going, eh? It's getting late.'

Bailey gulped and nodded.

It seemed neither of them quite knew the most appropriate way to say goodbye. For a moment she thought they were going to embrace with a kiss on the cheek, but they didn't. Instead they just ended up waving at each other.

'Au revoir,' she said.

He frowned. 'Eh?'

'It's French. It means "see you again".'

'Oh yeah. Indeed. See you again.'

And as she watched him walk off, she realised that she was looking forward to doing exactly that.

10

The piece of news was devastating. Bailey stared in horror at her father as he lay there in the hospital bed looking back at her with a grave expression on his face.

'Stage four pancreatic cancer?' she gasped.

He nodded slowly. 'The doctors say it has metastasised to my liver and spleen.'

Bailey swallowed. The words seemed unreal. She didn't need to be an oncologist to know that this was indeed a grim diagnosis.

'They say I've got six months. At the outside.' His voice, although level in tone, rung with a bleak finality.

Bailey blinked in disbelief and looked up at her mother who was sitting on the other side of the bed clutching a Bible in her hand. Janet Morgan looked small and frail, racked with fatigue, like she'd been up all night every night for a while. Her husband, ironically, looked in better form than she did, but Bailey knew appearances could be deceptive when it came to cancer, and people could switch from healthy-looking individuals to walking skeletons in the space of just a few weeks.

'I had all the tests last week,' he said. 'One of those full-body CT scans. An MRI for my liver. Various X-rays. I didn't want to tell you until I got the full prognosis back.'

'I tried to call you earlier, Bailey, but I couldn't get through,' said her mother.

'I'm so sorry,' said Bailey, remorse filling her. 'I was busy. Work. I'm currently on an operation. My normal phone was switched off.'

She was struck by a wave of self-reproach at the thought of her parents going through all this without telling her, and then cruelly being unable to get through to her when they finally had decided to break the bad news.

'That's okay,' said her father with a gentle smile. 'More important that you're out there catching criminals than worrying about me. Anyhow, it's a friendly enough place here.' He gestured around the ward at the other patients lying in their beds. He was currently residing in the gastroenterology ward in the Princess Royal Hospital in Orpington, not far from Bromley.

Bailey felt tears come to her eyes and everything went blurry. Her father. He had always been there for her. She loved him so much. And now he was going to die. In a short while, he'd no longer be there any more. Ever. She felt her inner world collapsing.

'No,' she whispered. 'There must be a way. There must be some treatment.'

He squeezed her hand and shook his head fatalistically. 'The cancer has spread too far through my body. It's too late to do anything now.'

'But what about chemotherapy or something?' she said desperately.

'I'm talking to the consultant about it at the moment. He told me I could choose to have the chemo if I wanted, but he explained that all it'll do is just keep me going for a bit longer. When the cancer is as advanced as mine, it's probably not worth it.'

Bailey sat there shaking her head, finding it hard to accept what he was telling her.

'I've got some important decisions to make,' he continued stoically.

'About where I want to spend my remaining time. They told me I could be moved back home if I wanted, or I could go into a hospice.'

She stifled a sob. He squeezed her hand gently again.

'But for the time being,' he said, 'they're going to keep me here in hospital while they tinker with the dosages of the drugs that they're giving me.' He nodded up at a device standing next to his bed. It was a box fixed atop a stand with a tube feeding from it into his upper arm.

Trying to process everything that her father had just told her, Bailey remembered then that it was only the sixth of January. If he'd just had the tests the previous week, that meant he must have had some inkling that something was wrong with him over Christmas.

She felt guilt start to well up inside her. During that argument they'd had over Christmas, the cancer had been growing inside him, its poisonous tentacles silently spreading through his body, dragging him away from her.

'I'm sorry, Dad,' she blurted, tears now running openly down her face.

He frowned and looked surprised. 'Sorry? Why?'

'For arguing with you.'

He shrugged it away with a smile. He handed her a tissue from the box on his bedside table. 'Let's not worry about that now. Let's think about happier times. While we still can, eh?'

And so they tried to talk about the old days, avoiding for the time being the subject of Jennifer, and instead harking back to the more innocent halcyon times before her disappearance. Holidays they'd spent together. Bailey's childhood. The little memories. The ones that mattered. They talked and they even laughed. And before Bailey knew it, several hours had passed and eventually, reluctantly, she stood up to leave.

Outside, it was completely dark overhead. It was almost five thirty in the evening and the sun had set over an hour before. As she walked through the hospital car park, the thought of how little time her father had left brought tears to her eyes once more. She felt like she hadn't spent nearly enough time with him, and what time she had spent, she had mostly spent arguing with him about Jennifer.

Bailey realised that she herself now had some important decisions to make. Should she quit this new undercover job right now so she could spend more time with her father before he died?

11

Bailey spent the next morning in the gym on the ground floor of the Stratford apartment block, trying to work off some of the emotional tension that was burdening her around her father and what she should do next.

After the gym, she came back up to the flat, took a shower, ate lunch, and was now sitting on the sofa holding her undercover phone in her hand, locked in a debate with herself about what would be the best thing to do.

She had Rick's number here and she could call him right now and kick off the operation immediately, but she knew that once she embarked on that course of action, there would be no turning back.

The problem was that she knew that time was now very limited for her father and that every day was valuable from this moment onwards. Instead of calling Rick she could call Frank and quit this assignment so she could spend more time with her father. She knew Frank and Dale would be hugely disappointed and the last thing she wanted to do was let them down. But she was sure they'd be able to find someone else to take her place.

It was a tough quandary and she was massively conflicted.

Her phone suddenly rang in her hand. She recognised the caller's number as Dale's. Hesitating a moment, she answered it.

'Hello Dale.'

'Hi Bailey. How are you?'

'Okay.'

By the brief silence, she could tell he was a little nonplussed by her taciturn response, but she had too much on her mind to worry about the niceties of social interaction. She waited for him to say whatever it was he was calling her about.

'Er... well, I was just calling to let you know that the murder investigation team have managed to locate a key witness. A homeless man who was in the vicinity of the car bomb. They've brought him in to answer a few questions. If you're interested, I can get them to hold off starting until you get here.'

She sat there silently for a few moments, mulling over whether to jack in the job right now whilst he was on the phone.

'Bailey, are you sure you're okay?' he asked, a tone of concern in his voice.

'Yeah, I'm fine.'

'It was just that it occurred to me that this homeless guy might have some information that could be of use to you in some way. You never know, right?'

She chewed her lip, torn by indecision. Should she quit the job?

'Bailey?' he said.

'Sure, Dale,' she said with a sigh. 'I'll be there in half an hour.'

12

Bailey stood behind the one-way glass peering into the interview room at the two detectives from the murder investigation team as they prepared to question the homeless man. They'd introduced themselves to Bailey a short while earlier – Detective Sergeant Adam Blake, who was white, and Detective Sergeant Joseph Charles, who was black. Both were clean-shaven and wearing smart suits, in polar contrast to the grimy bearded man swathed in tattered rags who was slouched opposite them across the table.

Dale, standing beside her, had shot her the odd curious look when she'd arrived, having clearly detected that something had been up with her over the phone, but he hadn't pressed her and for that she was grateful.

'When are you planning on getting in contact with Rick?' he asked expectantly.

She gave him an oblique look. 'When I'm ready.'

She was almost on the verge of telling him that she wanted to pull out of the operation, but couldn't quite bring herself to disappoint him. Instead, she turned her attention to the scene on the other side of the glass, allowing it to distract her from having to make that momentous decision.

In front of the homeless man was a steaming mug of tea, along with a plate of custard creams, which he was industriously munching his way through. He was looking around the room suspiciously, shifting uncomfortably on the chair, as if he was now beginning to regret coming here. She knew that as a witness he wasn't actually compelled to attend and was free to leave any time he wanted, though how far he was aware of that right now was another matter.

'They initially noticed him on public CCTV,' said Dale. 'So they knew he was there when the bomb went off. But it took them a while to track him down. They promised him a hot cup of tea and a biscuit and he was happy to come in. They thought it better to bring him into the station so they could record the statement.'

'Please state your full name,' said DS Blake.

'Dave Boakes,' said the homeless man after a short pause. Bailey detected a regional inflection in his voice. Bristol perhaps.

'What's your place of abode?'

Bailey rolled her eyes. 'Seriously...?'

Dave smiled at the question. 'I like to move around. But I would say my main *place of abode* is currently underneath the Westway.'

The Westway was a large elevated road leading into London from the West of England.

'I like West London,' he added, picking up another custard cream. 'You get a better class of person around there.'

'Can you tell us what you were doing in Chiswick the evening that the bomb went off?' said DS Charles.

'I was just sitting there in a doorway, trying to keep warm. As you do.'

'Can you tell us what you saw?'

'I didn't see anything,' said Dave, swallowing the biscuit.

'Nothing?'

He shook his head. He looked at the empty plate in front of him. 'Got any more biscuits?'

'When you tell us what you saw.'

'It was kind of dark. Couldn't see much. And it was cold. Very cold.'

'You must have seen something,' said Blake.

'We've got you on CCTV talking to the victims,' Charles added. 'What did you talk to them about?'

'I asked him if he had any spare change and he gave me fifty quid.' Dave smiled proudly.

Blake raised his eyebrows. 'Fifty quid? That's generous. What did you buy with it?'

Dave scratched his head quizzically and a perturbed frown settled on his face. 'I don't remember.' He glanced around the interview room. 'I don't like this place. I want to go now.' He crossed his arms and sat there with a sullen expression.

The two detectives looked at each other and sighed.

Dave scratched at a sore on his neck. As he did so, the cuff of his grubby coat fell aside to reveal an incongruously flashy watch.

'That's a nice watch you've got there,' said Blake.

Dave glanced down at his watch and cupped it defensively against his chest. 'It's mine,' he said.

'That's a Rolex GMT, if I'm not mistaken,' said Charles. 'They cost at least ten grand and I hear there's a three-year waiting list if you want to get a new one.'

Dave shrugged defiantly.

'Want to tell us where you got it?' said Blake.

'It was a present.'

The two detectives looked at each other sceptically.

Dale turned to Bailey.

'Interesting,' he murmured. 'Adrian had a blue Rolex GMT. Exactly the same as that one. I remember seeing it when I met him and thinking what flashy bastards these gangster types can be.'

'Looks like your watch has got a bit of damage,' Charles continued, peering at Dave's wrist. 'Looks a bit scorched. Like it was in a fire or something.' He frowned. 'And it looks like it's stopped.'

Blake leaned forward for a closer look. 'Well, well. It's stopped at exactly ten twenty-four. If I'm not mistaken, that's the exact time that the bomb went off. It's almost like it suffered a large fiery shock at exactly that time. Like...' He turned to Charles. They both made a big show of scratching their chins. 'Like a car bomb for example,' he finished.

'You want to get that watch looked at, mate,' Charles suggested.

'Yeah, I hear the Rolex shop on Bond Street does repairs,' Blake added. 'Maybe you should drop in.'

'Although I suppose it does tell the right time twice a day,' said Charles.

Blake leaned in, the sarcastic smirk dropping off his face. 'Did you take that watch from the crime scene?'

'N... no,' stuttered Dave. He clutched the watch tighter to his chest. As he did so, Bailey noticed that, with his other hand, he also protectively cupped a gaudy plastic keyring that was hanging around his neck from a shoelace. By his reaction, she idly wondered if he'd taken that from the crime scene as well. Looking closer, she saw that the keyring took the form of a cutesy manga-style kitten with an oversized head wearing pink dungarees. Perhaps the keyring had belonged to the female victim of the blast. Bailey couldn't imagine that Adrian Molloy would have possessed such an item.

'There was a body part close to where you were situated,' Charles continued. 'A human arm, to be precise, belonging to the male occupant of the vehicle that was blown up. A left arm. Did you remove this watch from that arm?'

'No!' said Dave. His eyes rolled around in panic and he now had a trapped look about him.

'The bloke was nice enough to give you fifty quid and you go and repay him by nicking his watch,' admonished Charles.

'Taking evidence from a crime scene is a criminal act,' said Blake. 'That constitutes two crimes. Theft by finding. As well as the much more serious charge of perverting the course of justice.'

Charles shook his head gravely. 'Perverting the course of justice. That's serious. Carries a heavy sentence. You can get up to life.'

Although technically true, Bailey knew a life sentence was highly unlikely. The maximum sentence was usually between four and thirty-six months, or sometimes just a fine, though she couldn't imagine he'd be able to stump up much in the way of cash.

Blake shrugged reasonably. 'You might like prison. Three square meals a day. A roof over your head.'

'Of course,' said Charles, 'if you tell us exactly what you saw, then we might believe your story about the watch.'

Dave eyed them both resentfully and swallowed nervously.

'I saw someone,' he muttered. 'Next to the car. He was kneeling down.'

Both detectives leaned forward eagerly.

'You saw a man kneeling down next to the car that got blown up?' Blake pressed.

Dave nodded.

'What did he look like?' asked Charles. 'Was he white, black, Asian?'

Dave shook his head. 'I couldn't see. Honestly. He was in the shadows. He did something to the car. And then he disappeared.'

Blake spoke up. 'CCTV footage showed that he had some kind of hat pulled down low over his face, which meant that we were unable to make out what he looked like. We were hoping that maybe you got a better look.'

Dave shook his head. 'I told you. It was dark. I couldn't see anything. Couldn't see his face. Nothing.'

The two detectives swapped disappointed glances.

Dave looked up hopefully. 'Can I have some more biscuits now?'

Dale turned to Bailey with an apologetic shrug.

'Sorry, Bailey. I hope this wasn't a waste of your time.'

She turned to him, still unable and still unwilling to make up her mind about quitting the job.

'That's okay, Dale. Thanks for thinking of me though.'

13

The next afternoon, still mired in indecision, Bailey was sitting on the sofa in her Stratford flat watching the news, having just switched on the TV.

After only a few minutes, a news item came on reporting the deaths of two young female university students, gunned down in a drive-by shooting in South Tottenham. They'd just emerged from a fast-food restaurant when they'd been caught in a hail of bullets from a passing car. It appeared that they were innocent victims trapped in the crossfire of a turf war between drugs gangs.

Bailey observed, sickened and angry. Both of the girls had promising academic futures ahead of them and now they were dead and their families were devastated. What a pointless waste.

It struck her forcefully there and then that as a policewoman she had a duty to undertake this operation, to stop those guns falling into the hands of ruthless criminals like these who would so callously extinguish the lives of innocent people in their quest for power and profit. Frank was right. They couldn't allow Rick to get away with selling those firearms.

It was time to make up her mind. And watching this news item had already tipped her decision. She could do this job and still manage to make time for her father. She'd make it work. Somehow.

With her resolve steeled, she picked her undercover phone up off the coffee table and called Rick's number.

Listening to the dialling tone, she realised that her heart was beating hard in anticipation.

A moment later, a man's deep voice answered. 'Yeah?'

'Is that Rick?'

'Who's this?' he said suspiciously. His voice had the raspy edge of East London going on Essex.

'I'm enquiring about the furniture.'

A pause.

'What furniture?'

'The Victorian oak dining set.'

A long silence. Her heart thumping hard. Her mouth suddenly dry. This was it. If Rick knew that his brother had been an informant, then he'd more than likely hang up on her right now because he'd suspect she was an undercover police officer.

She sat there nervously awaiting his response, one part of her almost wanting him to hang up so she didn't have to go through with it. Finally he spoke.

'I was wondering when I'd hear from you,' he said tersely.

A tiny burst of elation shot through her. It looked like the job was on.

'As luck would have it, we're in town this afternoon,' he continued. 'Come to a pub called The Admiral in Canning Town. Meet me there at three thirty. Ask for Rick.'

Bailey swallowed. Wow. These people moved fast.

'Sure,' she said. 'See you there.'

He ended the call. She realised he hadn't even asked her name. He sure did like to keep business talk to a minimum over the phone, just like Dale had said. Well, she was certain they'd want to know all about her once she got there. She felt a flush of excitement.

Looking at her watch, she saw that it was two forty-five. She gulped.

She had three-quarters of an hour to get there. That wasn't much time. Clearly these people worked to their own schedule and expected her to adhere to it.

Her phone still in her hand, she immediately called Frank to let him know.

'It's great to hear you've got the ball rolling,' he said. 'Do you want me to organise a back-up team for you?'

'There's no time for that.' She paused. 'I'll be fine,' she added, suppressing a pre-emptive twinge of trepidation.

There was a brief silence at the other end of the line.

'If you say so,' he said, a slight waver of uncertainty in his voice. Her safety was his responsibility and she knew he took it seriously.

She terminated the call.

Jumping to her feet, she went into the bedroom and hurriedly pulled on her undercover outfit. For this particular identity, along with the Hugo Boss black leather coat, she'd opted for classic straight-cut blue jeans, a white collared man's shirt and a pair of sleek leather boots with a discreet heel. As for the scar on her face, she decided to display it openly in a vaguely piratical manner, tying back the loose lock of hair which normally covered it.

Grabbing her bag and picking up her car keys, she made her way to the front door, praying that there wouldn't be too much traffic. It wouldn't do to be late to an appointment with people like these.

But she stopped then in front of the large gold-framed mirror by the hallway. She just had one last important thing to do before she left. She had to put on her game face.

'The name's Bailey Sharpe,' she said to the mirror. 'And I can sort you out with almost anything you want.'

She put on her Oakley sunglasses. All in all, she thought she looked pretty convincing.

The whole act might have looked a bit ridiculous to anyone watching, but it was all part of her way of psyching herself up, of believing herself into the role.

She whirled around to leave the flat and was just about to close the front door when something niggling at the back of her mind suddenly dropped on her like a block of concrete.

She stopped dead in the hallway, opened her bag and took out her purse. Opening it, she saw that her warrant card was in there. Her heart turned over at the sight of it. Schoolgirl error! She couldn't believe she'd made such a fundamental oversight. That had been close.

As a policewoman, it was second nature to carry your warrant card around with you. But on an undercover operation, it was a very bad idea. It was the one incontrovertible piece of proof that you were a police officer. However much you might deny it, there was no getting around a warrant card if it was discovered.

For her first meeting with the Molloys, she had no idea what would happen, but it was probably much safer not to have it on her. She plucked it out of her purse and stood there holding it for a few moments. She realised she should probably put it in the secret compartment in the bathroom. But she couldn't be bothered to do that right now. She was already running late and she had no idea what the traffic would be like. So she just tossed her warrant card onto the sideboard by the front door. But then, on second thoughts, just in case, she picked it up and put it in the bowl of Quality Street, shoving it right to the bottom. And then she left the flat, reminding herself to put it in the secret compartment when she got back.

She made her way rapidly down to the basement car park. The car she'd chosen for this assignment was a metallic orange BMW M3 with tinted windows and black spider alloys. It came from the police pool and out of all of the available vehicles it was probably the one best suited to her cover identity. Just like the outfit she was wearing, it helped to cement her own self-belief in her new persona. External appearance was crucial in undercover work, not just in conveying the right impression to those she was doing business with, but in making her feel psychologically aligned to the role she was playing.

She pulled out from the underground car park and up onto the road, gunning the BMW aggressively through Stratford, relishing the power of the twin-turbo three-litre engine beneath the bonnet, noticing the envious looks from the groups of young men hanging around on the street, wannabe gangsters perhaps, aspiring to own a car just like the one she was driving.

As she sped off in the direction of Canning Town, she prayed that the Molloys would buy her cover story.

14

The Admiral was an old-school boozer with a squat fortress-like appearance which stood on a street corner in Canning Town in East London. The poky, cramped terraces running away from it in either direction had been workers' homes in the last century and they stood in the shadow of what had once been a large factory which was now in the process of being developed into luxury housing. Large cranes towered up all around and the air reverberated with the loud clunking of an industrial jackhammer.

Bailey parked just across the road from the pub. A gang of Asian youths sitting on a nearby wall eyed her truculently and she hoped they didn't try and break into her car. She shot them a don't-fuck-with-me look and headed across the road to the pub.

Pushing open the door, she was confronted with the sight of a few elderly white men sitting here and there drinking ale from pint glasses. She got a few disinterested glances but nothing more. Motes of dust danced idly in the rays of sunlight coming in through the leaded windows. There was a TV on the wall, but it was switched off. The place was dead.

The traditional decor – dark wood panelling with brass fittings, a cream ceiling and a brown patterned carpet – possessed a ratty, threadbare feel, as if long in need of refurbishment. Or else the pub was trying its hardest to be as unwelcoming as possible to all but the most committed drinkers.

Looking around at the clientele, she couldn't see anyone who resembled Rick. But then she didn't actually know what he looked like. She could have researched him beforehand, but the problem with that was that if you showed recognition of someone who you weren't technically supposed to know, then it instantly raised suspicion. So saying, she was pretty sure none of the old men sitting in here were Rick Molloy.

She went up to the bar. Beneath a framed portrait of the Queen stood a young white barman with a narrow face and a spiv-like appearance.

'What'll it be?' he said with a rodent smile, his eyes darting over her.

'I'm looking for Rick.'

He didn't look at all disconcerted by her request. He stuck his thumb over his shoulder. 'He's in the back room. He's expecting you.'

She paused a moment. 'Is my car going to be all right parked out there?' she asked, thinking of the gang of youths she'd passed.

He glanced over her shoulder, then shot her a wink. 'If you're with the Molloys it will be.'

She nodded in acknowledgement and headed into the dark narrow passage which lay around the side of the bar.

So this was it.

That familiar fear spiked through her gut. She'd felt it on so many jobs and she'd still never got used to it.

Stopping in front of the heavy wooden door of the back room, she took a deep breath before pushing it open and entering.

The room was windowless, lined with mirrors to give it the illusion of space. Brown leather seating ran around the walls and in front of that were eight or so tables in a broken horseshoe, in the middle of which stood a solitary empty wooden chair.

Seated with their backs to the wall like spectators in a show were five members of the Molloy crime family.

Bailey's eye immediately gravitated to the only other woman in the room, sitting at the back in the centre, like she was holding court, which in a sense Bailey guessed she was. For this could be none other than Nancy Molloy.

Small and vulpine, she had a sharp angular nose and a scraggy craning neck. Her black hair was cut into a neat bob, quite obviously dyed, and she was dressed smartly in a dark purple blazer and matching skirt. On the lapel of the blazer was pinned a large gold and blue enamelled brooch in the form of a forget-me-not flower. She wasn't unattractive for a woman of her age, definitely well-kept, for Bailey estimated her to be somewhere in her early sixties. What stood out most, however, were her dark close-set eyes which were fixed on Bailey with a penetrating laser-like stare.

Sitting on her lap was a fluffy white dog which Bailey recognised as a Pomeranian, a yappy pointless breed that she particularly disliked. And on the table in front of Nancy was a bone china cup and saucer and next to that a packet of Lambert and Butler with a fancy-looking gold lighter on top of it.

Bailey acknowledged Nancy with a curt nod, then pulled her eyes away to cast her attention to the other occupants of the room. Immediately to the right of Nancy sat a tall man clad in a stylish dark blue suit and a pair of black snakeskin brogues. Bailey guessed the suit to be Armani, tailored to fit his muscular frame, and beneath the jacket he wore a charcoal slim-fit shirt with a button-down collar and a maroon tie. She clocked a plain gold wedding band on his finger. On his wrist, she noticed a gold watch with a black leather strap, elegant and understated, as opposed to the chunky showy Rolexes that these types usually favoured, and that small detail told some part of her this was probably Rick Molloy.

His hair was shaven close to the skull and a thin black stubble coated his large square jaw, and on first impression, Bailey thought he was quite handsome, in a dark, mysterious way. He observed her closely with a set of emotionless black eyes which revealed no clue as to what thoughts lurked in their inky depths. They reminded her of the dead black eyes of a great white shark; seeing as he was close to the top of the food chain in the underworld, the analogy wasn't totally inappropriate.

Sitting by the wall to the left side of Bailey was a burly man, also in a dark suit, although his style wasn't quite as voguish as Rick's. He was broad-shouldered and olive-skinned... and he looked faintly familiar to Bailey.

It took a few moments for her to recognise him from the MMA circuit. His name was Shane Reaper. His nickname in mixed martial arts circles, predictably, was 'The Grim Reaper' and she knew he had a large skeleton-themed tattoo on his back depicting just that. Herself an experienced martial arts practitioner, Bailey had caught him in a few YouTube videos when she'd been trying to improve her jiu-jitsu groundwork techniques. His *hadaka-jime* – rear naked choke – was unparalleled; it was an ideal submission technique to use against more powerful opponents, which is why she, as a woman, was interested in perfecting it. She was faintly surprised to see him here.

Sitting across the room opposite Shane, on her right, was a skinny sallow man wearing a large pair of black wraparound sunglasses which lent him a distinctly insectoid air. He had a tapered face, thin lips, a pinched nose, a widow's peak and a pronounced Adam's apple. He tapped gently on the table with long spidery white fingers. When her gaze passed over him, his lips peeled back slightly in a humourless chilling death's-head smile to reveal a set of brown rotting teeth. She suppressed a shudder of revulsion.

And finally, sitting next to Nancy on her left, was a small, baby-faced man dressed in a checked grey suit and a black polo neck. He had a round face with blubbery lips and a button nose. There was something underdeveloped about his features, to the point where Bailey wondered if he'd suffered from some kind of birth defect. With his tiny hands, he was absently playing with a small bottle of hand sanitiser. He was staring at Bailey, unblinking, much too intensely for her liking, even for a criminal. She got a deeply hostile vibe from him and immediately marked him as a potential problem.

Bailey's heart was beating hard and her mouth had suddenly gone very dry, making it difficult for her to swallow. Here she was back in the undercover game right in the deep end. These people were top-echelon criminals and she was being subjected to their close perusal. She forced her nerves under control and reminded herself that they couldn't see through her.

Shane pushed himself to his feet, came up to her and gestured for her to lift her arms so he could pat her down, presumably to check for a wire. His hands glanced professionally up and down her limbs and torso, not lingering any longer than was necessary. He peered in her bag, took out her purse and tossed it to the baby-faced one who began to rummage through her fake credentials. Thank God she'd taken out her warrant card.

Shane nodded wordlessly at the lone chair in the middle of the room. She sat down on it. It felt hard and uncomfortable. He then walked behind her to stand in front of the door with his arms crossed, blocking the room's only entrance and exit.

Something had changed in the environment and it took her a few moments to notice that the sound of the jackhammer on the building site had faded down to an almost inaudible muted thumping. She realised then that this back room had been deliberately soundproofed, no doubt to guard against possible surveillance. That meant the Molloys probably owned this pub. It also made her horribly aware that if they decided to do something to her here in this room then no one would be able to hear her scream.

Bailey felt an acute sense of isolation as the silent weight of their scrutiny bore down on her with a crushing oceanic pressure.

She was centre stage and the show was about to begin.

15

The baby-faced one placed his bottle of hand sanitiser on the table and stood up. He was short, almost to the point of being a midget. Walking into the centre of the room, he pulled a chair from one of the tables and spun it around so the back of it was facing her. He sat astride it, crossing his arms atop the back of it, his face no more than fifty centimetres from hers.

'Take off your sunglasses,' he ordered. His voice was squeaky and nasty sounding.

She did so and he stared into her face, peering directly into her eyes, examining her hard for what were several very long seconds.

'Who are you?' he said. His tone was sharp and aggressive. She could feel his hot breath on her face. She wanted to move her head away, but she forced herself to remain firm. The rest of them just watched, their faces cold and inscrutable.

'My name's Bailey Sharpe,' she said in a measured tone.

He smiled in disbelief, his eyes flaring angrily. He shook his head slowly as if she'd given the wrong answer.

'What's your real name?' he demanded, despite the fact he'd just examined her identification.

For a moment she wondered if her cover was already blown, if they somehow knew she was an undercover cop, or if her credentials were apparent to them as fakes. But then she pulled herself together. They were just trying to intimidate her. That was all. The old undercover mantra came back to her now. Never break cover. Whatever happens, whatever they might claim, you never break your cover.

'That is my real name,' she said.

'I've never heard of you,' said Rick. His voice, although soft in tone, emanated a very real sense of coiled menace.

She turned to face him. 'I'm guessing you're Rick,' she said.

He made no attempt to affirm or deny her supposition. He just stared at her, cold and enigmatic, like a Sphinx.

'He said he's never heard of you,' spat the baby-faced one.

Bailey ignored him and kept her attention fixed on Rick.

'I generally try and stay below the radar,' she said. 'I find it works better that way.'

From what she knew about him, that was exactly the kind of philosophy Rick took, but if he concurred, he made no indication that way. He just looked at her with his impenetrable black eyes and said nothing.

She swallowed nervously. On closer inspection, she now noticed little skulls dotting his maroon tie and recognised it as Alexander McQueen. She would have complimented him on it but felt that now wasn't quite the appropriate time.

'How did you know Adrian?' demanded Nancy in a husky smoker's drawl, her eyes boring into Bailey.

Bailey calmly met her gaze. Nancy was her target today, the one whose confidence she ultimately had to win if she was to get in with them.

'We did a bit of business together in the past,' replied Bailey.

'Business?!' exclaimed the baby-faced one, with a look on his face like she'd personally insulted him. 'What kind of business?'

With some insight from Dale into the sorts of things Adrian had been involved in, Bailey had come up with what she hoped was a suitable explanation.

'I got chatting to him at a party one time. Told him I had a few keys of coke I wanted to offload. He helped me out. Then he told me all about these guns. And here I am.'

They glanced at one another. With Adrian dead, they knew they wouldn't be able to verify her story. Obviously, if Adrian was alive, he'd be here and he'd be able to vouch for her, but all they had to go on were her words, and she could see they were wary.

'Adrian never got round to telling me who you were exactly,' said Rick. 'Unfortunately he was blown up before he had the chance to. I guess you probably saw it on the news.'

She wondered if she should commiserate about Adrian's death. It was hard to tell how they felt about it; their expressions were closed with no overt indication of grief. They were all dressed in blacks and dark colours which might have been because they were in mourning for Adrian, or it might just have been because that was the way they dressed normally.

'I was sorry to hear about what happened to him,' she said. 'I was hoping we'd get to do a bit more work together.'

They observed her aloofly, maybe even suspiciously. Nancy's eyes in particular seemed to drill into her with a glacial intensity. But if they were jumpy about one of their own being murdered, they did a good job of hiding it.

Rick spoke. 'Well, just because Adrian happened to think you were all right, that doesn't mean we're automatically going to trust you.'

'What other business have you done?' demanded the baby-faced one.

One thing Bailey had learnt working undercover was that if you started doling out your cover story unprompted, it was an instant red flag that you were a copper. No criminal worth their salt would ever readily give up details of their illicit undertakings without at least a little inducement.

'I do a bit of this and that, here and there,' she said, remaining intentionally vague in order to intimate that her activities didn't necessarily reside on the proper side of the law.

'This and that?' sneered the baby-faced one incredulously. 'Here and there?'

'Yeah,' shrugged Bailey defiantly. 'You know. Stuff.'

'Stuff?!' His voice rose an octave. His eyes widened even further and he shook his head in disbelief, throwing a glance over his shoulder at Nancy and Rick, but their faces, as always, remained unreadable.

He might have sounded pissed off, but inside Bailey was secretly pleased. Her reverse psychology seemed to be working. They were virtually begging to hear her justify herself.

The baby-faced one leaned closer so she could see right into his angry bobbing little eyes.

'You will tell us exactly what kind of business you've been doing,' he said, each word spat with venom.

In preparation for exactly this kind of question, Bailey had gone through police files to get ideas for a selection of plausible-sounding schemes that she'd been involved in. Her goal was to give the impression that she was a busy hustler juggling a number of deals at the same time. After all, she knew that a good villain could place you with just about anything you might want to acquire, the more illicit, the better.

She reeled off the list of schemes that she'd memorised, injecting just enough swagger to give them confidence in her abilities.

They listened intently without interrupting, five pairs of eyes piercing her all the while. When she'd finished, she waited apprehensively, holding her breath for their response.

After what seemed like an aeon it was Nancy who broke the silence.

'Diamonds. Cars. Drugs. Antiques,' she murmured softly. 'Got your fingers in a lot of pies.'

'A real grafter,' said Rick. Bailey couldn't work out if he was being sarcastic or not.

The room again lapsed into awkward silence.

Nancy picked up her gold lighter and flicked it open. It made a distinctive musical 'cling' as she did so. In the dead quiet of the room, it sounded like the ominous ringing of a church bell in a spaghetti western. She snapped it shut again without lighting it.

'Have you ever done time?' she asked.

'No,' retorted Bailey. The last thing she was going to do was mention HMP Foxbrook. Her cover had been blown there and if they probed around in any kind of depth they'd soon find out she was a cop.

'Never done time, eh?' said the baby-faced one. 'You've done all these things and you've never once been in the jug?' His voice dripped with scepticism. Again he was staring fixedly into her eyes, almost as if conducting some kind of retinal examination. She found it deeply unnerving.

'I'm very careful,' she replied.

She turned her gaze to Rick. She knew he was extremely careful, knew he'd gone to great lengths to ensure he'd never been caught for anything serious. But once again he gave nothing away.

'And I make sure I only deal with people who I can trust,' she added.

She was turning it back on them slightly, throwing them the implicit challenge that they had to be just as trustworthy as they were expecting her to be. She saw them bristle slightly, and wondered if she'd overstepped the mark.

Nancy took a sip from her bone china teacup and massaged the soft ruff of her Pomeranian, never once taking her eyes off Bailey.

The distant muted jackhammer thumped out its rhythm in parallel to Bailey's beating heart. She licked her dry lips and flexed her sweating palms as the adrenaline pumped through her system. Surrounded by villains, alone with no back-up, not knowing if she'd succeeded in outsmarting them, the fear drove a perverse exhilaration, that unique feeling she craved that only undercover work could give her.

The baby-faced one was now holding her fake driving licence. He looked from her face to the photo and back again like an immigration officer inspecting a passport at the airport. She could see him analysing the tiny writing on it. Her name. Her address. The date of issue.

'How long have you been in London?' he demanded.

'A few years.'

'Where were you before that?'

'Nottingham.'

She'd picked Nottingham as she was gambling it was far enough away from London for them to be less familiar with it, and therefore less likely to have contact with OCGs there. But it wasn't so far out that she would have required a regional accent. More importantly, she knew the city well, having been to university there; it was where she'd studied accounting. The less stuff you had to make up in a cover story, the better, because it meant fewer potential slip-ups.

'Nottingham?' said baby-face. He smiled unpleasantly. 'In that case you must know Barry Hale. Anyone who's done business up in Nottingham knows Barry Hale.'

Bailey cursed to herself. It was a test. He could have just made the name up on the spot, so if she said yes, then he'd know she was lying. On the other hand, it could be a real person who they would then corroborate her story with.

She'd done some research on the Nottingham underworld in preparation for this deployment and hadn't encountered that particular name, but that didn't mean he didn't exist, if he was careful and kept his identity hidden from the police.

'Yeah,' she said in an offhand manner. 'I'm pretty sure I've come across the name. I've never dealt with him directly or anything.'

She was betting on the fact they'd be expecting a certain amount of bluster from her in her desire to ingratiate herself with them. Hustlers like her would often make out that they knew people even if they didn't, if they thought it could make them appear more connected and thus more credible.

She waited tensely for their response. A few inscrutable glances flickered between them but nothing more.

'So whereabouts in Northampton did you live?' said baby-face, staring at her intently.

She caught herself. It was a trick question to try and trip her up.

'I lived in Nottingham, not Northampton,' she corrected him. 'And to answer your question, I lived in Thorneywood.'

It was the district of Nottingham just north-east of the city centre where she'd once shared a flat as a student.

Again a heavy silence filled the room. She wondered just how long they would continue questioning her. She wondered just how long she could keep up her act under their relentless gaze. Even the dog was now looking at Bailey, watching her with its brainless round eyes.

Finally, Nancy spoke.

'How did you get those scars?' she asked, her throaty voice exhibiting a pulse of interest.

As part of her cover look, Bailey was wearing her hair tied back in a ponytail to reveal her facial scar in all its entirety, so a question about it wasn't to be totally unexpected.

'I don't want to talk about it,' she said.

Nancy stared at her coldly. 'You don't have a choice.' Her tone turned to steel. 'Now tell me how you got those scars.'

For a moment Bailey wondered if news of her torture had drifted through the gangland grapevine. It was very possible. And if they already suspected she was a cop, then there was the distinct possibility that she might not be walking out of this pub alive.

'I told you,' she said. 'It's none of your business.'

She paused, closed her eyes theatrically, and conjured up the smell of clove smoke, letting it fill her with righteous anger and indignation.

She popped open her eyes and stared straight back at Nancy.

'But one thing I can tell you is that I'm not going to give up until I find him.' She twisted her face into a vicious sneer. 'And when I do catch up with him, he's going to pay. Big time.' Bailey said it from her heart, and she meant it. Any other response would have been false. And for someone as astute as Nancy only the truth would suffice.

She saw Nancy's eyes emit a tiny flare of approval, accompanied by a small affirmative nod of the head.

Bailey knew then that she'd judged her response correctly. Recalling the awful revenge that Nancy had supposedly wreaked upon the killers of her husband, Bailey knew that for someone like Nancy getting even was a big deal.

A sideways look passed between Nancy and Rick. Mother to son. Very subtle. Almost imperceptible. And that was when Bailey knew she'd won over Nancy.

She'd succeeded. She was in.

16

'So you want to buy some shooters?' said Rick.

He spoke softly but that only seemed to emphasise his innate hardness. This was a man who didn't need to shout. When Rick spoke, people listened.

'That's right,' Bailey replied. 'Seemed like a good earner.'

'What are you looking to buy exactly?'

He was aware that she already knew what he had for sale, but he was testing her anyhow, just to make sure.

'Adrian told me you had a hundred and twenty brand-new seven-point-six-two-millimetre CZ 805 BREN assault rifles, a hundred and forty brand-new nine-millimetre K100 pistols, seventy silencers and five hundred rounds of ammunition for each weapon.'

Rick nodded slowly, observing her with his jet-black eyes.

'Eight hundred grand,' he stated after a short pause.

With the preparation she'd done prior to the meeting, Bailey had been expecting a black market mark-up of anywhere between fifty and a hundred and fifty per cent. Based upon her research into the retail prices of these particular weapons and their ammunition, eight hundred thousand pounds was definitely sitting outside the high end of the spectrum.

It was a delicate situation. She didn't want to put up too much resistance and torpedo the deal before it had even been struck. But she couldn't capitulate too easily to his offer or else they wouldn't take her seriously, and might even become suspicious of her. She was aware also, of course, that she was by far the junior partner in any kind of dealings with them and thus had limited scope to dictate terms.

She stroked her chin and pretended to consider his offer. 'Six fifty,' she countered. She estimated that this was just over double the retail price, still a hefty mark-up and well within what might be considered a reasonable figure to demand.

Rick snorted a laugh and swapped glances with his mother. There was a twinkle of amusement in Nancy's eye.

He yawned. 'I could drop to seven nine five, maybe.'

To knock off a measly five grand meant he was taking the piss and she had the feeling they'd lose respect for her if she didn't make at least some attempt to push back on it.

Her jaw set firm, she shook her head. 'I'd consider going to seven hundred.'

She waited tensely for his response.

He looked away for a few moments, pensively twiddling his wedding ring. Then he turned back to eye her intently.

'Why do you want to buy so many guns?' he asked.

Her cover story rolled off her tongue just as she'd rehearsed. 'They're for these right-wingers I know. Very well-funded. They're kind of like preppers. They want to get their hands on as many guns as possible. They're stockpiling weapons for WTSHTF.'

Puzzled frowns flashed around the room. 'WTSHTF?'

'When The Shit Hits The Fan,' she said. 'They think there's going to be some kind of apocalypse. A race war. Something like that.'

Cover stories sounded much more plausible when they were integrated into the wider context of society. Bailey knew that with the global changes of the past few years, with Brexit and the fragmentation of old orders like the EU, there had been a rise in the politics of the right, along with an increase in individuals and groups preparing, or 'prepping', to deal with the uncertainties of the new era.

'These "preppers",' said baby-face. 'Where are they based?'

'They're out in the West Country. They live off-grid though. They're paranoid about state surveillance. They don't want anyone to know who they are or where they live.' She'd gone for the off-grid element to hopefully deter the Molloys from checking them out.

'How did you meet these "preppers"?' said Rick.

'I was doing a bit of business down in that part of the country. Driving for someone,' she said, implying that she was ferrying some sort of illicit merchandise. 'We got chatting around the pool table in the local pub one evening. They might live off-grid but they do like a pint. Anyhow, one thing led to another. You know how it is.'

Rick nodded slowly. 'So what do you get out of it?'

'A cut of the money for brokering the transaction.'

'These people in the West Country,' said Rick. 'We'll want to meet them.'

Bailey shook her head firmly. 'And cut me out of the picture? I don't think so.'

It was a risky move to make and one that could potentially scupper the deal right now, but she trusted her instincts and she knew how people like this operated. They always pushed for as much as they could take, and then some. Pushing back showed them she was a serious operator, not to be messed with.

A tiny smirk flickered across Rick's face. Was that respect in his eyes? He scratched his chin for a few moments, the sound of his fingers scraping on his stubble clearly audible in the quiet room.

'Seven fifty,' he said presently. 'And that's my final offer.'

It was still expensive, but for Bailey's purposes it was an acceptable price. Anyhow, if this operation went to plan, it wasn't like he was ever going to be seeing any of that cash.

Bailey gave a curt nod, sealing her agreement to the deal.

'Okay,' said Rick. 'We'll be in touch.'

Still watching her sullenly, the baby-faced one held out her purse containing her fake credentials. She took it from him, sensing that this was a signal that the meeting was now over and she was free to leave.

She stood up and cast her gaze around their faces one last time, letting it linger for a fraction of a second on Nancy Molloy, and then she turned and left the room.

17

The doner kebab rotated slowly on the skewer in front of the red glowing grill, the reconstituted brown meat dripping fat onto the pan below, while a balding Middle Eastern man in an apron intermittently carved slices off it with a large knife.

Bailey eyed the greasy hunk of meat distastefully through the window of the kebab shop as she stood by the poky door just adjacent, waiting for Frank to admit her.

Undercover operations were never actually run from inside a police station. If a criminal saw you go in or out, then you were in deep trouble, and they had been known to stake out police stations for that very purpose. Bailey didn't know how well the Molloys ran surveillance, but she wasn't taking any chances. So from now on all meetings with Frank and Dale were taking place in a temporary autonomous HQ specially designated for this operation. It had been set up in an empty flat situated above a kebab shop close to her new apartment.

Technically, it was only five minutes' walk away, had she followed a conventional route. However, to ensure that she wasn't being followed by the Molloys, she always took a slightly more circuitous route via the nearby Westfield Centre, a huge shopping complex in the middle of Stratford.

It was the ideal place in which to detect a potential tail, and to lose them if necessary. By covertly observing reflections in shop windows, doubling back along shop aisles and up and down the escalators, Bailey was able to check that she wasn't being followed by anyone. Only once she was satisfied that she was clean would she then emerge from a discreet side exit and proceed to the HQ. It usually added an extra ten to fifteen minutes to her journey but the hassle was worth it given the dangers associated with the alternative.

The door clicked open. Glancing over her shoulder furtively one last time to check for any tails, Bailey entered into the hallway, closed the door behind her and made her way up a narrow, dingy stairwell. Ascending the stairs, it occurred to her, not for the first time, that Frank seemed to have a habit of picking particularly grim places to serve as undercover HQs.

The flat was little more than a bare room with untreated floorboards and no carpet. A whiteboard had been set up in one corner and there were several laptops and mobiles on a large folding table in the middle of the living room space which was serving as the centre of operations. Beyond the table and accompanying chairs, the only other furniture was an old knackered sofa by the window with an upturned cardboard box in front of it which appeared to be functioning as a rudimentary coffee table.

Bailey threw herself down onto the sofa and looked up at Frank and Dale who were sitting on chairs at the table.

'Smells of kebab up here,' she said. 'I wouldn't be able to stand it for very long. I hate the smell of lamb.'

'Well, if you don't like lamb, Mustafa does a great chicken doner,' said Frank.

'Mustafa? Who's he? The proprietor?'

Frank nodded. 'He's a good bloke.'

'I remember seeing on the news one time that a kebab contains the equivalent of an entire wine glass full of fat,' said Bailey.

'If that's the case, then Frank'll be dead of a heart attack before this operation's over,' Dale replied. 'He's had about five already.'

'You've got a kid to think about, Frank,' chided Bailey. 'Think of Isabel before you have another one.'

They all laughed, then with the banter over, Bailey moved onto the progress of the operation so far. The faces of Frank and Dale tautened and went serious as they paid her their undivided attention.

From time to time, Dale chipped in, clarifying the identities of the people she'd encountered.

'The skinny pale one with the sunglasses sounds like Archie Steele. Contract killer. Associated with a string of murders and disappearances.'

'And like I said,' added Bailey, 'I recognised Shane Reaper from the MMA circuit. I didn't realise he worked for the Molloys though.'

'He's their lieutenant and head enforcer. Not as dumb as he looks.'

'He's got an excellent jiu-jitsu groundwork technique.'

'That other one you mentioned,' said Dale. 'The baby-faced one who did most of the interrogation. His name is Stephen Drood. He's their head of security. He's a former burglar and an expert breaking-and-entering man.'

Bailey shivered involuntarily. 'He made my skin crawl, the way he was looking at me. It was like he was almost trying to look inside my soul. I don't think he particularly liked the cut of my jib. But then I didn't particularly like the cut of his either.'

Dale raised one eyebrow knowingly. 'He's very close to Nancy, apparently. Her right-hand man, you might say. You want to be careful of him. He's dangerous.' He paused with a grave expression. 'And, of course, let's not forget the most important one. Ettie. She's the real brains of the whole outfit.'

Bailey's face creased quizzically 'Ettie?'

'Nancy's Pomeranian.'

They all laughed.

'Joking aside,' said Frank, 'it sounds like you've made some major headway, winning over Nancy and setting up Rick for the next phase of your infiltration. I'll put in an application to requisition the seven hundred and fifty thousand. We'll have it in cash ready for you to show him when the final bust goes down.'

'But unfortunately for him,' said Bailey with a thin smile, 'he's not going to have the pleasure of spending it.'

The three of them chuckled in satisfaction at the thought of Rick being led away in handcuffs.

'So far I'm really pleased with your progress, Bailey,' said Frank.

'Thanks,' she replied. 'But I've got this funny nagging feeling that it's not going to be a completely smooth ride.'

18

Dennis Morgan appeared to be in good spirits despite the fact that he was dying of a terminal illness. It tickled Bailey how her father had found it within himself to start dispensing health and safety advice to the hospital staff from his bed. Prior to retiring, he'd worked as a health and safety inspector for the local council and it appeared that old habits died hard. When Bailey had arrived at the hospital that morning, she'd found him lecturing one of the nurses on the dangers of electrocution, one of his personal bugbears, and one he'd lectured Bailey about no end when she'd been a child.

She'd come down from Stratford, driving around for a bit first in an unpredictable and random pattern to throw off any possible surveillance the Molloys might have placed on her. When she was satisfied that she was clean, she'd headed to Orpington and the Princess Royal Hospital.

It had been four days since she'd last spoken to him. And sitting there on a chair next to his bed, she didn't want to say it out loud, but her father did appear to be a little bit thinner, a little bit paler, than the last time she'd seen him – a grim portent of the illness consuming him. She remembered how he'd always hated going to the doctor and it bothered her to think that if he'd have gone earlier they might have caught his illness before it had managed to spread around his body. It was too late now.

'Where's Mum?' she asked.

'She's with some people from her church group this morning. She said she'd pop along later this afternoon.'

Bailey nodded and looked around the gastroenterology ward at the other sick people lying in their beds, being attended to here and there by nurses. She turned back to him.

'How's the food here?' she asked.

He grimaced. 'I can't eat much because I feel sick a lot of the time. The cancer's in my guts so that doesn't help, but it's the drugs that mostly make me feel ill.' He gestured at the stand next to the bed with the box attached that was dispensing the drugs into his system. 'This thing gives me the drugs automatically. I'm on so many different ones at the moment. I'm on two different painkillers: fentanyl and dexamethasone. The fentanyl makes me nauseous, so they're giving me special anti-emetic drugs to stop me feeling sick. The dexamethasone is some kind of steroid that apparently causes psychosis if you have too much, although apparently they're going to have to increase my doses as time progresses, so if I go crazy, you'll know why!' He laughed.

Bailey tried to laugh along with him but couldn't stand the thought of him being in pain, for that was surely the reason they'd be increasing the dosages.

He took her hand in his and smiled at her affectionately. 'I wanted to tell you that I've come to a decision about what to do next. I've decided to go into a hospice. It'll be less hard on your mother than if I'm at home hooked up to all these drugs with her having to take care of me. The hospice has its own doctors and nurses and a special palliative care team. And apparently I get my own room with my own TV. It sounds like a nice environment, a bit nicer than this hospital anyway, and it has a little garden and a café, which will be pleasant for you and your mother when you come and visit.'

Bailey swallowed hard, trying not to let her emotions overwhelm her.

'So when are you moving?' she asked.

'You have to be referred. The doctor's written a reference for me. He told me it should take two to three weeks before a place becomes available. It's kind of a one-in-one-out situation, if you know what I mean,' he said with a dry smile.

She managed to summon a limp smile at his gallows humour but she couldn't escape the unavoidable grimness of what he was saying.

She clutched his hand a little tighter in hers and prayed inside herself that against all odds he might somehow recover. But she knew it was a futile hope. He squeezed her hand in response and smiled at her from his position propped up on the pillows.

'I know we argue sometimes, Bailey,' he said. 'But did I ever tell you how proud I am of you?'

Bailey gulped and felt herself begin to well up. 'Stop it, Dad.'

He nodded in the direction of his bedside table. 'My book,' he said.

She saw that there was a paperback sitting on the bedside table, some big brick-like airport novel. She picked it up and handed it to him, but he shook his head.

'Open it,' he said.

She frowned, wondering what he was getting at. It looked like some trashy thriller. Did he want her to read to him from it? She shrugged and opened it to where it was bookmarked.

She looked at him quizzically.

'The bookmark,' he said.

The bookmark was a folded piece of paper. She took it out and unfolded it, and when she recognised what it was, her heart sank slightly.

It was a picture of Mister Snigiss. The only existing picture of Mister Snigiss. Drawn by eight-year-old Jennifer all those years ago, not long before she'd gone missing. Her father had kept it and he carried it with him everywhere he went. It was emblematic of his quest for Jennifer and it was the closest he had to any kind of clue as to the identity of Mister Snigiss. And it wasn't much of a clue.

The picture, crudely drawn in felt-tip pen by the hand of a child, depicted stick-figure renditions of Jennifer and Bailey being led on an adventure by Mister Snigiss. Mister Snigiss was little more than a stick figure himself, with two dots for the eyes and a slash for the mouth and he was wearing what looked like a fedora hat. He was, of course, accompanied by his pet snake, Sid, represented by a wiggly line down by his feet. The names of each of the characters in the picture were denoted beneath them in Jennifer's spidery handwriting.

Seeing the picture once more sent a tiny shiver down Bailey's spine as she remembered Jennifer's oft-quoted phrase whenever Bailey had questioned Mister Snigiss's existence: *You can't see Mister Snigiss but Mister Snigiss can see you.*

Bailey sighed as she studied the piece of paper in her hand. It was thin and fragile with age and had been kept folded so long that it fell open and closed along the folds. It saddened her to know her father placed such import on such a flimsy and tenuous item. She took a deep breath and braced herself, for she knew what was coming next.

'I want you to continue the search for Jennifer,' he said. 'After I'm gone.'

As she looked down at him in pity, she saw the desperation in his eyes, the inescapable knowledge that he was going to die soon and that he would never live to see his mission fulfilled.

'Take that picture to remember her by. Do it for me, Bailey. For your mother. For both of us. Promise me, Bailey.' He stared at her, the whites of his eyes tinged yellow because of the problems with his liver due to the cancer. There was a pleading tone in his voice and Bailey just didn't have the heart to argue with him. Not this time.

In light of his condition, the search for Jennifer seemed more fruitless than ever right now, but she knew how important it was to him and how happy it would make him if she just, for once, acquiesced to his wishes.

She carefully folded the piece of paper and put it in her purse.

'Sure, Dad,' she whispered. 'I'll carry on the search for Jennifer. I promise.'

'You mean it?' he whispered. 'You really mean it?'

She knew deep down it was a pointless waste of time. But as long as he believed she would try, that was all that mattered.

'I promise I'll keep looking for Jennifer,' she said.

And she kissed him on the forehead and stood up and left.

19

It was mid-afternoon by the time Bailey got back to Stratford. Emerging from the lift, still deep in thought about her father, she walked along the corridor to the front door of her apartment. She was about to put her key in the lock when her hackles suddenly went up. It was a kind of sixth sense she'd developed over her years working as an undercover police officer, to be able to smell impending danger. And right now something wasn't right.

The concerns about her father instantly receded as her physical senses attuned themselves sharply to every element of her immediate environment.

Gently inserting the key into the lock, she pushed open the door and peered cautiously into the hallway. It was empty, just as she'd left it.

She stalked slowly forwards, placing one foot softly in front of the other. And stopped.

She sniffed the air. A smell. Very faint. Alien to her apartment. A male cologne.

She tensed and dropped into a jiu-jitsu *yoi* stance. Crouching low to protect her centre of gravity, turning slightly side-on to offer less of a target, she edged forwards, leading with her left leg, her hands held up in front of her poised to parry or strike.

On entering the living room, she was confronted by the sight of Rick sitting on the sofa, his arms stretched expansively along the back of it, one leg resting up casually on the knee of the other. Standing by the floor-to-ceiling window was Shane. Archie was sitting on one of the kitchen breakfast stools. And leaning against the mantelpiece was Stephen.

There was no Nancy. Just the boys.

They all turned to look at her when she entered.

She straightened up, dropping her defensive stance. If they'd been planning to jump her, then they would have done so already, as soon as she'd entered.

She forcibly suppressed any expression of alarm. To display fear would look weak and that might be just what they were looking for.

For a moment she was puzzled as to how they knew where she lived. But then she remembered that this address was on her fake driving licence, the one Stephen had examined in such detail.

She guessed they didn't quite trust her after all. Things were never that straightforward working undercover. They had come here to check her out, to see if she really was who she said she was. And if they ascertained that she wasn't... she tried not to think about what they might do.

Rick observed her with his dead black eyes and gave her a bloodless smile. 'I hope you don't mind us paying you a little visit.'

For professional criminals such as these, breaking and entering into her apartment presented little problem. As she recalled, that was Stephen's particular area of expertise.

'Your alarm system isn't very good,' Stephen smirked. 'You'll get burgled if you're not careful.' He looked around at her sparse belongings. 'Not that you've got much to nick,' he added.

'Make yourself at home,' she said drily, moving into the living room warily, mentally marking their positions should she need to make a fast exit. 'Can I get any of you a coffee?' she asked, hoping to lighten the mood.

They ignored her and instead watched Stephen as he pushed himself off the mantelpiece, wandered over to a set of shelves and began to flip through her small collection of books of cryptic crosswords and sudoku.

'Looking for anything in particular?' she asked, attempting to sound casual.

But she knew exactly what they were looking for. They were looking for anything out of place, anything that might suggest that she wasn't who she claimed to be.

'Like I said, you don't have a lot of belongings,' remarked Stephen, turning around to fix her with his disconcertingly intense stare. 'Why is that?'

It was true. Your average person tended to build up a good deal of detritus over the course of their life. But as an undercover operative, Bailey was living a skeleton existence, having stripped away any possessions that might potentially contradict her cover story.

'In fact,' he continued, 'it looks like you've just moved in.'

All four of them observed her dispassionately, awaiting an explanation.

Thinking on her feet, she searched her mind for an appropriate response.

'I like to travel light,' she said. 'Clutter's bad for the mind. Simplicity. It's a Japanese thing. It's all the rage these days.'

'A Japanese thing?' sneered Stephen sceptically.

Bailey nodded enthusiastically. 'Yeah, I watched a show about it recently on Netflix. You chuck out anything that doesn't make you happy. The less stuff you've got, the happier you are. I just did a blitz and got rid of loads of stuff.'

'I think I caught that show one time,' murmured Shane from his position by the window.

Rick's gaze settled on the porcelain jaguar by the fireplace. A slightly perturbed frown crossed his face as if it offended him in some way.

'Well, if you're looking to declutter, I'd start by getting rid of that.'

Bailey had to agree with him. It was in exceedingly poor taste, but it was here in her apartment and she had to explain it somehow.

'I mean, what on earth possessed you to buy it in the first place?' he asked.

'I like wild cats,' she said. 'Predators. I love the way they hunt down and kill their prey. So graceful. So deadly. Someday I'll own a real one.'

He raised his eyebrows and nodded, conceding her point.

Shane had wandered over to her TV and was leafing through her DVD selection. He pulled one out and held it up for them all to look at.

'*Scarface*?' said Rick.

'One of my favourite films,' Bailey replied.

'What do you think of the ending?' asked Shane.

Bailey cursed inwardly. She hadn't got around to watching it yet so she didn't know what happened at the end. They were all looking at her, waiting for her response. Then she remembered what Frank had said about it.

'I like the bit where he shoots everybody,' she said.

Rick sighed. 'I've never been into gangster films myself. They never seem to get it right. Most of them are way too over the top. *Wall Street*. Now there's a good film. Gordon Gekko. You could learn a lot from him.'

She eyed Stephen with concern as he wandered off into the bathroom. She prayed that he didn't find the secret compartment. He would no doubt be rooting through the contents of the bathroom cabinet. He re-emerged a short while later, holding something in his hand. He held it up for them all to see. It was her packet of beta blockers.

'Beta blockers, eh?' he said in a spiteful tone. 'Do you suffer from anxiety?'

They all looked to her for an answer. She swallowed and tried to think how to explain the medication.

'You look like you could do with a few right now,' said Rick.

She forced a casual shrug. 'You know how it gets when you're juggling a lot of deals. It can sometimes get a bit stressful, keeping all those plates spinning.'

Rick nodded slowly as if he understood what she was talking about, although she got the impression he was the kind of person who kept a lid on that type of thing.

Stephen walked into the kitchen, tossed the beta blockers onto the kitchen top and began opening and closing the cupboards and generally poking around. Watching him as he opened the fridge and peered inside, Bailey was grateful she'd gone to the supermarket the previous day to fill it up; from that respect, at least, the place looked lived in. He closed the fridge, went over to the sink, squirted some anti-bacterial hand soap into one palm, turned on the kitchen tap and started to wash his hands.

'Washing your hands again, Stephen?' said Rick from the sofa. He turned to Bailey. 'Poor Stephen here has a rather serious case of OCD. What that does mean though is that he possesses superb attention to detail, which in his line of work is an excellent trait to possess.'

Obsessive compulsive disorder. That explained the hand sanitiser she'd noticed him fiddling with at their initial meeting. She guessed he fitted into the germophobe category of OCD sufferer.

'You've got low water pressure,' said Stephen, fiddling with the taps, watching the small dribble of water come out.

'I know,' she replied.

'You should get it looked at.'

'I will.'

'It's probably because you're so high up,' commented Shane, who had now moved back to his position by the window. 'Nice view though. Good fenestration. Know what that means?'

'Generous windows.'

'Very good,' he said with a patronising smile. 'But do you know what defenestration means?'

She could kind of guess. An unpleasant feeling came over her. 'Why don't you tell me?'

'It means to throw someone out of a window.' He laughed and shook his head. 'Funny how they've got a special word for it.'

He yanked on the latch and pushed the window open as far as it would go. He leant out and looked down.

'That's quite a drop,' he murmured.

Were they planning to throw her out of the window? It was ten floors down. No one could survive that kind of fall. She felt her palms beginning to sweat.

Leaving the window open, Shane pulled his head back in and wandered over to the entranceway, where he suddenly stopped and turned around, standing there solid and immobile with his arms crossed, cutting off her exit route from the flat.

Stephen strutted from the kitchen back into the living-room area, stopping right in front of her to glower up at her. He was at least five inches shorter than her.

So he was a stickler for detail. She didn't like the sound of that. A cover story was all about the little things at the end of the day, and if Stephen noticed some tiny detail that looked out of place...

She squashed down the anxieties and edged away from him and his hostile aura. With a jerk, she suddenly found that she'd almost backed into Archie, who was sitting on the breakfast stool. He was holding up a large knife right next to her face. She recognised it as one of her kitchen knives that he'd taken from the knife block on the counter top. She gulped and recoiled.

He drew his lips back in a smile, exposing his brown rotting teeth.

'Good steel,' he said, testing the edge of the blade against his thumb.

'Is it?' she replied, trying to sound nonchalant.

He hefted it from one hand to the other. 'And well balanced.'

The razor-sharp blade sparkled in the light only centimetres from her face.

'Archie's got an impressive knife collection,' said Rick. 'He likes sharp things. Maybe you could show her your knife collection one day, Archie?'

'Maybe I will,' replied Archie, a hint of menace in his voice. All she saw was her own convex reflection in the black lenses of his sunglasses.

A chill winter breeze blew in through the open window. Bailey analysed the situation. Shane was blocking her escape from the flat; Archie was right next to her with the knife. Stephen, now in the living room, was glaring at her intensely. And Rick was sitting on the sofa, smiling almost affably as he observed her with his obsidian eyes, appearing to relish her discomfort.

Four men. One woman. Much as she was good at jiu-jitsu, she doubted her ability to survive should they decide to stab her or push her out of the window, or both.

They still hadn't overtly addressed why they were here and it was making her nervous. As if reading her thoughts, Rick spoke.

'I guess you're wondering why we're here. Well, like I told you back in the pub, we don't just blindly trust everyone we meet.'

'What are you saying exactly?' Bailey infused her words with a slight tone of indignation, but inside her heart was pounding in apprehension.

'Have you heard of eye accessing cues?' said Stephen in his squeaky nasty voice.

Bailey shook her head, although in fact she knew exactly what he was referring to.

'Let me explain,' he said. 'When you're recalling a real event, your eyes look to the left. And when you're imagining something, your eyes look to the right. It's unconscious, see. You can't control it. Left means truth. Right means lie.'

That explained why he'd been staring so intently into her eyes when he'd been questioning her in The Admiral, why he'd demanded she take off her sunglasses.

She wanted to tell him that eye accessing cues had been discredited some time ago and that the police certainly no longer used them in interrogations. However, she had the feeling he probably wouldn't be very receptive.

'Well, the other day in the pub, I was watching the way your eyes moved.' He paused. 'You said you lived in Nottingham. And your eyes moved to the left. You weren't lying about that.'

He paused again, this time for longer, for dramatic effect. He pointed a tiny index finger at her accusingly.

'But when I asked you if you knew Barry Hale, your eyes moved to the right. You were lying.'

'I didn't say I knew him. I said I'd heard the name.'

'Well, the thing is, it doesn't surprise me that you were lying because,' his eyes widened triumphantly, 'there is no Barry Hale. I just made that name up to see if you were a liar. And it turns out that you are.'

Bailey forced herself to remain calm. She was really starting to dislike this guy.

'I must have got the name muddled up with someone else,' she said casually. 'You know how it is. You meet loads of people in my line of work. Barry Hale. Garry Bale. Harry Gale. It gets confusing sometimes.'

'Maybe we don't like dealing with people who get "confused",' said Stephen, looking to Rick for support. But Rick was just staring at her with that unfathomable expression of his. What the hell was going through his mind right now? She just could not tell.

She took a deep breath and decided to opt for honesty.

'Look, I just wanted to make a good impression on you, okay. You guys are major league. A big step-up in my operations.'

'What?' said Stephen, sounding deeply critical. 'So you thought—'

Rick waved for him to be quiet. Stephen looked put out and lapsed into a sullen silence.

Rick's coal-black eyes bored into Bailey.

'You're right,' he said slowly. 'Doing business with us will put you straight in the premier division.'

Bailey's tension ratcheted down a notch.

'My mother seems to approve of you,' he added. He glanced around the flat. 'And your place appears to check out. Doesn't it, Stephen?'

Stephen gave a sulky, reluctant shrug, indicating that he hadn't been able to find anything incriminating.

'I think we can do business together,' continued Rick. 'But I want you to remember one thing. The more we have to do with someone, the more we have to lose, if you understand what I'm saying. And if you turn out to have been stringing us along...' He left the threat hanging in the air. He didn't need to say any more.

Bailey knew from past experience operating with people at this level, that the deeper she got with them, especially with a deal of this size, the less able they were to just walk away from her if it all went pear-shaped. The only sensible option to them would be to kill her.

And with those menacing words of warning, Rick got to his feet and stretched, making ready to go. But then she noticed out of the corner of her eye that Shane had begun to rummage around in the bowl of Quality Street which was sitting next to him on the sideboard by the entranceway. He was picking through the chocolates clearly searching for a flavour that he liked.

With a sickening jolt of horror, she suddenly remembered that her warrant card was still in there. She'd been meaning to put it in the secret compartment but she'd forgotten all about it.

'Looking for any particular flavour?' she called, attempting to keep the concern out of her voice.

'I like the red ones,' he said. 'But there don't appear to be any in here.'

'The fudge ones? There's none left. I ate them all. They're my favourite ones too.'

He looked disappointed and ceased his rummaging. She breathed a sigh of relief.

But now Stephen was eyeing the bowl of Quality Street suspiciously. He must have picked up on something in her tone, some tinge of panic she hadn't quite been able to hide.

Shit. Was this it?

'Okay. Let's go,' said Rick, striding over to the doorway.

Archie pushed the kitchen knife back into the knife block, jumped off the stool and went to join them.

Rick turned to look at Bailey one last time. 'Thank you for your hospitality. As I said before, we'll be in touch.'

Stephen was frowning, looking at Bailey, then at the Quality Street, then back at Bailey again, like he couldn't quite work out what the significance was.

Bailey swore under her breath. She'd made too much of a deal about the chocolates. Stephen started to glide towards the bowl of Quality Street, his eyes narrowing in focus. Him and his bloody attention to detail.

'Yeah, sure, I'll talk to you soon,' replied Bailey, eyeing Stephen with increasing consternation.

'Get moving, Steve,' said Rick. 'We're leaving. Chop chop!'

Stephen unwillingly pulled himself away from the Quality Street, shot Bailey a final scowl and then followed Rick and the others out of the apartment.

Bailey stood there for a few moments, holding her breath. She listened to the front door slam shut, listened to their voices receding down the corridor. Her heart rate gradually began to slow and the flow of adrenaline began to subside.

Berating herself seriously for her near-fatal oversight, she crossed over to the window, which was still open, and peered down at the street ten floors below, aware once more of just how dangerously high up she was here. She waited for them to emerge from the apartment block, which they did presently, and she felt a heavy sense of relief as she observed them swagger away down the road.

Only after she was completely certain that they'd gone for good did she close the window and set about scouring the flat for any listening devices or miniature cameras they might have planted. It took a while to turn the place upside down, but when it came to an organisation as lethal as the Molloys, she wasn't taking any chances.

Once she'd established with some confidence that the place was clean, she finally went over to the sideboard, thrust her hand into the bowl of Quality Street and retrieved her warrant card. Marching into the bathroom, she pulled the cabinet away from the wall and secreted the warrant card in the hidden cavity.

Pushing the cabinet back into position, she caught a glimpse of her reflection in the mirrored door, noting for a moment the uncharacteristic flush of exertion across her cheeks.

'Bailey, that was a little too close for comfort,' she muttered.

20

Dale sat on the sofa and sipped the vodka that Bailey had given him. It was all she had in the flat, but he didn't seem to mind. Just like he didn't seem to mind the music – 'Save a Prayer' by Duran Duran, one of her top ten eighties power ballads – emanating softly from the Bluetooth speaker in the corner of the living room.

They'd gone for a few drinks earlier that evening in a pub just around the corner from the apartment in Stratford. If it counted as a date, then she guessed it was their second one, although she was wondering if all that was just in her head and it had been nothing more than just another informal work catch-up.

At any rate, she reminded herself that she should probably adhere to operational protocol and refrain from getting romantically involved with someone who she was working on a job with.

So saying, when he'd expressed an interest in seeing her undercover apartment out of professional curiosity, she'd found herself urging him to come back so she could show him. She hoped she hadn't given him the wrong idea.

He was sitting on the sofa now in close proximity to her. She swallowed nervously and brushed her loose lock of hair self-consciously across the scar on her cheek.

'That's crazy,' he was saying, shaking his head incredulously. 'I can't believe they came that close to discovering that you were a copper.'

Bailey had just been regaling him with an account of the Molloys' unannounced visit the previous day.

'Yeah, I know,' she said. 'If Shane had been satisfied with the coffee-flavoured ones, then I wouldn't have had to worry. There are loads of them in there.' She gestured at the bowl of Quality Street.

'Nah, but no one likes the coffee ones, do they?' he replied, wrinkling his nose in disgust.

They both laughed. He paused and looked at her inquisitively with his striking blue eyes.

'So there really is a secret compartment?'

She nodded. 'In the bathroom. Behind the cabinet. Nothing more than a hole in the wall really. I keep everything from my "normal" life in there. Warrant card. My regular phone, switched off. The keys to my flat in Crystal Palace. My real credit and debit cards. My real driving licence. Anything with the name "Bailey Morgan" on it.' She paused. 'But I'm sure you know all about this kind of thing already.'

He shook his head. 'Undercover work is quite different from what I do. And it never ceases to surprise me the kinds of things you lot get up to. You certainly don't live a normal life, that's for sure.'

'I don't think I'm able to,' Bailey admitted. 'It would drive me crazy. Two point four kids and whatever.'

'Well, I guess undercover work probably isn't that conducive to long-term relationships anyhow.'

She nodded resignedly. He was right about that. Working undercover could play havoc with relationships, as you often had to spend intense periods of activity away from a partner. Although, seeing as Bailey was currently single, that was less of an issue.

Dale eyed her closely. 'And I guess it must affect your ability to trust people.'

'What do you mean?' she said.

'Well, you always have to have your guard up. How do you know when to let it down?'

'When I meet the right person, I know when to let it down.'

They found themselves looking into each other's eyes. Bailey was suddenly acutely aware of his physical closeness, his arm draped along the back of the sofa behind her. She was glad she'd kept the lighting low to soften the impact of her scars. He edged a little closer still.

'Mind you,' she said, 'I'm a bit out of practice with all that stuff.'

He took a moment to scrutinise her. 'You know, what I like about you, Bailey, is that you're not a prima donna. Sometimes with these top-level undercovers, it goes to their heads. But not you. There's something special about you.'

She felt herself blush. Had he actually meant what he said about having a soft spot for her? Did he really genuinely fancy her? Even now with her scars? But then, sitting this close to her, he didn't seem bothered by her disfigurement.

His fingers brushed her shoulder lightly, his touch sending an electric tingle through her. Her breathing quickened. She wasn't used to this kind of intimacy.

She swallowed hard and sat up briskly.

'Any good at cryptic crosswords?' she asked.

Dale frowned, looking a little disconcerted. 'Uh... I can't say I ever really do them.'

She picked up a book lying on the nautical-themed coffee table.

'My dad bought me this for Christmas,' she said, leafing through it. 'Here. Look. I'm stuck on twelve across.'

Dale sat up and moved right next to her to look at the clue. She could smell the intoxicating scent of his musk. It made her heart beat that little bit faster.

'"Grandparents come from Lancaster",' he murmured, reading the clue.

'I can't think for the life of me what it is,' she said, trying to quell the stirrings inside her.

Dale frowned. 'That's easy. The answer's "ancestral". It's an anagram of "Lancaster".'

She slapped her forehead. 'Of course! The "grandparents" part means "ancestral" and the "come from" part tells you it's an anagram.'

She gazed at him with admiration. Not only was he good-looking, he was smart as well.

He shrugged modestly. 'I've always been an anagram man.'

They were only centimetres apart now, leaning over the book on her lap. He turned his head and smiled at her.

'I like your eyes,' he said.

She swallowed nervously. Her eyes were just grey and dull in her opinion. The colour of cold ashes. What could he possibly like about them?

She studied his handsome face and tried to think of a suitable compliment to reciprocate with. Up close, she noticed for the first time that his teeth were perfect and white.

'You have beautiful teeth,' she said.

'Why, thank you,' he replied, smiling even wider, flashing even more of his pristine enamel.

Realising that her heart was beating a little too fast, she clamoured for something innocuous to dial down the sexual tension a bit. She noticed a small gold ring on the little finger of his left hand.

'That's a nice ring.'

He looked at it as if it was the first time he'd seen it.

'Oh this?' He pulled it off and handed it to her.

She turned it over in her fingers. It was set with a flat black stone, which, she realised on closer examination, was actually reversible. She flipped it over to reveal a small symbol inlaid in gold on the other side. A set square and compasses. She'd seen those kinds of symbols before.

'Is this Masonic?' She looked up at him in surprise. 'Are you a Mason?'

He laughed. 'You got me. I am indeed a Mason.' He nodded at the ring. 'Don't you think it's pretty neat, the way it flips over like that?'

'A Mason, huh? The boys' club.'

Perhaps she shouldn't have been too surprised that he, as a police-man, was a member of the Freemasons. After all, that secretive

fraternal organisation had a long and well-known tradition of associa-
tion with the police force. Whatever little she knew about Freema-
sonry, her overriding view was coloured mainly by the perception that
it was an exclusively male affair.

'Women can also become Masons these days,' he said.

'No thanks.' She handed the ring back to him and he slipped it
back on.

He shrugged. 'I guess it's not for everyone.'

'Why did you join?'

'Well, I got asked, actually. A tap on the shoulder, if you know what
I mean. That's the way it works a lot of the time. And I thought, why
not?'

'Is that how you got ahead in your career so quickly?' she teased.
'Am I at a disadvantage if I'm not a member?'

He rolled his eyes. 'No, of course not. It's not like the old days any
more when the Masons virtually ran CID. These days, it's more of just
a social thing.'

She raised an eyebrow doubtingly, not entirely won over. The
whole thing still sounded a bit too cabalistic for her liking.

'But doesn't it still create competing loyalties?' she said. 'The law
and the public on one side and your fellow Masons on the other?'

He shook his head. 'That's all just paranoia. People are under the
impression that it's some sinister self-serving boys' club. But it's not like
that at all.'

She eyed him sceptically. 'If you say so.' She paused with a cheeky
smile. 'Do you really have a special handshake?'

He smiled and nodded. 'I'll show you if you want.'

He held out his right hand. She hesitated a moment and then
slipped her hand into his cool firm grip.

Staring at her intently with his bright blue eyes, he cupped his
hand slightly to allow his middle finger to curl inwards towards the
centre of her palm. He then slowly pushed it out towards her wrist,
then drew it back in again, then out again, softly caressing her palm.

Inwards. Outwards. Inwards. Outwards. She flushed, her breath turning ragged with arousal. It felt undeniably good...

She suddenly burst out laughing and tugged her hand away. 'That's not a Masonic handshake!'

He erupted into snorts of laughter. 'Okay, officer... I confess!'

She shook her head and rolled her eyes at his waggish behaviour. 'I think it's high time you were going.'

He made an attempt to look serious and stood up.

Watching him leave with a smile on her face, she realised that she was rather starting to like him. But at the back of her mind lurked the troublesome awareness that any intimacy that might arise between them would be tempered, if not completely hamstrung, by the torture and the sexual trauma she'd been through. Those hideous experiences were the main reason she hadn't been in any kind of proper relationship for the past few years, and she'd reached the point where she was wondering if she'd ever be able to have a normal relationship again. Hopefully he'd understand...

21

The hearse crawled slowly past on its way to the church. It was a shiny black vintage Daimler operated by a set of appropriately long-faced undertakers. The coffin, visible through the large rear windows, was topped with lavish floral tributes spelling out 'Adrian' on top, 'brother' on one side, and 'son' on the other.

Although it was a cold January morning, it was bright and fresh and the Romford street was lined with a mixture of people. Whereas some had turned out to pay their respects, many others were present purely out of curiosity.

Passing through the crowd, Bailey made her way in the direction of the Roman Catholic church where the service was being held, the cortège passing by next to her, the hearse trailed closely by a fleet of black limousines.

After her close encounter with the Molloys at her flat, Bailey had wondered what form the next contact from them would take. A few days later she'd found out. It turned out to be an invite to Adrian's funeral, sent through the post to her, printed on expensive gold-embossed card. It constituted somewhat of a curveball for her as funerals were hardly the most commonplace way of meeting up for business, but then, doing undercover work, she'd learnt to expect the unexpected.

It was now almost a month since Adrian had been blown up. From her experience as a police officer, Bailey knew that the delay in burial was likely due to various complications surrounding the post-mortem procedure and coroner's inquest that were required in cases of unnatural death such as his, not to mention the inevitable backlogs in the system that always built up over the Christmas period.

In keeping with the occasion, she was wearing a black French Connection trouser suit beneath her Hugo Boss jacket. The Oakley sunglasses completed the look, and today she wore her loose lock of hair down over the scar on her face.

Seeing the sentimental floral tributes in the back of the hearse, Bailey reflected that the maudlin nature of the whole affair was characteristic of the underworld. Whatever Adrian had been like in real life, in death he was elevated to near-sainthood. The event bore the nostalgic ring of a bygone era of blaggers and bank raids.

Glancing around, she knew there would be plainclothes policemen and unmarked cars watching the proceedings at Dale's behest, conducting surveillance, photographing everybody there, including her. She knew there would probably also be a few tabloid journalists here, their presence much less subtle.

Studying the people around her, she recognised a few well-known 'faces' from the criminal fraternity, clad much like herself in black leather jackets, suits and shades. Apart from the ones she knew from police files and past briefings, there were others there, clearly of a similar ilk, who she wasn't familiar with – up-and-comers perhaps, or just those who were good at maintaining a low profile. Watching them mingle with each other, she could only imagine what devilish schemes and internecine rivalries lurked behind the amicable handshakes and black sunglasses.

She arrived at the church just as the funeral cortège was disgorging various members of the Molloy family.

Nancy, stony-faced beneath a black veil, watched as Adrian's coffin was hoisted up onto the shoulders of Rick, Shane, Archie and several other thuggish-looking Molloy associates, all of whom were crammed into stylish black suits. Stephen, exuding his characteristic malice, followed next to Nancy, presumably too short to carry the coffin.

On entering the church, Bailey was suddenly struck with uninvited thoughts of her father's imminent demise and the fact that he too would be having a funeral at some point in the near future. She pushed the depressing contemplation from her mind and tried to focus on her surroundings.

Moving down one side, she positioned herself close to the front where she could have a better view of the mourners. The pews were full, with a number of children present alongside the adults, and the place buzzed with the murmur of low-level conversation.

The coffin was lying on the catafalque in front of the altar, where it was draped with a pall. Unlike some other Catholic funerals, Bailey reflected that this one would definitely be a closed-casket job; apparently they were still discovering body parts in the area where the bomb had gone off.

The Mass began with the priest reading a liturgy from the Old Testament and a psalm. Then he read a passage from one of the Gospels. After that, he delivered a short eulogy, praising Adrian 'for being the brother that they loved' and 'the son that they adored'. He made a point of saying how there should be no reprisals, quoting Romans 12:19 about leaving revenge to God and God alone. Listening to his words, Bailey wondered just how far he was aware of the exact character of the Molloy family and if they were really the kind of people who would pay heed to what he was saying.

As he gave the reading from the Bible, Bailey examined the Molloys. Nancy sat there staring straight ahead, her face dour and inscrutable. There were no tears, not even the smallest leak of emotion. Sitting beside her, Rick too bore a similarly impenetrable expression, his face cold and tough as granite. They hardly seemed riven with grief, but then they were hard people.

Once again Bailey wondered just who was actually responsible for killing Adrian. As far as she was aware, the police had made little progress in solving the murder. Seeing as it wasn't her priority, Bailey hadn't thought about it in too much depth up to now. However, being here in the heart of this villainous clan, she began to sense that the death of Adrian would, in some way, bear an inextricable influence upon the course of this operation.

22

The private room of the posh hotel was packed with mourners chattering loudly above the singing of some sixties-style crooner emanating from the sound system.

Bailey couldn't immediately spot any of the key Molloy family members among the crowds of people milling around and, never having been a big one for social occasions, she felt a little awkward, standing there by herself, not knowing anyone.

Spotting a table laid out with canapés, she sidled over to have a temporary excuse to find something to occupy herself with. She was examining the smoked salmon vol-au-vents when a female voice with a distinct Essex inflection spoke up in her ear.

'Don't wakes remind you of weddings? I suppose the only difference is that there's one less drunk standing at the bar.'

Bailey looked up to see a woman with long blonde hair and bright yellow fingernails wearing a large pair of Gucci sunglasses, and a Chanel handbag hooked over her right forearm. Bailey had noticed her earlier on in the church standing next to Rick. Now, looking at the woman's hand and seeing the engagement ring with its massive rock accompanied by a diamond-studded wedding ring, Bailey deduced that this woman was his wife. Although strikingly attractive from a distance, up close it was clear that she was quite heavily botoxed, that she'd had substantial work done on her nose, and that her large lips had been injected with so much filler they were in danger of making her resemble a duck.

The woman looked Bailey up and down with blatant curiosity.

Bailey reciprocated in kind. 'I like your nails,' she said. The lie came effortlessly.

The woman smiled, stretched out her long slender fingers and looked at them admiringly. 'Why, thank you. I had them done especially for the occasion.' She looked up at Bailey with a brittle smile. 'So who are you then?'

'My name's Bailey. Bailey Sharpe. I'm a business associate of Rick's. And you are?'

'Wendy. I'm Rick's wife,' she said, holding out her hand.

They shook.

Wendy pushed her sunglasses down onto the end of her nose and looked around with distaste. 'I find these things so tedious. And this music...' She rolled her eyes. 'Matt Monro. Nancy's obsessed with him.'

Bailey realised that the crooner was singing the song 'He Ain't Heavy, He's My Brother' and wondered if there was any special significance to that particular track, given the nature of the deceased.

'I prefer the Hollies version myself,' said Bailey, sizing up Wendy as a potential source of information. Working as a police officer, Bailey had learned how to read people in a fraction of a second and she already found herself warming to Wendy's refreshing lack of deference towards the criminals who surrounded her. 'So, what do you do?' asked Bailey, not really expecting her to have any kind of occupation whatsoever.

'I run a beauty salon,' Wendy replied. 'On Basildon high street. They don't let me get involved in any of their business.'

'That's because your gob's too big,' said a rough, gravelly voice behind them.

They both turned around to see Rick standing there, looming over them. In his black suit, he looked more menacing than ever.

Wendy emitted a frustrated sigh. 'A little respect wouldn't go amiss now and then.'

Bailey detected a very faint twinkle in Rick's eye, which suggested there was a small measure of affection in his criticism of his wife.

He twitched one eyebrow and jerked his head slightly to indicate that Wendy should leave them both to talk confidentially.

Wendy rolled her eyes, pushed her sunglasses back up her nose, gave Bailey a final brittle smile and then drifted away into the crowd.

Bailey duly offered Rick her condolences, which he accepted with a shrug and a nod, seemingly preoccupied with other things. He looked around to check that no one was within immediate earshot, then leaned in, settling on her with his soulless black eyes.

'The deal is on,' he said.

'That's brilliant news,' fawned Bailey, displaying what she hoped was the requisite level of gratitude. 'It's really great to be doing business with you.'

She recalled how Rick preferred to communicate face-to-face and realised now that the primary reason she'd been invited today was so he could convey this simple message to her. But she also felt that her presence here represented more than just that; a trust had been established which brought her one step deeper into their circle and, in a strange kind of way, she felt privileged to be here.

'So when can we get started?' she asked eagerly, keen to progress the operation to the next stage.

He eyed her silently for a few moments.

'I'll confirm the date of the transaction with you in due course.'

He scrutinised her reaction. She must have looked a bit dismayed, for a thought then seemed to occur to him.

'In the meantime,' he said, 'if your contacts are interested in a sample, I've got a few bits and pieces lying around. I could let you have it at a discount rate. Eight hundred quid, say?'

She realised he was trying to keep her sweet, and wondered if there was some delay or problem with moving things forward. Still, a sample would be a great way to confirm exactly what kind of merchandise she was obtaining. For eight hundred pounds, she guessed he was talking about a pistol rather than an assault rifle.

'That sounds like a great idea,' she said.

He nodded, satisfied.

'Here, why don't you come over and join us for a drink?' he suggested.

Without waiting for her response, he turned and strode away, leaving her to follow him. The crowd parted like water to let him through and, ahead of them, Bailey saw Nancy sitting in the corner. Although physically small, she seemed to command the room like a dark, malevolent spider at the centre of a web.

She patted the seat next to her with a predatory smile. 'Sit down for a drink with me, Bailey. What'll you have?'

'A vodka and blackcurrant.'

Nancy turned to Stephen who was sitting on the other side of her. He had already fixed Bailey with a moody stare and if there was one person she knew she hadn't won over quite yet, it was him.

'Go and get Bailey a drink, will you, Steve?' said Nancy. 'And you can get me another Courvoisier while you're at it.'

Stephen looked a little piqued at the request, but Nancy appeared not to notice. He stood up and went to the bar.

'Don't mind Steve,' she said with a wry smile. 'He's very possessive. I kind of adopted him when he was a young 'un.'

Sitting so close to Nancy, Bailey detected the odour of stale cigarette smoke, and on top of that she recognised the floral spicy tones of Black Orchid perfume by Tom Ford; it was a good choice for older women and Bailey had considered buying some for her mother but hadn't bothered in the end, thinking that it probably would have been wasted on her.

'I'm sorry for your loss,' said Bailey, reiterating her commiseration.

Nancy acknowledged her with a thin, bloodless smile, a marginally warmer response than she'd given in The Admiral.

'Tell me about your family, Bailey,' she said. 'Do you have any siblings, or are you a single child?'

When it came to small talk in situations like this, Bailey always found it best to try and stick to the truth where possible. It meant less false information to juggle and less chance of tripping up on your own lies later on down the line.

'I have... I had a sister.'

'You had a sister?'

Bailey hesitated a moment. 'She died when I was young.'

Nancy's dense close-set eyes scrutinised Bailey, some kind of cogitations taking place behind them. Nancy was quite obviously very shrewd and very astute, and, as Dale had warned, someone to be very wary of.

Bailey didn't particularly want to dwell on Jennifer, so she decided to steer the conversation in a different direction.

'So you like Matt Monro?' she said conversationally.

Nancy seemed flattered by her observation. 'I do indeed. My favourite track of his is "My Kind of Girl". My husband, Arthur, played it for me at our wedding.'

Nancy's eyes momentarily took on a dreamy far-off look, and Bailey noticed now that she was still wearing her wedding ring even though Arthur had been dead for many years.

'That pub you visited,' said Nancy. 'The Admiral. Arthur used to own it. He bought it many years ago and it's still in the family.'

That explained the soundproofed back room. Arthur had probably customised it especially for the purpose of having confidential business meetings in there.

'Adrian was buried in the same plot as his father,' Nancy added.

Bailey nodded, unsure how to respond. All she could think about right now was how the woman sitting just a few centimetres away from her had personally drilled holes in the heads of her husband's killers... or so the stories went. Bailey suppressed a shudder.

Nancy picked her lighter up off the top of the pack of Lambert and Butler on the table in front of her and began to absently fiddle with it in the same manner that she had done so in the pub, opening it with that distinctive 'cling' but not actually igniting the flame. The lighter was gold with a diamond-head pattern on its surface and a vertical striker wheel. Close enough to see it properly, Bailey recognised it as a Dupont. They were very expensive.

Nancy suddenly turned her head to Bailey. 'My son was murdered,' she spat. 'My own flesh and blood. And I'm going to get to the bottom of who did it if it's the last thing I ever do.'

Her words instantly dispelled the priest's eulogy about not seeking revenge. What with Nancy's past history, and now this, Bailey could tell that revenge was something that was very personal to her.

'I understand where you're coming from,' said Bailey, pushing her loose lock of hair aside to reveal the scar on her face, reminding Nancy of her own predisposition to revenge. Bailey half expected Nancy to enquire in more depth about her scars, but she didn't. Instead she set her jaw in a grim line and took it upon herself to dispense some gangland advice.

'In this world, if you don't take action you look weak. And that's fatal.'

'War is bad for business,' said Rick, who had sat down opposite them.

'Looking weak is even worse for business,' responded Nancy. 'That was one thing your father understood.'

'And look what happened to him,' said Rick.

Bailey detected a little discord between mother and son. The thirst for revenge versus the necessities of conducting business.

'You saw them all here today,' hissed Nancy. 'The Erkans. The O'Reillys. The Cromwells. Offering their condolences,' she said contemptuously. 'It could have been any one of them that blew up Adrian. They might be paying their respects, but what they're really looking for are any signs of weakness. They're like vultures circling.' She eyed her son gravely. 'And just remember, Ricky, it could be you they come for next.'

Rick shot his mother a warning glance, his eyes flickering to Bailey. It seemed that a mixture of emotion and alcohol had perhaps loosened their tongues more than was advisable in the presence of a newcomer such as Bailey who they didn't fully trust quite yet.

Bailey smiled innocently, deflecting their suspicious glances, and congratulated herself on breaking through to this new level. But she reminded herself not to get complacent, especially around people as deadly as this.

23

The remnants of a chicken doner kebab sat in a polystyrene carton on the upturned cardboard-box coffee table by the couch. Bailey turned up her nose at the sight of it.

'I'm not the culprit,' said Dale. 'Sadly they don't have much in the way of vegan options.'

'You could have had the falafels,' Frank intoned.

'I don't like chickpeas,' Dale replied.

'You're a vegan?' asked Bailey, eyeing Dale with surprise. 'Didn't figure you for the type.'

She guessed it explained his glowing complexion.

'I don't like cruelty to animals,' he said.

Bailey assessed him admiringly. Compassionate and handsome.

This was the first time they'd met since he'd visited her apartment a little over a week ago, and however each of them might have felt about the outcome of that particular evening, everything now seemed to be business as usual. And Bailey guessed that was probably a good thing.

'You know, I worked a case some years back,' said Frank. 'There was this chickpea who murdered another chickpea.'

They both looked at him blankly.

'It was a clear-cut case of hummus-cide,' he said with a straight face.

She and Dale groaned. It was a clear sign to get down to work.

'I had surveillance set up on the funeral,' Dale began. 'We got plenty of shots of you, Bailey. You looked like you fitted in just fine.'

'I'm glad my cover looks convincing to you, but I'm more concerned that it looks convincing to them.'

'Did you learn anything useful from being there?' asked Frank.

Bailey filled them in on the progress of the operation so far.

'He didn't mention anything about a date for the deal, but he did offer to get me a sample.'

'Getting a sample is a great plan,' said Frank. 'It could serve to confirm the provenance of the weaponry. I'll get hold of the eight hundred pounds for you as soon as possible.'

'I think the sample is a gesture of his sincerity,' she added. 'A way to make sure I stay on board. I think he's really keen to shift these guns.'

Frank thought about it for a few moments. 'If he hasn't confirmed a date, then that means it could be that the weapons aren't even in the country yet.'

Bailey nodded and pondered the possibility.

'Did you find out anything else?' asked Dale.

Bailey cast her mind back to the drinks reception in the hotel. 'I got the opportunity to talk to Nancy in a bit more depth.'

'And...?'

'I think she's warming to me.' Bailey paused. 'But she seems obsessed with the idea of getting revenge. She's determined to find out who killed Adrian and she'll go to war if necessary.'

'The last thing we need on our hands is a gangland war,' said Frank. 'Car bombs. Shootings. Innocent people getting caught in the crossfire. Tit-for-tat vendetta. Once this kind of thing kicks off, the reprisals just end up escalating back and forth.'

'Rick seems less keen on the idea,' she acknowledged. 'He said war is bad for business, and he's a businessman at heart, right? War costs money. It brings extra unwanted police attention to their operations. It forces people to take sides when they don't necessarily want to.'

Dale nodded to himself. 'Well, from what you've just said, and the fact that they seem to trust you, it sounds to me like they had no idea that Adrian was an informant. I wonder who did kill him though...'

Bailey hesitated in thought, staring down at the raw floorboards beneath her feet, then looked back up at Dale.

'You said Adrian probably had other schemes running on the side which he wasn't telling you about. Do you think one of them backfired on him in some way and that was the reason he got blown up?'

Dale sighed. 'Knowing him as I did, I wouldn't be surprised if he rubbed someone up the wrong way, or thought he was clever enough to rip someone off and think he could get away with it. If you find out anything, let me know. I'm sure the murder investigation team will be very interested.'

'Just remember though, Bailey,' interjected Frank, 'villains killing villains is one thing. But these guns are something else completely, with the potential to do real harm if the wrong people get hold of them. Don't forget your priority in this operation. And that's to make sure that these weapons do not hit the streets.'

24

_____

The hedgerows blurred past as Bailey pushed the BMW hard along the tight winding country lanes, following the directions on her GPS that Rick had given her in a coded phone message earlier the previous day.

It was the twenty-fourth of January. It had been almost a week since the funeral and she'd been starting to wonder just when she'd hear from him, worried that she'd inadvertently put a foot wrong somehow and had turned them off her.

She'd spent most of the previous few days at the hospital by her father's bedside. He was getting worse, and her mum wasn't coping too well with it, having retreated even further into the embraces of her church group. Bailey had also attended one of her scheduled appointments with the police psychologist. She'd talked a little bit about her father but had been reluctant to tell the psychologist just how much it was affecting her in case the psychologist thought she was too mentally overburdened to perform her undercover work properly and recommended that she be withdrawn. Fortunately, in that meeting she'd managed to stave off the prospect of being pulled out, but she knew she had to keep her head in the game, especially today.

It was a fresh sunny morning out in the Essex countryside and

Bailey reflected that at the very least this rendezvous was a good excuse to be getting out of polluted hectic London.

There was eight hundred pounds in cash in the glove compartment. Apart from an instruction to dress for a day out in the country, the only other thing Rick had said was to bring the cash, and then he'd hung up without even giving her the chance to respond. As was his habit, he kept business talk to the bare essentials over the phone. However, the request to bring the money was enough to tell her that the sample he'd offered would be awaiting her at this meeting.

So saying, there lurked the constant awareness at the back of her mind that at any point they could have discovered she was a cop and that this could be a trap, the conclusion of which would be her dead body being found in a car boot somewhere.

Her nerves jangled with a barely suppressed terror at the thought of being exposed and she couldn't help but recall the horrific torture she'd been subjected to after her cover had been blown with the car theft gang; in her undercover role, she was only ever one step away from that kind of thing happening again. On a wider level, the perpetual threat of exposure took an undeniable toll on her mental health, and that was the main thing the psychologist was interested in knowing – would Bailey burn out from the stress and lose the plot completely? But despite the incessant peril of her job, Bailey did know that she was too much of a restless soul to do any other kind of work. She was addicted too heavily to the fear and the adrenaline, and to the unbeatable satisfaction of seeing powerful crooks ending up behind bars all because of her.

And so long as she stayed alive, she'd carry on doing it. With undercover work, the key to survival was to be able to trust your gut instincts and if that inner voice told you something was off, you dropped everything and got out of there as fast as possible. So far, her intuition was telling her that everything was okay... so far...

She slowed down and turned off the lane onto an unpaved track, passing a sign indicating that this was private land. Driving slowly over the uneven ground along the edge of a field, Bailey soon saw a cluster of cars parked up ahead, along with a number of people milling around next to them.

She pulled up next to a large black Range Rover Velar and switched off the engine. Taking the wodge of cash out of the glove compartment, she tucked it into the pocket of her jacket, got out of the car and headed in the direction of the group of people.

It wasn't a large gathering and she immediately spotted Rick. He was dressed like a country squire in a Barbour jacket, a flat cap and Hunter wellies, and in the crook of his right arm, he was holding a shotgun, broken open. He noticed her at almost exactly the same time and turned to approach her.

'Glad you could make it,' he said, as if she really would have refused his invite.

'Nice to get out of the Big Smoke once in a while,' she replied, eyeing the shotgun with a little trepidation, wondering why he was holding it.

He looked her up and down, nodding in approval. 'Good to see that you're dressed appropriately.'

As per his instructions, she'd opted for a quilted jacket, jeans and wellington boots.

His black eyes scanned the horizon. 'We own all this land round here,' he said. 'This farm. Everything for miles. Old Bill won't have eyes on us out here, so you don't need to worry about them.'

For someone as paranoid as he was about being under surveillance, this was an ideal place to conduct illicit business. There were no buildings out here for the police to hide in and take photos, and any other vehicle could be spotted miles away.

That meant, of course, that Bailey, as an undercover police officer, was particularly vulnerable. When she'd informed Frank about this meeting, he'd offered her the services of a back-up team tailing her covertly at a distance to ensure her safety, but she'd refused. For one thing, savvy criminals could spot police surveillance if they knew what to look for, and if her cover was blown because her back-up team didn't keep a low enough profile, then she could suddenly find herself in a position of very real danger. Ironically then, it was often safer to operate completely alone in order to preclude those sorts of risks. All the same, in truth, being out here unprotected from potential peril did induce in her an undeniable sense of unease.

'What kind of things do you keep on your farm?' she asked in a tone of mild interest.

'Pigs mostly.'

'Pigs, huh?'

Rick gave her a cadaverous smile. Bailey knew pigs were a not uncommon way to dispose of bodies in the underworld. She wondered with a chill just how many of Molloys' victims had ended up as pig food.

'We make sausages,' he added. 'Which we sell to selected retail outlets. One of our more legitimate business ventures.'

'Of course,' she smiled nervously. 'So what's the plan for today then?'

'We're going shooting. Pheasants. It's almost the end of pheasant season, so we thought we'd have one last crack at them.'

She shrugged agreeably. That seemed reasonable enough, not that she'd ever hunted game birds before. She supposed this was the sort of thing you did for leisure if you came from these parts and had lots of money. And if you were like them, it didn't matter that it was a Thursday, because they didn't subscribe to the nine-to-five routine that most people were slave to. They could do whatever they wanted whenever they wanted.

Rick beckoned Shane over. Dressed in much the same way as Rick, Shane was holding two shotguns, also broken open. He handed one to Bailey, but she shook her head.

'Er... I think I'll just watch.'

'Not shooting?' said Rick, looking faintly disappointed.

'I'm probably more of a liability than anything else.'

Bailey's experience with guns was extremely limited. The last time she'd fired any kind of weapon, it had been an air rifle at the funfair in

Bexleyheath when she was fifteen years old with her boyfriend at the time, Neville. They had won a teddy bear though.

As an undercover police officer, firearms training was by no means mandatory, or even necessary, because, at the heart of it, undercover work was more about subtle human interaction and the art of infiltration. When it came to needing to shoot people, Bailey preferred to leave that kind of thing to the strike teams who swooped during the final stages of an operation. Ultimately, she'd never particularly liked guns or the idea of having to kill people. It was an ethos that had served her well so far and she wasn't inclined to depart from it any time soon.

'You want to buy all these guns from us and you don't like shooting?' said Shane, arching his eyebrows sceptically.

'Guns are just a commodity to me,' Bailey replied. 'Just something to shift to make cash.'

'Can't argue with that,' said Rick. He was a businessman. He knew the score.

The shoot commenced with the beaters driving the birds out of the bushes. Moments later, they tumbled from the sky, the sound of shots echoing across the flat, open landscape.

Bailey observed the shooters from a safe distance behind. The key members of the Molloy family were present, along with an assortment of other employees and associates. Nancy, dressed in a long tartan skirt, Barbour jacket and flat cap, enthusiastically plugged away at the flapping pheasants; Archie coolly and methodically blew them from the air one by one; Stephen, with his short little arms, struggled to manoeuvre the large shotgun but still managed to hit a decent number of birds. Bailey noticed that Rick was an excellent shot, not missing a single pheasant he aimed at. She saw Wendy standing off to one side, looking bored, not shooting either, idly checking her mobile phone from time to time.

Bailey wondered when Rick would give her the sample, but she didn't want to push him. She could see they wanted to make a day of it and she imagined he'd get around to it in his own time. At any rate, this was also a social invitation of sorts and she got the feeling this was their way of gauging her a little more.

However, with all these shotguns around, it had occurred to her that an 'accident' could happen very easily. But she quickly expelled the disturbing thought from her mind. They wouldn't try something so clumsy. If they suspected she was a cop and they wanted to kill her, then it would be something the authorities wouldn't be able to investigate quite so easily.

As they walked across the fields in pursuit of further game, Bailey caught Stephen watching her distrustfully. In fact, it seemed that every time she glanced in his direction, his little round eyes were glaring at her. Did he genuinely smell a rat or was he just naturally suspicious? The more concerned she got that he'd sussed her, the more she met his gaze, and the more she did that, the more suspect she realised she must have looked.

She forced herself to try and ignore him, and it was thus almost a relief when Nancy fell into step beside her, distracting her from her anxious thoughts. Nancy's shotgun was nestled in her elbow and she had an unlit cigarette hanging from the corner of her mouth. She opened her Dupont lighter with its distinctive 'cling', this time actually sparking the flame to light the cigarette.

Nancy was small, shorter than Bailey, who herself was only five foot six. Women grew smaller as they got older, as Bailey had noted with her own mother, who it seemed would eventually shrink out of existence altogether at some point. However, in Nancy's case, Bailey got the sense that as her size decreased with age, so her intrinsic malevolence increased, growing ever more potent and distilled.

Nancy blew out a stream of cigarette smoke and turned to look up at Bailey.

'As you probably know by now, Bailey, family is very important to me,' she said in her husky smoker's voice. 'And that means I'm curious about your family. Why don't you tell me a little bit more about them?'

While it might have seemed like quite an innocent question, Bailey was keenly aware that it could be a further more subtle way of probing her identity.

'Sure,' she said casually, concealing her inner wariness. 'What do you want to know?'

'You told me you had a sister. What was her name?'

Bailey hesitated a moment, but then reasoned to herself that information from her childhood was far enough removed from the present to be a relatively harmless thing to reveal to Nancy.

'Her name was Jennifer.'

'Jennifer,' echoed Nancy, her eyes narrowing.

Bailey saw Nancy soaking it up like a sponge and had no doubt that this woman's canny mind was adept at storing every tiny nugget of information for later retrieval, not dissimilar to how Bailey's own mind worked. After all, you never knew when a fact could come in handy or assume later significance.

'How old was she when she died?' said Nancy.

'She was eight. I was six.'

'Do you remember much about her?' said Nancy.

Bailey smiled. 'She loved the Ancient Egyptians. She was really into them.'

'The Ancient Egyptians?' Nancy laughed. 'Pyramids. Hieroglyphs. Tutankhamun. Yeah, kids love that kind of thing, don't they?'

'She was pretty,' added Bailey. 'She'd probably be really beautiful if she was alive today.'

Bailey wasn't lying about that, for it often crossed her mind what Jennifer would have been like as an adult.

'Did you get on well?'

'Yes, we did. As older sisters go, she was kind to me.'

Nancy perused her with curiosity, and if Bailey wasn't mistaken, also a glimmer of sympathy. 'Must have been hard for your parents to explain to you, at that age.'

'It was. I didn't really understand at the time. All I knew was one minute Jennifer was there and the next minute she was gone, and I didn't have anyone to play with any more.'

The large gulf of time had distanced Bailey sufficiently from those events to allow her to talk about them with a certain amount of detachment, as she was doing now.

Nancy paused for a few moments. 'Can I ask how she died?'

Bailey contemplated Nancy's question. Once again she saw no reason not to tell the truth.

'She was abducted off the street. Randomly. Just like that. She was never seen again. They never found her body. No trace of her at all. I think that's what my parents found most difficult. No closure.'

'That's awful,' said Nancy, shaking her head. 'To lose someone in that way.'

There was a sensitivity in Nancy's voice which Bailey hadn't detected before, something almost maternal and reassuring, and Bailey suddenly found herself wanting to confide in more detail about Jennifer's disappearance – her father's fruitless searching, her mother's descent into religion...

But then she caught herself. Nancy Molloy was a very dangerous person and this could all be part of some cunning ploy to draw Bailey in and get her to drop her defences. Opening up fully to someone like Nancy Molloy would be a very foolhardy thing to do indeed.

'I still feel her loss today,' said Bailey, keeping it vague. 'Some things you can't forget, however hard you try.'

'She was your blood,' said Nancy. 'And blood is important. I value it above everything else. And I can tell that you're the type who values it as well. Your family are all you've really got at the end of the day. That's why I have to find out who killed Adrian. And when I do...'

A pheasant flew out of the bushes. Nancy lifted the shotgun with a fluid dexterity and blasted the bird out of the sky. Bailey jumped at the loud report. The pheasant exploded in a mid-air puff of feathers and blood and cartwheeled into the ground.

Nancy marched over to it, Bailey in tow. Lying there in the grass, the pheasant, crippled beyond any kind of salvation, was still moving, twitching and panting its last breaths, its glistening viscera exposed, its small eyes darting in fear, acutely aware of its own impending demise.

Nancy lowered her shotgun so the muzzle was barely a few centimetres away from the trembling bird. She turned to look at Bailey.

'As I was saying, when I find them...'

She pulled the trigger. The shotgun roared and the pheasant disintegrated in a final explosion of gore and feathery down.

'... I'll show them no mercy.'

Bailey swallowed, shocked by Nancy's ferocity. Nancy stalked off, leaving Bailey staring down at the decimated remains of the pheasant. If Bailey had been having any doubts over Nancy Molloy's pitiless nature, this starkly laid them to rest.

Wendy came up beside Bailey and looked down at the dead bird. She made an 'ugh' face and sneered at Nancy's departing back.

'I thought she was supposed to like animals.'

'I think that only applies to Pomeranians,' muttered Bailey. She might have been quipping, but more than ever she now realised that to Nancy Molloy, her family was the most important thing, to the detriment of almost anything else.

When the shoot finished, they headed back to the cars. Rick beckoned Bailey aside, leading her away from the others, taking her over to the large black Range Rover Velar she had parked next to. With the two of them standing there alone, he took a key fob out of the pocket of his Barbour jacket and unlocked the car. Opening the rear, he lifted up the floor of the boot and took a brown paper bag out from beneath the spare wheel. He handed it to Bailey with an expectant, almost excited look on his face.

The bag was heavy, instantly causing her wrist to sag. Bailey peered inside. It contained a handgun. The sample. As expected.

'Take it out,' he urged. It was the first time she'd seen him this animated. She could tell he was getting a buzz out of it.

She hefted the gun in her hand, surprised at just how much it weighed. It was black and boxy looking.

'It's a K100 semi-automatic,' he said. 'Nine-millimetre. Made in Slovakia. There's some ammunition in case you want to test it. A full clip of fifteen rounds.'

Looking inside the bag, she noticed that, alongside the bullets, there was a chunky black metal cylinder.

'That's the silencer,' said Rick. 'I'll throw that in for free. You'll notice the gun's got a threaded barrel so you can screw it on.'

He turned his fingers into a gun shape, pointed them at Bailey and made a soft 'poufft' sound.

'Makes it nice and quiet,' he explained. 'Go on. Screw it on.'

Bailey clumsily screwed the silencer onto the end of the gun, which made the whole thing even heavier and bulkier. She realised that with the silencer, it constituted the ideal underworld assassination tool – quiet and deadly.

With that unpleasant thought on her mind, not particularly wanting to hold the weapon any longer, she removed the silencer and put both that and the gun back in the bag. She took the bundle of cash out of her jacket pocket and handed it to him. Rick pocketed it without counting it, barely giving it a glance. He knew she wouldn't rip him off at this stage as that would be counterproductive, given the large profits to be gained in the subsequent transaction. Anyhow, eight hundred pounds was a piddling amount to someone with his wealth, but she knew he had to ask for it out of a matter of principle. He'd probably spend that much alone on a bottle of champagne in a posh restaurant.

'So when exactly are we going to make the exchange?' she asked.

Rick eyed her mutely with a circumspect expression.

'I'll let you know the date all in good time,' he said, and turned and slammed shut the boot of the Range Rover.

She realised he wasn't going to elaborate any further than that. Starting to understand how he operated, she could see that he liked to be in absolute control of all information at every step of the process, never giving away any more than he had to at any time.

'I don't know about you,' he said, fixing her with his dead shark eyes. 'But I'm ravenous.'

25

They went for lunch in a country club a few miles down the road. Situated inside a Georgian stately home set in beautifully landscaped grounds, it couldn't have felt more exclusive. The place was built in a neoclassical style with tall pillars on the outside, while the interior had ornate plasterwork ceilings and antique hunting prints decorating the walls.

Bailey found herself sitting between Rick, on her left, and Wendy, on her right, while Nancy was sitting at another table chatting to Stephen and others. Smartly dressed waiters with impeccable manners glided between the tables serving them fine wine and exquisitely prepared food. The atmosphere was warm and pleasant, noisy with the sound of conversation and laughter.

Looking around her, Bailey contemplated how villains had to unwind too. Contrary to what people might have thought, they didn't spend all of their time engaged in nefarious acts of skullduggery. In fact, when they weren't locked up in prison, they spent a good chunk of their existence luxuriating in the fruits of their ill-gotten proceeds. After all, why bother making all that money in the first place if you couldn't enjoy it?

However, despite the convivial atmosphere, Bailey reminded

herself that their enjoyment was built on exploitation, intimidation, violence, murder and the trafficking of items that destroyed the fabric of society. She ate the delicious food with the knowledge that there was a gun in the glove compartment of her car, hard proof of their amoral activities, and it steeled her resolve to take them down for good.

Rick turned to her and smiled affably. 'Are you into restaurants, Bailey?'

'I like a decent bite to eat, but I can't say I'm much of a connoisseur.'

Although Bailey definitely appreciated high-quality food, her work schedule as a normal police officer often meant that takeaways were the only convenient option. When it came to working undercover though, things could be considerably more variable, her diet dictated largely by whatever environment she happened to be operating in. She certainly couldn't complain about this place, but in her last operation she'd had to stomach solely what had been on the menu in the prison canteen.

'Restaurants are one of my passions,' said Rick. 'In fact, I just purchased this new place. Asian fusion. You like Asian fusion?'

'Asian fusion? Never been quite sure what that is exactly.'

'Sushi pizza, kimchi quesadillas... that kind of thing. It combines the culinary traditions of Asian countries with those of various other countries. It's a very innovative cuisine, with the scope to create some really imaginative dishes.'

Bailey nodded, impressed by his expertise. Sometimes criminals, once they gained a bit of cash, liked to affect a certain degree of culture, like they were suddenly a cut above their fellow gangsters, but Rick seemed to have a genuine appreciation for haute cuisine.

'Of course, restaurants are just one element among many when it comes to my business ventures,' he said. 'I'm a property developer at heart.'

She knew property was one of the ways the Molloys laundered their illicit proceeds. Other ways included front businesses like restaurants, bars and bureaux de change; also, assets like jewellery, luxury cars and works of art; and, of course, hard cash, bundles and bundles of it, secreted around the place in various locations.

Bailey decided to flatter him a little, hoping to perhaps tease out some useful wisps of information.

'Property... wow. That's my dream. To get to the level where I'm doing big property deals.'

Rick puffed up a little. 'My latest undertaking is a luxury riverside development on the Thames Estuary. Six hundred top-of-the-range flats in Gravesend. The whole place is a building site at the moment, but they'll look fab when they're finished.' He paused. 'I do believe that's where the opportunity lies, further along the Thames Estuary as London expands.'

'That sounds like a really wise investment,' she said, nodding her head earnestly.

'I could sort you out with one off-plan if you're interested.'

'Ooh, tempting... although perhaps I should wait until we've concluded our forthcoming deal. Then I'll have a bit more money in my pocket.'

He gave her a magisterial smile. 'Carry on doing business with me, Bailey, and I'll make you rich.'

He left Bailey to ponder these words as he turned his attention to Shane, who'd come up that moment to ask him a question.

'Can you pass the salt, please?' said Wendy, breaking Bailey's train of thought.

'Sure,' said Bailey. She passed her the salt shaker, noticing as she did so that Wendy now had bright pink nails.

'What beautiful nails,' remarked Bailey. 'Again!'

Wendy fluttered her long eyelashes at the compliment. 'I deliberately wear pink to annoy her.' She nodded towards Nancy. 'She hates it. It's her worst colour. I mean, look at her. She's all blacks and dark purples. So oppressive.'

'I take it you two don't get on then?' said Bailey, probing a little, well aware that antagonism between individuals within criminal groups could be exploited to gain information or influence their activities.

Wendy lowered her voice and leaned in towards Bailey. 'Let me tell you, she's not the kind of mother-in-law you'd want to wish upon anyone. No one'll ever be good enough for her darling son. Him being the youngest and everything, they're always mummy's favourite. She scared away all his other girlfriends.'

'But not you?'

'Nah. I'm not scared of her, even if she does think I'm just some dumb blonde who's into beauty products.' She paused. 'I know exactly what their game is though. I know they're a bunch of villains through and through. I know my husband's no angel. Not that he ever tells me anything. But who cares? It's all boring anyway. Money, money, money.'

'Shame about Adrian, though,' said Bailey, angling for some further insight.

Wendy curled her lip in disdain. 'I can't say it surprised me that he came to a sticky end.'

'Oh? Why?'

Wendy peered over Bailey's shoulder to check that Rick wasn't listening. Bailey glanced around to see that he'd got up and was now standing at another table chatting to some other members of the gang.

'Well...' Wendy whispered conspiratorially, 'he was a bit of a nob. Always talking himself up. A bit too flash. A bit of a Champagne Charlie. Liked the nose powder a little too much, if you ask me. Always getting into trouble. Picking fights with people. Slagging people off in public. Something like that car bomb was bound to happen sooner or later.'

Bailey nodded to herself. It more or less corroborated what Dale had told her about Adrian.

'The problem was that he thought he was a proper player,' said Wendy. 'But that was just the drugs made him believe that about himself. Rick, for all his faults, doesn't touch them and he always despised Adrian because of his addictions. Saw him as weak.'

What she was saying only served to confirm Bailey's opinion of Rick – that he was a control freak; he didn't take drugs because they made you lose control, and for someone as powerful as him losing control could be fatal.

'Adrian used to push Rick around when they were kids,' continued Wendy. 'Always riding him. But then, when Nancy put Rick in charge, Adrian just went off the rails... not that he'd ever really been on them properly to begin with. And from then on it all built up to this huge blowout that happened just after he turned forty. That was about a year ago. He had a massive argument with Rick, they almost had a fight, but then they made up and it seemed like things were okay, but I'm not sure that they really were...'

Bailey absorbed the information with interest. Meanwhile, Wendy had taken out a small compact mirror and had started to apply some pink lipstick to her artificially large lips.

'So...' said Bailey carefully. 'Who'd you think killed Adrian then?'

Wendy glanced up from the mirror and shrugged. 'Ain't got a bleeding clue.' She continued to apply her lipstick, then paused and tilted her head thoughtfully. 'However, he did have this scuzzy coke-dealer mate called Marcus. They were always up to no good together. Marcus hasn't been seen since Adrian was murdered. Wasn't at the funeral or anything. Nancy and that lot are very suspicious that he's suddenly dropped off the radar like that. They reckon he might know who killed Adrian, and they're thinking he might even have been responsible himself. They're trying to track him down as we speak. I tell you, I wouldn't want to be in his shoes right now with this lot looking for him.'

Bailey processed the revelations, thinking that this was definitely a new lead that the murder investigation team would want to hear about.

Wendy pouted one last time into the compact mirror, then snapped it shut. She smiled her brittle smile at Bailey.

'You know, you should drop into my shop sometime. If you want to look good.'

She reached into her Chanel bag and took out a business card, which she held out to Bailey.

'Sure,' said Bailey, taking the card. 'I think I probably will. Thanks.'

26

Bailey sat down on the knackered old couch in the temporary HQ and tried to block out the smell of doner kebabs drifting up from downstairs.

With Dale and Frank standing over her, she proceeded to open her backpack and take out the brown paper bag that Rick had given her. She put it on the upturned cardboard-box coffee table.

Dale leant over to pick it up. He peered inside gingerly, smiled and nodded his approval.

'And a silencer as well. Great job, Bailey. I'll take this back to the station and get it checked out.'

Without touching the contents, he placed the entire brown paper bag into a large plastic evidence bag, ziplocked it shut and slipped it into his own bag.

'Rick still hasn't confirmed the date of the transaction with me,' she said.

'The more I think about it,' said Frank, 'the more it sounds like the guns haven't even entered the country yet.'

'Where do you think he's getting them from exactly?'

Frank nodded at Dale's bag containing the sample. 'Well, seeing as that pistol, the K100, is made in Slovakia, and the CZ 805 assault rifles are made in the Czech Republic, it doesn't seem too much of a leap to conclude that he's getting them from somewhere in Eastern Europe, which isn't that surprising. A lot of illegal guns entering the UK originate from that part of the world. If he is getting them from Eastern Europe, then there's a good chance they'll be entering the UK via Rotterdam. The Molloys will probably have done a deal with a Dutch OCG who, in turn, will have purchased the guns from an Eastern European OCG. But it'll be up to Rick's crew to determine exactly how the weapons will be smuggled into Britain.'

Bailey paused and thought back to something Rick had said during the meal at the country club.

'You know, Rick did mention that he had a property development in Gravesend.'

Frank and Dale both looked at her blankly.

'So?' prompted Dale.

'Well, what's just across the river?' she said.

Realisation dawned in Frank's eyes. 'Of course,' he whispered. 'Tilbury. Massive container port.'

Bailey nodded. 'It's a huge hub for stuff coming in from Europe. They process hundreds of thousands of containers a day. The guns could be concealed in any one of them. Hidden in fresh produce, car parts, you name it...'

'Yeah,' Frank agreed. 'Only one in a hundred containers is checked at Rotterdam anyway, and who knows, they might even have insiders over there in the Netherlands who make sure that it doesn't even go through those checks.'

'So once the guns are here, how do they get them from the container port to the property development?' asked Dale.

'They could also have insiders at Tilbury,' said Bailey. 'The containers come in. The insiders remove the guns before the containers go through the customs check they have to go through before being allowed out of the port. They load them onto a boat on the dockside in the middle of the night. The boat takes them across the river to the property development. It's an ideal place in which to transfer the weapons to a large vehicle before moving them wherever they're supposed to be headed. Everything will be hidden behind hoardings, and if it's a building site, then lots of big lorries going back and forth won't look unusual. The fact that the Molloys own the place means they can do whatever they want there.'

Frank and Dale both looked impressed.

'Interesting hypothesis,' said Frank.

The three of them paused for thought.

'Incidentally,' she added. 'I also found out something else the other day. Connected to Adrian's murder. It might be nothing. Or it might be something.'

'Go on...' responded Dale.

She recounted what Wendy had told her about Adrian's scuzzy friend, Marcus.

Dale raised his eyebrows. 'Sounds promising. Did you catch a surname or anything?'

Bailey shook her head. 'All I know is that the Molloys are going all out to find him, or rather Nancy is.'

'I can't imagine it'll be easy for us to locate him,' said Dale. 'He'll be lying very low indeed if he's trying to keep out of the clutches of the Molloys.'

'Either that or he's dead,' said Frank.

27

Lying asleep in the bed at the hospice, Dennis Morgan looked markedly more gaunt and wizened since the last time Bailey had seen him. The cancer ravaging his insides was now starting to show its toll.

He'd been moved to the hospice two days previously. The referral had taken just over a fortnight to come through. The hospice was located in Sydenham in South London, close to where her parents lived in Bromley, and just like he'd told her, it seemed like a really pleasant place despite the function it served, being basically a hospital that you went into and never left.

He was in his own personal room, hooked up to his drugs, and he had his own TV, attached to the wall, although at the moment it was switched off because he was asleep. Outside, through the window, Bailey could see the green and tranquil setting of the hospice garden. A few people were out there, sitting on the benches or wandering among the artful sculptures dotted here and there.

Bailey's mother was sitting on the other side of the bed. The cancer had taken its toll on her too – she looked drained and weary. Bailey tried to think what life would be like with just her and her mother. It saddened her greatly to see their little family unit crumbling like this right in front of her.

'How are you coping, Mum?' she asked gently.

'My church group are being very helpful,' said her mother. 'Very supportive.'

Janet Morgan clutched her King James Bible as she spoke. She'd been reading from it when Bailey had come in.

'I've been praying for him,' said her mother. 'As has everyone else in my church. We've all been praying for him. If anything, he'll be going to a better place soon.'

Bailey sighed within. As far as she was concerned, her father would die and that would be that. He would live on only in her memories. It was a rather existential view to hold, but she couldn't see it any other way.

With a pang of guilt, she recalled the picture of Mister Snigiss; it was still in her purse, untouched since he'd given it to her. At least now, while he was asleep, there would be no awkward conversations about that.

After a while, she and her mother stood up and went for a coffee in the hospice café, leaving her father lying there with his eyes closed, almost looking like he was in peace.

As they sat at the table sipping the coffee, Bailey reflected on how exposed she was, sitting here with her mother.

One of the strange things she'd found working undercover was that the more enmeshed you became in your cover identity, the more vulnerable you felt in your real life, because there was considerably more danger of compromising your identity if seen with people who were quite obviously not part of your cover. It was one of the main reasons Bailey refrained from meeting up with friends from her normal life when she was operating in an undercover role. It increased the risk of exposure, particularly in social settings like bars and pubs where you never knew if you might accidentally bump into someone who happened to be acquainted somehow with the criminals you were currently infiltrating; and that could be downright dangerous.

She wasn't expecting to encounter any of the Molloys here in this hospice, but they were a large organisation, so she couldn't completely rule out the possibility of meeting someone who knew them in some way. Even so, with her father in this critical phase of health, she couldn't allow herself not to visit. As for having an explanation to hand if she suddenly were to encounter one of them, she couldn't very well imagine rehearsing it with her mother, so she figured the best bet was to keep her head down and her eyes open and hope for the best.

Her mother gave Bailey a faint look of consternation mixed with sadness.

'Am I ever going to see any grandchildren, Bailey?'

Bailey got the impression her father's worsening condition had only served to exacerbate her mother's perennial pestering on this topic.

'I already told you, Mum, I'm not interested in having kids.'

'It just seems a shame, Bailey. You're of an age.'

'You're starting to sound like Mark.'

'He was such a nice young man. I can't understand for the life of me why you threw it all away.'

'I just didn't feel it was right,' said Bailey, not wanting to get drawn into a big debate about it.

'Is there no one else?'

She considered mentioning Dale, but she didn't because if she did, then her mother would be constantly 'Dale this' and 'Dale that', and, anyhow, Bailey wasn't sure that it was even going anywhere with him. So saying, he had asked her if she wanted to go out for a meal the day after tomorrow...

'No, there's no one serious at the moment,' said Bailey.

'Perhaps you should make more of an effort with the way you dress,' said her mother, looking critically at Bailey's Hugo Boss jacket. 'You look like some kind of... gangster.'

Bailey sighed, resisting the temptation to explain the reasons behind her appearance. When she was out and about like this, it seemed a safer bet to dress in character just in case she did randomly run into one of the Molloys, and if her mother thought she resembled a villain then at least Bailey was managing to pull that much off.

'If you want to attract men, you should look more feminine,' her mother continued. 'At the very least you could wear that hairgrip I gave you for Christmas. It wasn't cheap, you know.'

'Er...' Bailey sighed evasively. 'Sure, Mum. I keep forgetting to put it on. Anyhow, it's more the kind of thing I'd keep for a special occasion.'

However, her mother's nagging about the way she looked did remind her of something she'd been meaning to do...

28

The sleek walls of the salon were lined with glass shelves displaying a wide array of beauty products. Dance music played at a low volume in the background whilst the beauticians chatted softly with the clientele – women of various ages sitting in front of the mirrors having their hair cut and blow-dried or sitting at the back having their nails done.

A few of them looked up when Bailey came in. She felt a bit self-conscious, and not a little out of place, seeing as this wasn't normally the kind of establishment she'd make a habit of visiting. However, today was different; today she was here because of her job.

Looking around, she spotted Wendy at the back, standing by the cash register. On seeing Bailey, Wendy didn't appear to immediately recognise her, but then her face broke into a delighted smile.

'Bailey! It's so lovely to see you. You're lucky I was able to fit you in.'

It had only been that morning that Bailey had made an appointment with Wendy.

Bailey gave a buoyant shrug. 'I thought, what the hell, I'd give it a try. It's so hard to find a decent beauty salon.'

Wendy beamed. 'So what can I do for you?'

Bailey frowned, slightly stumped. She hadn't actually given it much thought. And she'd always been a bit clueless when it came to the finer points of beauty. She must have looked a bit bewildered.

'Okay,' said Wendy with a quizzical expression. 'Well, what's the occasion? Is there an occasion?'

'Er... yeah, I have a date,' said Bailey. It wasn't quite a lie. After all, she was due to go out for a meal with Dale later that evening, and although she wouldn't normally have bothered to doll herself up too much, it seemed like a good pretext under which to come here and see if she could extract any more useful information from Wendy.

'A date? Ooh how exciting!' She scrutinised Bailey with the sharp eye of a professional. 'Well, for a start, I think your hair probably needs a bit of work, if you don't mind me saying so.'

Bailey shrugged. 'You're the expert.'

Sitting Bailey down in a chair, Wendy got to work on her hair, chatting to her as she did so.

'I started off as a hairdresser, you know. In a place just down the high street. I'm a Basildon girl through and through.'

She lifted up the loose lock of hair which hung down over Bailey's left cheek.

'I see you normally wear a loose bit down the side of your face.'

'Yeah,' said Bailey, squirming a little self-consciously on the chair.

Wendy eyed Bailey's facial scar in the mirror and pursed her large lips thoughtfully.

'I'll leave that bit how it is, but I'll trim the ends a little. How does that sound?'

'Sounds good to me.'

'So who's the lucky fella?' asked Wendy as she snipped delicately at Bailey's hair.

'Oh... just someone I knew from a while ago who's kind of come back into my life.'

Bailey deliberately kept it a little vague as she wasn't keen on giving away too much information about her private life to someone like Wendy who had connections to her undercover operation.

'How romantic! Where's he taking you?'

'I think it's some trendy restaurant. It's had good reviews apparently.'

'So long as he's the one paying.'

They both laughed. Bailey decided to ease onto the subject of Rick.

'So... does Rick take you out much?'

Wendy's face darkened. 'Yeah... he does. But...' Her mouth tightened and she suddenly looked troubled.

Bailey sensed that something was wrong. She decided to explore this possible chink in their relationship.

'Is everything okay?' She injected a sympathetic tone into her voice.

The strained expression on Wendy's face grew more pronounced. Her good cheer had all but evaporated.

'You... you won't mention anything to him...' she said.

'Of course not.'

Wendy swallowed, her voice coming out in a whisper. 'I think he might be seeing someone else.'

Bailey sighed inside. That wasn't quite what she'd been hoping to hear. She hadn't come here to be the sounding board for Wendy's marital strife. But she couldn't back out now. In for a penny, in for a pound. She smiled gently.

'Well, you don't know for sure, do you...?'

Wendy shook her head in disagreement. 'I overheard him talking to one of his mates on the phone when he thought I wasn't listening,' she said, her voice wobbling at the edges. 'Often he goes out to the garden when he's talking business. But he didn't notice me when I was outside one time. I heard the tail end of his conversation. Her name's Kaia. He was talking about how he was off to see her in Torquay.'

It did sound kind of incriminating, Bailey had to admit.

Wendy glanced at the surrounding customers and staff, lowering the volume of her voice to try and maintain a modicum of professionalism. 'So I checked his diary secretly when he was in the shower,' she continued, the words tumbling out in an emotional stream. 'And there it was! Plain as day. Friday the eighth of March. He's taking her to

Torquay for a dirty weekend. Torquay! The same place we went on a little romantic getaway when we first met.'

She snipped away briskly at Bailey's hair as she spoke.

'He likes Torquay, you see. It's like a childhood nostalgia thing with him. His mum used to take the family there a lot when they were kids. And so he took me there when we first got together. Not Paris. Not Rome. But Torquay.' She sighed wistfully.

Then her expression curdled. 'And now he's doing exactly the same thing with another woman. Probably younger. Probably got big fake baps. Slut!

'And meanwhile he's at home making out like he's not doing anything wrong. We had dinner the other night, and I... I almost came out with it. But I... I couldn't... I know he'd just deny it. Or lie. He's good at lying. That's why he's never been caught. That's why he's never gone to prison.' She took a momentary pause from cutting Bailey's hair and met her eyes in the mirror. 'Kaia!' she hissed, clenching the scissors murderously. 'Fucking slapper name n'all!'

Now Bailey understood why Rick and Nancy never let Wendy know anything about their business activities. Wendy hardly knew Bailey and already she was confiding in her about the intimacies of her marriage.

'Has he done it in the past?' asked Bailey gently.

'Not that I know of. But after finding this out, I'm not so sure.'

Wendy hesitated and once more glimpsed around to check that no one was eavesdropping.

'I'm thinking of hiring a private eye,' she said. 'You know, to follow him. At least then I'd have some solid evidence to confront him with. Photos of them together and the like. What do you think?'

Bailey took a moment to contemplate the idea. 'I'm sure that whatever decision you make will be the right one.'

Wendy gave her a beatific smile, pleased at Bailey's apparent approval of her plan.

She stepped back to assess her work on Bailey's hair. She looked at Bailey in the mirror and nodded in appreciation.

'You know you're really pretty, Bailey.'

There was a sincerity in Wendy's voice that really touched Bailey. 'Oh, thank you.'

Wendy's brow creased a little as she perused Bailey's reflection.

'Have you thought about getting dermabrasion for the scar on your face?' she asked.

Bailey shifted self-consciously. 'Uh, yeah, maybe at some point.'

Undergoing surgery to mitigate her scars was something Bailey was planning to do eventually, but only after she'd caught up with, and taken revenge on, the person who'd given them to her. Up until then, she'd carry them as a reminder not to give up in that quest, and when she finally did take him down, she'd make sure he got a good look at them, just to remind him exactly what he'd done to her.

'Well, let me know if you do want to have the procedure done,' said Wendy. 'I can recommend a good clinic.'

'Thanks,' said Bailey. 'I'll make a note of it.'

She examined herself in the mirror. Her hair did look good. Wendy had done a sterling job. Maybe the trip to the beauty salon hadn't been a total waste of time after all.

29

They sat in a low-lit corner booth in the chic vegan restaurant that Dale had selected for their evening out. Bailey was eating a teriyaki-glazed tofu steak with glass noodle salad, while Dale had gone for the woodland mushroom pie with sweet potato fries.

The vegan food had been somewhat of a revelation for Bailey. She hadn't realised that meals without animal products could be this good, but at the same time she knew she was unlikely to ever become a strict vegan. She liked to keep her gastronomic options open.

She glanced around, scanning the other diners, trying to gauge if there might be anyone here with a potential connection to the Molloys who might question her presence with Dale. But then he was well aware of her situation and she was confident that he was smart and experienced enough to be able to come up with an on-the-fly explanation to back her up should this situation unexpectedly occur.

So far, though, things seemed to look fine. Just a load of other couples dotted around the tranquil interior of the restaurant, eating, drinking, chatting quietly. She turned her attention back to the table.

'The food here's very tasty,' she remarked. 'And this place is pretty classy. But surely there can't be that many vegan places around, so it must kind of limit you.'

'Not really. These days, most restaurants have at least a few vegan options. Anyhow, I always go online and check the menu before booking just to make sure.'

She took a mouthful of the delicious food and copped another admiring look at him, thinking once again just how handsome and stylish he was. Tonight he was decked out in a pastel blue linen Hilfiger shirt, which seemed to somehow enhance his healthy skin tone and lustrous blonde hair. Catching her glance, he reflected it back on her.

'You look good by the way,' he said. 'Have you had a haircut?'

Bailey blushed, secretly delighted that he'd noticed.

'I might have,' she said with a coy smile. 'Actually, I went to Wendy's beauty salon. To see if I could pick up any useful information.'

'And did you?'

She sighed and shrugged. 'Well... she thinks that Rick is cheating on her. But beyond that, I didn't pick up anything particularly useful. I kind of like her though. Although I'm not surprised that the Molloys keep her well away from their business ventures. She's definitely what you'd call a sharer.'

'Cheating on her, eh? Mmm...' Dale rubbed his chin thoughtfully. 'Do you think we could turn her? Use his infidelity as leverage to make her an informant?'

Bailey winced. 'I don't think so. Not at this stage. It would be too risky. I'd have to admit to her that I was a police officer. And if she didn't bite, then we'd have to immediately end the operation, because she'd probably tell Rick.' Bailey paused. 'To be honest, much as I've warmed to her, I don't think she has access to the kind of information we need. Like I said, they make sure not to tell her anything sensitive, precisely because she's not all that discreet.'

'Sounds like a wise decision on their part,' said Dale with a smile. 'Okay. Fair enough.'

Bailey took a moment to observe the other couples dining and conversing softly in the warm, intimate space of the restaurant.

'Anyway, let's stop talking work,' she suggested. 'We should be unwinding, right?'

'Sure. Good idea,' Dale agreed. 'So what did you get up to over the weekend?'

'The weekend...?' She hesitated. 'I went to visit my father in the hospice.'

'Your father's in a hospice?'

Bailey realised that she hadn't told Dale about the situation with her father.

'Yeah. He's really ill. Stage four pancreatic cancer.'

'Oh my God! I had no idea.' His eyes widened in concern. 'I'm so sorry to hear that.'

She gave a disconsolate shrug.

'Do you want to talk about it?' he asked gently.

She started to shake her head and began to explain why he probably wouldn't want to hear about it. But then somehow she found herself talking, and telling him more and more until the words were spilling out in a ceaseless torrent. And all the while, he listened silently, his calm blue eyes wide and receptive, paying firm attention to everything she said.

She halted suddenly, realising she'd been talking at him non-stop for almost ten minutes.

'I'm sorry. This must be really boring for you.'

'Not at all,' he said.

'I'm not used to talking about these kinds of things with other people. I guess it's all just built up inside of me.'

'It's good to get stuff off your chest.'

'You're a good listener,' she said.

'It's a crucial skill to have when you're working with informants.'

They both laughed.

That was what she missed about intimacy. To be able to confide in someone close to you. But did the fact that she was now confiding in Dale mean that they were becoming intimate?

'I like it when you tell me about yourself,' he said. 'It's interesting.'

'You don't know the half of it,' she said.

'What do you mean?'

She snorted a laugh. 'I haven't even started telling you about my sister.'

He raised his eyebrows in curiosity. 'I'm all ears...'

And so she found herself telling him all about Jennifer's disappearance and her father's futile quest to find her and his irrational obsession with Mister Snigiss. It felt good to talk. Cathartic. Once again, Dale listened intently, giving her his full attention. However, as she was drawing to a close, she noticed that a preoccupied frown had settled on his face.

'I'm sorry,' she said, shaking her head. 'I think I really have bored you this time. I just told you all this crap from my childhood.'

'No, that's okay.' The furrows on his forehead deepened. 'It's just that...'

She saw his lips flex and tighten like he was about to say something but had suddenly thought better of it. As a police officer, she was good at noticing these little behavioural cues.

'What is it?' she asked.

'Ah, it's probably nothing.'

'You look perturbed.'

He shook it off and smiled. 'Like I said, it's probably nothing.'

Now she was intrigued. 'You can't say that and then not tell me.'

He smiled and sighed. 'Okay... I'll tell you, for what it's worth. But don't place too much stock in it... because it might not be anything, okay?'

He took a deep breath to speak. She leaned forward in anticipation.

'Well...' he said. 'When he was alive, Adrian was always trying to tap me up for information, stuff that was probably connected to schemes that he was secretly running on the side. You have to be careful when you're running informants that they don't end up running you. They're crafty sods. Instead of you getting information out of them, it's them getting information out of you. The balance can easily tip the other way. That's what these people are like.'

Bailey nodded. She understood only too well how the criminal mind operated, with its innate deviousness and cunning.

He paused and took another deep breath.

'Anyhow, it was a few days before Adrian got blown up that I met up with him and he asked me if I could "look into" someone for him. Now, what that usually means is that he's got some rival, or someone he's looking to screw over, and he wants to know details of their criminal record, convictions, known associates, and so on, to give him some kind of advantage. So this bloke he wanted me to look into... well, he implied that he was some kind of pimp, or at least operating in that general milieu. Made out like this guy was a fairly serious player. He gave me a name...'

Bailey felt the hairs on the back of her neck rising.

Dale stared at her with his unblinking bright blue eyes.

'The name was Mister Snigiss,' he said softly.

Bailey's breath caught in her throat and a powerful shiver went through her. She felt as if someone had walked over her grave.

It couldn't be. Surely not.

'Mister Snigiss?' she whispered. 'Are you sure?'

Dale nodded. 'Adrian did refer to him as exactly that – "Mister Snigiss". Not "Snigiss", but "Mister Snigiss". No Christian name. Just "Mister".' He raised his palms. 'But then it could just be a coincidence.'

Bailey found that she was shaking her head. She'd never been a big one for coincidences. Snigiss was an odd enough name as it was, but the precise appellation of 'Mister Snigiss' took it beyond what in her eyes could be considered a coincidence.

She blinked as she tried to grasp the ramifications of Dale's revelation, that Mister Snigiss wasn't a figment of Jennifer's childhood imagination, that, God forbid, her father had actually been right in his assumptions all along...

'I assumed that this Mister Snigiss character was connected to one of Adrian's schemes,' Dale was saying. 'I figured that perhaps Adrian was trying to get into prostitution or sex trafficking or something like that. I asked him why he wanted to know about Mister Snigiss, but he was extremely cagey. I warned him he wasn't supposed to be involved in any kind of criminal enterprise that he hadn't told me about, and that he'd be liable for prosecution if he was. I told him that I didn't know the name... because I didn't. And I refused to check it out for him.'

'But you did, didn't you?' said Bailey.

Dale nodded. 'To satisfy my own curiosity. So I checked the Police National Database but—'

'The name threw up nothing,' she said, interrupting him.

'You've already checked?'

Bailey nodded slowly.

A heavy silence descended over them.

Dale looked at Bailey in concern.

'You really do look like you've seen a ghost, Bailey. I'm worried that I've spooked you.'

Bailey was indeed spooked. More than she'd been in a very long time. For so many years she'd been confident that her father had been chasing nothing more than a phantom of his paranoid guilt-riddled imagination. But now she wasn't so sure.

'Maybe I shouldn't have mentioned it,' said Dale.

'I think I need another glass of wine,' said Bailey.

Dale sighed. 'Anyhow, I've already passed the name onto the murder investigation team on the off-chance this Mister Snigiss might have some involvement.'

Bailey blinked and frowned in confusion. 'What are you talking about?'

'Remember you asked if I thought one of Adrian's schemes might have backfired on him and that was the reason he got blown up? Well, if Mister Snigiss is connected to one of Adrian's schemes, then that makes him a potential suspect in the car bomb.'

Bailey nodded and swallowed, still trying to take it all on board. 'So has it led to anything?'

Dale shook his head. 'Nothing so far. The whole murder investigation has basically hit a dead end. But I'll let you know if anything changes.'

For Bailey, though, everything already had changed.

30

Later that night, Bailey sat alone on the sofa in her apartment, locked in a stupefied trance, staring out of the large windows at the glittering lights of the city beyond.

Her evening with Dale had eventually petered out into long, pensive silences on her part as she'd wrestled with what he'd told her. Despite his attempts to talk about other things, she couldn't shake it from her mind. Eventually they'd parted ways stiltedly, and now she was sitting here unable to sleep, her mind churning ceaselessly in a furious tangle of speculation.

Mister Snigiss.

The revelation had stripped her raw on the inside, shattering her emotionally. The name she'd repeatedly dismissed for all these years had now returned with a vengeance, resonating right through to the very core of her being.

Could this really be the same Mister Snigiss? Had Mister Snigiss been more than just an invisible friend? Had he really been responsible for Jennifer's abduction?

In the light of what Dale had told her, it all now seemed to make a horrible sense. It had always been Bailey's notion that Jennifer had been swallowed into some dark, sordid world of sexual exploitation, never to re-emerge. But now she knew there was someone called Mister Snigiss in that world, it only served to confirm those unpleasant suspicions.

At first, it had seemed unbelievable that she should encounter, here, on one of her very own undercover police operations, the very same Mister Snigiss from her childhood. But then the more she thought about it, the more likely it seemed that sooner or later their paths would cross, for he was a criminal and she was a policewoman, and the world, perhaps, wasn't such a big place.

But who was he?

Reaching for her purse on the sofa next to her, she took out the picture of Mister Snigiss that her father had given her. Unfolding the delicate paper, she examined the crude felt-tip drawing, seeing it in a new light now, seeing it as her father saw it – as some clue to Mister Snigiss's identity. But it was no e-fit, that was for sure. A stick figure in a little fedora hat with his pet cobra wriggling along beside him, drawn by an eight-year-old girl who'd never been particularly strong at art. How could Bailey even begin to identify Mister Snigiss on the basis of this?

You can't see Mister Snigiss, but Mister Snigiss can see you.

Jennifer's tinkling voice now returned to Bailey like a childhood taunt. It had frustrated Bailey all those years ago that she'd never been able to see Mister Snigiss, and now that same frustration resurfaced.

She traced her fingertips over Jennifer's spidery handwriting, over the name 'Mister Snigiss' that was scrawled beneath the loping hat-wearing stick figure and his pet snake. What kind of name was 'Mister Snigiss' anyway? Ever since she was young, Bailey had never really liked the way it sounded. 'Snigiss' sounded like the cross between a snigger and a hiss. And with her father characterising him as some sinister abductor of children, and now Dale implying that he was this underworld pimp, the disagreeable connotations of the name seemed more apt than ever.

She stared down at the picture, battling to make sense of it. A part of her seriously wanted to reject the whole thing, to stubbornly maintain the view she'd held all these years that her father's theories had been baseless and crazy and nothing more. But this time she knew that there was something in it.

Much as she was reluctant to pursue Mister Snigiss, her conscience was telling her otherwise. Her filial loyalty to her dead sister arose from deep within to override any other considerations. This new revelation presented the tantalising possibility of finding out what had really happened to Jennifer and maybe even the hope of exacting some kind of justice. Surely she owed her sister's memory that much. And as for her father, it was the least she could do for him... and probably the last thing she could do for him.

31

Going back to Bromley always depressed Bailey. The drab suburban streets with the rows of pebble-dashed houses with their net curtains seemed to try their utmost to crush her spirit. But in lieu of talking to her father, returning to the landscape of her childhood seemed like the next best thing in terms of unearthing further information about Mister Snigiss.

It was ironic that at the very time she most needed to discuss Mister Snigiss with her father, she was prevented from doing so due to his poor health. It wasn't that he was physically unable to talk, at least not yet; it was more that she didn't want to unduly excite him, in his weakened state, with something that could in fact lead to nothing. And, at any rate, she would be unable to discuss any matters pertaining to Adrian, as those formed part of an ongoing undercover operation and were thus totally confidential. As a matter of course, she never revealed anything more than the most cursory details of her job to her parents.

As for her mother, Bailey had never really broached the subject of Mister Snigiss with her. Bailey knew her mother didn't like to dwell too much on Jennifer's disappearance; her primary method of dealing with it had been to bury herself ever deeper in her religious beliefs. But now, as they both sat at the kitchen table drinking mugs of tea, Bailey thought it an appropriate time to raise the issue.

Taking advantage of a pause in their current conversation in which her mother had been lecturing her on the tenets of her Christian faith, Bailey took the opportunity to speak.

'Mum, do you remember much about Mister Snigiss?'

Her mother frowned. 'You normally hate talking about that, Bailey.'

'Well... I was just curious, that was all.'

Her mother tilted her head in recall. 'Yes. I remember Mister Snigiss. I remember when Jennifer first started going on about him. Your father and I were a little worried at first. Jennifer would suddenly start talking to someone who we couldn't see. Or she'd tell us that he was in the car with us. She'd say "You can't see Mister Snigiss—"'

'But Mister Snigiss can see you,' chimed Bailey, completing the sentence.

Her mother sighed. 'Yes. We thought it was a sign of mental illness, so we went to the doctor, but he told us that it was normal for a child of her age to have an invisible friend. Apparently it's most common between the ages of three and eight, and it's usually the older child who does it, and it happens more often with girls than boys. So, all in all, Jennifer was nothing unusual. When we asked why she was doing it, he said that kids do it in order to practise their social skills, or something like that. And I suppose Jennifer was always a very imaginative little girl.'

Bailey nodded slowly. 'But you never...?'

Her mother shook her head. 'Not once did I ever harbour the kinds of suspicions that your father developed about Mister Snigiss after Jennifer went missing. No. My view was, and still is, that Mister Snigiss was just an imaginary friend and nothing more.'

Bailey looked out through the kitchen window into the back garden, the setting for most of the fantasy adventures that she and Jennifer had embarked on under the auspices of Mister Snigiss. Bailey couldn't help but smile at the sight of the apple tree in the corner, still there after all these years. When she was five years old, she'd climbed to the top, and promptly got stuck, causing her parents to have to call in the Fire Brigade to rescue her.

But now the garden was overgrown. Her mother had neglected to maintain it, and with her father ill, it would no doubt get even shabbier. Seeing the old shed where he kept the lawnmower evoked a sudden pressing sadness, not helped by the drizzly overcast weather. God, suburbia could be so grim.

Bailey rose from the kitchen table.

'I'm just going upstairs for a bit,' she said.

Her mother nodded absently and continued to drink her tea.

Leaving the kitchen, Bailey trudged up the stairs and padded along the carpeted landing to stop outside Jennifer's bedroom. Stuck to the door was a ceramic plaque inscribed with the words 'Daddy's Little Princess' surrounded by pink hearts and yellow stars. Jennifer had always been her father's favourite. It was a fact Bailey had accepted from an early age, to the extent that she never really questioned it, although as she'd grown older she'd occasionally wondered if her father would have demonstrated quite the same determination to find her had she been the one who'd gone missing instead of Jennifer. However, despite those occasional misgivings, she knew her father did love her deeply, and that was the important thing.

With some reluctance, Bailey pushed down the door handle and entered the room for what was probably the first time in almost ten years. She'd long made a habit of avoiding Jennifer's bedroom, mainly because of the way her father insisted on preserving it exactly the way it had been the day she'd gone missing. It seriously creeped Bailey out.

The bed was neatly made with a My Little Pony bedspread and pillows, above which perched a row of soft toys lined up along the headboard. Bailey remembered the name of only one of them now – Claude, a loveable elephant standing at the far end of the row.

Hanging from the ceiling was the dinosaur mobile Jennifer had made in school from coloured felt, coat hangers and bits of cardboard. Now it was draped with a fine grey gossamer of cobwebs undulating in the air currents generated by Bailey's presence.

On the floor by her desk were her collection of Barbie dolls, their plastic faces frozen in miniature pouts, waiting patiently for their owner to return.

Stuck to the walls were a variety of Jennifer's crude and garish felt-tip drawings, the paper now curling and yellowing with age, the corners discoloured from the oil leached out of the ancient Blu Tack. It was one of these pictures that now resided in Bailey's purse, taken from the wall by her father, the only depiction of Mister Snigiss he'd been able to find.

She moved closer to the wall to pore over the pictures. She herself featured in a fair few of them – a little stick figure, smaller than the one which was Jennifer, both of them engaged in adventures of one form or another.

It had been Jennifer who'd always initiated their games, who'd been the prime architect of that fantasy world, with Bailey, two years younger, running around after her, looking up to her older sister. On any given day, the two of them might be princesses, pirates, or even animals of some sort, playing along with a host of imaginary beings whom Jennifer had endowed with names and whole lives of their own, drawn up from the wellspring of her fertile imagination.

Stepping back, Bailey glanced around, noticing that on the wall above Jennifer's desk was tacked a fashion poster with a Roaring Twenties theme. Her parents had brought it back from a fashion exhibition at the Victoria and Albert Museum, knowing at the time how much Jennifer was growing to adore fashion and glamour. The picture was a stylised depiction of a tall, dashing man wearing a black fedora hat accompanied by a slender, glamorous-looking woman clad in a long slim gown. Bailey had always thought the reason Jennifer had given Mister Snigiss a fedora hat was because it was what the man in the poster was wearing.

Underneath the window was a bookcase stuffed with a collection of children's books. There were a fair few on fashion, along with several on the Ancient Egyptians – a subject Jennifer had reserved a special passion for – and also a number of books on snakes and reptiles. As she'd grown older, Jennifer had wanted a pet snake, but her parents had refused, so Mister Snigiss had got one instead, and he'd called it Sid. Just like Mister Snigiss, Bailey hadn't been able to see Sid either.

For all these years, Bailey had assumed that Mister Snigiss had been nothing more than an amalgamation of various elements of Jennifer's childhood interests, mashed together into a fantasy figure who could fulfil the demands of her powerful imagination. All those elements were present in this room right now. The man with his fedora hat... The books on snakes... But maybe Bailey had got it wrong. Maybe there really was more to Mister Snigiss, just like her father had always said. There was only one way to find out.

She rolled up her sleeves and got to work. Pulling open the drawers of the dresser, she began to riffle through Jennifer's possessions, taking out all of her clothes and running her hands through the pockets, hoping to find some fresh clue as to the true identity of Mister Snigiss. Soon the floor around her was strewn with Jennifer's garments. Her father would have been furious at the mess she was creating in here, but there wasn't a lot he could do about it now.

Kneeling down by the bookcase, she pulled out all of the books, flicking through each and every one of them, seeing if they concealed some hidden note or photograph, then dropping them on the carpet when she was done.

Standing up, she went over to the desk and rummaged through all of Jennifer's schoolwork – the exercise books containing her project on snakes, her project on the Ancient Egyptians and her primitive efforts at creative writing. There was a pile of Jennifer's sketchbooks and Bailey leafed through every one of them, examining all of the pictures in detail, and then she turned her attention back to the pictures that were stuck up on the wall and scrutinised all of them as well.

A good hour or two had passed by the time she'd finished. Her hair was ruffled and she'd broken into a sweat. The room was in complete disarray, Jennifer's belongings piled hither and thither around her. It felt like she'd gone over every square inch of the bedroom.

And she'd found absolutely nothing that gave her any further insight into Mister Snigiss.

Bailey blew her hair out of her face with a huff of frustration. Perhaps she shouldn't have been too surprised. After all, her father had probably done much the same thing some years previously and he hadn't found anything apart from that one picture that she now carried in her purse.

She looked around at the mess she'd created. She supposed she should try and clear it back up. But then she doubted her father would be coming back here to check. And her mother wouldn't care. In fact, maybe her mother would finally actually get rid of it all when her father passed. It would probably be the best thing for her mental health.

As she sat there among the piles of clutter, Bailey assessed her remaining options. If there weren't any clues to Mister Snigiss here... well, that left one other place she definitely had to check.

32

Wendy Molloy sat at one end of the long oak dining table in the living room of their palatial Essex mansion and watched her husband over the top of a glass of Châteauneuf-du-Pape as he wordlessly ate his dinner.

Cheating bastard, she thought, taking a sip of the expensive red wine.

'How was your day, darling?' she asked in a tone of fake bouncy enthusiasm.

Rick grunted dismissively, barely even bothering to make eye contact with her, and took another mouthful of the eye-wateringly expensive Kobe beef steak she had meticulously prepared for him that evening.

It wasn't anything new, this paucity of small talk. She sometimes wondered if it was because he was partially autistic or something; she'd read an article about it a few months earlier in one of the lifestyle magazines she kept in her beauty salon. Either that or he just couldn't be bothered.

He cut two generous chunks of meat off his steak and tossed them onto the polished mahogany floor. Seconds later, two huge Neapolitan Mastiffs bounded out of the neighbouring room and eagerly gobbled them up. He petted them both, rumbling affectionate words into their ears.

Her face soured. 'You know, you talk to those two dogs more than you do to me.'

He looked up at her, his face dropping. 'Okay,' he growled. 'So what do you want to talk about?'

It almost popped out. The accusation of infidelity. It was there on the edge of her tongue. But somehow she couldn't quite bring herself to articulate it.

'I was thinking that perhaps we could have some of the neighbours round for dinner or something,' she said brightly.

'What's the point?'

She rolled her eyes. 'To be sociable. Remember I have a life to live too.'

Wendy spent much of her social time mixing with neighbouring housewives whose husbands worked mostly in finance.

Rick stared at her silently with his emotionless black eyes.

'You need to make more effort with people,' she said. 'If it's not about business, then you're just not interested.'

'I don't like the neighbours. They're too nosey, for one thing.'

She knew Rick didn't like her hanging out with them. He hated the way they gossiped and he was paranoid she'd give something away about his business. He himself stayed well away from them, and on the few occasions he did end up having to talk to them, she'd cringe as she watched the conversation dry up in a matter of seconds.

'Well, having them round might help to dispel some of their... suspicions about you.'

His eyes narrowed warily. 'What suspicions?'

'Like after the cat incident for example...'

Most of the neighbours didn't know what Rick did for a living. As far as they were concerned, he was just a well-to-do businessman. But she knew that some of them suspected that he was a major-league crook, particularly the people who lived directly next door. Their cat had strayed into the grounds of Rick and Wendy's mansion one evening and had promptly been chewed to pieces by the Mastiffs – Vito and Frankie – who he put out on guard patrol every night. The neighbours had complained bitterly, but their complaints had soon melted away after some of Rick's associates paid them a visit.

She sighed. She might as well be banging her head against the wall, trying to get him to act like a normal person.

Sometimes she wondered if having children might change things for the better, might make him a little bit more human. But he'd never once expressed interest in going down that route and she'd never particularly been the maternal type, so it didn't look like kids would materialise any time soon.

'You know, Bailey came into my shop the other day,' she said idly.

Rick looked up sharply. 'Oh yeah?'

At last, something that piqued his interest.

'Yeah. I gave her my card. She came in to have her hair done. She was going on a date.'

'And?'

'And what?' She paused. 'I like her.'

It was true. Wendy did like Bailey. Certainly, the two of them were very different people and Bailey wasn't at all like the kind of women that Wendy normally socialised with. She'd thought Bailey slightly awkward and tomboyish, and Wendy had wondered if she might even be gay. After all, she hadn't actually specified that it was a bloke she was going on a date with. But she seemed genuinely down-to-earth, and with those unfortunate scars, she didn't seem to present much of a threat to Wendy in terms of Rick.

Not like this fucking Kaia. The bitterness surged up again inside Wendy like bile in her gullet.

She took another large gulp of her wine.

That was the problem with men like her husband. Their money and power were like an aphrodisiac. Should she really have been surprised that he had some young nubile replacement waiting in the wings?

She twiddled the huge diamond engagement ring on her finger.

She remembered when he had proposed to her on the terraces at Amalfi. It had been the happiest day of her life. And now it had come down to this.

'What the eye can't see the heart can't grieve,' one of her friends had told her when she'd confided in her about it.

So long as it wasn't in her face, she should just get on with her life and be grateful for the lavish lifestyle he provided her with. But Wendy wasn't like that. She just couldn't stop thinking about it and it was eating away at her. Sometimes she saw him talking on his phone out in the garden and she could never be sure now if he was talking business or whether he was talking to his mistress. The paranoia had crept in and it was growing larger by the day, fed by her insecurities, contaminating his every last action.

She knew if she was ever foolish enough to start seeing another man and Rick found out about it, he wouldn't hesitate to get rid of the man… permanently. She knew enough about her husband to know he possessed a very deep and very dark streak of violence. She'd heard enough about his organisation, just through the mainstream media, to know about all the murders and disappearances it was linked to; it was something she tried not to think about too hard.

She'd thought about trying to work it out with him, but she knew he'd outright reject the possibility of ever going to a marriage counsellor. At any rate, she'd never been able to fathom those couples who stolidly and masochistically worked through the issue of one partner's infidelities. As far as she was concerned, once that special trust had been broken, the relationship was over for good and there was no point trying to salvage it. What she needed was a clean break and a new start. What she needed was a divorce.

Well, they were married, and she had the law on her side, even if he didn't have much regard for it. She'd been secretly researching getting a divorce and she knew she was entitled to a big pay-off. She didn't know how much her husband had exactly, but she knew it was at least in the tens of millions, probably a lot more. So saying, he'd hinted that a fair chunk of that was secreted in stashes of cash buried all over

Essex and Kent... and getting hold of that could prove to be compli-
cated. She had the annoying feeling that a divorce settlement would
only include those assets of his that were both visible and legal.

She wasn't quite sure how he would react if she asked for a divorce,
but she was expecting the response to be volcanic at the very least. The
thought of broaching the subject filled her with a fair amount of trepidation, but she knew she had to be strong and stick to her guns.

The solicitor she'd spoken to had emphasised the importance of
having photos or some kind of solid evidence that her husband was
having an affair. Apparently it would stand her in good favour in court.
So, just as she'd planned, she'd gone ahead and hired a private eye to
follow her husband around.

And as soon as she had some proof... then he'd be sorry.

33

Bailey scratched her head in vexation as she surveyed the sea of paper that surrounded her. She took a sip from the cup of coffee which stood to one side. It had gone cold. Yuck. Had she really been here that long? She looked at her watch. Several hours had passed already.

She was sitting at a table in a small room in the police station in Bromley analysing the original case files on Jennifer's disappearance. She'd had to come down here in person as this was an old case and the files hadn't been digitised.

There were piles of empty boxes stacked around her. They'd contained interview statements, police reports, photographs and other documents relating to the investigation into Jennifer's disappearance over twenty years earlier. Now the contents of those boxes were spread out all over the table as Bailey meticulously searched through them for evidence of Mister Snigiss. Just like the drawings in Jennifer's bedroom, the material was getting yellow and curled at the edges with age.

It wasn't the first time Bailey had looked at these files. She'd come here once before, not long after joining the police, hoping to uncover the truth behind her sister's disappearance, but, just like the investigating detectives at the time, she'd been unable to pinpoint anything indicating how her sister had gone missing or who had taken her. It was in every sense a cold case.

This time, she was inspecting the documents through the prism of the recent Mister Snigiss revelation, hoping to detect some scrap of evidence that she might have missed the first time around, some clue as to who he was, or who he might have been, some reference to the name Snigiss or perhaps some innocuous mention of a fedora hat buried in an interview statement somewhere, or even an allusion to a pet snake. She was hunting for something... anything...

She'd been trawling laboriously through the whole lot, back and forth, again and again, going over it with a fine-tooth comb, hammering it with all the analytical skills she could muster, everything she'd learnt as a detective over the past few years. But so far she hadn't managed to uncover a single crumb of information related to Mister Snigiss.

The problem with Jennifer's case was that there'd been no witnesses to the actual abduction, despite the large number of people the police had talked to. No suspicious vehicles had been seen in the area and no similar events had occurred in the vicinity. And the police had been unable to identify any potential suspects. A subsequent *Crimewatch* reconstruction, broadcast across the entire nation, had still failed to generate any viable leads.

It seemed as if Jennifer had just disappeared into thin air. Walking the short distance home from her friend's house just around the corner, she'd been snatched from the street in the blink of an eye and never been seen again. Bailey had always been of the opinion that it had been an opportunistic abduction by some predator cruising the area for solitary children, probably driving some kind of van with no windows in the back. He'd swooped extremely quickly and had been very careful not to get spotted.

However now, what with recent developments, she had to reconsider her father's theory that Jennifer had been acquainted with her abductor. Her father believed that Jennifer had been groomed by him over the period of time leading up to her abduction. On that fateful day, it could have been that she'd actually arranged to meet him at his suggestion, or possibly she'd innocently revealed details of her movements to him so all he'd had to do was lie in wait for her. Whichever way it had happened, he must have been an extremely crafty and duplicitous character to have managed to obscure his real existence from everyone but her; and the way he'd done this, it seemed, was to have posed as an 'invisible friend' called Mister Snigiss.

Bailey tried to think how Jennifer might have come into contact with him. Had he been one of the neighbours? A teacher at school perhaps? Or maybe a relative of one of her friends who she'd encountered at a party or barbecue or something like that – a cousin or uncle, or perhaps an older brother? The possibilities revolved through Bailey's mind, but none of them were anything more than pure speculation. And what was the likelihood of being able to track down those people today, over twenty-four years later, to see if any of them bore the name Snigiss?

But then, seeing as the name Snigiss hadn't emerged in any of the material from the case files, it seemed very possible, as her father had suggested, that his real name wasn't Mister Snigiss at all. But that of course made it all the more difficult to discern his true identity.

Though if his real name wasn't Mister Snigiss and he'd just made up that name in order to deceive an eight-year-old child, why was he still calling himself Mister Snigiss all these years later? Did he just like that name or was it actually in fact his real name?

Bailey felt like she was going in circles. She felt like her brain was going to explode. She clenched her fists in frustration. At the very least it looked like these case files weren't going to yield anything fruitful, just like the visit to Jennifer's bedroom.

Scratching her head, Bailey tried to think of what other avenues she could pursue in her quest to track down the infuriatingly elusive Mister Snigiss...

She jumped as her undercover phone rang, trilling loudly in the oppressive silence of the small room. Taking it from her pocket, she looked at its small screen.

It was Rick.

She took the call.

'Hello, Bailey,' he rasped in his rough voice. 'Are you up for a fight?'

34

The air was thick with testosterone as the mostly male crowd roared aggressively, cheering on one or other of the two heavily muscled men pummelling each other in the boxing ring.

The arena was located in East London and the Molloys owned a private box which offered a generous panoramic view of the proceedings. Bailey was tucked between Rick on her right and Shane on her left; on the other side of Shane, Nancy was sitting with Ettie the Pomeranian on her lap, chatting to Stephen.

Shane was observing the fight with a faint expression of contempt, his arms crossed, and unlike the others he wasn't cheering. 'I've never been that into boxing myself,' he grunted. 'They might be able to punch hard, but that's all they can do.'

'You think you could beat one of them in a fight?' said Bailey.

'Piece of piss,' he scoffed. 'I could take either one of them easily. I'd neutralise him immediately with a single-leg takedown. Then, once he's on the ground, he'd be toast.'

When it came to mixed martial arts, Bailey knew that Shane's speciality was groundwork, in particular his *hadaka-jime* – a special blood choke that cut off blood to the brain, resulting in the extremely rapid submission of opponents. She would have liked to discuss the subject in more depth with him, but thought it wiser to keep her jiu-jitsu knowledge to herself. Talking about it might look suspicious and, anyhow, she preferred people to underestimate her abilities when it came to self-defence.

Next to her, Rick had no such reservations about the boxing. He was cheering loudly and gesticulating passionately and it sounded like he had money on the fight. Here, again, she was seeing a more animated side of him.

The bell rang, signalling the end of that particular round. Taking a breather, Rick turned to face her, flushed and slightly out of breath. He leant in close to her, speaking in her ear, his words just audible over the loud noise in the stadium.

'We're set to go,' he said. 'The ninth of March. I'll clarify the precise details of the exchange closer to the time.'

Finally. The date of the transaction. So it was going to go down on the ninth of March. Bailey memorised the date, feeling an inner satis-faction at getting another step closer to the guns.

She nodded with an obliged smile. Rick nodded back, then turned his attention away from her to Archie, who was sitting to his right.

That was it. The message had been conveyed. Rick had invited her here basically just to tell her this small but very important piece of information; all because he didn't like revealing the specifics of busi-ness over the phone.

She looked at the date on her watch. Today was the second of February. The ninth of March was still over a month away. The delay made her almost certain now that the guns still hadn't entered the country yet.

'I'm going for a piss,' said Shane, getting up and leaving the box.

After a few moments, Nancy moved into Shane's seat to sit directly next to Bailey. She leaned in close.

'Rick loves boxing,' she said, eyeing her son with affection. 'Both of my sons went to the local boxing gym in Ilford when they were kids. Rick was pretty good at it. Adrian was hopeless... but he turned out to be very good at gambling, and losing, money on it.' She sighed with a slight expression of dismay. 'That was his problem really. Adrian had no impulse control. Too short-term. No sense of the bigger picture. He was under the illusion that crime was the shortcut to wealth, but no one told him that you have to graft if you want to succeed. Crime is no different from any other business in that respect. That's why I like you, Bailey. You're a grafter.'

Bailey smiled at the compliment. 'Why, thank you. I'm just trying to earn a crust, like anyone else really. After all, there's no pension in what I do, so I want to make as much money as I can now.'

With Nancy opening up to her in this way about her family, Bailey realised that this ruthless gangland matriarch was beginning to actually trust and like her. On the basis of her previous undercover experience, Bailey had found that she could sometimes end up developing an emotional attachment to these people, almost becoming friends with them, or at least being in the position where they perceived her as their friend. But, unbeknownst to them, her only reason for being with them was to make sure that they got locked up. After an operation finished, she was sometimes struck with a feeling of sadness at betraying them, along with a discomforting awareness that they were stewing in thoughts of revenge and hatred as they rotted away in some prison cell somewhere.

When it came to the Molloys, and in particular, Nancy, Bailey was very wary of allowing herself to feel anything approaching affection for them, but given what she knew of them, that wasn't too much of a stretch. At any rate, if the operation did tie up as planned, she could only begin to imagine just how dangerously aggrieved and enraged someone like Nancy would be on discovering her duplicity.

'As you'll understand if you ever reach our level,' continued Nancy, 'operating a business like ours requires a great deal of nous and it takes a lot of energy. I'd reached the point where I was keen to take more of a back-seat role and I had to decide who would be best to pick up the reins... and Adrian just didn't have the strategic wherewithal to run an organisation of our magnitude.'

Bailey listened intently as Nancy spoke in her throaty voice, absently petting her Pomeranian as she did so.

'Of course, Adrian took it pretty hard when I put Rick in charge. Adrian felt like he should have been the one to take over, being the eldest. But I knew Rick was the best choice.

'Adrian accused me of showing favouritism towards Rick. And I suppose he wasn't wrong. Parents always have their favourites... and I guess Rick was mine. You'd understand if you had kids.'

Nancy paused and scrutinised Bailey. 'Did your parents have favourites with you and your sister?'

Bailey thought about the visit she'd recently made to her parents' house and the 'Daddy's Little Princess' plaque on Jennifer's bedroom door.

'My father always preferred Jennifer,' she said. 'He was devastated when she went missing and he's still not over it.'

'And your mother?'

'My mother's gone a bit doolally.' Bailey paused. 'It's a pity really, as I would like to be able to talk to her more about things.'

Nancy placed a bony desiccated hand on Bailey's forearm. 'I've often wondered what it would be like to have a daughter. I always wanted a girl. At least just one. To balance out all those men in the house. It would have been nice to have a daughter to talk to. The closest I've got is Rick's dumb bint. And she's not worth my breath. I really can't understand why he married her...'

Bailey once again sensed the maternal emanations coming from Nancy. In a strange way, Bailey almost felt reciprocal, for she could talk to Nancy on a level that she couldn't with her own mother. But then she had to remind herself that letting someone this dangerous get too close to you was very risky indeed.

'You intrigue me, Bailey. I feel like we can do business together. Maybe after this deal is done, you can even come on the firm.'

Bailey realised that Nancy was implying that she could join their criminal family as an associate. Given Nancy's obsession with the importance of blood, Bailey realised just what a significant gesture this was.

'Would you like that?' asked Nancy. 'To come on board?'

'I would be honoured,' said Bailey, radiating what she hoped was the suitable amount of deference and gratitude.

Nancy stared hard at her with her small dark eyes. 'Of course, when you're playing at our level, you need to have a tolerance for certain things.'

It sounded ominous. 'What kinds of things?'

'Have you ever attended a gangland interrogation?'

Bailey swallowed and suppressed the involuntary shudder that went through her as she tried not to recall her agonising torture at the hands of the car theft gang in their scrapyard.

'Not exactly,' she whispered, reflexively brushing the scar on her face.

'I'll invite you along to the next one,' said Nancy. 'Show you how we conduct business.'

'I'll look forward to it,' replied Bailey, forcing a grateful smile onto her face.

35

'The ninth of March, huh?' said Frank. 'That's still a way off. We're only just into February.'

Bailey was sitting on the knackered old sofa in the temporary HQ. It was a Monday morning, two days after the boxing, and she was filling in Frank and Dale on the latest developments in the operation. They were both sitting on chairs at the folding table.

She scratched her head. 'Like you said, it sounds like he's waiting for the guns to arrive. Otherwise we'd be closing the deal a lot sooner.'

Frank stroked his moustache and thought about it. 'It makes a kind of sense though. Looking at it from his perspective, he doesn't want to risk holding the weapons here in the UK any longer than he has to without a buyer. All those guns lying around are a bit of a liability. It's a safer bet for him to secure a buyer first before proceeding with bringing the weapons here. I imagine they'll probably be arriving on, or around, the ninth of March. He'll want to transfer them to you and get them off his hands as soon as possible after they enter the country.'

She nodded. Frank's explanation seemed very feasible.

'Talking of which,' he added, 'I got the seven hundred and fifty thousand signed off. You're going to need a big suitcase for that much cash.'

Bailey rubbed her jaw. 'When it comes to the actual exchange, Rick said he'd clarify the precise details closer to the time. So, at the moment, we don't know the location or the ins and outs of how it will actually go down.'

'He's very cagey about giving out any more information than he needs to, isn't he?' said Dale.

'He's very careful,' Bailey replied. 'That's why he's never been caught.'

'Well, this time we'll get him,' said Frank. 'And we'll make sure he doesn't get to put any more guns on the street for a very long time.'

The three of them paused for a moment, reflecting on how important it was to nail Rick.

Dale looked up and snapped his fingers as if he'd just remembered something.

'Oh, by the way,' he said, 'I got contacted by the Essex police this morning. You remember that shipment of ecstasy pills that was supposed to be coming into that airstrip on the third of February?'

Bailey looked at the date on her watch. 'That was yesterday, right?'

Dale nodded. 'Yeah. Well, they swooped on the hangar but it turned out there were no ecstasy pills. Either Adrian gave me dud information or the Molloys got suspicious about something and changed the date or the location.'

Bailey digested the news, trying to think if it might alter anything in relation to her infiltration. She couldn't envisage any immediate problems.

'It might not mean anything,' Dale continued, 'but I thought it best to mention it to you all the same, just in case it turns out to have some bearing on what you're doing.'

'Thanks,' she said, nodding. 'I'll keep it in mind.'

36

William Buttmeal had been working as a private detective for a few years now. He'd come up with a tagline for his business which read 'Where there's a Will there's a way'. As well as being a rather clever pun on his name, he thought it conveyed exactly the kind of positive, can-do attitude you'd expect from a highly efficient private detective and he bet that no other private detectives called Will had been clever enough to think of it.

Sitting in his deliberately anonymous-looking Toyota Prius, he covertly observed the subject of his latest assignment. The man's name was Richard Molloy and Buttmeal had been following him around since the beginning of February. It was now the sixth of the month and he was wondering just how much longer he'd need to continue tailing Molloy. Despite the romantic impressions Buttmeal liked to project to other people regarding his job, most of his time as a private detective was taken up with sitting around in his car and it required a great deal of patience.

He was currently parked across the street from an expensive steak restaurant in Ilford that Molloy had entered an hour and a half earlier along with two other men. Now he watched as they left the restaurant, crossed the street and climbed into a large black Range Rover Velar with tinted windows. Lifting up his digital camera, he discreetly took some photographs of them.

Buttmeal hadn't been able to ferret out a great deal of information about his subject; there was a marked dearth of anything useful on the internet and the other sources he normally utilised hadn't yielded anything particularly insightful either. It was almost as if the man was intentionally trying to maintain a low profile. As far as Buttmeal could ascertain from his movements, Molloy appeared to be some kind of businessman, with interests in a wide variety of enterprises, spending much of his day travelling between them in his black Range Rover.

The woman who'd hired Buttmeal had been extremely reticent in providing personal details. He'd spoken to her only over the phone and she'd refused to reveal her name or the nature of her relationship to the subject. This kind of thing wasn't that unusual in his line of work. However, from the nature of the assignment, he guessed she was the man's wife as she'd instructed him to focus on capturing evidence of any liaisons with women, particularly anyone going by the name of Kaia. Cases involving marital infidelity constituted much of Buttmeal's daily bread and butter as a private detective.

So far, though, Molloy appeared to have been blameless in that respect as Buttmeal hadn't yet managed to observe any evidence of meetings with any women. If Molloy was being unfaithful to his wife, he was doing a good job at keeping it below the radar. But it was early days yet, thought Buttmeal, as he started the engine of his Toyota, ready to commence following the Range Rover as it pulled away from the kerb.

Driving slowly through the afternoon traffic, Buttmeal carefully kept a distance of a few cars between himself and the Range Rover, wondering where Molloy was headed off to next.

After about fifteen minutes of wending their way through town, Molloy pulled into a large multi-storey car park. Buttmeal followed the Range Rover into the car park, closer to it now, as it ascended the various floors, each one a little emptier than the last, until it reached the almost deserted eighth storey, where it pulled into a bay and stopped.

Buttmeal continued past and parked up a few spaces down and across from it. He switched off his engine and, sinking down a little lower into his seat, watched in the rear-view mirror as Molloy emerged by himself from the Range Rover and made his way to the lift area.

Could this be it? thought Buttmeal. Perhaps Molloy had left the other two men in the car in order to say a quick hello to his girlfriend. But if Buttmeal was to find out, he was going to have to follow Molloy on foot and possibly even accompany him down in the lift. Deciding that he didn't want to lose out on the opportunity, he grabbed his digital camera and thrust it in his bag, got out of his car and hurried through the dim area, a chilly breeze blowing in through the open sides of the building.

He reached the lift area a few moments later, praying that Molloy hadn't taken the lift yet. But to his surprise the lift area was empty. There was no sign of Molloy anywhere. Then Buttmeal noticed a sign taped to the lifts saying that both of them were out of order. He realised Molloy must have taken the stairs and saw that on the other side of the lift area was a door leading to the stairwell.

Buttmeal pushed open the door and entered the stairwell, where-upon somebody slammed into him hard. He crashed up against the wall, stunned, and found himself looking into the dense black eyes of Richard Molloy.

'You've been following me,' growled Molloy, baring his teeth.

Buttmeal gulped, finding it difficult to swallow with Molloy's elbow pressing across his throat with the force of an iron bar. A heavy fear plopped into his guts like a big boulder as he realised that he'd seriously underestimated Molloy's powers of observation.

A moment later, the door to the stairwell swung open and the two other men entered, flanking Molloy on either side. A brawny one with a Mediterranean complexion and a skinny pasty one wearing a large pair of wraparound sunglasses. All three of them leaned up against him in an extremely menacing fashion.

'Er...' stuttered Buttmeal. 'I don't know what you're talking about.'

'Rubbish!' rasped Molloy, pressing his elbow harder across Buttmeal's throat.

The brawny one lifted a thick finger and prodded him hard in the side of the head.

'Who the fuck are you working for?' he spat aggressively.

Buttmeal's eyes flicked around in panic as he realised that there were no CCTV cameras here in the stairwell. It then hit him with a sinking dread that this had been a set-up. They'd lured him here deliberately. The sign on the lifts was probably fake.

'I... urgh... I'm not... urgh...' he struggled to breathe.

'Sorry?' hissed the pasty one, peeling back his lips in a nasty smile to reveal a set of rotting brown teeth. 'I didn't quite get that.'

'I want some answers,' said Molloy. 'Now.'

Buttmeal stared back fearfully into Molloy's eyes; they brought to mind the dead black eyes of a great white shark, and under their predatory gaze Buttmeal felt like little more than a hapless minnow that had foolishly swum into its path.

Maybe he hadn't worked as a private detective for long enough, or maybe he'd just been lucky, but Buttmeal had never found himself in this kind of situation before, and he now felt completely out of his depth. Before becoming a private detective, he'd worked in marketing where you just didn't meet people like this, and it now occurred to him with a pang of alarm-filled regret that perhaps he should have just stayed in that profession – the only reason he'd left marketing was because he'd thought it sounded cooler to tell people he was a private detective.

The brawny one snatched his bag and began to riffle through its contents. The pasty one reached into his pocket and pulled out his wallet.

'I'm... urgh... I'm a private detective,' he managed to force out.

The pasty one held up Buttmeal's business card, of which he kept several in his wallet. Molloy turned his head to scan the card.

'"Where there's a Will there's a way".' He looked back at Buttmeal. 'Very catchy.'

Buttmeal smiled nervously, but Molloy didn't smile back.

'Who hired you?' asked Molloy.

Buttmeal frowned. 'In the interests of client confidentiality, I am unable to disclose—'

'Oi,' the brawny one suddenly cut in. He had been browsing through the contents of Buttmeal's digital camera and was now showing Molloy the camera. 'He's got a load of photos of you on here.'

Molloy's head swung round sharply to look at the camera. 'You what?'

The brawny one nodded with a grave expression on his face.

If Buttmeal already had a bad feeling, that bad feeling now just got a little bit worse.

Molloy turned back to Buttmeal, his eyes bulging dangerously.

'I don't like people taking pictures of me,' he said. 'Why the fuck were you taking pictures of me?' He spoke in a worryingly quiet tone, the voice of someone who had gone beyond anger to something much worse.

Buttmeal gulped. 'Look, I can explain... just let me explain.' The words tumbled out in a panicky torrent.

Molloy leaned in closer to Buttmeal, so close that Buttmeal could make out every pore on his face, every bristle of his black stubble.

'I don't like people following me,' said Molloy. 'And I don't like people taking pictures of me.'

Buttmeal's heart was beating furiously and his mouth had gone unbearably dry. The fear that had gripped him just moments earlier had now transmuted into an all-consuming terror at the thought of what these men were going to do to him, as it had become quite clear that they obviously didn't operate on the right side of the law. What the hell had he got himself into?

Maybe he should break client confidentiality. Make an exception. Just this once. But then what exactly would he tell Molloy? That the woman was his wife? She might not be though. She might be someone completely different. If only he knew her name...

He was trying to think how best to explain it when Molloy suddenly let go of him and took a step back. Buttmeal slumped against the wall, drawing several deep breaths. Maybe it was okay after all. Maybe they were going to let him go. Maybe...

'You know what?' said Molloy. 'I don't care who you're working for. But whoever they are, they're going to need to start looking for a replacement.'

Molloy nodded to his two associates, who both stepped in and seized Buttmeal roughly by the arms.

'No!' squealed Buttmeal. 'Please don't hurt me.'

They tugged him sharply across the concrete landing to the open balcony. A panoramic view of the town stretched out beyond. Buttmeal's eyes widened with horror as he realised what they were planning to do.

'Oh God! No!'

He struggled to break free, but they were holding him too firmly.

'Please!' he screeched. 'I can explain! My client—'

He felt them grab his legs and lift him off the ground. He flailed and screamed as they manoeuvred him onto the rim of the balcony. He reached out in vain, but there was nothing to grip onto, just smooth cold concrete.

And then they tipped him over the edge. And he was falling downwards. Tumbling down. Cold air blowing through his hair. The car park blurring past storey by storey. The pavement coming up below. Closer. And closer. And closer.

The tagline went through his head. Where there's a Will there's a way. Maybe there was a way out of this.

Or maybe not...

37

Dave Boakes looked up at Bailey from the dog-eared science-fiction novel he'd been reading. His messy beard was perhaps a little longer than it had been in the police interview room, but it was definitely him. And he was still wearing that Rolex on his wrist.

'Spare some change?' he asked nonchalantly.

It was a cold but sunny February morning, and Dave was reclining outside on a worn yoga mat in front of a red mountaineering tent that had definitely seen better days. His worldly belongings, including various items of clothing, an umbrella and a number of tatty paperbacks, were piled in a nearby shopping trolley.

A few metres above them, traffic roared along the busy elevated road known as the Westway. Down here among the graffiti-covered concrete stanchions and the weeds resided a small community of homeless people. It had taken Bailey a good hour of driving around the area in her BMW before spotting their impromptu campsite.

She knew it was a bit of a long shot, but Dave Boakes was really all she had left to go on. Although the murder investigation had uncovered absolutely no connection so far between Adrian's death and Mister Snigiss, Bailey had taken it upon herself to probe into it a little further, aware at the back of her mind that a certain amount of desperation on her part was pushing her down this avenue.

Reviewing the CCTV footage of the bomber that had been taken on the night of the explosion, she'd seen that the figure had been wearing some kind of hat which concealed their face. The images had been somewhat indistinct, but the more she'd looked at them, the more she'd convinced herself that it kind of looked like a fedora...

Was it a case of wishful thinking? Was she just clutching at straws in a vain and desperate bid to find anything that could lead her closer to Mister Snigiss? Or was she actually onto something?

The only way to try and solidify her conjecture was to talk to someone who'd been there in person.

Dave Boakes.

Kneeling down in front of him, she flashed her warrant card, trying not to inhale his rank odour of unwashed body. Acting overtly as a police officer whilst she was still working undercover didn't worry her too much in this instance as she figured that Boakes and the Molloys were highly unlikely to move in the same circles.

'I'm a police officer,' she said, in as non-confrontational a manner as she could muster.

His face twisted into a suspicious frown and he shrank back defensively.

'I've come to talk to you about the car bomb,' she said. 'I was there at the police station. Behind the one-way glass. But we were never introduced. My name's Detective Constable Bailey Morgan.'

Dave gave her a suspicious scowl and cupped the Rolex protectively.

'Don't worry,' she assured him. 'I'm not interested in your watch.'

'I've already talked about the bomb,' he declared grumpily. 'I told them everything.'

'Yes,' she said gently. 'And you were very helpful. I was just hoping to get a few more details from you though. About the person you saw. The bomber.'

'I didn't see anything,' he said. 'It was too dark. And it was too cold.'

'The bomber was wearing a hat, right?' she pressed.

Dave nodded. 'That's right. That's why I couldn't see his face.'

Taking out her phone, she opened the search engine and tapped in 'fedora hat', and showed Dave the resultant gallery of images.

'Was it a hat like one of these, in this kind of style?'

He squinted at the small screen. She watched him intently, anxiously awaiting his response.

He rubbed his beard and then nodded slowly. 'Yeah... yeah it was. One of them ones. Just like that.'

She felt a burst of elation. A breakthrough. Finally.

'Are you sure?' she whispered.

'Yeah. I'm sure. I remember now. It was definitely one of them.' He grinned at her. 'Did you say you had any spare change?'

She nodded to herself with interest as she absorbed the ramifications of what he'd told her. If what he was saying was true, then it presented the tantalising possibility that Mister Snigiss himself had personally planted the car bomb.

Putting her phone away, she reached into her trouser pocket to see if she had any spare coins. As she did so, she noticed, hanging around his neck from a shoelace, the pink manga-style kitten keyring she'd seen him wearing in the police interview room.

She paused a moment. The hungry look in his eyes started to change to one of dismay.

'Just a moment,' she said. She nodded at the keyring. 'What's that around your neck?'

Dave frowned and looked down at it. 'It's a kitten, innit?'

She recalled his instinctive protection of it back in the interview room when the detectives had been grilling him about his watch. And looking closer now, she could see that the plastic did bear faint scorch marks and was slightly melted around the edges.

'You got that from the car bomb, didn't you?' she asked.

'No!' he said, shaking his head a little too vehemently. He was a poor liar.

Up close to it now, getting a better look, she started to get an idea of what it actually was. And if she wasn't wrong, it was more than just a keyring. Hmm... Interesting.

'That was in the man's hand, wasn't it?' said Bailey.

Dave eyed her mutely, not denying it, and Bailey knew her supposition had been correct.

'You took the Rolex off his wrist,' she said. 'And you took that kitten out of his hand.'

His eyes flickered shiftily from side to side as if searching for an escape route.

'Look, I'm not going to arrest you,' she said. 'And you can keep the watch because I'm not interested in it. But that...'

She reached gently for the keyring, but Dave snatched it away, clutching it close to his chest.

'It's my little kitten,' he whispered.

Bailey sat back on her haunches and paused for thought.

'I'll tell you what,' she said. 'I'll trade you.'

She reached into the pocket of her jacket and took out her car keys. Attached to the keychain was a mini-torch, a handy little gadget which had an extremely bright LED as well as a laser pointer.

She unclipped it from the keys and shone the red dot of the laser pointer onto the ground, dancing it around a little in front of him, watching him eye it covetously.

She dangled it before him and raised her eyebrow suggestively. He reached for it, but she pulled it away out of his grasp. He shot her a sullen glare, then reluctantly unhooked the shoelace from his neck and handed her the keyring, his hand wavering recalcitrantly. As soon as her fingers closed around the keyring, he snatched the mini-torch from her other hand and immediately began to play with it.

Bailey examined the keyring in the palm of her hand. It weighed very little. She pulled at the kitten's oversized head, and just as she'd suspected, it came off with a little 'pop' to reveal a USB jack. It was a novelty memory stick. She'd seen these kinds of things before for sale on Amazon, pitched at the female market.

Now maybe this would hold some answers, perhaps something more than just a fedora hat...

She looked up at Dave with a grateful smile. 'Thanks.'

'How about that spare change?' he said.

38

Bailey tapped her fingers impatiently on the table as she waited for the laptop to boot up. She was using the laptop Frank had given her as part of her undercover identity as that was the only computing device she had in the Stratford apartment.

Picking up the kitten-themed memory stick, she examined the scorched and melted edges of the plastic. It didn't seem too badly damaged and she guessed it had been shielded from the worst of the blast because it had been enveloped within Adrian's severed hand. She knew a memory stick like this was just a lump of silicon with no moving parts and was thus, hopefully, quite robust. She'd find out soon enough.

With the laptop ready to use, she pulled the head off the kitten to expose the USB jack poking from its neck. She inserted it into the USB port on the side of the computer, her heart beating hard with anticipation at what she might discover on it.

The file window opened. The memory stick appeared to contain just a single MPEG4 file called 'meeting'.

Her fingers trembling slightly, she double-clicked on the file. The video player programme opened up on the screen and the file began to play.

The picture quality was slightly grainy, the camera optimising for low-light conditions. Filling the screen was a large double bed, neatly made, unoccupied, with headboard fittings that suggested it was located within an upmarket hotel.

A woman entered the frame. Probably in her late twenties, she had long blonde hair and a strikingly beautiful face. She was clad in expensive-looking black lingerie which did little to conceal her extremely well-proportioned physique.

She climbed onto the bed, stretching in a seductive feline manner. She then appeared to mouth something to someone off-screen.

Moments later, another woman appeared. She was a black woman with a svelte appearance and lithe, colt-like limbs. Of a similar age and with comparably attractive looks, she too was wearing a set of highly revealing lingerie, although hers was white in colour. She climbed onto the bed and the two women immediately began to kiss and fondle each other.

Bailey swallowed as she watched, finding that her throat had gone dry, the small laptop screen pulsating with the erotic writhing of the two women on the bed.

It was a show they were putting on and they were doing it very well. However, they didn't appear to be playing to the camera, having not acknowledged its presence in any way. By the static position of the camera and its grainy quality, Bailey sensed that it was small in nature and probably concealed.

Breaking off from their copulation, the black woman looked up with her dark doe-like eyes, turned her head to her right and beckoned with an alluring slender finger.

Seconds later, a man joined the fray. Middle-aged with neatly combed grey hair and a generous tan, he was clad in just a pair of white boxer shorts and black socks. It appeared that he had been the intended audience of their Sapphic display.

He eagerly clambered onto the bed, positioning himself between the two women, who then started to kiss and caress him passionately. He looked as happy as a pig in mud.

Bailey was transfixed, strangely fascinated, and perhaps a little repulsed, as these two stunning young women lavished themselves upon this less attractive older man. They appeared to be expert at what they were doing and Bailey got the impression they did this for a living, which meant they were either porn actresses or prostitutes, or possibly both.

They undressed the man completely and then they too peeled off their lingerie so that all three of them were naked. A long and energetic bout of three-way sex then followed. And it was towards the end of this session that Bailey noticed an interesting detail that confirmed what she was beginning to suspect.

The blonde woman sat up for a moment while the man was slobbering over her black companion. She flicked her sweat-soaked hair out of her face and just for a fraction of a second her gaze flickered directly into the camera. It was enough for Bailey to realise that she was aware of its existence.

By now it had become quite clear to Bailey what this was. It was a sex tape and it was being secretly recorded without the knowledge of at least one of the participants. It was prime blackmail material and she was guessing that the man was the target.

Bailey absently fiddled with her loose-hanging lock of hair, as she was wont to do when trying to solve a puzzle. What was Adrian's connection to this sex tape? Was this part of some scheme he'd been running? Was this the reason he'd been blown up? Discovering the sex tape had thrown up more questions than answers.

Bailey paused the video on the man's face and studied it in more detail. Who was he exactly? The more she looked at him, the more she realised there was something familiar about him. She'd seen him somewhere before, she was sure of it. But he wasn't someone she'd met personally. She must have seen him on TV somewhere.

And then it was with a powerful jolt that she recognised him. She'd seen him on the news one night when she'd been unable to sleep.

It was Lewis Ballantyne, the prospective Conservative candidate for Mayor of London.

39

The three of them huddled around her laptop on the table in the temporary HQ above the kebab shop.

Bailey wryly observed Frank and Dale as they watched the video play on the small screen. At first they both looked a bit taken aback at the graphic nature of what they were seeing. Dale seemed somewhat bemused and Frank had gone a bit red.

'This was in Adrian's possession when he was blown up,' explained Bailey.

As the two women and the man writhed around on the bed, Bailey waited with bated breath for either Frank or Dale to recognise Lewis Ballantyne, but neither of them did. Either they didn't keep track of the news or their attention was too taken up by the women.

Instead, Dale nodded at the screen and said, 'You know that's Tiffany, right?'

Bailey frowned and peered at the blonde woman. 'The one who got blown up with Adrian?'

'One and the same.'

Bailey nodded to herself with interest. Pieces were starting to fall into place...

'I thought she was just Adrian's floozy,' said Frank.

'She was some kind of model apparently,' Dale clarified. 'According to the murder investigation team.'

'Model?' said Bailey. 'Hooker more like. Watching the video, you can see that they're professionals.'

She leant forward and tapped on the laptop to pause the video on the man's face.

'I'm surprised you haven't recognised him,' she said.

They both looked at her blankly.

'He's just some rich older bloke,' said Dale. 'Presumably he'd have to be pretty wealthy to get two babes like that to sleep with him.'

'He's no ordinary older bloke,' Bailey replied. 'He's Lewis Ballantyne.'

Dale's eyes widened as he gaped at the screen. Frank bore much the same expression.

'Holy shit!' exclaimed Dale. 'You're right. It is.'

Frank and Dale lapsed into stunned silence as they absorbed the potential ramifications of what they were watching.

'The Met's golden boy,' murmured Frank. 'This isn't going to do much for his political career.'

'This is a blackmail tape if ever I saw one,' said Dale.

'Do you think Adrian had a plan to try and blackmail him?' asked Bailey.

Dale raised his eyebrows. 'I knew he had various schemes running secretly on the side, though I never had any idea he was into anything this heavy.'

'He was holding that memory stick in his hand when he was blown up,' said Bailey, explaining how she'd acquired it from Dave Boakes. 'Seeing as Tiffany is the girl in the tape, I think she gave this memory stick to Adrian just before he got blown up. I reckon that it belonged to her. It's my belief that the reason Adrian and Tiffany were together that evening wasn't because they were on a date; it was so that she could meet him and give him this. But clearly someone else had other plans for them.'

'You think they got blown up because of this?' asked Frank.

Bailey shrugged. 'Seems like more than a coincidence.'

'This is obviously very important and highly sensitive material,' said Dale. 'I'll pass it onto the murder investigation team with the utmost priority. May I take this?'

Bailey nodded. She closed the video player and extracted the memory stick from the laptop and handed it to Dale.

Frank watched Dale secrete the kitten-themed memory stick in his pocket. He seemed to be caught in thought. He looked at Bailey with a frown.

'Why were you even pursuing this in the first place, Bailey?' he asked. 'You're supposed to be focusing on the guns.'

She glanced at Dale and took a deep breath.

'Well, I'm glad you asked because that's the other big thing I was about to tell you. I recently became aware of an angle in Adrian's murder case that might relate to my sister's abduction.'

Frank raised one eyebrow. He knew all about Jennifer. Bailey had mentioned it to him a number of times in the past. Up until today, she'd only ever talked of it dismissively, rolling her eyes as she'd told him wearily of her father's obsession with finding her missing sister. However, now she elaborated on what Dale had told her about Adrian's connection to Mister Snigiss. Frank listened patiently, with Dale interjecting at various points to support her explanation.

After she'd finished, Frank sat there in silence for a bit, mulling over what she'd told him. He fixed her with one of his characteristically sceptical looks.

'An invisible childhood friend and abductor of children who's now some underworld player?'

Bailey paused for effect. 'I have a very strong feeling that Mister Snigiss was behind the car bomb. And if he was, then that means that he's somehow connected to this sex tape, if we assume that the sex tape was the reason that Adrian and Tiffany were blown up.'

'You think Mister Snigiss blew them up?' said Dale with a puzzled frown. 'How did you come to that conclusion?'

'When I talked to Dave Boakes, he more or less confirmed that the bomber was wearing a fedora hat.'

'So?' said Frank. 'A hat is a hat. So what?'

Bailey archly raised one eyebrow, reached down into her purse and, with a flourish, pulled out Jennifer's picture of Mister Snigiss. She pushed it across the table. The two men peered down at it in puzzlement.

'What's this?' said Frank, visibly nonplussed.

'It's a picture of Mister Snigiss. Look. See. He's wearing a fedora hat.'

'It looks like it's been drawn by a kid,' he said.

'It was. Jennifer drew it.'

Frank looked at the picture in disbelief. 'Bailey, you cannot expect me to take this seriously. A picture drawn by a... How old was she?'

'She was eight when she was abducted.'

'A picture drawn by an eight-year-old kid over twenty years ago.' He paused to regard her sympathetically. 'Bailey, I have a five-year-old daughter. Now I love her dearly, but I wouldn't trust her to come up with an accurate—'

Bailey banged her fist on the table angrily. Frank and Dale both recoiled, looking shocked, almost a little scared.

'Look at the picture!' she said, punching her finger at it.

'I am!' said Frank.

'What's that wiggly thing?' Dale asked.

'It's his pet snake. Mister Snigiss had a pet cobra called Sid.'

Frank and Dale swapped glances in a way two people might do if they thought they were dealing with someone who was mentally unhinged.

Bailey huffed in annoyance. 'I'm serious!'

Frank was shaking his head incredulously. 'So you're saying that because your sister's invisible friend wore a fedora hat, it must have been him who planted the car bomb?'

Dale spoke up. 'Bailey, are you suggesting that we put this picture in front of seasoned murder detectives? You met those two – Adam and

Joseph. Can you imagine how they'd react? They'd laugh you out of the room. You'd never live it down.'

Bailey sighed in frustration. She could see how crazy it must have looked to them. She folded the picture and put it back in her purse.

'Look,' she said, in a more reasonable tone. 'All I'm saying is that I think I'm onto something. I'm not sure what, yet. But I'll find out eventually.'

Frank evinced an expression of concern. 'Look, I know how important your sister is to you, Bailey, but I don't want you getting sidetracked. Your priority is to focus on the guns. Okay?'

He fixed her with a stern expression.

She rolled her eyes. 'Okay, Frank. Don't worry. I'll make sure the guns take top priority over anything else.'

He nodded, apparently mollified, but he didn't look like he entirely believed her.

'Just leave it with us, Bailey,' said Dale. 'I'll make sure this sex tape finds its way to the murder investigation team and I'll keep you posted on what they find out. Okay?'

She sighed. She guessed it would have to be okay. For the time being.

Nancy Molloy glared at the group of Asian youths hanging around near the entrance to The Admiral. This area really had gone down the toilet, she thought. She pushed past them haughtily and entered the reassuring warmth and security of the pub.

She bestowed a warm smile on the slim young bartender.

'Hello, Ronnie, how are you?' she said.

'I'm fine, thank you, Mrs Molloy. They're waiting for you in the back room.'

She nodded and made her way past the side of the bar through to the soundproofed back room. As expected, Rick was sitting there, along with Shane and Archie on his right and Stephen on his left. The core crew.

Her son had called her to this meeting, but she didn't know what it was about, but then it was his wise habit never to explain anything in any detail over the phone. She did have a feeling it was important though as he'd told her it was urgent and they only really ever met here in this room when they had super-confidential things to discuss.

'So what's the occasion, Ricky? I was supposed to be taking Ettie to the vet this afternoon. I've had to reschedule her appointment.'

She'd called him Ricky ever since he was a boy and she continued to do so now, even though no one else referred to him by that moniker.

He looked back at her with his black eyes and rubbed the dark stubble on his square jaw. He had his father's strong jaw and his mother's dark eyes. She could tell instantly that something was troubling him and he looked uncharacteristically hesitant.

'You're not going to like what I'm going to have to say, Mum. Probably best if you sit down.'

She settled herself on one of the leather seats, a sense of unease growing within her.

'Do you want to hear the bad news or the really bad news?' he asked.

The unease swelled into a distinct feeling of dread and she braced herself for something unpleasant.

'Okay, I'll start with the bad news,' he continued. 'I had some private investigator following me around.'

She frowned. 'Private investigator? Sent by who?'

'One of our rivals probably. He was taking photos of me.'

Her eyes widened. 'Taking photos of you?'

'Building up a picture of my movements. Setting me up for a hit, I reckon.'

Her heart went cold at the thought of it. 'Maybe the same bastards who killed Adrian?' she whispered.

He gave a grim shrug. 'Maybe. But that kind of brings us, in a roundabout way, onto the second bit of news. The really bad news.'

She swallowed. How could it get any worse than this?

Rick took a deep breath. 'Adrian was a grass.'

The news totally blindsided Nancy. She blinked, momentarily unable to breathe, as if someone had punched her in the guts. Denial immediately welled up inside her. No member of her family could be a grass. It just wasn't possible. Hatred of the law was bound up in their very DNA.

'I don't believe you,' she said stoutly.

'I said you wouldn't like it.'

Deep down though, she knew he was right. Rick wouldn't come out with something like this unless he was a hundred per cent certain. That was one of the reasons she'd put him in charge. She felt a lurching sense of nausea. This was really bad news indeed.

'He was talking dirt on us?' she hissed through gritted teeth. 'How can you be sure?'

Rick's eyes flickered to Stephen. 'The police hit an airstrip in Essex a few days ago, on the third of February. Customs too. They were under the impression that a planeload of ecstasy pills were coming in.

'But it was fake information. There were no pills. I told different people different locations, different dates. Adrian was the only one who knew about that airstrip in Essex. He was the only one who knew that the ecstasy was supposed to come in on that particular day. He was the only one who could have leaked that information to the police.'

Nancy absorbed what her son was saying. She knew how careful he was and this was typical of his way of operating.

'Have you got any proof?' she asked, desperate to keep Adrian's name intact. 'Maybe he just accidentally blabbed it to the wrong person?'

'Blabbed it to the wrong person? I don't think so. He knew the rules. Even he wasn't that stupid. Even with all those drugs he took. No... this was calculated and deliberate.'

'Was there a specific reason why you decided to lay this trap?'

'I wanted to flush out any rats before we close this upcoming gun deal,' he said. 'There's a lot of cash at stake.'

'You thought there was a rat?' she said doubtfully. Back when he was alive, Arthur had run a pretty tight ship, and after his demise she'd run an even tighter one, and in all those years grasses had been few and far between, and those that they had rooted out had been dealt with in the harshest way possible. Anyone possessing more than half a brain cell and the slightest modicum of self-preservation knew that it was a very dumb idea indeed to try and stitch up the Molloys.

'Little things here and there,' retorted Rick. 'Seizures when people were supposed to have been paid off. Raids on places that were supposed to have been secret. Old Bill just seemed to be one step ahead and I felt that something was wrong. So I had Stephen come up with this little plan to locate the leak.'

Nancy glanced at Stephen sitting there twiddling his bottle of hand sanitiser. Trust Stephen to come up with such a sneaky plan, she thought. But then he excelled at that kind of thing. That's why he was their head of security.

'I can't accept that Adrian was a grass,' she persisted, but her voice was starting to waver now.

'Believe it,' said Rick. 'I didn't want to either. But it's the only explanation.'

She frowned. 'The third of February?' she said. 'That was last week! Why didn't you tell me sooner?'

'I would have told you sooner, but I wanted to check the details and make double sure. You know how I like to be certain.'

They both gazed at each other in silence for a long while, two pairs of jet-black eyes staring into one another.

'I'm sorry, Mum,' he said finally. 'I really am.'

Shane, Stephen and Archie kept their heads bowed diplomatically. This was about family – blood – and they all knew just how much that meant to her. And now Rick was telling her that her own son – her own flesh and blood – was a Judas of the first order.

'Adrian always hated me,' Rick continued. 'You know how he was. He couldn't accept it when you put me in charge. It must have twisted his mind.'

As she slowly let the reality sink in, a deep sense of sadness pervaded her. Her eldest son had committed the cardinal sin and his betrayal cut deep. She tried to rationalise it in her head. It was the drugs. It must have been all that cocaine he took. It had made him sick. He hadn't been acting in his right mind. When she framed it like that, it made his treachery slightly more palatable.

'This has to remain within these four walls,' she whispered. 'No one must know about this. If it is true, then it is a stain on our family.' Her eyes then widened speculatively. 'Unless people already knew he was a grass,' she murmured. 'And that was the reason he got blown up. Maybe someone else thought he was dishing dirt on them and killed him because of it.'

She, better than any of them, knew that in the underworld anyone exposed as a grass developed a very short life expectancy, regardless of who they were.

'Could be,' muttered Rick. 'Difficult to know.' A dismal look settled on his face. 'I tried to give him a chance,' he said. 'You know I did. I know he had his problems. His addictions and all that. But I tried to include him in our business where I could. Especially after that big argument we had last year after his fortieth. I tried to get him involved in more of the deals, thought it might help to calm him down, straighten him out. But I guess that was a mistake. I trusted him and he tried to fuck me over. Never in a million years would I have thought he would stoop so low...'

'Traitor or not,' she said, 'he was still our blood and someone murdered him.'

'You place too much of a premium on blood,' Rick replied.

'Blood is what makes us strong. It's what ties us together. Without blood, we're nothing.'

There was a tense pause between them.

'I followed all the way through when it came to catching your father's killers,' she said firmly. 'And I'm going to do exactly the same with whoever killed your brother.'

'I understand your need for revenge, Mum, but like I said before, war is bad for business.'

She raised her voice in exasperation. 'Don't you understand anything I've taught you? Your father would turn in his grave if he could hear you right now. If we let them get away with it, then it makes us look weak. If they think they can get away with murdering an actual member of the Molloy family, it'll be open season on us. We have to find out who killed Adrian and we have to make them pay. Whether they killed him because they thought he was a grass, or whether they just killed him because they're trying to move in on our business, it makes no difference to me. Either way, we need to find them and deal with them.' She punched a pointed finger emphatically as she spoke.

Rick sighed in capitulation. Nancy knew she'd always win out in this kind of situation. Her son ultimately always deferred to her, especially on this particular subject which he knew was so close to her heart.

'Okay, Mum. But we do have a problem though.'

'What's that?'

'The police use informants as a way of infiltrating businesses like ours. It's very possible that Adrian...' He left the implication hanging in the air.

Nancy chewed her lip pensively. It was an exceedingly unpleasant but very valid point. Had Adrian gone so far as to contaminate their organisation with an undercover police officer?

'What we need to do,' said Rick, 'is focus our attention very closely on anyone who's recently entered our orbit.'

He turned to his left.

'And Stephen here has got a very good idea who we should start with.'

41

'I was thinking that you should get a manicure, Bailey.'

Bailey looked down at her nails as she stood there in the warm aromatic environs of the beauty salon. She'd never really bothered that much with her nails before.

'Um... sure,' she said. 'Why not?'

Wendy smiled at her amenably. 'What colour would you like?'

'Er... aquamarine?' It was Bailey's favourite colour.

Wendy frowned and shook her head. 'Aquamarine?! No, no, no.'

She turned to the rack of nail varnishes next to her and scanned them thoughtfully, eventually picking one out.

'I think a dark metallic grey would do you right.'

Bailey shrugged and let her get on with it, waiting for her to get around to sharing more details of her marital issues.

Wendy had been pestering her by text for a few days now, inviting her to come in for a session that Wendy had said would be 'on her'. Although Bailey had concluded that there wasn't a great deal of mileage to be gained in pursuing Wendy as a source of information, she'd finally agreed to come in as she sensed that Wendy wanted to unburden herself of her problems, and Bailey figured it was best to try and stay in her good books for the sake of the operation with Rick.

Sitting at the table, Bailey observed Wendy carefully apply the nail varnish whilst the customers and the salon employees chattered softly around them.

'So what did you get up to over the weekend?' asked Wendy lightly.

Seeing as it was a Monday, this was no doubt the main topic of light conversation filling the beauty salon this morning.

Bailey had spent a considerable portion of the weekend down at the hospice visiting her father. With his strength fading, and with all the painkillers being pumped through his system, he'd spent much of his time slipping in and out of sleep, unable to engage much with her. It was therefore a relief, in some ways, that he hadn't been in any state to badger her about Mister Snigiss, and even if he had, she wouldn't have disclosed the nature of what she'd discovered so far; it was all too tied up with a confidential investigation, and at any rate, she still had no clue as to Jennifer's ultimate fate.

'Oh, nothing much. I just chilled out,' said Bailey, unwilling to discuss her father's situation with Wendy. 'How about you? Have you been up to anything exciting since I last saw you?'

It was all the prompt Wendy needed. She looked up from Bailey's nails with a slightly strained expression.

Here it comes, thought Bailey.

'I hired that private eye. Like I mentioned before.'

'Oh?' Bailey was faintly surprised, having half expected Wendy not to bother following through with it.

'Yeah,' said Wendy.

'And?'

'He's dead.'

Bailey did a double take. 'Dead?!'

Wendy took a deep breath. Her lip wobbled and she suddenly looked like she was about to start crying.

'He jumped off the top of a multi-storey car park. The local news is saying it's probably a suicide.' She swallowed hard. 'But that's bullshit. I know it was my husband. Him and his cronies. They did it.'

Bailey shuddered. Knowing what she knew about Rick and his

organisation, it seemed utterly plausible. Many of their victims had died in circumstances that made their deaths extremely difficult, if not impossible, to tie back to the Molloys. Many others, of course, had just disappeared completely.

'You can't be sure,' she said, trying to sound breezy. 'Maybe it was just a suicide.'

Wendy shook her head. 'I might not know much about what my husband does, but I know my husband, and I know he's very capable of killing someone.'

She paused and suddenly glanced around at her colleagues, aware that she was talking in rather a loud voice. She dropped the volume a little.

'We were sitting there eating dinner the day afterwards. I was watching him closely and there was no emotion whatsoever. They chucked that poor bloke off the top of that car park, but to look at Rick's face, you'd think nothing had ever happened. I'm starting to think he's some kind of psychopath.'

Bailey was surprised it had taken Wendy this long to reach that conclusion.

A thought suddenly occurred to her. 'Does Rick know that you put the private eye onto him?'

Wendy shook her head firmly. 'No, not as far as I'm aware. He would have said so. He would have hit the bleeding roof. Hopefully he won't find out.'

Bailey eyed Wendy with concern, her police officer sensibilities kicking in. 'Are you scared?' she asked. 'Are you worried for your own safety?'

Wendy hesitated a moment. 'I don't think he'd ever hurt me. But that man is dead because of me and I feel terrible about it.'

Bailey nodded grimly. Today's revelation was a stark reminder to her of the sheer ruthlessness of the people she was dealing with. For Rick to kill a man just for poking into his life meant that her demise would be a veritable certainty should he ever discover that she was an undercover cop.

42

Bailey walked along the corridor to her apartment admiring her finger-nails as she did so. Wendy had done a good job. The metallic grey colour did indeed suit her. She wondered if Dale would notice and comment on them. She was due to catch up with both him and Frank later that afternoon at the temporary HQ.

Unlocking her front door, she walked into the apartment to be confronted by the sight of Rick, Shane, Archie and Stephen. Her breath caught in her throat. Her sixth sense had failed her, or else she just hadn't been paying close enough attention to it.

Shit. What was going on?

She smiled nervously. 'Hey guys. This is the second time you've invited yourselves in here. Have you heard of a thing called a doorbell?'

None of them said anything. Their faces were cold and unsmiling.

Shane, who'd been standing closest to the door, deftly stepped behind her into the hallway and positioned himself with his arms crossed, squarely blocking off her exit route.

She gulped and shrank a little, her heart suddenly beating harder. This wasn't looking promising. Something was up. Something serious.

Stephen, who'd been leaning against the mantelpiece, pushed

himself forward and swaggered over to her. There was an almost gleeful glint in his little round eyes as he spoke in his squeaky voice.

'We think you're Old Bill,' he said.

An icy chill stabbed through her like a dagger. Those words were ultimate anathema to any undercover cop.

She swallowed, trying to maintain a semblance of calm while her mind furiously analysed the possible reasons for their accusation. Her thoughts were immediately wrenched back to the time her cover had been blown when she'd been working undercover in the car theft ring. In that particular case, the gang had claimed to have had a source inside the police who'd tipped them off as to her real identity. Was it going to be the same with the Molloys, or was it going to be something else? Some inconsistency in her cover story perhaps? Or perhaps some police operation against them that they'd decided could only have been possible with the aid of an infiltrator?

Whatever their reasoning, there was only one course of action she could take to try and dispel the seeds of doubt. And that was to deny it totally and completely.

Never break cover.

'Old Bill?' she sneered. 'You must be having a fucking laugh.'

'Do you see us laughing?' rasped Rick, his face like stone.

He'd been sitting on the sofa, but now he stood up. In the small confines of the flat, she realised just how big he was.

'The police and Customs hit an airstrip in Essex recently,' he said. 'They'd heard that we were bringing in a large shipment of ecstasy pills.'

Bailey's hackles went up. It was that drugs shipment Dale had mentioned. The one scheduled for the third of February which had never materialised.

'The thing is,' said Stephen, 'it was fake information designed to flush out a rat. We know that the person who provided this information to the police was a grass.'

'Who's this grass?' she said, well aware that it was Adrian they were referring to.

'Never you mind,' growled Rick.

'The problem we have,' said Stephen, 'is that this grass could have planted an undercover police officer inside our organisation.'

Shit. This was exactly the kind of thing she'd been afraid would happen should the Molloys ever discover that Adrian had been a confidential informant.

She put on an act of shocked realisation. 'Wait a minute! Are you telling me that Adrian was the grass?'

'We're not telling you anything,' spat Stephen. 'We just want to know if you're Old Bill.'

'For some reason my mother seems to trust you,' said Rick, 'and normally I respect her opinions. But Stephen here convinced both of us that we should take some extra precautions. Just to be on the safe side. After all, you know how careful I am.'

She glanced at Stephen. He had a self-satisfied smirk on his face. God, she really detested him.

'All we want you to do is answer some questions truthfully,' he said.

'Are you going to use eye accessing cues?' she asked with a faint tone of disdain.

Stephen smiled unpleasantly and shook his head. He nodded to Archie who was sitting on one of the breakfast stools. Archie reached inside his jacket and withdrew a small black pouch from his inner pocket. Bailey eyed it with trepidation.

He unzipped the pouch and took out a hypodermic syringe. A horrible sinking feeling went through Bailey. She had a bad track record with needles.

'What's that?' she whispered.

He smiled his death's-head grin. 'It's scopolamine. It's a truth serum.'

Shit. Bailey knew what scopolamine was. It was a drug that induced a state of total compliance, as well as completely wiping your memory. It was more commonly used to facilitate robbery or rape. She knew that under the influence of scopolamine she could very easily end up revealing that she was an undercover cop.

'Why don't you take a seat?' said Archie, gesturing at the sofa which Rick had just vacated.

Bailey got the idea it wasn't so much a request as a demand. And if she didn't obey...

She glanced behind her. Shane was still standing in the hallway, blocking her exit. Mentally, she started to choreograph her escape from the flat, trying to work out which jiu-jitsu moves would give her the best chance of escaping. It would be tough, perhaps even impossible to incapacitate four grown men. But if she was fast...

She stopped herself. Maybe there wasn't the need to resort to that quite yet. There might just be a way out of this.

She smiled amenably, stepped forward and sat down on the sofa. Archie got up from the breakfast stool and sat down beside her. Brandishing the syringe, he gestured for her to roll up the sleeve of her left arm.

Bailey held up a hand.

'Just a moment. Maybe we don't need to do this. Before you inject me with anything, why don't you check who I am with one of my former bosses? I worked for him for several years as a sales manager for his financial services company. Now, I wouldn't have been able to do that and be a copper at the same time, would I? I've got his card in here somewhere.'

She rummaged around in her purse and pulled out a slightly crumpled business card. She held it out to Rick. He looked down at it emotionlessly, making no effort to take it.

Out of the corner of her eye, she could see Archie eagerly poised to inject her, the sharp point of the needle wavering in the air.

She breathed a sigh of relief as Rick plucked the business card from her fingers and scanned it with his black eyes.

'Donald Ferguson,' he murmured. 'Chief Executive Officer. Wycombe-Ballard Limited.'

'He'll verify that I used to work for him. You can check the dates and everything.'

'I don't think—' started Stephen.

But Rick held up his hand and Stephen lapsed into a reluctant itchy silence. Rick took his phone out of his jacket pocket and dialled the telephone number on the business card.

He stood there waiting for it to be answered, staring directly at her. Then his eyes flickered away as someone answered at the other end.

'I'd like to talk to Mr Ferguson, please,' he said.

A pause. Probably some kind of holding music. His eyes locked back onto hers. She could feel her heart thumping hard inside her ribcage. Then someone came on the line.

'Is that Mr Ferguson?' said Rick.

Another pause.

'Yeah,' he said. 'I'm calling from an organisation who's offering a job to someone called Bailey Sharpe. We'd just like a reference. Over the phone is fine. We just want to confirm that she worked for you.'

He listened for a few moments.

'Oh, she did work for you, huh?'

He nodded and listened.

'And you say she was a good hard-working employee as well. A self-starter.'

He stared at Bailey, a small dry smile on his face, as he listened to Ferguson extolling Bailey's virtues.

'Okay, yes I'm sure we'll be very lucky to have her. And one last thing – what dates did she work for you?'

Again he listened and nodded.

'Okay, well, thank you very much for your time.'

He ended the call. The smile dropped off his face.

'Well, well. Isn't that convenient?'

He tossed the card contemptuously into her lap.

'The thing is though,' he said, 'that could be a fake company. We know how the Filth operate. That number probably goes through to the police switchboard. I was probably talking to a bleeding copper just now.'

Bailey kept her expression firm, shaking her head vehemently. 'I'm not a fucking pig, okay.'

'Yeah right. Do you think I was born yesterday?'

'I told you. I'm not a copper.' She bristled indignantly, trying to look insulted, which any real criminal would be. She had to front it out and do her best to remain in character.

Rick sighed. 'I think a dose of scopolamine should clear things up pretty quickly.'

Stephen smiled triumphantly.

Bailey's heart dropped. She knew any resistance on her part might be interpreted as a tacit admission of guilt. And if she did attempt to resist, they'd more than likely hold her down and forcibly inject her with it anyway. Either way, she was screwed.

'Go ahead,' she said defiantly. 'See if I care. I've got nothing to hide.'

But on the inside her heart was racing furiously, her mind frantically going over her very limited options. She would doubtless give herself away, and if that happened, what would they do to her? If she failed their test, then she was quite certain they'd kill her here and now. She'd gained too much of their trust by now for them to just walk away like they would have done at the very beginning had they discovered she was a cop. Wounded pride would also play a big part in their retribution.

She glanced nervously at the large windows, recalling with a chill how the private eye had died. Falling from a height was a sure way to dispatch someone and it was near impossible to prove as murder.

If, by some miracle, she got out of this, she made a mental note to recommend to Frank that all undercover apartments be situated on the ground floor from now on.

She turned to look at Archie. He smiled at her, revealing his brown decaying teeth. Holding up the needle, he flicked the tip. A dribble of liquid oozed out of the top.

The other three stared down at her, their faces grim and forbidding. She rolled up her left sleeve and stared back at them insolently, not breaking eye contact as Archie leant forward and injected her with the drug.

She suppressed a wince at the bite of the needle. And almost immediately she felt the drug hit her system.

Her vision started to blur slightly while her heart rate seemed to increase even further. A feeling of drowsiness descended upon her and the rest of her body started to drift away from her control, like a boat cut loose from its moorings.

Rick knelt down in front of her. He stared at her with those blacker-than-black eyes. Mesmerised, she could not tear herself away from their terrible gaze.

She tried to analyse the situation, but her thoughts had lost the ability to cohere, scattering hopelessly like oiled marbles slipping through her grasp.

Rick opened his mouth, his gravelly voice emerging in a soft almost gentle tone.

'Are you an undercover police officer?'

43

It was an easy question. She knew the answer to that one. The answer was very simple. Just one word would suffice. And that word was 'yes'.

Are you an undercover police officer?

Some vague instinct deep within her told her that she had to deny it. But right now lying seemed like so much effort, almost insurmountably so.

It was so much easier just to answer in the affirmative because, after all, that was the truth.

Her brain started to formulate the word, her neurons sending signals to her vocal muscles.

She opened her mouth to speak.

And at that very moment they were interrupted by the metallic sound of a key entering the front-door lock.

The four men spun around sharply.

The door creaked open and a man emerged from the hallway into the living room.

In his late forties perhaps, he had a pale countenance topped with reddish hair going to grey and a short moustache.

Recognition blossomed. She knew this guy. His name was Frank. He was a policeman. He was her boss.

Frank was wearing some kind of faded blue boiler suit with splotches of paint on it, and he was holding a bag of tools in one hand. He was panting, slightly out of breath.

He surveyed them all, his face breaking into a welcoming grin.

'Afternoon all,' he said.

'Who the fuck are you?' growled Shane menacingly.

'I'm the plumber. The estate agency sent me.'

He turned his attention to Bailey.

'I presume you're Ms Sharpe. I'm here to fix the low water pressure. Just as you requested. The agency gave me the keys as they weren't sure whether you'd be in or not.'

Bailey stared at him, her mouth hanging open vacantly.

The four men exchanged suspicious glances. They seemed unsure how to react.

'Come back later,' grunted Rick.

'I can't,' said Frank jovially. 'I've got a whole load of jobs on my list.' He held up his phone. 'Talk to my boss if you want. He'll go spare if I don't get them all done today. I'll dial him right now and you can talk to him.'

Before they had a chance to respond, he squeezed past Shane and blundered through the living room, halting in front of Bailey. Beneath the happy-go-lucky demeanour, his watery blue eyes assessed her in a cool and calculating manner.

'Which tap has the problem, Ms Sharpe?'

She gazed up at him. She slowly frowned. She wasn't Ms Sharpe. She was Ms Morgan. She began to shake her head.

Frank's eyes narrowed as he saw that something wasn't right. He quickly rephrased the question. 'Your name's Bailey, right?'

That was an easy question. Her name was indeed Bailey.

'Yes,' she said. 'That's right. My name's Bailey.'

'Bailey, where's the tap with the low water pressure?'

Another easy question. No effort. No problem.

'It's in the kitchen,' she said slowly, her voice slurring slightly.

Shane marched up to Frank. He looked him up and down, taking in the manky boiler suit... and the incongruous pair of shiny black Oxfords.

'You're a plumber?' he said, his face screwing up sceptically. 'You don't look much like a plumber to me.'

'We come in all shapes and sizes,' said Frank, easing past him into the kitchen.

Shane frowned angrily and walked in after him, watching Frank closely as he put the bag of tools down on the kitchen worktop.

Shane eyed him suspiciously. 'You look like you should be on *Rogue Traders*.'

Frank shrugged agreeably and turned his attention to the sink.

He fiddled with the tap, turning it on and off. A dribble of water came out. He nodded gravely.

'Mmm,' he murmured. 'Definitely low water pressure.'

Shane stepped in closer, moving well into Frank's personal space, looming over him in the small kitchen. He put his face right up close to the side of Frank's head in a blatantly intimidating manner. Frank studiously ignored him, appearing to focus all of his attention on the tap. Shane suddenly frowned and his nose wrinkled.

'You smell of doner kebab, mate.'

Frank glanced up at him and smiled. 'I just had lunch.'

'How can you eat that revolting shit?' muttered Shane.

'Sod him,' said Rick, who'd been observing with a dark expression. 'Let's just get on with it.'

With a final sneer of contempt, Shane wandered out of the kitchen and back into the living room.

Rick turned his focus back to Bailey. He cleared his throat and spoke to her once again.

'Are you an undercover police officer?' he said.

The answer started to rise up in her throat. Once again, some deep primitive urge inside her screamed at her to resist, but her strength to do so had atrophied to virtually zero.

There was a sudden metallic groan, followed closely by a loud hissing. They all recoiled, turning in shock as water sprayed across the living room, coating them with a fine shower of cold droplets.

Bailey saw Frank standing in the kitchen, clutching a wrench, drenched in water, while a large geyser sprayed uncontrollably from the top of the tap. It appeared that he'd somehow pulled the top off it with the wrench.

'What the fuck?!' snarled Rick, looking down at his wet Armani suit in outrage. He looked up at Frank, a truly murderous expression on his face. 'You muggy cunt!'

Frank put his hands over the top of the tap, vainly trying to stem the fountain of water spraying upwards from the exposed valve.

'I'm terribly sorry, gentlemen! Please forgive me.'

Violent looks bounced between the four men and there was a dangerously tense pause. Then Rick's murderous expression subsided and he brushed off his suit jacket.

'It's only water,' he said dismissively. 'Anyhow, we're done here.'

'Wait a minute—' protested Stephen.

'I said we're done.'

Rick nodded at them all to leave. And so they did, leaving Bailey and Frank alone in the flat, water coming down like rain around them.

44

Bailey's memory started to return sometime later, coming back sluggishly in bits and pieces.

The first thing she saw was Frank sitting on the sofa next to her, dressed in a paint-spattered blue boiler suit, peering into her face with an expression of concern.

She groaned softly. Her mouth was unbearably dry, she felt excessively nauseous and she had a headache far worse than any hangover she'd ever experienced.

'Urghh... oh my God,' she muttered. 'I feel terrible.'

She slowly gazed around the interior of the apartment. Her face twisted into a puzzled frown.

'Why's everything wet?'

'You really don't remember anything, do you?' said Frank.

She rubbed her head, grimacing in discomfort. God it hurt. She tried to cast her mind back. She could recall everything up until just before they injected her.

'They gave me scopolamine,' she said. 'It wipes the memory.' She squinted at him with a perplexed look. 'What's with the boiler suit?'

He looked down at it. 'Oh, this? I was pretending to be your plumber. I think they bought it, although I imagine any real plumber would have been out of here like a shot.'

'Where did you get it?'

'Mustafa had a pile of old decorating overalls in the cupboard at the back of the kebab shop, along with the tools. It was all I could come up with at such short notice. Seems to have done the trick though.' He sniffed at the sleeve of the boiler suit. 'Although this does smell of doner kebab.'

She smiled. 'Glad to see you're still able to think on your feet, just like you taught me to all those years ago.'

'When I came in, it didn't take me long to clock that something was wrong with you. I figured they'd drugged you in some way... probably some kind of truth serum. I knew you were in trouble though. Why else would you have contacted me?'

She raised one eyebrow. 'Well, you got here just in the nick of time "Mr Ferguson".'

He snorted a laugh. When setting up the operation, she and Frank had established a number of operational emergency security protocols. Wycombe-Ballard Limited was a fake company set up for exactly this kind of scenario. Any call coming through to that number was routed via the police switchboard directly to Frank. Regardless of who was calling or what they were saying, any call to Wycombe-Ballard Limited would instantly indicate that the undercover officer was in the process of being compromised and in imminent danger of physical harm. It had been a gamble convincing Rick to call the number and she dreaded to think what would have happened if he hadn't.

'Lucky I was close by,' said Frank. 'There wasn't time to call the full back-up squad.'

'That would have put an end to the whole operation anyway.' She paused. 'Do you think the Molloys think I'm a cop?'

He shrugged. 'Hard to tell. From what I could hear, you didn't reveal anything incriminating. They gave up on the interrogation after I messed up your tap and got them soaked. Anyhow, I guess they didn't want a witness here in case they ended up having to kill you. And they couldn't very well have killed me. Killing you and making it look like an accident is one thing. Killing me as well and also making it look like an accident would have been stretching it just a little bit too far.'

He paused, gazing at her with his watery blue eyes.

'What made them suspect that you were a police officer?' he asked.

She explained to him about the non-existent shipment of ecstasy pills that was supposed to have been coming into the airstrip in Essex.

'So that whole piece of intelligence was nothing more than a clever set-up on Rick's part with the aim of flushing out a snout?'

She nodded. 'It's becoming quite clear to me how Rick operates. He's a very crafty individual. We're going to have to tread a lot more carefully from now on. He knows that Adrian was an informant, but that doesn't mean he knows that I'm a cop. If he had solid proof that I was a police officer, he would have just killed me outright. He wouldn't have bothered with all this scopolamine malarkey. So I think we still have a chance here. I don't think the operation's over just yet.'

He scrutinised her apprehensively and rubbed his chin. 'Hmm. I don't know. Maybe we should pull you out. This job seems to be getting quite hazardous.'

She knew his concern for her was rooted in a deep-seated guilt he'd held ever since the fiasco with the car theft gang. Operational security was something he prided himself on, and on that occasion it had been breached catastrophically. It had been his operation and he felt responsible. She knew he'd made it his mission ever since to get to the bottom of how her cover had got blown on that job, although as far as she was aware he hadn't come up with any tangible leads.

'Every undercover job is hazardous,' she replied. 'That's the nature of what I do. You should know that.'

'There's no guarantee they don't think you're a cop,' he said. 'They could just be waiting for a more opportune moment to kill you.'

'I'll take that risk. I want to stay. I feel like I'm close to nailing them.'

Frank sighed. 'If you say so. But I also have a feeling you're sticking this out for personal reasons. Because of your sister.'

'You're not wrong. I do have a personal stake in this and that's one thing I'm not willing to give up on either.'

'Just don't let it cloud your judgement,' he said, standing up to leave.

She sat there on the sofa pondering his words as he walked over to the door.

'Frank,' she said, looking up.

He stopped in the hallway, turning around. 'Yeah?'

'Thanks for saving my bacon.'

He smiled at the police-related pun. 'Glad to see you haven't lost your sense of humour, Bailey.' He paused. 'Anyhow, I know you'd do the same for me.'

45

Dennis Morgan lay asleep in his bed in the hospice while Bailey sat by his side watching him and thinking about how he seemed to be sleeping a hell of a lot these days. She guessed it must partially be due to all the drugs he was on. All those painkillers. As she recalled, he'd said the doctors would progressively increase the dosages as his condition got more serious.

It concerned her to see how much he had deteriorated since her last visit. He was substantially paler, thinner and more deeply lined than before, and she knew it would only get worse. It broke her heart to see him looking so frail, remembering how active he'd been not so long ago, going on hikes in the countryside with her mother and playing tennis with his friends.

She knew he would be dead soon. Gone forever. Everybody died sooner or later, but you never got used to it when it was someone close to you, especially when it felt so out of the blue – after all, it was only two months ago that they'd been sitting together having Christmas dinner.

She opened her purse and took out the picture of Mister Snigiss he'd given her. Once again she examined the crude felt-tip drawing, tracing her finger over the depiction of Mister Snigiss leading her and

Jennifer on one of their imaginary adventures. Mister Snigiss was where her family life and work life now converged. Mister Snigiss was where the past met the present. Mister Snigiss wouldn't bring her father back from the brink. No, her father would die anyway. But she couldn't let him die without finding out who Mister Snigiss was first. She had to find out the truth about Jennifer before her father was lost to her forever.

She'd always told herself she didn't believe in the supernatural, but she was now gripped by the irrational conviction that if he died without knowing the truth about Jennifer, then he would end up as a ghost stuck between this world and the next, tormented for all eternity by the unresolved question of his missing daughter.

Bailey tried to think what her next move should be. What was the best way to progress her search for Mister Snigiss? What about the sex tape? Would that turn out to be connected to him? She felt sure that it was. But things seemed to have gone a bit quiet on that front. She made a mental note to chase up with Dale to see where the murder investigation team had got with it.

With Dale on her mind, she noticed from the date on her watch that today was the fourteenth of February. Valentine's Day. In terms of romance, things between them had cooled off quite a bit since her recent sudden absorption with Mister Snigiss. Perhaps he thought she wasn't interested any more. Perhaps she was deluding herself about how he really felt about her. Anyhow, she told herself it was probably for the best. After all, they were work colleagues first and foremost and it was important to keep things professional.

46

Rick's black Range Rover Velar was already parked up in the lay-by when Bailey arrived. He was the kind of person who liked to get to meetings early.

The sky was grey and overcast and it was spitting lightly as she pulled in behind him and switched off the engine of her BMW. He had called her that morning with the sole instruction for her to come to this lay-by on an A-road in Essex. She knew that a lay-by was a good way to avoid police surveillance and thus an ideal place to discuss sensitive business matters.

She had been relieved to hear from him. Following the scopolamine incident, she'd been anxious that they'd decided they were done with her, but now it seemed that Rick wanted to commence with business as before. Obviously, the possibility had also occurred to her that he'd invited her here so they could pick up the interrogation where they'd left off – after all, in this lay-by there wouldn't be any plumbers close by to conveniently interrupt them. Either way, she'd told Frank where she was going.

She got out of her car and walked over to his Range Rover, droplets of rain pattering on her skin while traffic roared past just a few metres away. Pulling open the passenger door, she climbed inside. The interior was warm and dry and it smelt of leather and the seat was large and comfortable.

Rick was sitting there all by himself, leaning on the steering wheel. She wondered where the others were, but felt vaguely reassured by their absence, figuring that it meant a further interrogation was off the table.

He gave her a thin smile, but those black eyes were dead as ever.

'Sorry about the other day,' he said. 'I hope you understand.'

'To be honest, apart from the horrific headache, it's kind of a blank in my memory.'

'Yeah, well that's scopolamine for you.'

'Did I answer your questions correctly?'

Rick was silent for a few moments, staring at her with a characteristically inscrutable expression.

'We were interrupted unfortunately. By your plumber. But the fact you were willing to undergo the experience is what counts.'

Was he being honest with her? Or was this just the entrée to some further test or trap?

Shifting uncomfortably in the car seat, she suppressed her misgivings and attempted to project a confident front.

'I'm presuming you didn't invite me here just so we could admire the countryside,' she said, nodding at the flat featureless fields on either side of the busy A-road.

He smiled. 'As I mentioned previously, the transaction will take place on the ninth of March. I'll provide you with the location on the day itself. It'll be a safe neutral indoors location. All you need to do is bring the paperwork.'

Paperwork. Cash.

'Seven fifty. As agreed,' she said. 'And the merchandise?'

'After we've checked the paperwork and we're happy with it, then we'll bring in the merchandise in a truck and hand you the keys. Sound good?'

Bailey shook her head. 'Uh-uh. That's not the way I normally do things. I'll have a man with the paperwork. He'll bring it to the location but he'll keep it outside in the car. One of your men will go outside to check it. In the meantime, you'll have the merchandise inside for me to check. If I'm happy with it, then I'll go outside and give the nod to my man to hand the paperwork over to your man. And then I'll go back inside and you'll hand me the keys to the truck.'

Rick eyed her silently. She was fairly sure he wouldn't try and pull a fast one on her, but with ruthless Machiavellian people like this you could never be quite sure. The way he'd originally planned it left too much margin for him to double-cross her, take the cash and potentially kill her as well in order to limit any comeback.

And she was certain he was well aware of that. If she was as professional as she was trying to make out, then he'd expect her to push back. Not doing so could flag her as an amateur who was asking to be screwed over... or an undercover cop.

After a short, tense silence, Rick broke into a mirthless smile.

'Okay. We'll do it your way if it makes you feel better.'

She nodded slowly, satisfied with the arrangements, tentatively congratulating herself on sealing the final elements of the deal. It seemed like everything was going to plan. She was about to say goodbye and get out of the car when Rick's phone rang.

He answered it. Bailey couldn't quite make out the voice on the other end.

'Really?' he said, raising one eyebrow in surprise. 'About time. Don't do anything until I get there.'

Bailey feigned disinterest but was secretly wondering who he was talking to.

He turned to look at her whilst still talking down the phone. 'Yeah, she's with me right now actually. Just finalising some arrangements with her.'

Bailey was genuinely curious now. Rick smiled inertly at her.

'Sure, okay,' he said to the person on the other end of the phone. 'See you in a bit.'

He ended the call.

'Who was that?' said Bailey.

'My mother.'

'What did she want?'

'She says she's got a little treat in store for you.'

A vaguely ominous feeling descended upon Bailey.

'Get in your car and follow me,' said Rick. It sounded more like a command than a request. Unless she wanted to risk messing things up at this crucial stage of the operation, Bailey knew she had no choice but to obey.

47

Rick drove fast, aggressively, bullying other smaller cars out of the way. He travelled in a circuitous and unpredictable manner, presumably to throw off any potential surveillance, and Bailey sometimes had trouble keeping up with him.

The rain was now coming down more heavily, spattering on her windscreen, the wipers flicking industriously from side to side.

Somewhere on the outskirts of Romford, just past a derelict gasworks, he turned off into a grim-looking industrial estate. Big boarded-up warehouses that had seen better days interspersed with wide stretches of cracked weed-strewn concrete. The whole place looked to be completely deserted. Driving along behind him, Bailey was suddenly hit by a flashback to her torture session in the scrapyard at the hands of the car theft gang. Just like that place, this was far enough away from civilisation to ensure that your screams would never be heard...

The car wobbled as her hands suddenly went weak on the steering wheel, the horrific memories forcing themselves unbidden upon her.

She inhaled sharply, clenching the steering wheel and, with the greatest effort, forced herself back into the present. To succumb to that toxic disabling fear right now would not be productive... and could even be fatal.

Rick eventually slowed and turned into the loading bay of one of the large disused warehouses. The brickwork was covered in mould and big rusting metal shutters covered the entrance where the goods would have been unloaded. There were three other vehicles parked there – a white Transit van, a dark blue Jaguar XJ6 and a silver Audi TT.

Bailey parked next to him and switched off the engine. She sat there for a few moments breathing deeply, attempting to regain her composure fully. Still she wondered if this was a trap and whether she should make a break for it right now.

Rick climbed out of his Range Rover and jumped up onto the platform of the loading bay. He turned and beckoned at her. She hesitated for one last moment before getting out of her car, locking the door and going to join him.

The rain splattered down around them as he glanced about surreptitiously, then knelt down and pulled up the rusty metal shutters with a loud clanking noise, leaving just enough room for them to duck underneath into the black interior beyond. He crouched down and entered the warehouse.

Bailey stood there in the rain, trying to make up her mind whether this was a very bad idea or not. Her sixth sense wasn't ringing red alarm bells just yet. Maybe it was fine. Maybe...

'What are you waiting for?' he said from the other side.

Fuck it. She ducked down underneath the shutters and followed him in.

Straightening up on the other side, she blinked as her eyes adjusted to the dim cavernous interior. A second later, the smell hit her – that distinctive stench of burnt hair and toasting flesh, rounded off with a discernible odour of shit. It was the indisputable smell of pain and fear and it sent a powerful bolt of dread through her.

She trailed after Rick as he strode ahead through the chilly gloom, making his way through a doorway at the back into a dingy corridor with a yellow light at the far end. She could now make out the sounds of voices ahead of them, and the closer they got, the more the acrid smell grew in pungency.

The corridor opened out into a stark concrete room illuminated solely by the glare of a single bare bulb hanging from the ceiling. In the centre of the room was a naked man tied to a chair. His hands were bound behind his back with cable ties and silver duct tape was wrapped around his mouth. His heavily muscled body glistened with perspiration. He was slumped forward, his head hanging downwards, his hair matted with sweat, and he was shivering uncontrollably. There was a large puddle of urine on the floor and globules of faeces dribbled down the side of the chair.

Standing around him were various members of the Molloy family, the yellow light from the bare bulb casting demonic shadows across their features. Nancy, clad in a dark fur coat holding Ettie in the crook of her arm; Shane, arms crossed, chewing gum with a sadistic grin on his face; Stephen, holding a video camera trained on the man in the chair; Archie, clutching a steam iron in one hand, still wearing his sunglasses. By the almost jocund expressions they bore, it seemed like they were enjoying it as a family day out.

'I told you not to start before I got here,' said Rick angrily.

'I'm sorry, Ricky. I got ahead of myself,' Nancy replied. 'And Archie here was just raring to go.'

Archie grinned and pressed a button on the iron making it emit a gust of steam. The man in the chair flinched reflexively at the hissing noise. Bailey knew the steam iron wasn't here because they wanted to keep their clothes neat and pressed.

Nancy turned to Bailey with a welcoming smile. She looked genuinely pleased to see her.

'I'm so glad you could make it, Bailey,' she said.

Trying not to look at the man in the chair, Bailey forced a smile and a nonchalant shrug as if this was nothing she couldn't handle. But inside she fought against the revulsion at what she was seeing, trying to keep a lid on the simmering recall of her own experiences of torture.

One thing she could not afford to do right now was let a flashback overwhelm her.

'I wouldn't have missed it for the world,' she said.

'Remember I told you I would show you how we operate,' said Nancy. 'Well, you're party to a prime example of a gangland interrogation. Molloy-style.'

Bailey knew from personal experience that there were no bounds to what could be done in this kind of situation. And it looked like they'd only just got started. She wondered who the poor victim was. He looked to be quite young, maybe in his thirties, and was possibly even quite handsome, although in this state it was hard to tell. He twisted his head slowly to look up at Bailey from beneath his matted hair, his wide eyes filled with pure unadulterated fear. She knew exactly how he felt.

'Have you even let him talk?' said Rick.

'Not yet. We were just softening him up for you,' said Shane.

'We caught up with him in Leeds,' said Stephen. 'He'd been lying low up there since Christmas. Some of our contacts up there alerted us to his presence.'

Bailey was starting to get an idea who this was. This was Marcus, Adrian's scuzzy coke-dealer friend who Wendy had mentioned. The one the Molloys had been searching for in connection with the car bomb.

'Well, let's hear him talk,' said Rick.

Archie stepped forward and viciously ripped the duct tape off Marcus's mouth. He immediately expelled a snort of snot and saliva, the drools hanging down off his face. He began to whimper and babble incoherently.

Archie slapped him hard around the face, then, grabbing a handful of his hair, wrenched his head around so he was facing Rick.

Marcus instantly stopped his babbling and stared at Rick transfixed.

'We know you were involved in Adrian's murder,' said Rick.

'I... No... I wasn't... No... I didn't...' Marcus's voice came out in panting fits and spurts.

'Why were you hiding from us then?' demanded Stephen.

'You'd better give us some answers,' growled Shane.

'Or do you want me to carry on ironing your bollocks?' whispered Archie.

Marcus twitched convulsively and squirmed against his bonds, making an animal-like keening noise.

'What was that?' said Rick, cupping his ear. 'I couldn't quite make that out.'

'Mist... Mister... Mister Snigiss...'

The utterance sent an ominous prickle through Bailey. Her breathing quickened.

The Molloys exchanged looks of confusion.

'You're not making any sense!' said Shane, giving Marcus a sharp prod in the head.

'Mister Snigiss!' blurted Marcus. 'It was Mister Snigiss!'

'Mister Snigiss?' said Stephen, pushing the camera into Marcus's face. 'Who's Mister Snigiss?'

'Mister Snigiss killed Adrian!'

Bailey's thoughts churned wildly at what she'd just heard. Marcus's admission only served to strengthen what she'd been increasingly suspecting all along. Mister Snigiss had been behind the car bomb. Notwithstanding her deep repugnance towards the torture, Bailey couldn't help but lean in closer to listen to what Marcus had to say next.

Nancy stepped around in front of Marcus, softly stroking the top of Ettie's head. Marcus looked up at her, a pleading and desperate expression on his face.

'Who is this Mister Snigiss?' she asked softly in her husky voice. 'And why did he kill Adrian?'

Marcus started speaking, the words tumbling out breathlessly.

'It all started when Adrian met Tiffany at a party—'

'Tiffany?' cut in Stephen. 'You mean that bird who got blown up with him?'

Marcus gulped and nodded. 'He met her at a party. Just some party y'know. She was there. Lots of fit birds. Top-end brasses. She was one of them. He ended up doing lines with her. You know what Adrian was like. And then—'

'Get to the fucking point!' shouted Shane.

'She was a hooker,' gasped Marcus. 'Worked for this high-end outfit run by Mister Snigiss.'

'So this Mister Snigiss is a pimp?'

Marcus nodded. 'That's right. Mister Snigiss runs the whole thing. High-class hookers, that's what they are. He's got a whole stable of them.'

Despite her abhorrence at the methods being used to get Marcus to talk, Bailey absorbed his information with mounting excitement, her picture of Mister Snigiss growing clearer by the minute.

'So why did he kill Adrian?' said Nancy.

'These hookers... Mister Snigiss uses them to make blackmail videos. He secretly films the punters. All these rich, powerful blokes. And then he uses the videos to control them. To get influence. That kind of thing.'

Marcus's words resonated strongly with what Bailey had discovered so far. It seemed very plausible to her now that it was in fact Mister Snigiss – a pimp – who lay at the heart of the blackmail focused on Lewis Ballantyne.

'So how did Adrian get caught up in all this?' demanded Rick.

'Adrian met Tiffany at this party and she told him she'd got this shit-hot video of her and this politician and that she was going to sell it to one of the tabloids and make loads of money. But Adrian was like, no no no, if you do it my way you'll make even more money. Of course, you know what Adrian was like, he just wanted a piece of the action. But he spun her a line and she bought it.'

'Stupid little boy,' growled Nancy. 'Getting mixed up with cokehead brasses, bringing our family name into disrepute. You should have been keeping a closer eye on him, Ricky.'

Rick ground his teeth angrily at his mother's reprimand.

'That's how I got involved,' stammered Marcus. 'I've got loads of media contacts, see. Adrian thought he could play them off against each other for the video, like an auction, drive the price up. At least that's what he told Tiffany. And she went along with it cos she wanted to make as much money as possible.'

As she eagerly digested the revelations, Bailey felt a strange sense of satisfaction as the disparate elements of the story began to cohere more fully in her mind.

'So what the fuck happened with Adrian then?' growled Shane menacingly.

Marcus cowered fearfully. 'Well, normally Tiffany would have just done her business with the politician and Mister Snigiss would have filmed it and Tiffany would have got paid and that would have been that. But Tiffany thought she wasn't making enough money. So she secretly set up her own camera and made her own video, without telling Mister Snigiss. And that was the video she took to Adrian.'

Bailey thought back to the kitten-themed memory stick, understanding now that the MPEG4 file was Tiffany's own sex tape that she'd saved on there in order to give to Adrian.

'But somehow Mister Snigiss found out about it,' continued Marcus. 'And he wasn't too pleased, cos I guess if it all got out into the media it would have messed up his plans to secretly control the politician. So that's why he blew them up.'

Nancy nodded slowly. 'So let me get this straight. Mister Snigiss blew up Adrian and Tiffany because they were going to sell this sex video to the tabloids. And that would have ruined Mister Snigiss's plans to have some kind of secret influence over this politician.'

Marcus nodded frantically, desperately eager to assuage them in any way possible.

'Who is this politician?' said Stephen.

'Lewis Ballantyne.'

'That cunt who's running for Mayor?' said Rick, raising his eyebrows in surprise, shooting a glance at Nancy.

Marcus nodded.

'So where is this sex video?' said Nancy.

'Dunno. Got blown up in the bomb probably. Mister Snigiss blew them up on the day that Tiffany was supposed to give Adrian the video. She only agreed to give it to him after she was sure that him and me had got everything sewn up at our end. As soon as I heard they'd got blown up, I left town like a rat up a drainpipe. I knew they'd got blown up cos of the tape and I knew Mister Snigiss would be looking for me next.'

Bailey slyly reflected on what she'd just heard. Little did they know that the memory stick had survived the blast, and little did they know that she herself had viewed its contents.

'Mister Snigiss?' Nancy rolled the name contemptuously around her mouth. She looked around at the rest of the gang. 'Have any of you heard of this Mister Snigiss?'

She was met with shrugs and shakes of the head. Bailey proffered a similar response although inwardly she was just as curious as Nancy, if not more so, to know more about who he really was.

'Mister Snigiss,' muttered Nancy. 'Pfuh! Sounds like the baddie from a panto. What's his first name?'

'I dunno!' squealed Marcus. 'No one knows his first name. No one knows anything about him and he likes to keep it that way.'

'Tiffany never met him?' said Rick.

Marcus shook his head. 'None of those hookers ever met him. She said he just gave them their instructions remotely. Signed it off as Mister Snigiss, nothing more, nothing less. That's what Tiffany said.'

Bailey processed what she was hearing with profound interest. Invisibility. It had been a hallmark of Mister Snigiss all that time ago and it was a trait he appeared to have retained all these years later... if this was the same Mister Snigiss who'd kidnapped Jennifer. And there had to be a very high chance that it was the same individual, given the distinctiveness of his name, as well as the type of person she was starting to understand him to be.

'This high-class hooker outfit,' said Stephen. 'Has it got a name?'

Marcus nodded. 'Ophidia. That's what it's called. Ophidia.'

'Ophidia?' said Nancy derisively. 'Swanky name for what is basically just a bunch of prozzies at the end of the day.'

She gave a nod to Stephen, a mandate for him to check it out in more detail.

Bailey herself memorised the name. Later on she'd be doing her own bit of research.

'Whoever this Mister Snigiss is,' said Nancy, stroking her Pomeranian, 'we'll find him and we'll kill him. No one murders one of the Molloys and gets away with it. No one.'

48

Barely had Bailey sat down on the knackered old sofa in the temporary HQ than she was explaining to Frank and Dale what she'd learnt at the gangland interrogation, the words spilling out in an excited torrent.

The two men listened patiently, unable to get a word in edgeways.

'And I checked out what "Ophidia" meant,' she said. 'It's not just a fancy-sounding name. It's also the scientific word for "snakes". This Mister Snigiss has to be the same one who abducted Jennifer. The snake connection is too much of a coincidence. If you recall, Jennifer's Mister Snigiss used to keep a pet snake...' She opened her purse and once again reached for Jennifer's picture of Mister Snigiss.

Frank held up his hand for Bailey to stop. She paused. The two men exchanged uncomfortable glances. She detected a strained edge to the air. Something wasn't right. Why weren't they as enthused as she was?

'What's the matter?' she asked, her face dropping in dismay.

'Adrian Molloy's murder investigation has been shut down,' said Dale bluntly.

'What?!' she exclaimed.

'It's come down from higher up.' He jutted his thumb at the ceiling.

'Why?!'

'Why do you think? You saw who was featured on that sex tape. If this comes out, then there is absolutely no chance that Lewis Ballantyne will be elected as Mayor of London.'

'But—' started Bailey.

'Do you know how much money he's pledged to pour into the Met?' Frank interrupted. 'Millions and millions. The top brass are dead set on him getting elected. He's currently the front runner and they want him to stay that way. And they're not going to let something like this murder investigation get in the way. As far as they're concerned, Adrian was a relatively unsuccessful villain who's now dead, end of story.'

'You mean they're just going to brush it under the carpet?' she said incredulously. 'This is a murder we're talking about! A car bomb!'

'Look at it from our perspective, Bailey. All we have linking this sex tape and Mister Snigiss to this murder is the say-so of a homeless bloke and the testimony of some poor bastard being tortured in a gangland interrogation... and as we all know, people will say anything under that kind of duress.'

His last point was one that she was painfully well aware of.

'Where is this Marcus bloke anyway?' said Frank. 'Has anyone seen him since the interrogation?'

Bailey frowned. She had no idea what the Molloys had done with Marcus after the interrogation, but she didn't rate his chances of survival very highly.

'We'll probably find him floating face down in a canal in a few days' time,' said Frank, 'Or, knowing the Molloys, we'll probably never find him at all.'

Bailey swallowed and blinked, still trapped in a state of shocked disbelief that the powers-that-be could show such monstrous self-interest at the expense of the truth.

'But covering this up won't put Ballantyne in the clear,' she said. 'Okay, so Adrian and Tiffany aren't around any more to go to the media. And Marcus is very possibly dead. But Mister Snigiss is still out there and if you were listening to what I just told you, the whole point of that sexual liaison in the first place was so that he could film Ballantyne with two hookers and use that footage to secretly exert influence over him. I mean, Jesus, if Ballantyne does get elected as Mayor, then there's a good chance he might even end up as Prime Minister one day. Do you really want Mister Snigiss to be able to secretly control not just the potential Mayor of London, but possibly even the future Prime Minister of England?'

She paused for breath. Frank and Dale stared at her in silence, momentarily stunned by her outburst.

'We have to find Mister Snigiss,' she continued. 'If not to solve Adrian's murder then at least to stop him getting his claws into our political system.'

Frank gave her a sympathetic, almost sad look. 'Bailey, as I recall, the reason you've been looking for this Mister Snigiss is because of your sister. You're doing this for personal reasons. And that's never a good idea with undercover operations.'

Bailey chewed her lip in frustration. He was completely right of course, not that it altered her desire to follow through with this.

'The top brass might be able to shut down the murder investigation,' she said, 'but they can't shut down the Molloys. I know Nancy Molloy. She won't give up until she finds the person who killed her son, and as far as she's concerned that person is Mister Snigiss. And when she finds him, she'll kill him. More specifically, she'll drill a hole through his head with a power tool. And if she does that, I'll never find out what happened to Jennifer.'

Frank shook his head. 'I'm sorry, Bailey. You'll have to desist in any kind of investigation of this matter. That's an order. Or we'll pull you off the job altogether, which would be a shame, as you seem to be making good progress with the guns.'

She stared defiantly at Frank, her jaw set. Unyielding, he stared back at her with his watery blue eyes. A tense silence settled upon the room. Dale glanced awkwardly between the two of them.

'I can't believe you're just going to fold like this, Frank,' she said. 'I'm really disappointed in you.'

He eyed her with concern. 'As your line manager, I'm worried about your mental health, Bailey. This obsession with a missing person's case that's over twenty years old. This elusive abductor who was also your sister's invisible friend. You should listen to yourself.'

It occurred to her suddenly, with some sense of irony, that he was addressing her in much the same manner as she'd talked to her father up until not so long ago.

'I assure you I'm perfectly sane,' she replied. 'I know you set a high bar for evidence and proof, Frank. That's why I respect you. But you have to understand what this means to me, and I genuinely think we're onto something.'

'Look,' said Frank gently. 'Dale told me about your father's medical situation. I understand that it's probably placed you under added psychological pressure. Maybe you should pencil in an appointment with the psychologist.'

Bailey sat back in her chair with a huff of frustration and crossed her arms. She looked away from them to stare moodily out of the window. Frank and Dale both sat there watching her apprehensively. After a long few moments, she turned back to them.

'Okay,' she said with a big sigh. 'I'll let it go and I'll just focus on the guns. After all, that's the reason you brought me in.'

Both men breathed audible sighs of relief.

She was, of course, lying through her teeth just to placate them. There was no way she was going to give up on this.

49

The glittering panoramic vista of the night-time city stretched out beyond the windows. But Bailey wasn't looking at the view. For the past few hours she'd been sitting at the table hunched over her laptop trawling the internet for any mention of a high-class escort service going by the name of Ophidia. So far she'd found absolutely nothing. But then, given the shady nature of Ophidia's activities, was it any surprise they liked to stay out of the limelight?

She sat back in her chair with a frustrated sigh. Time was ticking down. The Molloys were no doubt cracking on with their search for Mister Snigiss whilst she seemed to be getting nowhere.

After a minute or two of heavy contemplation, an idea occurred to her. Closing down the internet browser, she navigated to the folder on her computer which contained the MPEG4 file of the sex tape that she'd copied from the memory stick.

She knew keeping a copy of it on her undercover laptop constituted a serious breach of operational security should the wrong person happen to discover it. Not only that, she knew making an unauthorised copy of something this sensitive was probably in itself highly irregular. However, she'd gone ahead and done it anyway, just in case she'd wanted to investigate further outside official channels. As it turned out, her forethought had paid off.

She clicked 'play' on the video, once again immersing herself in the carnal entanglements of the two women and the politician, studying it closely for any clues that could somehow bring her closer to Mister Snigiss. It felt furtive and voyeuristic watching this on her laptop late at night in the low-lit apartment yet it was also strangely mesmerising, in part because Bailey now knew that the blonde woman in the video had subsequently been blown to pieces. Poor Tiffany.

As she watched the recording though, Bailey found herself focusing increasingly on the black woman, her supple flesh writhing and pulsating in a primal sweat-drenched rhythm. Finding herself unexpectedly aroused, Bailey sat up sharply and took a deep breath, shaking her head clear of the erotic daze that had crept up on her all of a sudden.

Turning her attention back to the screen, she forced herself to be objective. With a slightly trembling finger, she hit the mouse button to pause the video on the black woman's face, her elegant features twisted in passion. Bailey took a screenshot and then zoomed in on her face, cropping out the rest of her body. With the low quality of the recording, the close-up was pretty grainy. But hopefully it would be enough for what Bailey had in mind.

50

It was a Sunday morning and the office was dead, which suited Bailey just fine considering the reason she was there.

Using her standard police credentials, she logged onto the computer system, and then, surreptitiously glancing around the near-empty office to check no one was looking, plugged in a memory stick containing the screenshot she'd taken the night before. She logged into the Police National Database and uploaded the black woman's picture to see if the PND's facial recognition technology could match it to the faces of any of those in custody records.

It turned out there was indeed a match.

The mugshot which appeared on the screen was unmistakably that of the woman in the video. Even under the circumstances of a police mugshot, her striking looks were apparent.

Bailey scanned through the information attached to the record. The woman's name was Claudia Figaricca and she'd been arrested around three months previously for the possession of cocaine. Bailey tore a piece of paper from a notepad on the desk and copied down the address that was associated with the record.

Once again she cast a guilty glance around the office, mindful of the fact that she was misappropriating police resources to pursue her own forbidden personal investigation. She had wrestled with the ethics of it before making the decision to come here. One part of her conscience was indentured to the strictures of her job and the need to abide by the law, while another part was obligated to Jennifer and her father, and that sense of duty ran much deeper.

51

Bailey had collared enough burglars in her time to pick up a few tricks of the trade, so breaking into Claudia's apartment had proved to be relatively straightforward.

For a high-class hooker, the place was surprisingly basic – a small one-bedroom flat on the second floor of a nondescript block in Hammersmith in West London. But then Bailey wondered if Claudia didn't make quite as much money as popular opinion made out when it came to these kinds of women.

She didn't bother poking around. That wasn't why she was here. Instead she sat down in an armchair in the corner of the living room with the lights switched off and waited for Claudia to return home.

Normally she'd have favoured a slightly softer, more oblique approach, with the aim of building up some kind of rapport. However, time was of the essence so she'd decided to resort to much blunter methods. She had to reach Mister Snigiss before the Molloys did and Claudia was her only lead.

It was perhaps an hour or so later that the door opened and the light clicked on. Claudia bustled in, dressed informally in jeans and a Puffa jacket, clutching a bag of shopping and humming to herself. She turned to go into the kitchen, caught sight of Bailey sitting in the armchair, emitted a small shriek and jumped back in shock, dropping her shopping on the floor with a loud clunk.

'Who the fuck are you?!' she gasped. Her face twisted from alarm to anger. 'How the hell did you get in here?'

Bailey stood up. Claudia took two steps back, her eyes widening in fear.

'I'm not going to hurt you,' said Bailey gently, holding up both palms.

'I'll call the police,' said Claudia, her voice wavering uncertainly.

'I am the police,' said Bailey, pulling out her warrant card and holding it up.

Claudia peered at the card and then frowned suspiciously. 'You're not allowed to just bust in here like this. Even I know that much.'

Bailey ignored her. 'I need some answers.'

'I haven't done anything wrong,' said Claudia defensively.

'I need to talk to Mister Snigiss.'

At the mention of the name, Claudia's doe eyes grew larger still and she shrank a little.

'Who are you?' she whispered.

'It doesn't matter who I am. I just need to talk to Mister Snigiss.'

'Are you with them?' she asked warily.

'Who?'

'There was someone else asking about Mister Snigiss. A man. Hassling some of the other girls.'

The Molloys, thought Bailey. It had to be. Only a few days had passed since the gangland interrogation of Marcus and already their hunt for Mister Snigiss was well under way. The sense of urgency swelled within her.

'I'm not with them,' said Bailey. 'All I want to do is meet with Mister Snigiss. I need to talk to him for personal reasons. And I know you can get in contact with him.'

Claudia shook her head with a horrified expression.

'No one meets Mister Snigiss. No one! That's the whole point. You never see him. No one sees him. I've never seen him. I've never even talked to him… not directly anyway.'

'Mister Snigiss is in danger. Those other people who are looking for him. They're out for revenge. There was a car bomb. Mister Snigiss was responsible.'

On hearing the words 'car bomb', Claudia blanched and swallowed.

'You need to get out of my flat now,' she whispered hoarsely. 'I can't talk to you about that.'

Bailey eyed Claudia closely. 'Tiffany. She died in the car bomb. You knew her, didn't you?'

Claudia now looked overtly distressed, her beautiful face suddenly sallow and drawn.

'I said I can't talk about it.' She looked around fearfully. 'Please leave.'

'I saw the sex tape you made with Tiffany and that politician.'

Claudia's jaw dropped. 'How could you have seen that?' she gasped.

'Mister Snigiss murdered Tiffany because she made her own tape, didn't he?'

'Tiffany made a mistake,' stammered Claudia. 'She betrayed us. She paid the price. Mister Snigiss punished her.'

Bailey scrutinised Claudia with a detective's eye, noting the microscopic quivering of the lower lip, the slight shaking of the head in self-denial.

'You ratted on Tiffany, didn't you?' said Bailey. 'That's how Mister Snigiss found out about the tape she made. You knew about it and you told him.'

Claudia put her hand to her mouth, aghast, and Bailey knew she'd hit the nail on the head.

'I had to,' gasped Claudia. 'I had to tell him. He would have punished me too otherwise. I didn't know he was going to kill her though. I swear.' Her face creased up with guilt and remorse and she looked like she was about to start crying.

'How did you know about the tape?' Bailey asked.

Claudia's voice started to wobble. 'Stop questioning me. I don't want to talk about it. Just get out of here and leave me alone.'

'Just tell me what happened and I'll leave you in peace. I promise.'

Claudia stared at her in silence for a few long moments, then her shoulders sagged in defeat. 'We'd just done a job. The two of us. Together. I had to make a call, but my phone had died, so I borrowed hers whilst she was in the shower. I knew her PIN because I'd borrowed it before. Anyway, I was just flicking around on her apps, and there was this video app. And that's how I found the video she'd made. The one with the politician. I knew she shouldn't have had it on her phone. We never normally see the videos that Mister Snigiss makes. Only he gets to see those. We don't even know where he hides the cameras. We just meet who he tells us, do what they want, and that's the end of it.'

She swallowed hard and continued. 'When she came out of the shower, I confronted her about it. And she got all defensive. Then she pleaded with me not to tell Mister Snigiss. So I made her explain. She said she was sick of working as a hooker, wanted to make enough money to get out of it for good. So she thought she'd make her own video, make some of her own cash off these punters that Mister Snigiss was filming. They're all rich, powerful, y'know. So she bought this little miniature camera, one of those that feeds back to an app on your phone. And she hid it in the room and made her own video. I mean, I understood where she was coming from with wanting to get out and everything, but I knew it was a bad move. You don't cross someone like Mister Snigiss.'

Claudia's large dark eyes were wide with fear.

'I tried to tell her, I tried to warn her. She was my friend, you know. But she wouldn't listen. I think she figured she'd have enough money to split for good and go somewhere where Mister Snigiss would never find her. She offered to cut me in if I didn't tell Mister Snigiss, a cut of all this cash she said she was going to make from selling it to the media. But I didn't want any part of it, so I refused. But I also told her I wouldn't tell Mister Snigiss. Because she was my friend.' Claudia took an emotional gulp.

Bailey gave an empathetic nod, encouraging her to continue.

'But then, later, the next day, when I thought about it, I got scared. Even though I'd refused to be part of it, I realised that if Tiffany's tape was all over the news, then Mister Snigiss would think that I was involved even if I wasn't and then he'd punish me too. Mister Snigiss once had acid chucked over this hooker who stepped out of line and I didn't want to end up like that. So then I did tell Mister Snigiss, and the next evening Tiffany got blown up. But I didn't know he was going to do that, I swear. I had to tell him though. You understand. I had to. Or else he would have hurt me as well.' At that point, her voice broke completely and she started sobbing outright, large tears streaming down both cheeks.

Bailey stepped up to her and placed a soft hand on her shaking shoulder.

'You did what you had to do,' she said gently. 'And I need to do what I have to do. I have to talk to Mister Snigiss and you're my only way in.'

'You don't want to talk to him,' whispered Claudia, looking at her through tear-rimmed eyes. 'He's dangerous. He's ruthless. He'll kill you. You don't know what he's capable of.'

'I'll take my chances,' said Bailey.

52

Nancy Molloy lived in an unassuming semi-detached house on a quiet suburban street in Wanstead. Her son was always pestering her to move into a larger place in a nicer area, but she wasn't interested in some big flashy mansion like the one he had. This was where she'd grown up and she felt that it was important to stay in touch with your roots. Plus the place held lots of memories for her, not least of her beloved Arthur, and the older she got, the more valuable those memories became.

'Bolo de Mel,' she said. 'From Madeira.'

Stephen Drood, perched on the settee in her front room, nodded as he took a bite of the cake that she'd given him, along with a cup of tea, served, as always, in one of her best bone china teacups. She'd always possessed a sweet tooth and recently she'd become enamoured of this traditional Madeiran dessert.

Sitting in a high-backed leather swivel armchair by the window with Ettie on her lap, Nancy patiently waited as Stephen munched on the cake and swallowed. She watched him with a certain measure of affection. How time flew. It seemed only yesterday that she'd caught him breaking into this very house as a delinquent teenage burglar. Under other circumstances, he might have ended up paying for it with a good maiming, or even his life, but she'd spotted something in him – a latent potential – a seed that if properly watered and tended to would one day bear fruit. And so it had, for he was now one of her most efficient and trusted employees.

In a small symbolic gesture of gratitude, he made an effort on her birthday and every Christmas to get her a new Royal Worcester porcelain figurine to add to her ample collection in the glass-fronted display cabinet which stood in one corner of the living room, for it had been one of these figurines that he'd been clutching in his hand the very first time they met.

'So please tell me you have good news, Stephen,' she said.

It had been several days since she'd sent Stephen out on a mission to investigate Mister Snigiss and she was itching to know what he'd discovered.

'I followed up on Ophidia,' he began. 'Ophidia is the name of a high-end, very exclusive escort service. They're so exclusive that they operate by word of mouth only. So it wasn't easy to find out information about them. But I asked around here and there – some of Adrian's former acquaintances. And I eventually managed to track down a few of the girls. But when I mentioned the name Mister Snigiss, they clammed up pretty quickly. From what I gathered though, none of them has ever met him in the flesh.'

She nodded with interest. 'This Mister Snigiss really likes to keep a low profile, doesn't he?'

Nancy had mulled long and hard over what Marcus had said about Mister Snigiss, for she didn't just accept everything she was told at face value. Eventually, though, she'd decided that he'd probably been telling them as much as he honestly knew – torture had that effect on people. What had impressed her most from his account was just how anonymous this Mister Snigiss had managed to remain, and it surprised her that, given his aspirations, this blackmailing pimp hadn't come to her attention sooner. In any other circumstances, she might almost have been impressed by his ability to stay out of reach, but he'd made the big mistake of killing her son, and for that reason she wasn't prepared to afford him any kind of esteem whatsoever.

'But I don't give up that easily,' said Stephen. 'So I've been asking around elsewhere. Various underworld contacts. To see what the rumour mill threw out.'

'And...?'

'Well, despite the low profile, he's still managed to leave behind him a distinct trail of death, disfigurement and disappearances. Rival pimps and madams, prostitutes who've crossed him, and just about anyone else who's gotten in his way.'

'Like Adrian...' she muttered. 'So what's he playing at? What's his game?'

'Good question. To just call him a pimp is perhaps reductive. I get the impression he's aiming for more than that. He's got ambition. These hookers, this escort service, they're really just a means for him to gain power and control.'

'Through these blackmail sex videos?'

Stephen nodded. 'He's using them to gain leverage over the right people, which in turn allows him to conduct his criminal activities more freely and consolidate his position in the underworld. He's kind of like a hidden puppetmaster, pulling the strings from behind the scenes.'

'Clever...' murmured Nancy. She frowned as a thought occurred. 'So I'm curious. Where did he come from? Surely he didn't just pop up out of nowhere.'

'Well, that's the thing. No one really knows. He emerged from the shadows a few years back, but he's just so secretive that it's hard to find out anything about him beyond hearsay.'

'Anonymity is a wise strategy in our business,' said Nancy, 'but it's not going to save his skin when it comes to me. I will find him and I will kill him.'

'There is one other thing, for what it's worth.'

'Yes?'

'Apparently he has a penchant for poisonous snakes. According to what I heard, he keeps a load of pet cobras. Rumour has it that some poor bastard who crossed him got chucked in a pit of cobras.'

'Cobras? You're having me on! Sounds like a James Bond villain,' she said with a laugh.

'You don't say,' murmured Stephen drily, watching her sitting in the black high-backed leather swivel chair stroking the fluffy white dog on her lap.

'Poisonous snakes! How ostentatious,' she said. 'I think I'll stick to Pomeranians myself.'

Nancy knew all about villains and their predilections for dangerous pets. Usually it was lions or crocodiles or something similar that they kept in their mansions to impress and intimidate guests. The kinds of animals that ate other animals or presented some lethal threat to humans. So poisonous snakes weren't such a stretch...

'The problem,' said Stephen, 'is that we don't know his real name. We don't know what he looks like or how old he is, or even what race he is. We don't know anything about him. And until we do, I don't see how we can find him.'

'There's always a way to get to someone if you really want to,' Nancy replied. 'No one is completely invulnerable.'

They both lapsed into momentary silence. It seemed they'd hit an impasse. Nancy sat there stroking Ettie, looking down at the little Pomeranian as she meticulously analysed the situation in her mind.

After a minute or two she looked back up at Stephen, a sly enigmatic cast to her face.

'You told me this Mister Snigiss keeps cobras,' she began. 'Well, I had to have Ettie's ears syringed the other day.' She looked down at Ettie. 'Didn't I?' she said to the dog in a cooing tone, rubbing her ears. 'And it wasn't cheap either, was it? Oh, no it wasn't.'

Stephen watched patiently, waiting for her to make her point.

Nancy looked up from Ettie. 'Just because Mister Snigiss is this wannabe gangland kingpin, it doesn't mean that his pet cobras don't get ill from time to time. And if your pets get ill you have to take them to the vet. I mean, look at me. I have to take Ettie to the vet just like everyone else. She doesn't go to a special underworld dog vet, she goes to a regular normal vet.'

Stephen looked a bit mystified. 'So his cobras get ill sometimes? So what?'

'Well, I bet you there aren't that many vets who specialise in deadly poisonous snakes like cobras. I bet your run-of-the-mill vet doesn't.'

He nodded, a smile spreading across his face. Now he was beginning to get it.

Nancy continued, 'And I bet you there aren't that many people who are licensed to keep cobras. Because you definitely do need a licence for dangerous creatures like those.'

'I think I see where you're going here,' said Stephen. 'But how do you know Mister Snigiss doesn't just keep them illegally? I mean, he sounds like the kind of person who does what he pleases.'

Nancy nodded. 'A good point. But it's my contention that this Mister Snigiss wants to appear as normal as possible on the surface. Totally legitimate. Just like we do. After all, to the wider world, we are just successful businesspeople who run a string of very profitable enterprises. And I reckon Mister Snigiss operates in exactly the same way if he aspires to be a major-league villain.'

'It takes one to know one,' smiled Stephen.

Nancy grinned. 'Exactly. To all intents and purposes, Mister Snigiss will resemble a model citizen, if he's as clever as you're making out. Of course, he won't be going under the name of Mister Snigiss. That's just his gangland moniker, something to obfuscate his proper identity. In reality, he'll have some regular boring name and a seemingly regular boring existence. But that's exactly how we can get to him.'

'Through his snakes,' murmured Stephen.

'He wouldn't risk getting in trouble with the authorities on account of his exotic pets because that might draw attention to his illicit business activities. No, he'll be all above board. We just need to get our hands on the patient records of vets who specialise in cobras. We could also get hold of the lists held by local councils of people who are licensed to keep cobras. Do that and we might just have ourselves a list of possible contenders for Mister Snigiss. I'm sure a little bit of cash to oil the wheels should do the trick, and if that fails, a bit of "creative" questioning, if you know what I mean. Take Archie with you if that's what's required.'

Stephen smiled and cracked his knuckles. 'It'll be my pleasure. Leave it with me.'

53

Bailey sat at the folding table in the temporary HQ looking at the whiteboard that Frank had set up in the corner of the sparsely furnished room. It was covered in a scrawl of notes and arrows relating to the next and final phase of her undercover operation. She, Frank and Dale had been putting together a plan, trying to work out if there were any angles she'd missed and determining what resources she'd need in order to complete the transaction. It was Monday the twenty-fifth of February and strike day was scheduled to take place in just under two weeks' time. Very soon, the Molloys would be going down.

'Something on your mind, Bailey?' asked Frank, who was standing next to the whiteboard holding a marker pen.

'Eh?'

'You look distracted. Is everything okay?'

The past week or so, Bailey had been preoccupied with Mister Snigiss almost twenty-four hours a day, unable to sleep, unable to concentrate on almost anything else. But of course she couldn't mention that to Frank.

'My green cashmere scarf,' she said, hurriedly pulling up a suitable excuse. 'I mislaid it recently. It's kind of annoying because it's been pretty chilly the past week. I'm trying to think where I left it. Have you seen it around?'

Frank shrugged and shook his head. He looked at Dale who also shrugged.

It was technically true. She had actually lost her scarf. She could swear she'd left it draped over the back of one of the chairs in her apartment. But maybe she'd lost it before that. Maybe she'd left it in that vegan restaurant she'd gone to with Dale. For the life of her, she couldn't recall. There were too many things on her mind and she was starting to make mistakes. And mistakes could be dangerous. She needed to stay on the ball.

Her undercover phone suddenly started to ring in her pocket. She took it out and looked at it. The screen said 'No caller ID'.

'Hello,' she said carefully.

'Bailey Morgan?' A woman's hard steely voice.

With a flash of horror, Bailey realised that the woman had called her on her undercover phone yet was addressing her by her real name. That meant that operational security had somehow been breached. Bailey's stomach turned over in anxiety. She hesitated whether to answer in the affirmative.

'Who is this?' she whispered.

There was a pregnant pause on the line.

'Mister Snigiss will meet you,' said the woman.

Bailey's breath caught in her throat and for a moment she was lost for words. Frank and Dale were now both staring at her, intrigued. They could see that something was up.

Bailey hurriedly got to her feet and made her way out of the front room into the poky bathroom at the back and locked the door behind her.

She swallowed nervously, her mind racing. Now it made sense why the caller knew her real name. She'd told Claudia her real name, had flashed her warrant card, and had given her the number to her under-cover phone. That meant that Claudia must have conveyed her message to Mister Snigiss about wanting to meet. Bailey guessed that the woman she was now speaking to was some kind of intermediary operating on his behalf.

'That's all I'm asking for,' she said, trying to keep her voice steady. 'To meet Mister Snigiss.'

'Mister Snigiss knows about your sister, Bailey,' said the woman matter-of-factly. 'Mister Snigiss knows all about Jennifer. Mister Snigiss knows that's the reason you want to talk.'

Bailey felt dizzy, the walls of the cramped bathroom pressing in on her. She hadn't mentioned Jennifer in anything she'd said to Claudia. That meant Mister Snigiss must have conducted some serious background intel on Bailey. She realised that she was dealing with someone with a very long and dangerous reach. And that scared her.

'Where's Jennifer?' she gasped breathlessly.

'You'll find out everything you need to know when you meet Mister Snigiss,' said the woman. 'Abney Park Cemetery in Stoke Newington. Tomorrow morning at seven o'clock. By the gravestone of Nelly Power.'

'But—'

'And one other thing. You must come alone.'

The woman terminated the call.

Bailey stared at her phone, her thoughts churning. There had been no physical description of Mister Snigiss, no indication of how she might recognise him. It would be Mister Snigiss who approached her. It would be Mister Snigiss who would be in control of the situation.

Standing there in the poky bathroom, Bailey was hit with a wave of misgivings as she recalled everything she'd heard about Mister Snigiss... how he'd had acid thrown over a hooker who'd stepped out of line, how he'd personally planted the car bomb that had blown up Adrian and Tiffany, how he'd deceived and abducted her very own eight-year-old sister and done God knows what to her. Claudia, Marcus, Dave Boakes, her own father... their fearful testimonials swirled together into a dark coalescence of this shadowy evil figure. Mister Snigiss was a vicious pimp who employed blackmail, coercion and murder in a heinous quest for dominance. He was devious, nasty and ruthless, and people were scared of him for very good reason. And she was going to meet him by herself in the middle of a cemetery with no one else around. Was she crazy?

She was well aware that this could be a trap – the chance for Mister Snigiss to conveniently silence the nosey policewoman sister of the little girl he'd abducted all those years ago. And that's why the woman on the call had mentioned Jennifer – just to make sure that Bailey definitely did go along tomorrow. Bailey knew she had no choice but to go anyhow if she was to stand any chance of finding out about Jennifer, and it looked like Mister Snigiss knew that as well...

Emerging from the bathroom, she re-entered the front room to be met by inquisitive gazes from Frank and Dale. She tried to pull herself together and act as if nothing was amiss.

'So who was that then?' said Frank.

'Oh, no one,' she said, trying to keep the stammer of trepidation out of her voice. 'Now, where were we with these guns?'

Frank and Dale swapped glances with each other. Neither of them looked convinced, but they didn't probe any further.

54

That same morning, in St James's Park in central London, Stephen was ambling along next to Nancy, appreciating the sunny weather, observing Ettie as she scampered in front of them on the lead.

The good thing about the Pomeranian, thought Stephen, was that at least she was small and non-threatening. Whenever he was round Rick's house, those two Neapolitan Mastiffs scared him shitless.

Stephen had always liked St James's Park, not least because of its associations with espionage, the corridors of Whitehall being just a short hop away. He often contemplated that, in some other life, with the right upbringing, he could have ended up working as a spy. But as fate had it, he worked for the Molloys and that certainly wasn't a bad gig by any means.

The park seemed an apt location in which to update Nancy on the progress of his investigation. It had been almost a week since their last meeting, and knowing her as he did, he imagined the waiting must have driven her to distraction. He'd worked as fastidiously as possible and he was looking forward to sharing his efforts with Nancy.

'I take it that self-satisfied smile on your face means the last few days haven't been a total waste of time,' she said.

'I did a bit of bribing here and there,' he replied. 'Complemented by a bit of breaking and entering. And I took Archie with me for good measure. And I've come up with a few results.'

'I knew you were the man for the job,' she said.

On conducting the work, he had found himself once again admiring her prescient insight. 'You were right,' he said, puffing up a little. 'There aren't many vets who specialise in cobras. And there definitely aren't many people who own them. In fact I could only find five people in the London area who are licensed to own cobras. I checked each of them out, did a bit of initial recon, managed to get basic personal details on all of them, and I think you'll be interested to hear what I found out.'

'Go on...' said Nancy, barely able to conceal the excitement in her voice.

'The first one is a twenty-five-year-old man living in Neasden with his parents,' said Stephen. 'Likes to enter his snakes into competitions. Crufts for snakes, that kind of thing.'

Nancy shook her head. 'Unlikely. Sounds too young to be Mister Snigiss.'

'Next we've got a thirty-two-year-old woman living in West Kensington. Got the impression she's some kind of spoilt fashionista into Louis Vuitton bags and Gucci sunglasses who also dabbles in dangerous snakes.'

Nancy wrinkled her nose. 'I don't think so.'

'Then we've got a forty-five-year-old man living in Hackney. He's married with kids. Also owns a number of other poisonous snakes. Works for the council in waste disposal.'

'Hmm. Waste disposal? Doesn't sound like Mister Snigiss to me. I don't think he'd have kids either.'

'Next up is a seventy-four-year-old woman living in Bermondsey. She's currently confined to a wheelchair.'

Nancy snorted a laugh. 'Nope.'

He could tell she was starting to wonder if he actually had come up with anything useful after all.

He raised one eyebrow with an impish smile. 'And finally we have a fifty-five year-old man living alone in a large apartment on Edgware Road in an exclusive block populated mostly by rich Lebanese. Seems to be fairly wealthy but not ostentatiously so. Doesn't appear to go to work, as far as I could gather. From what I observed, he's a bit of a recluse. Goes by the name of James Grecken.'

Nancy smiled. 'You were keeping the best till last, weren't you? He sounds like he could be our man. I think we should check out this James Grecken in a bit more detail.'

Stephen couldn't have agreed more. He had the feeling he would quite enjoy paying James Grecken a little visit in the very near future.

55

Dale scrutinised Bailey over the top of his latte. They were sitting in a café in Stratford, Bailey having suggested that the two of them grab a coffee following the planning session earlier that morning.

'Is this about what I think it's about?' he asked.

'What?'

'That phone call.'

'Was it that obvious?'

'You went off into the bathroom and then when you came back in, you looked even more shell-shocked than when you'd answered the phone. Who was it?'

Bailey chewed her lip in debate, still unsure about telling Dale the truth of the matter. But then telling him about it was the whole reason she'd dragged him here in the first place.

He stared at her inquisitively with his bright blue eyes.

'Bailey?' he said in a warning voice, raising his eyebrows. 'Are you up to something you shouldn't be?'

She took a deep breath. 'I couldn't tell Frank because I know he wouldn't approve.'

'Tell Frank what?'

'Promise you won't tell him.'

He looked puzzled. 'Well, you haven't told me what this is all about yet.'

She stared at him steadfastly.

He threw up his hands. 'Okay, I promise not to tell Frank.'

She paused and took an even deeper breath.

'I'm going to meet Mister Snigiss tomorrow morning.'

Dale's eyes widened and his mouth dropped open. 'Bailey, you were explicitly told to desist in that investigation!'

'I have to go. I have to find out about my sister. I have to talk to Mister Snigiss before the Molloys get to him. I know they're working hard to identify him, and I don't know how close they are. If they kill him, I'll never find out about Jennifer.'

Bailey knew her father didn't have much longer left, his condition having deteriorated substantially in the past few weeks, and she was therefore more conscious than ever of the urgency driving her quest to confront Mister Snigiss.

Dale shook his head incredulously. 'You are one stubborn person, Bailey Morgan. You just don't give up, do you?'

'I'm placing my trust in you, Dale. You won't tell Frank, will you?' she pleaded.

He looked conflicted for a few moments, then sighed. 'No, I won't tell Frank. But I feel that what you're doing might be dangerous, Bailey. You might get hurt. Or worse...'

'That's why I'm telling you,' she said. 'There's no one else I can tell who I trust enough.'

A modest flattered smile twitched across his face.

She fixed him with a long look. 'You know how when a girl goes on a date with someone she's never met before, she tells her friends and family where she's going, just in case something happens to her? Well, that's what this is. I wanted to let you know where I was meeting him just in case something happens to me.'

His eyes widened in consternation. 'This is no date, Bailey. By all accounts, this is someone really dangerous.'

She sighed. 'I know. But I have to meet him. He knows about

Jennifer. He's going to tell me all about her tomorrow. I've got no choice but to go.'

Dale eyed her gravely. 'Okay, so where are you meeting him?'

'Abney Park Cemetery. Tomorrow morning. Seven o'clock.'

He raised his eyebrows. 'A cemetery, huh? And an abandoned one at that. Abney Park hasn't been used for years.' He scratched his chin. 'Well, seeing as you've been expressly forbidden from pursuing this investigation, I imagine any kind of official back-up team is out of the question. But I'll tell you what, I'll come with you. I'll follow at a distance, just to make sure that you're safe.'

'No!' she exclaimed. 'He said to come alone.'

'But it could be some kind of trap!'

'There is that possibility. But I can't afford to mess it up at this stage. It's a risk I'll just have to take.'

'I'll make sure he doesn't see me. I'll make sure to keep a really low profile.'

Bailey shook her head. 'He said to come alone and he meant it. I can't afford to jeopardise this opportunity to find out about Jennifer. It might be the only chance I get. I don't want you to follow me.'

He looked perplexed. 'If you don't want me to be there with you, then why did you tell me?'

She took a breath. 'People who go looking for missing people sometimes end up going missing themselves. My parents already have one missing daughter. And it's completely torn them up inside not knowing what's happened to her. If I tell you where I went and I go missing, you can at least let them know some of the details. It won't be a complete mystery, like it was with Jennifer. If something happens to me, I want you to visit them... and you know... tell them...'

After what had happened to Jennifer, Bailey felt guilty about potentially having to put her parents through the emotional wringer like this, especially her father right now, but she knew she had no choice.

Dale nodded grimly 'Okay.'

'But please promise me you won't actually follow me there.'

'I promise.' He held up three fingers in a Scout's salute. But his face was deadly serious.

56

A fine miasma of early morning fog blanketed the Edgware Road. Stephen squinted through the windscreen of his car at the entrance to the luxury apartment block where James Grecken lived. He had been parked there since six o'clock. It was now almost six thirty and the faint glow of sunrise was beginning to edge through the mist. He wondered how much longer he'd have to wait before Grecken showed any signs of activity.

'This is so fucking boring,' grunted Shane, who was sitting in the back seat. 'I'm sure I could have spent an extra hour in bed. I mean, is this bloke really going to be out and about at this time in the morning?'

'Are we even sure that this is the bloke?' said Archie, who was sitting in the passenger seat cleaning his nails with the tip of a switchblade.

'That's the whole point of us being here,' Stephen replied. 'As soon as he leaves, I'll break in and have a snoop around his flat. If it looks like he's our man, then I'll call you guys to come up. And he'll have a nice welcoming committee when he returns.'

'What does he look like?' asked Shane.

Stephen was about to answer when he noticed the door of the apartment block swing open and a man emerge.

'He looks exactly like that,' he said.

Shane and Archie looked up sharply.

The middle-aged man who'd just walked out of the building was of medium height, slim and well groomed, with the patrician demeanour of a silver fox. Clad in a beige linen suit and clutching a leather port-folio case, he moved with the casual self-assured stride of someone either wealthy or powerful enough never to need to hurry anywhere. He wasn't accompanied by any minders and he didn't look particularly bothered that anyone might be observing him, but then, thought Stephen, perhaps he was so confident in his anonymity that these things just weren't a concern.

'That's him?' asked Shane.

'That's him,' confirmed Stephen.

'Maybe he's just nipping to the corner shop to get a pint of milk,' Archie suggested.

Grecken walked up to a black Bentley, opened the door and got in. Moments later, the car pulled away from the kerb, growled off down the street and disappeared around the corner.

'Or maybe not,' said Archie.

'Why don't we follow him?' said Shane.

'No point,' Stephen replied. 'It'll be much quicker and easier to work out who he is from what's inside his flat. Trust me, I've done this kind of thing many times before.'

Leaning forward, he opened the glove compartment and took out his set of breaking-and-entering tools. He pushed open the car door then paused a moment and turned back to them.

'And if you see him return while I'm still in there, then give me the heads-up pronto.'

'Yeah sure,' yawned Shane. 'Just get on with it.'

57

At around the same time, just over six miles away, Bailey was standing outside the large iron gates of Abney Park Cemetery, peering through the railings into the misty undergrowth beyond.

Once again she was starting to have second thoughts, consumed as she was by a cloying sense of dread at the impending encounter with Mister Snigiss. She suddenly regretted not allowing Dale to be here watching her back. Too late for that now though.

She suppressed her fear and looked up at the sky. At least the sun was starting to rise. She didn't fancy trekking around inside that cemetery in the pitch-black with only a torch to guide her.

She blew on her hands, tucked her baseball cap lower and huddled deeper into the collar of her Hugo Boss jacket. It was a chilly morning and a damp fog shrouded the streets of North London. There was a bit of early morning traffic along Stamford Hill just behind her, but other than that, things were still pretty quiet.

Abney Park Cemetery was located in Stoke Newington in the London borough of Hackney. It hadn't functioned as a working cemetery for well over a hundred years and was now largely overgrown. These days it was a heritage site and a nature reserve... and also, apparently, a popular gay cruising spot.

It didn't open until eight in the morning, so Bailey knew she had to find her own way in. She looked up at the imposing gates, then glanced around to check that there was no one else in the vicinity. Grasping the iron railings, she hauled herself up, minding not to accidentally impale herself on the spikes at the top.

Dropping down on the other side, she straightened up and looked around. Paths stretched off into the tangled woods, disappearing into the vaporous murk. Without further ado, she set off at a quick pace, her heart thumping nervously in anticipation of the meeting which lay ahead of her.

All around stood gravestones from another era, receding into the tangled thickets, protruding from the ground at odd angles, skewed by decades of subsidence. From grand mausoleums to humble headstones, all were now left to the embrace of nature, the crumbling stone covered in moss, the carved cherubs and angels wreathed in ivy. Many of the names inscribed on the decaying masonry were no longer legible, having been slowly erased by the ravages of time.

The further she advanced into the sepulchral gloom, the more the noise of the traffic on Stamford Hill faded, until she was left walking alone in an eerie silence punctuated only by the sounds of her footsteps crunching on the gravelly dirt. She found herself shivering, distinctly aware that the chill she felt was due to more than just the cold air. This place was spooky to say the least.

She stopped for a moment, trying to gauge her whereabouts. She'd googled the rendezvous point beforehand and she was fairly sure she was heading the right way. Nelly Power, all but forgotten these days, had been a music hall performer back in the nineteenth century, and was one of the better-known occupants of this place. Her gravestone apparently lay somewhere along the trail that Bailey was walking along.

There was a sharp crackle in the undergrowth. Bailey spun around, dropping into the jiu-jitsu *yoi* stance, her legs apart, slightly bent at the knee, and her arms in front, fists clenched. She tensely scanned the bushes, bracing herself for a potential assault, acutely aware of just how vulnerable she was to some kind of ambush.

She held herself like that for perhaps ten seconds or so, her eyes flickering nervously from side to side, before slowly straightening up and relaxing a little. It had probably just been some animal scuttling through the shrubbery.

She continued on her way, paying close attention to the names on the wonky moss-covered stones. The sky was lighter now, the sun having risen fast behind the thick veil of fog, allowing her to read the faded writing more easily.

With a burst of relief, she finally stumbled across it – a relatively plain marble headstone bearing the inscription:

In Loving Memory of Nelly Power who departed this life January 20th 1887 aged 32 years

followed by a short religious epitaph.

She looked around her. There was no one else here... yet. Glancing at her watch she saw that it was six fifty-eight. Two minutes to go. Two minutes until—

She froze.

The unmistakeable sound of footsteps. A soft rhythmic crunching growing ever closer.

Then, out of the mist ahead, the outline of a figure began to coalesce.

Bailey's breathing quickened and her heart rate increased. She peered desperately into the fog, and as the person became clearer, she started to make out the distinctive profile of a fedora hat.

'Mister Snigiss?' she whispered.

58

Stephen squeezed the trigger on the lock-pick gun. Once. Twice. Three times. Sufficient to automatically align the pins inside the tumbler of the door lock. Twisting on the small torque wrench that he'd also inserted, the door clicked open smoothly and he slipped quietly into Grecken's apartment.

Standing there in the hallway, he took a moment to savour the thrill of successfully breaking and entering into a stranger's residence. It brought back that old buzz from his teenage years when burglary had been his primary occupation, his small stature suited perfectly for wriggling in and out of difficult places. That had been before he'd moved up in the world. Before he'd met Nancy Molloy.

He inhaled deeply. He liked to breathe in the smell of whatever place he broke into, as if by imbibing it he somehow made the ground his own, albeit temporarily. He wrinkled his nose. This place smelt... weird. The strong aroma of air freshener didn't completely succeed in masking a distinctly foetid odour emanating from somewhere in the apartment.

He immediately started to analyse his surroundings, his mind rapidly breaking down and categorising everything he saw. Whenever he broke into someone's house, he found it best to operate on the assumption that they could return at any minute, so it was his habit to move as fast as possible.

The apartment was spacious, with high ceilings and at least six rooms by the looks of it. The polished wooden floor was covered with expensive Persian rugs and the white walls were decorated with numerous framed photographs of snakes, mostly artful close-ups of cobras in various poses. It was immediately obvious that Grecken was into snakes in a big way.

Stephen moved down the hallway, treading softly with the stealth and grace of a cat. His intention was to methodically go from room to room until he found what he was looking for. He didn't know exactly what that was, but he'd know when he found it.

The kitchen lay immediately to his right, but he decided to leave that until last. Instead he headed down the hallway and turned into the first room off to the left.

Immediately he recoiled in disgust. On all sides, he was confronted with racks of glass cages full of snakes. The foetid odour was particularly strong in here and Stephen realised that it must be coming from the snakes. Up until now he hadn't known that snakes smelt of anything, but now that he did, it only increased his dislike of the creatures. He'd never liked them very much in the first place – the way they slithered and hissed, and it just seemed wrong to him that they had no limbs.

Some of them began to respond to his presence, rearing up and spreading their hoods, whispering sibilantly, their horrible forked tongues flickering in and out. He shuddered in revulsion and carefully retreated backwards out of the room.

Turning around, he entered the room across the hallway. Going by the thick oak desk and numerous bookcases, Stephen deduced that it was probably a study. Lying both on the desk and piled on the floor was a collection of sophisticated and expensive-looking camera equipment – lenses of varying sizes, tripods and a number of camera bodies.

Glancing at the wall, he noticed a framed certificate. Peering closer, he saw that it was an award to Grecken for being 'Reptile Photographer of the Year'. He frowned, struck by a jab of doubt. Would someone of Mister Snigiss's repute really be the same kind of person who won awards for taking photographs of reptiles?

Turning his attention to the bookcase, a large hardback caught Stephen's eye, one of those expensive coffee-table books, placed face-out for full effect. The title was *The Cobra: King of Snakes*. On the front cover was a big colourful photo of a cobra with its hood spread, baring its fangs. Looking closer, beneath the title, Stephen saw the words, 'Photographs by Jim Grecken'.

Scanning the spines of the other books in the bookcase, he saw several similar ones that also credited Jim Grecken. Most of them seemed to be about cobras.

Stephen scratched his head. It appeared that Grecken was some kind of wildlife photographer who specialised in snakes, specifically cobras.

He felt a sharp pang of frustration, annoyed with himself that his preliminary research hadn't picked up on Grecken's profession. He supposed he could snoop around a bit more, but his instincts, plus what he had seen so far, told him Grecken was not the ruthless underworld player that they were looking for.

With a sinking heart, he took out his phone and prepared to call Nancy. He knew only too well how she hated hearing bad news. It would put her in one of her moods and she was never fun to be around when she was like that.

59

As the figure emerged from the mist, Bailey began to make out more details. Below the black fedora hat, the person was slender, swaying slightly from side to side on heels.

It was a woman.

Her features became distinct as she moved closer. Probably in her early thirties, she had an angular but pretty face with hard grey eyes that scrutinised Bailey intently from beneath the brim of the hat. She was dressed stylishly in a figure-hugging black trench coat with the collar turned up against the cold.

The woman stopped around two metres away from Bailey. They both stood there in the misty graveyard staring at each other in silence.

Bailey's mind swam with confusion, her expectations totally confounded. Was this Mister Snigiss? It couldn't be. Surely. Not only was this a woman, she was way too young to have been the person who'd abducted her sister. She concluded that Mister Snigiss must have sent someone else in his place. But who was this woman and why was she wearing Mister Snigiss's hat?

The woman examined Bailey with her steely grey eyes, the gaze cutting through her like the blade of a knife. She had presence, that was for sure. But there was something else. Something about her that tugged at Bailey on some deep instinctual level.

'You came alone.' It was a statement rather than a question. The woman spoke brusquely in a neutral accent.

Bailey nodded in affirmation. 'I recognise your voice,' she said. 'It was you I talked to on the phone, wasn't it?'

The woman inclined her head fractionally, confirming to Bailey that her supposition was correct.

'But you're not Mister Snigiss,' said Bailey. 'I came here to see Mister Snigiss.'

'You're looking at Mister Snigiss,' the woman replied.

Bailey screwed up her face and shook her head. 'That's impossible.'

'Why?'

'I thought you would be a man. And much older. You're not at all what I expected.'

The hint of an amused smirk flickered across the woman's face.

'And you're not quite how I expected you to be either,' she said. 'Mind you, twenty-four years is a long time.'

It took a few seconds for the implication to sink in, such was the gravity of it. And when it finally did, it was like a nuclear bomb had gone off inside Bailey's head, instantly decimating the foundations of the entire worldview she'd carefully constructed for herself over the course of the past two decades.

'Jennifer!' she gasped.

She staggered on her feet, stunned by the realisation, the world suddenly spinning around her. Forcibly composing herself, she looked at the woman anew, physical recognition now surging up from deep within to hit her square-on with the force of a speeding truck.

Superimposing the cherubic face of her eight-year-old sister onto the features of the woman before her, the traces of resemblance, though very faint, now became apparent – the distinctive small upturned mouth, the pronounced cheekbones, and the grey eyes so similar to Bailey's own.

Jennifer was a little taller than Bailey. She always had been. And thinner. And more beautiful, in the classic sense. But a Baltic harshness underlay this woman's beauty, as if it had been honed to a fine edge on cold sharp rocks.

'You're alive,' whispered Bailey. A choked sob issued from her throat and tears came to her eyes. Overcome by emotion, she rushed forwards to embrace Jennifer. But Jennifer stiffened and took a step back, holding up a hand defensively.

Bailey stopped in her tracks, blinking the tears from her eyes to scrutinise the woman standing in front of her. She saw now that there was something cold and stand-offish about her, an aversion to physical contact. But that was okay. After all, they hadn't seen each for twenty-four years. No need to hurry things. There would surely be time to get to know each other again. Time to catch up. There was so much to talk about, Bailey didn't know where to start.

And at this very moment, rendered inarticulate by the flood of sentiment overwhelming her, all she could say once again was: 'You're alive.'

'Not in the way you think,' said Jennifer.

'I don't understand.'

'Jennifer Morgan died twenty-four years ago. The person you see now is someone completely different.'

'But... but... how...' stammered Bailey. 'How did you...?'

There were questions suddenly. So many questions.

Jennifer smiled calmly. 'All in good time, Bailey. I'll tell you everything. After all, that was the whole reason I agreed to meet you.'

She stepped up to Bailey and peered closely at her face. She lifted a hand, and with the tips of her slender pale fingers, gently pushed Bailey's loose-hanging lock of hair aside to reveal the scar on her cheek.

'What happened to you?' she asked.

Bailey drew her head back. 'What happened to me?' she said indignantly. 'What happened to you?'

Jennifer sighed. 'It's a long story.'

'I need to know. I deserve to know.'

Jennifer stared at her silently for a few moments, then gave a small shrug and started to speak.

60

'What's there to say? Except that Jennifer was in the wrong place at the wrong time. There was no conspiracy or master plan to abduct her. She was just plain unlucky, that was all. How could she have known that evil would be lurking there on a dull suburban street on a quiet Sunday afternoon?

'You see, she'd been playing Barbie dolls with her friend, Sarah, who lived just up the street when she remembered that her mother was planning to make one of her special carrot cakes that afternoon. Jennifer was keen to get home and try a slice before her little sister, Bailey, gobbled it all up, so she said goodbye to Sarah and headed back to her house.

'So there she was, walking along the pavement, her head so filled up with thoughts of carrot cake that she didn't even notice the dirty white van that had suddenly appeared on the kerb, crawling along just behind her.

'With a loud clunk, the door of the van swung open and rough hands reached out and grabbed her right off the street. And before she knew it, she was bundled up in the darkness in some kind of smelly sack and the van was speeding off. And that was the last anyone ever

saw of Jennifer Morgan.' She paused a moment, her grey eyes boring
into Bailey.

Bailey stared back, transfixed, holding her breath in horror, as she
finally learned the truth of Jennifer's abduction. Hearing her sister
refer to herself so clinically in the third person made it seem all the
more disturbing.

Jennifer continued, her voice quiet but penetrating.

'The men who took her were the worst kind of men. Sick, evil men.
They made Jennifer do things. Awful things. Things that she didn't
understand. That she wasn't ready to do. Things that no child should
ever do. They kept her captive for many years, bringing other men in
from time to time, letting them use her body as they saw fit.'

Having occasionally come across similar such cases in her career,
Bailey registered with a deep sickening realisation that her sister had
been subjected to the most appalling type of fate, and it revolted her to
know that she'd been used in this way. She listened in mute shock as
her sister carried on speaking in her weirdly detached manner.

'Jennifer knew that if she was going to survive all the bad things
that were being done to her then she had to become strong and fearless... just like Mister Snigiss.

'Mister Snigiss had been her friend before, and Mister Snigiss had
always been there for her. And now that Jennifer was in this awful situation, Mister Snigiss was there with her too, by her side, giving her
strength, urging her not to give up. But Jennifer knew she wasn't strong
enough. Not like Mister Snigiss, who was brave and strong and fearless,
and capable of doing things that Jennifer was unable to do. So, in that
dark place, just as Jennifer had reached the very limits of her endurance,
Mister Snigiss offered to take over. Mister Snigiss would become Jennifer.
And so that's what happened. Jennifer "died" and all that was left in her
place was Mister Snigiss. And she's been Mister Snigiss ever since.'

Bailey stared at her sister, hardly believing what she was hearing.
Now, in the depths of those grey eyes, she detected a hint of derange-
ment. Bailey was no psychologist, but she knew enough about trauma

to understand that an internal dissociation had taken place within Jennifer in order to allow her to cope with the severity of her experiences, and this dissociation had manifested itself in the form of the Mister Snigiss persona.

As if to confirm Bailey's thoughts, Jennifer spoke once more. 'Looking back, I suppose it wasn't such a hard transition really. Jennifer had always known deep down that Mister Snigiss had come from inside her, had always been a part of her. Whenever she summoned Mister Snigiss, Mister Snigiss would come.' She paused. 'Only this time, Mister Snigiss stayed for good.'

'Why didn't you come back?' gasped Bailey. 'You're alive. You survived. Why didn't you return? I thought you were dead. All these years. Mum. Dad. They—'

'Return?' Jennifer raised an eyebrow. 'How could I? After what I'd been through. No. It changed me. Forever. Irrevocably. I came of age in that dark, twisted world. I was a prostitute, you know. From the age of eight until the age of twenty-eight. It was all I knew. To be sold to men, to be used by them. But I perfected my craft. Became an expert. And ultimately I graduated to something better. I set up my own business, with a whole stable of women working for me.'

'Ophidia,' whispered Bailey.

'In regular parlance, you'd probably refer to me as a "madam".'

Jennifer's voice was cold and dispassionate, revealing not a single residual trace of the warm chirpy little girl Bailey had once known.

'People are scared of you,' said Bailey. 'That car bomb. Tiffany. Did you really do all of that? Is it really true? I can't believe it, Jennifer. Tell me it isn't true.'

Jennifer sighed. She looked at Bailey with pity. 'Mister Snigiss has done some very bad things. But they were necessary in order to survive, in order to prosper. It's the way of the world... or at least it is in the world that Mister Snigiss occupies.'

'But it was you who planted the car bomb, wasn't it? You personally. You killed them.'

Jennifer gave a light shrug, as if it wasn't a big deal. 'If you want to get something done quickly with the least amount of trouble, I generally find it's better to do it yourself. Anyhow, it was a very simple device. A child could operate it.'

Bailey shook her head in disbelief. Her own sister was an out-and-out murderer.

'Are you going to arrest me?' said Jennifer. It almost sounded like a challenge.

'I can't. The murder investigation has been shut down. To protect Lewis Ballantyne.' Bailey paused. 'And I guess that suits you just fine. Once he gets in, you'll have him in your pocket, because you've got that footage of him, haven't you? You'll have City Hall at your beck and call.'

Jennifer smiled coldly. 'I was onto him as soon as he announced his candidacy for Mayor last November.' She gave a contemptuous sneer. 'He was weak. He was so easy to set up. These politicians. These men. They're easy prey. They're asking for it.'

Bailey couldn't believe how twisted her sister had become.

'I became a policewoman because of you,' said Bailey hoarsely. 'To get justice. And now it turns out that you're little more than one of the common criminals I've spent my life trying to lock up.'

'Considering what I went through, I didn't have a lot of choice in the matter. So much was taken from me. Now I want something back. And I'm going to take it and no one's going to stand in my way. Not even you.'

Bailey swallowed. 'Are you going to kill me, Jennifer? Your own sister?'

Jennifer eyed her for a few long moments. 'The reason I agreed to meet you here today, Bailey, was to warn you. Don't pursue Mister Snigiss any further. Mister Snigiss doesn't like people poking into his business matters and Mister Snigiss doesn't want you to get hurt.'

The threat was more than implicit.

They both stared at each other mutely for what seemed like a long time, then Bailey broke the silence.

'Well, maybe Mister Snigiss should be more concerned about his own safety,' said Bailey. 'I don't know if you're aware, but one of the people you blew up in the car bomb was a member of a powerful crime family called the Molloys and they're out for your blood.'

'Pah!' sneered Jennifer. 'I can take care of myself.'

Bailey suddenly felt emotionally drained. Surely there was still some spark of something from before left in her sister.

'Dad's got cancer,' said Bailey. 'He hasn't got long to go. It's serious. It's stage four. He's been moved to a hospice down in Sydenham.'

Jennifer shrugged indifferently. 'I barely remember him. Or Mum. They died a long time ago, along with Jennifer. That life means nothing to me any more.'

'He never gave up on you,' said Bailey, angered at Jennifer's dismissive tone. 'He's been searching for you all these years. Everyone else thought you were dead, including me. But not him. He was convinced you were still alive somewhere out there. And it turns out he was right.'

'Well, I don't think he'd like what he finds. Better that he goes to his grave remembering the innocent little girl from twenty years ago.'

Bailey disliked what she was hearing. Unwilling to believe it, she desperately tried to think of some way to connect with the old Jennifer.

Suddenly remembering, she eased the folded scrap of paper out of her jacket pocket, having secreted it there earlier that morning. It was Jennifer's felt-tip drawing of Mister Snigiss. Bailey opened it up and handed it to her sister.

A faintly quizzical expression crossed Jennifer's face, to be replaced by a smile of recognition.

'Well, well...' she murmured.

'Dad carries it with him everywhere he goes... Or at least he used to. It's like his special charm. It symbolises his belief in you, that you're still alive.'

Bailey paused to contemplate the cruel irony of it. How would her father react on hearing that Jennifer was alive but completely disinclined to see him? It would probably devastate him.

Jennifer scrutinised the piece of paper with the hint of a smile, tracing her fingertip over the wiggly line that was Mister Snigiss's pet snake. 'I do have my very own pet snake now, you know. I had to get one, obviously, as Mister Snigiss. I have several in fact. Cobras to be precise. Just like Mister Snigiss had. Magnificent creatures.' She looked up at Bailey, handing her back the piece of paper. Then, pausing a moment as if thinking something over, she reached inside her collar and unhooked a thin gold chain from around her neck. She handed it to Bailey. 'Here, I want you to have this.'

Bailey took the necklace. Attached to the chain was a small pendant made of dark green stone, set into a gold mount. Looking closer, she could see that it was carved in the form of a coiled snake.

'It's a cobra,' said Jennifer. 'It's an Ancient Egyptian amulet.'

Bailey examined it, turning it over in the palm of her hand. On the back of the amulet, there was some form of inscription – a series of tiny Egyptian hieroglyphs cut into the green stone.

'You always loved Ancient Egypt,' she murmured.

'They used to worship snakes, you know. Especially cobras. Held them in very high regard.'

'Is it genuine?' asked Bailey.

'Oh yes. It's Middle Kingdom. About three and a half thousand years old. It's a protective amulet. It'll keep you safe.'

As she stared down at the amulet, Bailey felt completely disoriented by everything that had happened this morning, and she was finding it hard to get a grip on things.

'First you threaten me, now you want to protect me.'

Jennifer shrugged off the contradiction. 'Keep it to remember me by because you won't be seeing me again.'

Bailey looked up sharply. Jennifer bore a grave expression.

She spoke in her hard, steely voice. 'Don't ever try and find me again, Bailey. And remember my warning. It's a dark and very dangerous world that I live in, and you don't want to go there.'

First bewilderment, then crushing disappointment swept across Bailey.

'No, Jennifer! Please! We can still—'

'This is where we say goodbye, Bailey.'

A kaleidoscope of childhood memories tore through Bailey and she was gripped by a reflexive primal love. This was her sister. For so long they'd been apart. And now, too soon, she would be gone again forever.

'No!' she exclaimed. 'Please, Jennifer! Don't go!'

But Jennifer had already turned on her heels and had begun to stalk off through the mist.

Bailey started to follow, but her steps soon petered out for she knew deep down that it would be futile to pursue her.

'Jennifer,' she whispered sadly. 'You don't know how much I missed you.'

But Jennifer had gone, the mist closing like curtains behind her.

61

Bailey left the cemetery in a daze, walking along the pavement oblivious to the world waking up around her. It was getting on towards eight o'clock and it looked like the mist was starting to lift. The streets were busier now and the traffic was picking up as people headed to work and went about their ordinary lives. But that all seemed like a meaningless facade to Bailey right now.

She reached her car but kept on walking. She needed to walk. She needed to think. She needed to get her head straight. The shockwaves of the meeting were still reverberating through her.

Jennifer was alive.

One part of Bailey desperately wanted to rejoice at the fact. But at the same time she was profoundly disturbed. Her sister was rotten to the core, irredeemably damaged. Bailey could understand this in part, given the disgusting and awful things Jennifer had been put through as a child, but it distressed her deeply to see that there was absolutely no light left inside her sister that she could grasp onto.

How could she ever tell her parents? The truth of it would probably finish her dad off for good. In some ways, Bailey wished she'd never gone down this road.

The thoughts turned over and over in her mind. Enough to drive her crazy. It was like a rug had been pulled out from under her. Her whole world had collapsed in a single encounter and she wondered if she'd ever be able to rebuild it. Right at this moment it didn't seem so.

She trudged along the pavement, robotically putting one foot in front of the other. And after a while she became aware of a car driving along slowly beside her. She turned to look, recognising the midnight-silver colour of Dale's Tesla Model S.

Bailey stopped. The window wound down. Dale looked out at her with an expression of concern on his face.

'You promised not to come here,' she said accusingly.

'I was worried about you.'

'Did you follow me into the cemetery?'

He shook his head. 'No. I didn't want to risk messing up your meeting. So I waited up the road in my car. It seemed better than nothing.' He eyed her anxiously. 'I've been following you for the past five minutes or so. You've been walking along in a complete daze. What the hell happened in there? Thank God you're safe at least.'

She stood there for a few moments, looking into his bright blue eyes, unable to put words to what she'd just experienced.

'Why don't you get in?' he said. 'I'll drive you back to your car.'

She hesitated for a few moments, glanced around instinctively to check if anyone was watching her, then got in the Tesla.

Dale turned to study her for a few moments.

'Are you okay, Bailey?'

But she just stared straight ahead without replying, still lost in thought.

'You look really out of it, Bailey. I've never seen you like this before.'

'I'm fine,' she murmured, blinking herself out of her trance.

'Did you meet Mister Snigiss?' he asked tentatively.

She finally turned to meet his gaze, her grey eyes boring into him. She nodded slowly.

'And?' he whispered nervously.

'I can't talk about it.'

He frowned. 'But did you find out about your sister?'

She nodded, remembering the snake necklace in her pocket. Was it still there? Did it really exist? It was physical proof of something so unbelievable to Bailey that she had to convince herself right now that it hadn't been some dream or hallucination. She slipped her hand into her pocket to feel for it. It was still there.

Dale glanced at her pocket curiously, then up at her face. He looked deeply puzzled. Then his eyes widened in realisation and his mouth dropped open. 'She's alive, isn't she? Your sister's still alive.'

Bailey looked up at him sharply, taken aback by the incisiveness of his guess. But she shouldn't have been too surprised; he was a smart guy and very perceptive. She desperately wanted to tell him all about it. But she knew she couldn't. Not the full truth of it. Not now. Not yet. It was too much for her, let alone anyone else, to take on board.

So she just bit down on her lip and gave him another nod.

'So where is she?' he asked breathlessly.

'Right now,' she said. 'I haven't the slightest clue.'

She stared into his concerned handsome face.

'Someday I'll tell you what happened, Dale,' she said. 'But I can't right now. So please don't ask me anything more about it.'

He smiled sympathetically. 'You can talk about it whenever you're ready, Bailey.'

As he pulled away from the kerb, Bailey realised that was the problem – she didn't know if she'd ever be ready.

62

Nancy Molloy reflected bitterly on Grecken. She'd been so sure that he was their man. It had been so disappointing to find out that he wasn't. Maybe they needed to cast their net further afield. Or maybe they'd just been barking up the wrong tree with all that snake stuff. She hated it when she was wrong about things.

There had to be another way to find Mister Snigiss. She was certain of it. She wasn't just going to give up. Oh no. She wasn't that kind of person. She had grit and determination. That was why the Molloy family were still holding the whip hand after all these years.

She was sitting in her high-backed leather armchair, facing out of the window with Ettie on her lap, fiddling with her Dupont lighter, repeatedly flicking it open and closed, each 'cling' causing the dog to give a tiny twitch.

Nancy ground her teeth and stared through the net curtains with her small dark eyes at the quiet suburban street outside. A young couple walked past pushing a baby in a stroller. The sight of them brought back memories of her early days with Arthur when she'd been a young mother having just given birth to Adrian.

Time passed so quickly and before you knew it all that was left were the memories and the photos. The mantelpiece behind her was cluttered with a display of framed photographs, the most prominent of which was a large one of her and Arthur on their wedding day, the happiest day of her life. Others depicted her two sons at various stages of their lives, from childhood to manhood. And there were older pictures still, her mother and father back in the sixties, and her grand-parents in the forties...

In the corner of the room was an old-style vinyl record player on a cherry-wood stand accompanied by her treasured collection of original Matt Monro records. She liked nothing more than to stick on 'My Kind of Girl', relax back in her leather armchair with a glass of Courvoisier and lose herself in the memories of her wedding night all those years ago. But not tonight.

As dusk set in outside, the room was starting to grow dim. The Royal Worcester figurines, frozen in their poses in the glass display cabinet, mutely observed their brooding mistress. A little drummer boy. A woman in a hooped dress holding a bouquet of flowers. A soldier carrying a musket over his shoulder.

Sitting there in the armchair, consumed by the thirst for revenge, Nancy savagely contemplated what she would do to Mister Snigiss once she caught up with him. His evasiveness infuriated her, only hardening her desire to track him down and get even with him.

Nobody got away with crossing Nancy Molloy. Nobody.

It was the first of March and a Friday morning and whilst most people in the city were going to their normal nine-to-five jobs and looking forward to the weekend, Bailey was sitting in the temporary HQ with Frank and Dale finalising plans for the bust. Mustafa hadn't yet opened the kebab shop so for the time being she was spared the stink of reconstituted lamb wafting up from the floor below.

It had been three days since the bombshell meeting with Jennifer and Bailey had spent every waking minute since then trying to piece her inner life back together and make sense of it all.

For the meeting today with Frank and Dale, she'd been doing her best to try and put it out of her mind whilst she focused on this crucially sensitive stage of the operation. Now that it had entered the arrest phase all that remained was for the three of them to go over the final details again and again until they were confident that all possible scenarios and contingencies had been mapped out.

The whiteboard had accumulated even more dates, places and photographs of key players, all connected by a plethora of arrows in a big spidery diagram. Frank was standing next to it, gesticulating with a marker pen.

'Strike day is just over one week away,' he was saying. 'The ninth of

March. Next Saturday. We'll have a meeting the day before where we'll coordinate plans with the strike team leader and the rest of his crew. There'll be a lot of people present at the bust. This is a big operation and there's a lot at stake.'

'And the seven hundred and fifty thousand?' said Bailey.

'I'll give that to you on the day itself, just beforehand,' he said.

'He's worried that you might run off with it,' joked Dale.

Bailey shot him a droll smile.

There was a large question mark in a circle on the whiteboard. Frank tapped on it with the end of his pen. 'All that remains to be known is the location of the transaction.'

Bailey nodded at the question mark. 'Rick said he'd confirm the location on the day itself. He said it would be indoors. So with a quantity of weapons of this size, I'm guessing the venue is likely to be somewhere big and fairly secluded, like an empty warehouse or a disused aircraft hangar.'

She knew the reason Rick was keeping the location to himself until the last minute was so if he thought he was being followed he could call the whole deal off.

So far though, seeing as she'd heard nothing from the Molloys since the interrogation of Marcus, she was presuming no news was good news, and it saved her the trouble of having to dance around them. But from another more worrying perspective, she knew they'd probably been spending their time searching for Mister Snigiss, and despite Jennifer's claims she could look after herself, the thought of them catching up with her terrified Bailey as she was acutely aware of the lengths they'd be capable of going to in order to quench Nancy's thirst for revenge.

'Well, wherever he ends up taking you,' said Frank. 'We'll have eyes on you the whole way. From beginning to end.'

'I don't want to know where they'll be though,' retorted Bailey, aware that an unconscious flicker of her eyes in the direction of the strike team could alert the Molloys to their presence and thus blow the whole operation.

'Sure,' he replied. 'And I'll make sure they keep an extra-low profile as well.'

'Presumably I'll be wired up,' she said.

Frank nodded. 'As well as a microphone, you'll also be wearing a miniature camera. We want to catch Rick on film conducting the transaction. That'll ensure he definitely won't be able to squirm out of it like he normally does.'

'So how will the strike team know when to take action?' asked Dale.

Bailey had already given this some thought. 'Basically, when I come out to give the signal to my man to hand the money over to Rick's man, that's when the strike team will know whether to move in or not. If the weapons are there as planned, I'll be wearing my sunglasses. But if I'm not wearing my sunglasses, then that means that the weapons aren't there, and that the strike team should hold off for the time being. It means that Rick might be holding the weapons in a secondary location just to be on the safe side.'

'What about an emergency signal?' said Frank. 'Just in case something drastic happens.'

Bailey paused and pondered a few seconds. 'If the shit hits the fan, I'll put my baseball cap on backwards.'

Dale's eyes twinkled. 'Things would have to be pretty drastic for you to make a fashion statement that extreme.'

They all laughed.

'Okay, well assuming the guns will be there,' said Frank, 'the strike team will swoop in and arrest all the members of the gang that are there. We'll also have a firearms team at the ready.'

'Just make sure they know what I look like,' said Bailey. 'If it all goes south, I don't want to end up with a bullet inside me by accident.'

'Don't worry,' Frank replied. 'Like I said, we'll have a final meeting the day before it goes down. Only then will we reveal your identity to the rest of the team. For the sake of good OPSEC, we want to keep your identity secret until the very last minute.'

Bailey nodded in approval. She trusted Frank's planning skills and knew he placed the utmost importance on operational security. She'd been through this kind of situation with him many times in the past on previous undercover jobs.

'Who will "my man" be?' she asked, referring to the other under-cover officer who'd be functioning as the money man in the transaction.

'We're still confirming details of who that will be,' said Frank. 'But don't worry. It'll be someone dependable.'

She nodded in assent.

'As you already know,' he added, 'we're coordinating very closely with the National Crime Agency on all of this and some of their officers will be present at the bust. I can tell you they're very excited about this, Bailey. You know, if this all goes down as planned, I reckon you'll be looking at yet another commendation.'

'Now let's not get ahead of ourselves,' she muttered. For all their careful preparations, she knew from experience that these things never went quite to plan. And she had a nasty feeling that someone as cunning as Rick Molloy would have something unexpected up his sleeve.

64

Wendy Molloy eyed her husband sitting at the other end of the long oak dining table. It was a Tuesday evening and they were eating dinner – a Bluefin tuna steak accompanied by a bottle of grand cru Chablis – but the expensive food and wine tasted like ashes in her mouth, such was the bitterness that consumed her.

And the flowers had only aggravated her foul temper. A lavish bouquet of roses which now stood in one of the antique Chinese vases on the sideboard. They'd just served to confirm her worst suspicions about her husband. He never normally bought her flowers. It was so out of character that she knew he must be compensating for something. And she knew exactly what that was. It was that fucking slut, Kaia. He was seeing her next weekend.

'So why the roses, darling?' she asked, struggling to keep her voice light and cheerful-sounding.

He shrugged and smiled. 'I'm in a good mood. I thought I should buy you a little treat to celebrate.'

A good mood?! What rubbish! He was just trying to butter her up. It made her even angrier to know that he thought she was that stupid. They said hell hath no fury like a woman scorned. Well, he'd scorned her and now she was furious.

She couldn't hold it inside any longer. The time of reckoning had come.

'I can't believe you,' she muttered through clenched teeth.

He frowned, looking genuinely puzzled. 'What? I thought you'd be pleased. You're always going on about how I never buy you flowers.'

'Up to much next weekend?' she asked, her eyes flaring with anger.

He shrugged. 'I'm doing some business, that's all.'

'"Business"?!' she said sarcastically, making quote marks with her fingers. 'That's bullshit and you know it!'

His mouth dropped open. For once he looked quite taken aback. He clearly hadn't been expecting an outburst of this magnitude. Well, let him have it.

The accusation finally burst from her lips, fuelled by the pressure of having been held in for so long. 'You're meeting that bitch, Kaia! You're meeting her next Friday, aren't you? The eighth. A dirty weekend in Torquay. I heard you talking about it on the phone. And I saw her name in your diary!'

Rick gulped at her, his black eyes wide with shock. He looked like he'd been punched.

'What do you know about Kaia?' he whispered dangerously.

'That private eye. The one you murdered. It was me who sent him.'

His features darkened and his jaw clenched. 'That was you?!' he whispered.

'Yeah, that was me! I've had enough of your bloody lies and deceit!'

'You. Silly. Fucking. Bitch,' he growled.

'I wanted to find out the truth about you and this Kaia. I wanted to prove it.'

'It's not what you think,' he said. 'I'm not having an affair.'

She wasn't going to believe that. He was a liar.

'Then who the fuck is Kaia?' she demanded.

'None of your fucking business!'

'You're cheating on me!'

'No, I'm not!'

'They say "happy wife, happy life". Well I'm not happy! And that means your life is about to get really unhappy. Because I want a divorce!'

'You what?' he looked at her incredulously.

'You heard me. It's over!'

65

Sitting on the sofa in her undercover apartment, Bailey once again examined the amulet that Jennifer had given her, the small green stone cobra twisting slowly on the thin gold chain as she held it up in front of her.

It was unbelievable to think that it had been created over three millennia ago. She peered at the hieroglyphs, making out amongst them a kneeling man, a bird, a flower, a zig-zag line of water. They were tiny pictures that were also words with meanings and she wondered what they said exactly. Being a protective amulet, she supposed they formed some kind of magical inscription.

She debated what to do with it. It didn't feel right to wear it around her neck. At least not yet. But, in keeping with Jennifer's intentions, she would try and keep it somewhere on her person. Opening her hand-bag, she carefully placed it into one of the internal pockets.

She suddenly felt worried for her sister, seized by the fearful certainty that the Molloys would eventually succeed in finding and killing her. Much as she was repulsed by what Jennifer had become, Bailey still possessed a strong filial urge to protect her. And she knew that if strike day went down as planned, then the Molloy family would be seriously crippled and thus present much less of a threat to

Jennifer. The best Bailey could do right now to protect her sister was to make sure that she pulled off the operation to the best of her ability.

It occurred to her then that she should probably call Frank. She imagined he was probably still fretting about her preoccupation with Mister Snigiss and the sex tape investigation. He was a bit of a worrier by nature, and although he hadn't raised the subject during their last meeting, she knew it had probably been on his mind. After all, despite her statements to the contrary, he knew she wasn't the type to quit on something of such personal significance to her. Given the importance of this operation, the less unnecessary things he had weighing on his mind, the better.

She picked up her undercover phone and dialled his number. He answered a few moments later, sounding uncharacteristically cheerful.

'Bailey! How are you?'

She could distinguish the sound of a young girl laughing in the background.

'Is that Isabel I can hear?' she asked.

'Yes. We're having a bit of a father-daughter bonding session. Joanna's going away for a few days with Roland and she's left Isabel in my care for the rest of the week.'

Joanna was Frank's ex-wife and Roland was her new partner – a stable and reliable businessman who Bailey knew Frank shared absolutely nothing in common with.

'I'll be quick then,' said Bailey. 'I just wanted to put your mind at rest about that whole thing with Mister Snigiss and the sex tape and Jennifer and all that. I just wanted to let you know I've put it behind me and I'm one hundred per cent focused on the operation, because that's all that counts at the moment.'

There was a brief silence on the other end of the phone.

'You know me only too well, Bailey. To be honest, I had been a little concerned. And I did voice those concerns to Dale, actually.'

'Oh yeah? What did he say?' she asked with a little twinge of anxiety.

'He told me not to worry. He told me that he thought you had a handle on everything regarding the operation.'

Bailey felt a burst of gratitude towards Dale for having her back. And it didn't sound like he'd spilt the beans.

'Oh good,' she said, relieved.

'But I appreciate you calling me, Bailey. I really do. Thanks.'

'Well, I hope you and Isabel have a nice evening,' she said, and ended the call.

Almost as soon as she had done so, and before she'd even had a chance to put it back on the table, her phone rang. It was Dale.

'Hey, Bailey, how are you?'

'So-so. I went to visit my dad today.'

'How is he?'

'Getting worse,' she sighed. Knowing what she now knew about Jennifer, she'd kind of been dreading the visit, afraid that he'd ask about Mister Snigiss and she'd somehow blurt it all out to him, but he had been asleep for the most part, so she'd been spared the trouble. But it made her sad seeing him like that, knowing the end was worryingly near, and that she wouldn't be able to give him the resolution with Jennifer that he so desperately wanted. As for letting him know that his eldest daughter was alive, and not mentioning the rest of it, she knew that wasn't an option as he'd just be tortured by the knowledge that Jennifer wasn't interested in seeing him, and Bailey knew that would be worse for him. She paused. 'Is everything okay with you? Why did you want to talk to me? Was it important?'

'Kind of.'

'Oh?'

'I wanted to ask if you wanted to go out for dinner tonight.'

She smiled.

'I know it's a bit short notice,' he said. 'But you know, special occasion and all that.'

She frowned. 'What special occasion?'

'Let's make the special occasion "Bailey Morgan".'

It sounded like a proper date. A beam of gratification struck her as she realised that he hadn't given up on her after all, despite all the drama she'd been immersed in recently.

'Sure,' she said with an eager smile. 'Why not.'

'Phew. I've already booked the table.'

'Oh? Where are we going?'

'It's called House of Bamboo. It's just opened. Have you heard of it?'

'No, I don't think so. Sounds fancy.'

'It is apparently. Pick you up at seven?'

'See you then.'

She ended the call and held the phone to her chest for a moment. What a great guy. It was almost like he knew she'd been feeling anxious. Her beneficent feelings towards him increased even further.

She looked at her watch. She had forty-five minutes or so to get ready. She jumped up off the sofa and went into the bathroom to take a shower.

Afterwards, she stood in front of her dresser wrapped in a towel trying to decide what to wear.

There was a pleasant feeling in her stomach, like warm butterflies, as she realised that tonight was the night that she would surrender herself to Dale... if the evening panned out that way. For the first time in some years she felt ready to get intimate with a man again. Maybe it had been the emotional catharsis of the encounter with her sister that had triggered the change. Either way, tonight was going to be his lucky night. And as for that whole thing about maintaining a professional distance... to hell with it!

Bailey opened one of the drawers and took out a lacy black thong and matching bra. Poking around a bit more, she found a garter belt and a pair of stockings to go with them. Tonight she'd go for the full set-up. She'd bought the lingerie in Agent Provocateur back when she'd been with Mark but had never worn it since then. Ever since the torture and the scars, she'd been too self-conscious to. And she'd never thought she would wear it again. But subconsciously some part of her had told her not to throw it away – a good decision because now it seemed the time had come to try it on again.

She slipped on the underwear, sitting on the side of the bed to slide on the stockings. Standing up, she clipped the tops of the stockings to the garter belt and looked at herself in the full-length mirror which stood in the corner of the room. She suddenly felt burningly self-conscious, dressed like this, all too aware of the cigarette burns and the razor scars that crisscrossed much of her torso. The thought of Dale looking upon her body as she was looking upon it now filled her with both deep apprehension and sensuous excitement. Shaking off any misgivings, she pressed on.

She took out her tight black shoulderless cocktail dress and pulled it on. She wouldn't normally have worn something as revealing as this on a date with Dale as it displayed too much of her disfigured shoulders and cleavage. But tonight would be a test of sorts. If he was fine seeing more of her scars than usual, then he was probably fine seeing her naked.

Likewise with the scar on her face. Tonight she wouldn't be hiding it behind her loose-hanging lock of hair. She pulled her hair up and looked for something to tie it back with. Lying there on the top of the dresser was the Christian-themed hairgrip that her mother had given her for Christmas. She smiled to herself. That would do perfectly.

Pouting in the mirror, she put on a dash of lipstick, then applied a touch of eyeliner, and then, to finish, a squirt of Coco Mademoiselle perfume. And, last but not least, she slipped on a pair of sharp black heels.

She assessed herself in the mirror. Even if she said so herself, she looked pretty damn hot.

There was one last thing she needed and that was a phone. Seeing as this was just a date, she decided to bring her normal phone rather than her undercover phone. She went into the bathroom and opened up the secret compartment. Pushing aside her warrant card, she took out her normal phone and switched it on. However, it appeared that the battery had gone dead. Not surprising really, considering it was tucked away in here most of the time.

Cursing under her breath, she took it out into the living room and started to search for the charging lead. At that point the entry buzzer rang. She lifted her head with a little thrill of anticipation. He was here.

Giving up the search for the charging lead, she discarded her normal phone on the sofa and picked up her undercover phone instead. The undercover phone would suffice for this evening. At any rate, that was the phone she currently used most of the time anyway.

Dropping her undercover phone into her handbag, she excitedly went over to the intercom panel by the front door and pressed the button.

'Dale?'

His voice came out of the small tinny speaker. 'Hi, Bailey.'

'I'll be down in just a minute,' she said breathlessly.

'Actually, do you mind if I quickly come up for a sec?'

She frowned, then shrugged. 'Sure.'

She pressed the button to unlock the main entrance door of the apartment block to let him in and wondered why he wanted to come up.

66

When she opened the front door of her flat, Dale's eyes almost popped out of his head.

'Holy crap, Bailey, you look amazing.'

She squirmed bashfully under his gaze, then gave him a reciprocal once-over.

'You brush up pretty good yourself,' she said.

He had clearly made an effort as well, with a grey herringbone blazer jacket, a button-down sky-blue shirt, dark-wash indigo jeans and a pair of tan loafers. And he seemed to have done something to his blonde hair to make it look even more lustrous than normal.

'Why did you want to come up?' she asked.

'Do you mind if I quickly use your bathroom?'

'Oh.'

He smiled sheepishly. 'I drank way too much coffee today. Guess I should have gone before I left, but I didn't want to be late.'

'Sure,' she said with a smile and a small roll of her eyes.

She waited in the hallway as he dashed inside. Glancing in the gold-framed mirror hanging there, she examined herself one last time, preening slightly, delighted at his response to her appearance. A short while later, she heard the toilet flush, and he reappeared.

'Sorry,' he said with an apologetic grin. 'Right, let's rock.'

They took the lift downstairs and went outside to his car, which was parked just in front of the building. The door handles of the dark metallic Tesla popped out automatically as they approached. He stepped forward with a gentlemanly flourish to open the passenger door for her.

She got in and settled into the spacious seat. The car had a sleek black interior with ash-wood panelling, cream-coloured seats and a glass roof.

Dale climbed into the driver's seat and as he did so she caught a tantalising whiff of his cologne – hints of sandalwood and cinnamon if she wasn't mistaken.

'I don't think I fully appreciated your car the last time I was in it,' she murmured, glancing around, admiring the minimalist hi-tech design.

'You had bigger things on your mind, as I recall,' he said, tapping on the large touchscreen which dominated the dashboard, bringing up a route map.

'So where is this restaurant?' she asked.

'It's a little out of the way,' he said. 'Just on the edge of Epping Forest. We should be there in about half an hour or so.'

He pulled away smoothly from the kerb and she relaxed back into the comfortable seat, glad to be driven for once, marvelling at how quiet the electric engine was compared to a normal car.

He drove confidently, with the self-assurance of someone experienced in commanding patrol cars at high speed, deftly weaving through the evening traffic, keeping just within the speed limit, knowing exactly which parts of the road to use.

As they pulled onto the dual carriageway, he tapped the touchscreen again and music flooded the car. It was Berlin's 'Take My Breath Away'. She turned her head to him with a smile and he gave her a wink. He had her down when it came to music.

She gazed contently out of the window, letting the superior sound system envelope her with the pristine music. The car seemed to block out all other outside noise, and with its perfect climate control, she felt like she was cocooned in some kind of speeding spaceship.

Before she knew it, they were there, Dale slowing the car and pulling into the restaurant car park. She saw that one or two other cars were parked there. Set back slightly from the road, the restaurant stood alone, with no other buildings in close vicinity. It seemed to Bailey like a nice quiet location, even a little romantic, and certainly somewhere she'd never have discovered herself.

They got out of the car and she shivered a little in the chill of the evening. Over to her right, she saw the silhouette of trees – Epping Forest no doubt. It almost felt like they were in the countryside, even though it was just suburban Essex. Much as she enjoyed the noise and bustle of the city, she was happy that Dale had chosen somewhere cloistered and special for their evening out.

Dale put his arm out and she took it and together they walked up to the entrance of the restaurant – a single-storey modernist box-shaped building with the name 'House of Bamboo' written above the door in simple elegant font.

They walked up a set of shallow marble steps to the door. Dale stepped ahead of her and held it open. A sensor triggered a little electronic 'ping' as she entered and, moments later, a lanky, bald-headed maître d' appeared with a fawning smile on his face.

The place was tastefully clad in dark lattice woodwork with gold dome-shaped lamps hanging low over the tables. The restrained decor encapsulated a meld of styles – Chinese scrolls hung from the walls, while Japanese-style paper screens separated the tables and Malaysian rattan blinds covered the windows. In keeping with the name, earthenware pots of bamboo stood here and there, the greenery pleasantly offsetting the stark simplicity of the modern Eastern design. To Bailey's eyes, the restaurant represented the essence of understated cosmopolitan sophistication.

The place seemed quite empty though. In fact, they appeared to be the only diners there.

'Seems very quiet,' she said. 'Though I suppose it is a Monday night.'

'It's only just opened,' said Dale. 'Probably still finding customers. Let's hope the food's good though, eh?'

She squeezed his arm. The maître d' conducted them over to a choice booth – a round table set into the wall where they could sit as close to each other as they wished. Sitting down, they gravitated towards one another so their knees and elbows were brushing, the physical contact sending a delectable quiver of pleasure through Bailey. The maître d' clicked his fingers and a waiter came over holding a bottle of sparkling water, two menus and a wine list.

After a few moments of perusing the menu and the wine list, Dale patted his pockets and gave a frown.

'Bollocks. Left my wallet in the car.'

'Haven't heard that one before,' said Bailey, teasing him.

He smiled as he stood up and eased himself out of the booth. 'I'll just nip out and get it. I won't be a sec. Why don't you look at the menu and see what you fancy ordering. And remember, don't skimp because I am most definitely paying!'

She nodded obediently and watched him with a glow of affection as he walked off. It felt good to be spoiled. It had been so long. Maybe just for tonight she could allow herself to forget about all those concerns that had been playing on her mind recently – about her father, about Jennifer, about the upcoming operation – and just let herself go with the flow of what was shaping up to be a very promising evening.

She turned her attention to the menu. From a gastronomic perspective, it was definitely more high-end than what she was normally used to. And the prices... well, they were definitely right up there as well. But what the hell. It was a treat and Dale was paying, though of course she wasn't planning on going mad or anything.

She scanned through the options, contemplating what to choose, and found herself both amused and a little intimidated by the strange array of dishes on offer. Venison satay. Shanghai pork dumplings with

Mexican salsa. Miso jellied eels... That was the thing with these fancy places – some of the stuff they served was a bit out there.

She scanned the vegan options, wondering what Dale was going to have, but it seemed like they didn't have a lot of choice on that front. In fact, looking at the main courses, it appeared that the only vegan option was the Indonesian chickpea curry. And she knew he didn't like chickpeas.

She frowned. He wouldn't be too happy about that. But then, for a special night out like this, she would have thought Dale would have researched the vegan options in advance online, like he told her he normally did. Why bring her to a place where there was nothing for him to eat... apart from a side order of chips, but she doubted a place this swish even did chips.

She sighed and turned the menu over, trying to work out just what kind of cuisine this was, with its weird selection of dishes. She began to read through the blurb.

House of Bamboo offers an eclectic mix of both classic and contemporary Eastern fare refracted through a truly global prism to give you an Asian fusion experience that you will savour forever.

Asian fusion.
That rang a distant bell.
Asian fusion? Where had she last heard that? She couldn't remember...

A waiter came over and placed a plate in front of her, momentarily breaking her train of thought. The plate was covered by a silver dome.

'A taster, madam.'

She absently smiled without looking at him, staring at the plate as he lifted up the silver dome.

Beneath the dome, lying on the plate, wasn't a serving of food, but a rectangular sliver of plastic.

It was her warrant card.

She gaped at it, utterly confounded. What was this? Some kind of joke? How on earth had her warrant card got into this restaurant? And why was it being served to her on a plate?

She looked up at the waiter quizzically. But it wasn't the waiter who'd given them the menus.

She knew that voice had sounded familiar...

It was Rick.

He was standing there dressed in a waiter's white shirt and black waistcoat smiling down at her with his dead shark eyes.

And Dale was nowhere to be seen.

67

Bailey blinked and did a double take, not quite believing what she was seeing.

But Rick was still standing there looking down at her with his cold black eyes and a nasty grin on his face. He was no hallucination.

She looked back down at the table.

And that was definitely her warrant card lying on the plate. Incontrovertible proof that she was a policewoman, it bore the logo of the Metropolitan Police, beneath which were the words 'POLICE OFFI-CER' stated boldly in red. It showed her current rank – detective constable – and, quite crucially, the name 'Bailey Morgan' clearly printed right there in black and white, accompanied by a little photograph of herself.

How the fuck had her warrant card got here? Why the fuck was Rick here? What the fuck was going on?

With a horrible sickening lurch, it all clicked into place.

Asian fusion.

This must be the Asian fusion restaurant that Rick had talked about acquiring back when they'd been having lunch after going pheasant shooting. He'd never actually mentioned the name of it, but this had to be it. It meant this was his turf – an environment totally under his control.

That's why there were no other customers here.

It was a trap. And the jaws had closed on her.

She gasped, finding it hard to draw breath all of a sudden as the true horror of the situation dawned upon her.

Like actors appearing on a stage, the rest of the gang emerged from behind a paper screen. Shane Reaper... Archie Steele... Stephen Drood... and finally Nancy Molloy. The sight of each one struck a further hammer blow of dread into Bailey's heart.

They stood around the booth, looking down at her, their faces cold and unforgiving.

Her mind turned to Dale. Where was he? Were they going to jump him when he came back into the restaurant? Or had they already done so? Was he already dead?

Then, stunned, the penny dropped.

She had been betrayed by Dale.

How else could the Molloys have got hold of her warrant card? Only Dale knew about the secret compartment where she kept it. He must have removed it earlier that evening when he'd made that excuse about needing to use the bathroom in her flat.

And the restaurant. That was why Dale had asked her if she'd heard of it. Just to double-check that Rick hadn't mentioned the name to her.

And this date? Nothing more than a devious ploy to deliver her into the hands of the Molloys, for he knew she wouldn't have arranged any kind of police back-up for something as ostensibly innocent as a simple date.

The devastating shock of his betrayal was almost too much for her to grasp and at this moment in time she couldn't even begin to grapple with the reasons why. She had considerably more pressing concerns on her mind right now. Like how to get out of this situation.

She looked around desperately for a way to escape. But there was no way out. She was trapped in the booth.

Shane sat down next to her, blocking her exit to her left. And then Rick and Archie sat down on her right.

Nancy remained standing, with Stephen by her side. She fixed Bailey with her dark close-set eyes and smiled unpleasantly.

'It looks like you've been served up, my dear,' she said, nodding at the warrant card.

Bailey stared speechlessly down at it, racking her mind for a solution. The options were looking pretty limited.

In fact, there was only one option.

She looked up at Nancy. 'I'm not a cop.'

Nancy snorted contemptuously. 'Do you really expect me to fall for that crap? I know how the undercover Filth operate. Never break cover. That's what you're taught, aren't you?'

'I swear it,' said Bailey. 'There is no way that I am Old Bill.'

'That warrant card looks like pretty damning evidence to me,' growled Rick.

Bailey attempted a dismissive shrug. 'It's a fake.'

'It's a fake,' mimicked Nancy in a nasty tone. 'This girl just won't give up, will she?'

Bailey's heart hammered in her chest, panic threatening to overwhelm her. They weren't buying it. But of course they weren't going to buy it. They weren't stupid.

Nancy shook her head sadly. 'Bailey, I'm disappointed in you. I can't tell you how disappointed I am. I feel hurt more than anything else. Because I actually kind of liked you. And you've let me down in a big way.'

'I am not a copper,' declared Bailey belligerently, 'and that warrant card is a fake.'

Inside, she knew that her denials were pointless, but her cover story was all she had and if she gave up on that, then her fate was sealed beyond all doubt.

'I admire your verve, Bailey *Morgan*,' said Nancy, placing particular emphasis on her real surname. 'And your resourcefulness. You played me well. You really had me going. And I'm angry with myself that I fell for it, for letting you get one over on me.' Nancy gave Stephen a side-ways glance. 'I should have listened to my boy, Stephen, here. He had his doubts about you right from the very beginning.'

Stephen took a step forward, his eyes filled with a mixture of vitriol and triumph. He leant towards her, placed his hands on the table and spat in Bailey's face.

Bailey recoiled in shock, blinking the strands of saliva out of her eyes.

'You're a dirty liar,' he hissed, 'and you're going to get your come-uppance.'

Nancy stroked his hair. 'Come now, Stephen. Calm down. The poor girl is going to be dead quite soon. We should let her come to terms with it.'

Rick leaned forward and plucked the warrant card off the plate.

'I suppose you're wondering how we got hold of this. Although it must be pretty obvious by now.' He smiled at her. 'I get the impression that you two were almost an item.'

Dale, conspicuous by his absence, returned once more to Bailey's consciousness with a sting of anguish.

'Normally it's such a challenge to find a plod to corrupt,' continued Rick. 'You've got to find a weakness, like a gambling addiction, or a drug addiction, or some kind of embarrassing sexual proclivity to blackmail them with. Or else you can just try and buy them... because everyone has their price.' He paused. 'But it's a process fraught with risks and difficulty. You just have to be so careful these days.

'But your gentleman friend, he just turned up on my doorstep yesterday afternoon. Out of the blue. Very entrepreneurial of him. Normally I wouldn't have given him the time of day. I would have been way too suspicious. But when he promised me this warrant card, I knew he meant business.'

Bailey felt like she was going to throw up. Hearing it directly from Rick's mouth unequivocally destroyed any last vestige of hope that Dale was not the agent of her betrayal.

How could she have misjudged him so seriously? How could she have been so blind? And, more to the point, what had driven him to do such an awful thing? The questions pummelled her remorselessly.

'Shame about those guns,' said Rick. 'I was so pleased to have found a buyer... and you turn out to be the bloody Filth.' He paused philosophically. 'Still, it's not going to stop me from selling them. I'm too far down the road not to. Luckily for me though, your bent-copper friend said he already knew a few people who might be interested. Genuine criminals.'

A heavy nausea suffused Bailey at the thought of all those guns flooding the streets with Dale's connivance.

'Now, normally,' Nancy intervened, 'we'd just kill you straight away because you're Old Bill. That's just par for the course. As I'm sure you understand. However...' She paused, her eyes narrowing slyly. '... Your fella told us something very interesting. He told us that you've been looking for Mister Snigiss too. Something to do with your missing sister, who apparently, according to him, is actually still alive...'

On top of everything else, a deeply worrisome feeling now gripped Bailey. If things were already bad, they had just got even worse.

'Fancy that?' said Nancy. 'All along, we've both been looking for Mister Snigiss. And you know what?' The thin smile on her face blossomed into a horrible grin. 'Your fella told us that you've actually met Mister Snigiss, that you know who he is... and that you can positively identify him.'

Bailey swallowed. This was not good.

She shook her head. 'I don't know what you're talking about.'

Nancy paused and scrutinised Bailey with a curious frown. 'You're protecting him. Why?'

Bailey tried to control her breathing, tried to remain calm. The Molloys might end up killing her, but there was no way she was going to concede the slightest piece of information that might help them kill Jennifer as well.

Nancy sighed. 'I don't know why you're protecting him... but you are. For some reason. Not to worry. We will find out. We'll find out everything. That's because instead of killing you straight away, we're going to torture you until you tell us everything you know. And then we're going to kill you. Because you're a cop. Then we're going to kill Mister Snigiss. But as for the torture, it's your choice. You could save yourself a whole lot of pain and discomfort if you tell me right now. If you do, we'll make your death quick and relatively painless.'

'I don't know anything,' said Bailey.

Nancy sighed. 'I had a feeling you'd say that. Oh well, have it your own way. I'm sure Archie here will be able to extract the information we need.'

Archie tilted his head at her and grinned his death's-head smile, displaying his brown rotten teeth. All that Bailey could see were the miniature reflections of herself trapped in the shiny black lenses of his large wraparound sunglasses.

All the while she'd been talking with the Molloys, one small cool-headed part of Bailey's mind had been monitoring their physical juxta-position, mentally choreographing the most appropriate jiu-jitsu moves to try and get her out of this situation. All she needed to do was get out from behind this table and get through that main door and make a run for it.

She realised that it was now or never. And with that her body unleashed a colossal dose of adrenaline into her system. Instantly, everything slowed right down. Every tiny detail suddenly became super-enhanced. In a bizarre way, it made her feel calm, in control, even though that couldn't be further from the truth right now.

Below the table, very gently, very subtly, she removed her feet from her heels.

She took a deep breath, tensing slightly...

Then, in a single sharp movement, she twisted sideways, brought up her knees so her feet were on the seat, then, using them as leverage, jettisoned herself upwards.

Standing upright on the seat, she pushed herself away from the wall to launch herself across the top of the table in an attempt to escape from the booth, the plate with her warrant card skittering off the table to smash on the floor.

Shane, his eyes widening, made a lunge for her, but he was too slow, his hands closing on thin air where her ankle had been a fraction of a second earlier. Archie, slightly faster, swiped at her leg, knocking her off balance. She spun around atop the table and then crashed sideways through the flimsy paper screen into the neighbouring booth, landing heavily on the table there.

Already they were on their feet, fanning out to block her exit from the restaurant. By this point, several more associates of the gang had appeared, alerted by the ruckus.

Recovering swiftly, she rolled off the table onto the floor, and bounced to her feet, orienting herself in the direction of the door.

But her way was blocked by two of the Molloys' thugs. They were meatheads she'd barely exchanged two words with since the beginning of her infiltration, but however dumb and unimportant they were, the next few seconds of interaction with them could prove to be the most important few seconds in her life.

The nearest one, shaved bald with a ginger beard, resembled nothing less than a human bowling ball. He smiled condescendingly at her petite form and made a grab for her with a huge beefy hand. She nimbly evaded it, his hand gliding harmlessly past, leaving him wide open for a *tenohira soko-uchi* – open-hand palm strike. She delivered it with her right hand, the heel of her palm impacting the base of his nose with an audible crunch. He reeled backwards, stunned, with blood pouring from his nostrils.

She darted around his lumbering figure to find herself facing the second thug, a thickset boxer type with cauliflower ears and black curly hair. Not quite as complacent as his colleague, his hooded eyes watched her warily as he moved in for the attack. He suddenly feinted with a blow to her left, then swung a lightning-fast right hook at her face. But she had already determined her next move.

Koshi guruma – hip wheel.

Utilising his own kinetic energy against him, she caught the inside of his striking arm with her left hand, simultaneously sliding her right arm around his neck. Then she pivoted on her foot, pushing her hips backwards into his, her small stature working in her favour as she dropped beneath him, breaking his balance, pulling him around in a circular motion at the same time. Propelled by the force of his own punch, he tumbled straight over her hips and crashed onto the floor. He lay there blinking in shock, but she gave no respite, following up with a hard stamp downwards into his groin, hearing him squeal in pain.

She caught a glimpse of the rest of the gang goggling at her, completely taken aback by her hitherto unannounced self-defence skills.

She swung back around to the door…

And saw that Shane had somehow already got there ahead of her. He was standing blocking the exit, with his arms crossed and a wide smile on his face.

'I see you possess jiu-jitsu skills,' he said admiringly. 'You kept that quiet. I'm impressed with your technique. But I feel I could still teach you a few things. So come on then, copper. Let's have you.'

He dropped into a professional fighting stance, completely in his element.

She sagged. Fuck. He was going to present considerably more of a challenge than the two gorillas she'd floored just now. This was Shane Reaper, a fourth-dan jiu-jitsu black belt who'd won more UFC bouts than she could count on both hands. Against someone of his expertise, she rated her chances very low indeed.

He sidled forwards with a fluid grace that belied his brawny frame. She mirrored his stance, hoping to give the impression that she was going to engage with him, even though she had no intention of doing anything of the sort.

As he got within about two metres of her, she dodged sharply to her left, then suddenly switched back to her right, attempting to side-step around him. But he was too fast. His hand shot out to grab her left arm and jerk her forward; at the same time, he spun himself forward to drop down in front of her whilst kicking the inside of her left leg to somersault her expertly across his body.

Yoko otoshi – side drop.

She slammed into the marble floor, the hard surface knocking the air out of her. And before she had a chance to respond, he was on top of her.

Shit. She was done for.

Groundwork was his forte. The vast majority of MMA fights ended in a clinch on the ground. And when it came to beating someone in that kind of situation, jiu-jitsu stood head and shoulders above any other type of fighting system. That's why the jiu-jitsu guys always won at MMA. Guys like Shane.

She struggled to move, but he'd already wrenched her around in front of him and got her in a *hadaka-jime*, his speciality. His forearm was locked across her throat like a vice.

'Familiar with *hadaka-jime*?' he asked, his mouth just millimetres from her ear. 'Also known as the "rear naked choke", in case you're not acquainted with it.'

She squirmed and strained against his grip, already feeling herself starting to go dizzy, as the hold cut off the blood supply to her brain.

'They also call it the "lion killer",' he whispered.

She pushed in vain against him, trying to arch her body up and out of his grip, but he held her firm.

'The key thing about this hold is the importance of getting your hooks in early,' he said in a conversational tone as he folded his legs in over hers, rendering her almost completely immobile.

He increased the pressure on her throat. She choked and gasped.

'And the other thing to remember is to always get the arm under the chin rather than across the chin. That's a mistake people often make with *hadaka-jime*. They never quite get the arm under the chin properly.'

He pressed his forearm into her throat even harder. A light-headedness seized her and a blackness began to descend like a curtain across her vision. And the last thing she remembered thinking before she passed out was how annoying it was that she hadn't watched more YouTube videos on how to counter this particular hold.

68

Bailey awoke to find herself tied to a chair. Her hair was hanging down over her face, having become loose in the struggle with Shane.

She blinked and attempted to orient herself, blowing her hair out of her face to try and get a better look around. The room she was in was relatively bare, lit by several strip bulbs overhead. She wasn't sure if she was even in the restaurant any more, but then she noticed some metal racking against the wall stacked with large sacks of rice and giant cans of cooking oil and she figured she was still inside the restaurant but in some kind of storage room out the back.

Glancing down, her heart sunk as she remembered why she was here. The floor all around her chair was covered in heavy-duty polythene plastic sheeting. There was only one reason for that to be there. It was to make sure that all her blood and guts didn't make a permanent mess everywhere.

It struck home with a harsh force just how feral the underworld really was, and she knew that in her situation she could not expect any kind of mercy, not least because she was Old Bill.

The one small blessing was that she appeared to be alone in here, and there was currently no sign of the gang, which meant she had a small window of opportunity in which to try and do something. She wrenched at her bonds, but doing so only made them cut deeper into her wrists and ankles. Looking down, she saw that her legs had been secured to the chair with cable ties, and by the feel of it so had her hands, tied behind her.

She thought about screaming at the top of her voice, but then she recalled that the restaurant was quite remote and it was therefore unlikely that anyone would hear her. Better to conserve her energy in order to try and think of some way out of this.

Her mind frenetically churned through the options. Maybe if she knocked the chair over, she could somehow wriggle herself towards something to cut her bonds with. But the cable ties would be incredibly hard to cut, not helped by the fact that her hands were bound behind her back. No, that wouldn't work. What about if—

The door to the room swung open. Her thoughts froze and she stiffened in the chair.

It was Dale.

He strode in with an arrogant swagger. Stopping at the edge of the plastic sheeting, he took a moment to absorb the tableau. A smile of overt gratification crossed his face.

From beneath her ruffled hair, she stared at him with a mixture of hatred, disbelief and revulsion.

'Did you find your wallet?' she growled.

'Did you decide what you wanted to eat?' he enquired. He then put on a fake miserable face. 'Or have you lost your appetite?'

'I knew something wasn't quite right when I looked at the menu and saw that there weren't any vegan options you could eat.'

Dale raised his eyebrows. 'Oh really? I never even bothered to look at the menu. After all, it's not as if I was planning on eating here.'

Viewing him with abhorrence, she now knew that she should have trusted her gut feeling from Hendon all that time ago. That taint of arrogance he'd possessed back then had never quite sat well with her, and she realised now that it had never really gone away. She should have smelt it. A signal of the rot within. But, like the best manipulators, he'd hidden it well.

'You gave me up,' she hissed. 'Why?'

He sighed. 'You know, I didn't have to come in here. I could have just left. But I thought you at least deserved some kind of explanation before you die.'

'What a gentleman you are,' she spat sarcastically. 'Thank you so much.'

'Well... actually,' he said with a suppressed glee in his voice, 'I can't not tell you really.' He gave the lapel of his grey herringbone blazer jacket a self-congratulatory tweak. 'The whole thing is almost beautiful in its conception.'

'Beautiful?' she sneered. 'The explanation seems pretty simple to me. You're a bent copper and that's all there is to it.' She eyed him with contempt. 'You're probably just doing it to pay for all that cosmetic surgery you've had. I knew something had changed about you since Hendon. For one thing, your teeth look a bit too white to me. I reckon they're implants. And they cost a tidy packet, don't they? And your ears, they definitely used to stick out more. You've had them pinned back, haven't you? I bet that wasn't cheap.'

He patted his ears self-consciously. A hurt angry look flickered across his face. But then, just as quickly, the smug smile returned.

'Oh dear,' he said, shaking his head condescendingly. 'You really don't get it, do you?'

She frowned, puzzled. What was he going on about?

'You know, I had to pull a fair few strings to get you assigned to this operation. So much bloody red tape to go through. Luckily though I managed to convince Frank you were the one we needed.'

'Get me assigned?' she said, bewildered. 'What do you mean? What are you talking about?'

'It had to be you, Bailey. It always had to be you. Ever since you made it out of that scrapyard alive.'

Her eyes widened as it hit her with a gut-wrenching heave of realisation.

'Oh my God,' she gasped. 'It was you! You're the one who betrayed me to the car theft gang. You're the one who blew my cover.'

He nodded very slowly, his bright blue eyes boring into her, a mocking smirk on his face. 'Now she realises. You see why I had to come here and explain. It would almost have been unfair not to tell you.'

The devastation was complete. The room spun around her. She could barely breathe. His treachery was even more profound than she could have imagined. Her scars, the torture, the trauma, all those sleepless nights... it was all because of him.

'You should have died in that scrapyard, Bailey.' He shook his head, his face serious now. 'I just couldn't rest knowing that you were still alive, probably trying to work out who'd betrayed you. It was keeping me awake at night, you know. You have no idea how that kind of thing eats away at you. I knew you would discover me eventually. And if not you, Frank. He'd been sniffing around. Getting closer. Too close. So I knew I had to do something.'

'I can't believe it,' whispered Bailey. 'I just can't believe it.'

'That car theft ring had me on their books for several years, and they paid me very handsomely for information... about things like undercover cops, for example. Luckily I was careful to keep contact with them to a minimum, so when they went down, thanks to you, there was only one person among them who was able to identify me. But that was one too many, and the problem was that after he got caught, this bloke started threatening to give me up unless I got him off the hook. But I knew it was too late for that.' He paused and smiled. 'But you know what? Fate was on my side. This bloke had a congenital heart problem, you see. And all that stress of being caught meant he had to go to the hospital for an operation. And who should be the surgeon doing the operation, but a fellow Mason from my very own lodge who owed me a favour or two. Needless to say, the bloke died on the operating table.' Dale absently twiddled the Masonic ring on his finger as he spoke. 'But you were still out there alive, looking for me, you and Frank. And I had to do something about it.'

'So right from the get-go this whole operation has been nothing more than a giant trap?' she said, trying to get her head around the sheer audacity of his scheme.

Dale nodded smugly. 'They say that luck is the crossroads of preparation and opportunity. Well, I've been preparing to get rid of you for ages so, when the opportunity to infiltrate the Molloys came up, things just kind of fell into place.'

Bailey shook her head in bafflement. 'It seems like a heck of a lot of trouble to go to. Why didn't you just shoot me or something?'

He waved his finger at her. 'No. That would have looked way too suspicious. No, this way is perfect. I wanted to wait until you were in deep with the Molloys before blowing your cover. That way, they'd have no choice but to kill you because you'd know too much about their business by that stage.'

She had to admit, his logic was impeccable. 'Getting them to do your dirty work,' she muttered.

'I like to keep my hands clean,' he said. 'But that's not the half of it. When I paid my little visit to Rick yesterday, I told him that his brother had been an informant, which of course he'd already worked out. But when I told him that Adrian had helped to insert an undercover police officer into his organisation, you have no idea how grateful he was. You see, when I first met Adrian, not only did I see the opportunity to solve the Bailey Morgan problem, I also saw that by doing so, I could ingratiate myself with Rick Molloy. Ever since the car theft ring went down, I've been looking for a new employer, and Rick Molloy fits the bill perfectly. Adrian, of course, wasn't wise to any of this. The stupid fool thought he was dealing with a kosher police officer, but I was merely using him to get my way. When he got blown up, that did throw a bit of a spanner in the works initially, but it actually turned out to be for the best – he's one less headache for me to worry about now this thing's finally come to fruition.'

She stared in disbelief and loathing. 'Where did it all go wrong, Dale? Back at Hendon?'

His face twisted bitterly. 'They lied to us, Bailey. They told us it would be exciting. They told us it would be rewarding. But what did we get? Long hours. Low pay. And an ungrateful public. Some reward!' He exhaled derisively. 'I don't understand how you can put up with it.' He smiled unpleasantly. 'But then I guess you won't have to for very much longer.'

'If you hate being in the police so much, then why don't you leave?'

He shrugged. 'Because I got used to being corrupt. That's why. It has its own rewards, you know. I was doing it for years, and it was all going swimmingly... until the car theft ring got busted. And then I had to cease all my activities. I just couldn't risk doing anything that might expose me, couldn't risk doing anything that might possibly flag me to you and Frank. So since then I've been lying dormant, and spending my time working out the best way to get rid of you.'

Staring at him in disgust, Bailey felt soiled by the intimacy they'd shared. And to think she'd been planning to sleep with him later tonight. She felt like she was going to puke.

Apparently reading her thoughts, he rolled his eyes and emitted a nasty snicker. 'You probably thought tonight was going to be your lucky night, didn't you? I can see you dressed up especially. Probably put on some sexy underwear as well.' He looked away and snorted in condescension. When he looked at her again, he had an expression of disdain on his face. 'I wouldn't fuck you. I wouldn't lower myself. You're disfigured for one thing. Ugly. And I heard you were raped. And that means you're dirty. Damaged goods.'

His cruel words cut into her like acid. She felt tears surge up and forced herself to bite them back, but he hadn't finished just yet.

'I mean... look at you. You tried to make a real effort and everything.' He gestured at her dress. 'But it's kind of pathetic really. You'll never be a real woman.'

'You cunt,' she whispered.

'Oh, I'm sorry,' he said sarcastically. 'Did I hurt your feelings?'

It was clear as day now that the only reason he'd made such an effort to get close to her had been so that he could work out exactly the best time to betray her. But she'd been so blinded by her insecurities that she hadn't seen him for what he really was. She cursed her fatal lack of judgement.

He looked at his watch. 'Anyway, I've said what I wanted to say. Got it off my chest. I have to be going now. I've got a few loose ends to tie up before the evening's over.'

'What loose ends?' she muttered.

'Frank, of course. Like I said, he's been getting a bit too close for comfort. Now that you're out of the picture that just leaves him for me to deal with. Once he's out of the way, I'll be home free.'

'What are you going to do?' she gasped, her heart turning over in her chest at the thought of something happening to Frank.

'I'm going to kill him, of course. And I'm going to frame you for his murder. I'm going to use that gun that you got off the Molloys. That sample you gave me. It has your fingerprints all over it. You know, I never even checked it into the police property storeroom.' He smiled pleasantly. 'You're going to be fitted up in the finest tradition of police corruption. And there's absolutely nothing you can do about it.'

He reached into his pocket and took out a mobile phone. He held it up and twiddled it in front of her. She recognised it as her undercover mobile.

'I got this out of your handbag just now,' he said with a self-satisfied smirk. 'I'll have it with me when I kill Frank. When they're investigating his death, they'll triangulate the location of this phone and find out, lo and behold, that you were there.'

She shook her head, revolted by his cunning. Then, with a shocking jolt of realisation, she remembered that Frank's five-year-old daughter, Isabel, was staying with him. Dale would have no choice but to kill her as well and from what she knew of him now she knew he wouldn't baulk at it.

He had to be stopped. She had to stall him.

'Why would I kill Frank?' she said hoarsely. 'It doesn't make sense.'

'No, it makes perfect sense,' said Dale, his blue eyes staring maliciously into hers. 'You've been mentally unstable recently. What with this obsession with your sister. Frank told you to desist in your investigation of this Mister Snigiss. You went round Frank's house to argue with him about it. The argument got out of hand and you lost your temper and shot him. And then you went on the run. I will, of course, provide ample supporting testimony for all of this. Meanwhile, the Molloys will have killed you and disposed of your body. Fed it to the pigs or whatever it is they do with people they don't like. But to everyone else it'll look like you've fled abroad... because I'll have planted plenty of rumours to that effect. They'll be looking for you for years. But of course they'll never find you...'

He chuckled to himself, tickled by the cleverness of his own plan.

He sighed. 'Au revoir, Bailey Morgan.' He frowned. 'Oh, wait a minute. That means "see you again". I think the correct word is "adieu". That means "goodbye forever".'

And with that he turned on his tan loafers and exited the room, the door swinging shut behind him.

'Bastard,' muttered Bailey. 'This isn't over till it's over.'

69

Bailey listened to his footsteps fade away down the corridor, heard another door open and close, and then all was silent save the sound of her own ragged breathing in her ears.

She reflected on her situation. It had gone from really bad to even worse. If her own death wasn't enough, Frank's life and that of his daughter now hung in the balance. And she was the only person who could do anything about it. But she was stuck in this room tied to this blasted chair and these cable ties just weren't going to give way any time soon.

She tugged one more time at her bonds, but it was no good. They held her fast. The sharp edges of the plastic bit into her flesh, but that pain was nothing compared to what she knew would be facing her in the very near future.

Despair gripped her. If she didn't manage to make it out of here, then Frank and Isabel would die. And even if she did get out of here, there was no guarantee she'd be able to get help in time to prevent something happening to them, for Dale was no doubt heading over to them right now. Her situation seemed beyond all hope.

She gritted her teeth. She would not allow herself to give up. Not yet. All the while she was alive, there still existed a glimmer of hope, however small.

There was a creak as a door opened somewhere outside. Then a few moments later the door to the storeroom opened. *This is it*, thought Bailey, feeling a stomach-churning fear. The moment of reckoning.

Archie stood motionless in the doorway for a few moments, surveying the room through his insect-like black sunglasses. She observed him tensely, noticing that he was clutching a leather holdall by his side.

Without saying anything, he walked over to a small table on one side of the room. He placed the bag on the table. It made an ominous clank.

'Did you have a nice little chat?' he said, glancing over his shoulder at her.

She said nothing, eyeing the bag with concern.

He shrugged and turned back to the table. He unzipped the bag and began to take out a variety of items, laying them out methodically on the tabletop.

'I said I might show you my knife collection one day. Well, here it is. Not all of them, of course. I've got way too many for that. Just some of my choice favourites, as well as a few other tools of the trade.'

The knives and tools clinked as he arranged them neatly side-by-side on the table.

Craning her head, Bailey could make out some kind of dagger, a meat cleaver, a bone saw and a pair of pliers amongst other things. And he was still taking stuff out of the bag.

'I used to work as an apprentice in a butcher's shop,' he said, without turning around. 'I got to be quite an expert at the art of dismemberment. Cutting a carcass down into its constituent joints of meat. Once you've taken apart a pig, a sheep, a cow, humans are easy. And I've done a fair few of them. I've got the whole process down to forty-five minutes, start to finish.'

'Well, I guess you've got to have transferable skills in today's job market,' said Bailey conversationally, attempting to keep her voice level. The more she engaged him and the more he talked, the more time she had to try and figure a way out of here.   .

'Indeed,' he said, turning around to face her. 'Obviously, the reason I'm going to cut you up is to make your body easier to dispose of.'

'Of course,' she nodded agreeably. 'That makes perfect sense.'

He scrutinised her mutely through his black sunglasses and she wondered if she'd overdone it.

'Before I cut you up though, I'm going to have to kill you. I'll be cutting your throat. Ear to ear. You'll be all done and bled out in less than three minutes. I can't say it won't hurt, but it is my favoured method. Legacy of working in the meat industry, I suppose.'

He picked up the meat cleaver and the bone saw and held them up for her to see.

'After you're dead, I'll use these to take off your head, then all four of your limbs. I'll have to chop up your torso a bit, as that's always the most challenging part to dispose of.'

He placed the tools back on the table and then held up the pair of pliers.

'When it comes to your head, I'll use these to pull out all your teeth so they can't do that dental records identification thing.' He gave her a grin. 'Don't worry though, I'll make sure to do that after you're dead. I know how some people hate having their teeth interfered with. I for one detest the dentist.'

She guessed that explained the poor condition of his teeth.

He began to screw a vice onto the edge of the table. 'This will hold your severed head whilst I extract your teeth,' he explained.

She watched him in disbelief, finding it hard to understand how someone could treat horrific acts like these in such a workaday manner. But then he was clearly a psychopath, plain and simple. Pleading for your life with someone like this would be a total waste of time, so she wasn't even going to bother.

He finished screwing the vice onto the table and turned to face her. 'It's nothing personal, you know. I hope you understand. This is just business.'

'Sure,' she said reasonably. 'You're just doing your job.'

He nodded with a contented smile. Then, for the first time ever, he took off his sunglasses to reveal a pair of pale blue eyes so light in colour that they almost seemed albino. An icy shiver went down Bailey's spine as she saw the complete absence of empathy in them and beyond that, dancing behind the black pupils, a tiny spark of insanity.

'But first,' he said, 'I believe you have some information that Mrs Molloy wants.'

70

With her hair hanging down messily over her face, Bailey sat there furiously wringing her brains for a way to resolve her predicament, but she wasn't having much luck and it looked like time was running out fast.

'Now, we can make this as long or as short as you want,' said Archie. 'It's really up to you and how soon you decide to give up what you know.'

'I told you I don't have any information about Mister Snigiss,' she said.

'You should really know better,' he chided. 'Because, by the looks of those scars, it appears that you've already been tortured at least once before.' He frowned curiously. 'Did you tell them what they wanted to know? Or were they just doing it for fun?'

The hideous memories of that experience started to resurge. She tried to push them from her mind. Her head had to remain clear. The priority was to think of an escape.

He assessed her disfigurement with the dispassionate eye of a professional, his bleached blue gaze running down over her face, neck, shoulders and cleavage.

'Hmm. A tad crude perhaps. A cigarette and a straight razor, I'd guess. Am I right?'

Images and sensations flashed unbidden through her mind. That deadly sliver of metal slicing into her flesh. The glowing tip of the clove cigarette. That sickly sweet smell... the lascivious grin on her torturer's face...

'Personally I find straight razors a little awkward to handle,' said Archie. 'They work better as a psychological tool, in my opinion. Not that I don't have one or two in my collection.'

By sheer force of will, Bailey steered her mind back to her current situation, attacking it from every possible angle, pushing her problem-solving skills into overdrive. There had to be a way out of this. There had to be.

'Often, when I meet someone,' Archie continued. 'I'll visualise the wounds on them before I've even started. It's like when Michelangelo was talking about how he saw the statue of David contained inside that block of marble. Because I guess it's a bit like sculpting in some ways.'

Bailey couldn't help but roll her eyes at his conceit. 'Give me a break. The next thing you're going to tell me is you're an "artist", aren't you?'

He looked a little bit hurt. 'I think of myself more as a craftsman.' He licked his lips, once again revealing his brown rotting teeth. 'I'd like to say it doesn't give me pleasure. But it does. They say if you love your job, you'll never work another day in your life. And I love my job.'

'Where do they find you fucking people?' she said.

He frowned. 'I possess a highly sought-after skillset.'

'Yeah right,' she muttered.

He nodded in the direction of the door. 'That lot are all into household appliances and power tools,' he said, referring to the rest of the gang. 'Me, personally, I'm a purist. I think that there's nothing better than doing a bit of carving with a nice sharp knife. I love cutting bits off. When it comes to human beings, there are so many nice sensitive bits that you can cut off.' He nodded at her scars. 'You think those look bad? After I'm done with you, you'll be completely unrecognisable.'

She swallowed hard, her mouth dry, her heart thumping against the inside of her chest. She sensed the foreplay was coming to an end and very soon Archie would be getting down to business. Time was running out very rapidly and she still hadn't thought of a way out of this quandary.

'For the purposes of this evening's torture,' he said, 'I'll be using one of the latest additions to my collection. I've been absolutely dying to test it out. It's from Japan. It's known as a *tanto*.'

He selected one of the knives lying on the table and held it up for her to see. It was a short dagger with a slight curve to the blade and a very sharp angular point. The style was reminiscent of a samurai sword.

'Isn't she beautiful?' he said. 'Hand-forged in laminated carbon steel.'

Bailey looked at the knife and gulped nervously.

'You can get an incredible edge on carbon steel,' he explained, softly testing the blade with his thumb, 'Although for what I have in mind tonight, she could probably do with even more of a sharpen.' He addressed the knife as if it was a person. 'Do you want me to sharpen you, baby?'

Bailey stared at him in disbelief.

He turned his back on her and picked up a whetstone from the table. Humming a little tune, he began to hone the edge of the knife on the whetstone. Schwip. Schwap. Schwip. Schwap...

Think, Bailey, think. There must be a way out. Think think think.

She blew her hair out of her face. Bloody hair, getting on her nerves. As she did so, she felt something knock against the back of her neck and realised that it was her hairgrip. It had become loose in the recent struggle and was now hanging down behind her head.

Her poor mother, she suddenly thought. Despite her fundamentalist Christian ways, she'd meant well and she'd only ever wanted what was best for Bailey. And now look at Bailey – tied to a chair on the verge of being tortured and murdered. She wondered if it was too late to suddenly become a Christian. That would make her mum happy. After all, people often did convert when they were close to death and—

Bailey's fevered musings suddenly jerked to a halt as something occurred to her.

The shape of the hairgrip.

The ancient fish symbol. A single line traced in thin silver, the end of the tail formed of two divergent strands of metal with nothing joining them together.

An idea began to take form in her mind.

She remembered that cable ties could be unlocked if you found something narrow enough to insert in the lock. Maybe there was the very slim chance she could use one of the metal ends of the fish tail. If memory served her right, it was slender enough to fit inside the mouth of a cable tie. All she had to do was somehow get the hairgrip out of her hair and into her hands. But that was no easy task.

She glanced at Archie. He was still sharpening the knife, talking to it in a breathless whisper. 'Oh, you like that, don't you? Oh, yeah...'

Praying that he would keep going for a few minutes longer, she began to shake her head until the hairgrip started to come loose. Her aim was to try and catch it in her hands behind her. But it would be exceedingly difficult. Not only were her hands bound, she wouldn't be able to see what she was doing. But it was imperative she caught it, for if she dropped it, or if it bounced off the top of the chair, then she was finished for good.

She jerked her head again. She felt the hairgrip loosen a little and slide down a bit further. Almost there...

She eyed Archie warily. He was still sharpening the knife with his back to her.

Schwip. Schwap. Schwip. Schwap.

He appeared to be completely absorbed in the process, lost in a dreamy rapture as he whispered sweet nothings to his knife.

He just needed to stay that way for a few moments longer, just long enough for her to...

She jerked her head again. The hairgrip moved once more. She could now feel it hanging from her head by just a thin strand of hair.

Contorting her arms and stretching out her fingers to catch it, she gave her head one more jerk.

The hairgrip came loose completely. Flexing her fingers, she managed to catch it. But only just. She was gripping it by the very tip of the nose of the fish between her thumb and forefinger.

She held her breath. If she dropped it now she was done for. She felt it slipping out of her fingers, but then very slowly... very gently... she eased it into a more secure position until she was holding it firmly in her bound hands.

Whew! That was close. But she didn't have much time. Archie would soon be finished and ready to start on her. She could not afford to mess this up. Her life, Frank's life, his daughter's life – all of their fates hinged upon her very next actions.

Trying to keep her hands from trembling, she bent her right wrist to insert the tip of the tail into the lock of the cable tie of her left hand. It was an incredibly awkward manoeuvre and she had to try several times before she felt the narrow tip of the fish tail enter the mouth of the cable tie. Slowly working it inwards, she probed for the tiny ratchet that locked it shut.

She glanced up. Archie appeared to have finished sharpening the knife and he was now holding it up and admiring it, turning it one way and then the other, watching the light shine off the blade, entranced by the silvery sparkle of the steel. *Please let him stay in that world of his own*, she thought. Just for a few seconds more. That was all she needed...

Pressing down with the hairgrip, Bailey felt the ratchet give way. Gently, she pulled her wrists apart, feeling the cable tie feeding back through the lock. As soon as there was enough room, she eased her hand from the plastic loop.

Again she looked at Archie. He still had his back to her and he was still peering intently at the blade. Now he was testing the edge of it with his thumb.

Not taking her eyes off him for a second, she leant down and used the hairgrip to release the cable ties attaching each of her ankles to the legs of the chair.

She was just in the process of slipping her left ankle out of the final cable tie when she noticed Archie looking at her in the reflection of the blade. A pale blue eye occupying the mirrored surface of the steel... looking directly at her. The eye widened in alarm and Archie whipped around to face her.

He immediately hurled himself at her, bringing the knife down in a deadly arc towards her neck. She boosted herself to her feet, going into automatic jiu-jitsu mode, throwing her left arm up just in time to parry the blow, the vicious point of the blade halting just a few centimetres from her face. Already she knew the next move to make...

Ude garami – bent arm lock.

She snaked her right arm under his knife arm and grasped her left wrist, trapping his arm in a figure-of-four entanglement. She took a step forward past him and exerted a sharp downward pressure, twisting his elbow and shoulder in a painfully unnatural direction.

He gasped in agony as he bent over backwards. She held him immobile in the armlock, and for a moment they both stood there wrapped in a frozen snapshot of combat. Archie blinked up at her from his excruciating position, his pale eyes wide with astonishment, stunned by the speed and dexterity of her reaction.

Then she saw him draw breath as if to scream. And she couldn't afford to let that happen. She paused for the fraction of a second that it took her to make that lethal decision.

Nukite uchi – spear-hand strike.

Disengaging her right hand from her left wrist, she compressed her extended fingers into a point and drove them hard into his Adam's apple.

The blow crushed his larynx, stopping the scream in his throat before it had a chance to escape. His eyes bulged as he choked, the knife clattering uselessly to the floor beside him.

She released him and he fell to the ground clutching his neck, making grotesque gargling noises as he suffocated to death.

She stood there watching him writhing his last movements at her feet.

'I'm sorry,' she whispered, looking into his pale bulging eyes. 'I hope you understand. This is just business.'

71

The plastic sheeting crinkled beneath her stockinged feet as Bailey walked to the door of the storeroom.

Bitterness at Dale surged up once more in a painful reflux of emotion. How could she have been so stupid as to trust him? How could she have fallen for such an absolute piece of shit? How could she have been so blind? The stinging thoughts only strengthened her resolve to try and stop him. *Please let it not be too late to do so...*

Standing by the edge of the door, she opened it a crack and looked out. A brightly lit corridor lay beyond. Just across and to her right was the door to another room. Through the glass panel in the door, she could make out at least two men in chef's hats and clouds of steam rising up amidst hanging pots and implements. It looked like the kitchen. A few seconds later, the kitchen door swung open and a waiter emerged carrying a tray of food. She quickly eased back into the storeroom, pushing the door almost closed, watching through the thin crack as he passed. The tray was laden with appetisers and they looked and smelt delicious. Bailey realised that the stress of the situation had made her ravenous. But now wasn't the time to be thinking about food.

The waiter walked to the end of the corridor and passed through a set of double doors. The warm light of the restaurant was visible for a moment through the doors, then it was gone as they swung closed again.

Looking up the corridor in the other direction, she saw a blank wall. A dead end. Unless she went through the kitchen, where there were people working, and where there was no guarantee of an exit, the only way out of here was through the restaurant. Either way was going to be supremely risky.

Bailey chewed her lip. Time was of the essence. If she was going to move, she needed to move now, before the waiter returned.

She crept out of the storeroom and sneaked along the corridor, her stockinged feet padding silently on the concrete floor. Stopping at the double doors, she pushed one of them open a fraction and peeked into the restaurant.

Over to her right, she could see the various members of the gang sitting at a long table embarking on a meal, the waiter moving between them serving appetisers from his tray. In any other context it might have resembled a birthday celebration or a group of people from work out for an evening meal. They were chatting and laughing boisterously and clinking beers, as if it was no big deal that just a short distance away on the other side of a wall, they were having a female police officer tortured, murdered and dismembered.

Nancy was sitting at the head of the table. Stephen was sitting to her right, holding court, telling everyone how he'd always suspected that there was something off about Bailey. Shane was laughing loudly. The bald-headed, ginger-bearded thug who she'd punched was sitting among them holding a bloodied napkin to his nose but still smiling all the same.

Bailey watched them as they triumphantly toasted the benefit of having yet one more copper in their pocket, and how things were really looking up for their organisation, and how they'd find a new buyer for the guns, and how lucky they were to have found out about Bailey before the deal went down, and how the information she was going to provide on Mister Snigiss would finally help secure them the requisite justice for Adrian. But Bailey didn't have time to hang around and

listen to them, being concerned with rather more urgent plans of
her own.

She peered over to the left, where the exit was. By it was a small
alcove containing a coat rack. Seeing the coats hanging there, it
occurred to her that at least one of them might contain a mobile phone
with which she could call the police to warn Frank. And failing that,
one of them might contain car keys, for if she couldn't call ahead from
here, she'd have to get to some location where she could, and fast. The
restaurant seemed relatively remote and she didn't want to bet on the
chance of waiting for and waving down a passing car.

She eyed the layout of the restaurant with concern. To reach the
exit and the coat rack she would have to cross a large open stretch of
floor where she would be fully exposed to view for a distance of at least
five metres or so. She would just have to move as stealthily as possible
and pray that none of them happened to look in her direction at that
particular moment.

She saw that the waiter had almost finished offloading his tray of
appetisers and would probably be heading back through the double
doors in just a short moment.

Kneeling down, she eased one of the double doors open a small
way and squeezed out into the restaurant. Getting down on her belly,
putting a large pot of bamboo between herself and the gang, she
crawled forwards and rolled beneath a table just as the waiter made his
way back to the kitchen. Lying under the table holding her breath, she
watched his shiny black shoes pass by just a metre or so from her nose.

As soon as he had gone back through the double doors to the
kitchen, she slithered forward in a commando crawl, emerging from
under the table to cross the centre of the restaurant. Her heart beat
furiously as she pulled herself along on her stomach, trying not to
make any sharp movements that might attract their attention. Glancing
up at them, she saw that they were still wrapped up in chatter and
laughter.

Never had she felt more exposed in her life as she did crawling
across the middle of the restaurant in full view of the gang, her black

dress sharply defined against the light-coloured marble floor. At any moment any one of them – Nancy, Stephen, Rick, Shane – could turn and notice her out of the corner of their eye and then all would be lost.

Bailey gritted her teeth and pushed herself forwards across the cold marble, each second seeming to stretch out into an agonising eternity. Finally she reached the alcove with the coat rack, pulling herself into the small space with a huge sigh of relief. Momentarily she was once again concealed from their view.

Getting up on her knees, she began to riffle through the pockets of the jackets hanging on the rack. In the first one, no phone, no keys. The same with the second. Nothing in the third. She cursed. Then, putting her hands in the pocket of the fourth jacket, her fingers closed around a bristling metal bundle. Yes! She pulled them carefully out, trying not to make them clink. A key fob displaying the Range Rover icon told her that these were likely the keys to Rick's car, and looking at the jacket she'd taken them from, she now recognised it as his black Dior cashmere overcoat. Checking the rest of the coats for a mobile phone, her search came up empty. Still, at least she had the car keys – one out of two wasn't bad. Her priority now was to proceed with all haste to some place where she could make an emergency call.

Standing up, she peered around the corner of the alcove at the gang. They were still occupied in noisy conversation. The door was only around two metres away, but she would be exposed once more when she went to open it.

Clutching the car keys in her hand, she took a deep breath and tiptoed from the alcove to the door. Through the glass panel of the door, she could see the welcoming darkness outside. She was almost there. She was almost free. Just a few steps more.

Wrapping her fingers around the door handle, she carefully pulled it open. And as she did so there was a sharp electronic 'ping'.

It was the bell, triggered by the automatic sensor, that informed the maître d' whenever someone entered or exited the restaurant.

Shit. She'd forgotten all about that.

She froze and looked over her shoulder. And saw that Rick was staring directly at her. His jaw dropped open in disbelief.

Bollocks.

He drew breath. 'It's that fucking bitch!' he roared.

The race was on.

She wrenched open the door and sprinted down the marble steps, looking around frantically for Rick's Range Rover. But she couldn't see it parked out in front of the restaurant. But then, of course, it wasn't going to be there. That would have given the game away when she'd arrived with Dale. She would have recognised it immediately. No, it had to be somewhere else. There had to be some other parking area. Out the back.

Adrenaline driving her forwards, she ran towards the corner of the restaurant, the sharp stones of gravel biting into the soles of her stockinged feet. Seconds later the Molloy entourage spilled out of the restaurant in pursuit, panting and shouting, their breath frosting in the cold night air.

'There she is!' she heard someone shout.

'After her!' shouted someone else.

But she had already rounded the corner and was racing along the side of the building, praying that she was heading in the right direction.

The path she was running along suddenly gave out into a small open area behind the restaurant in which several cars were parked, among them, to her great relief, Rick's black Range Rover Velar.

She made a beeline for it, pressing the button on the key fob as she did so. The car lights flashed as the door unlocked and a fraction of a second later she was there, yanking the driver's door open and climbing inside.

When being in the car previously with Rick, she'd noticed that, as well as the fact that it was an automatic, it was also one of those vehicles where you didn't need to insert a key in order to start it. She pressed the 'start/stop' button and the car started immediately.

Flicking the drive selector into reverse, she jammed her foot on the accelerator, the large vehicle jumping backwards. Almost immediately, she felt a juddering crunch as the rear of the Range Rover ploughed into the side of one of the cars parked behind it. Whoops! She swung it round, dialled the selector into the 'drive' position, and sped forwards, clipping the front of another car before hurtling back down the path to the front of the restaurant and the road beyond.

Rick's men scattered aside as she cannoned forward in the heavy vehicle. She wasn't stopping for anyone.

The tyres skidded loudly on the loose gravel as she aggressively steered the powerful car through the front car park in the direction of the trackway leading to the main road. There ahead of her she saw Rick standing by the open boot of one of the cars holding something in his hands. Something long and sticklike...

As she whizzed past him, she saw that it was a shotgun which he'd just loaded and snapped shut. She caught the grim determination on his face as he raised it to his shoulder and brought it to bear upon her.

She pressed down harder on the accelerator, the car flying ahead, simultaneously ducking down as the shotgun roared behind her, blowing out the back window of the Range Rover.

Sitting up again, unscathed by the shotgun blast, she glanced in the rear-view mirror to see his tall figure receding into the distance as the car sped away from the restaurant.

Pulling out sharply onto the main road, she turned the vehicle in the direction of London and Frank's house, and just hoped, against all odds, that it wasn't too late to save him.

72

Frank picked up a handful of Texas BBQ Sauce-flavoured Pringles from the bowl on the coffee table and put them in his mouth. They were Isabel's favourite flavour and he'd purchased them especially for her visit, along with the Haribo Tangfastics which filled yet another bowl. He himself had consumed more of both of them than she had so far this evening though. Whenever his five-year-old daughter came round to visit it provided a good excuse for him to buy junk food that he secretly enjoyed under the auspices that it was for her. He'd have to watch it though – his waistline had been growing somewhat larger recently, what with all those kebabs he'd been getting through. On reflection, perhaps it hadn't been the best idea to set up the temporary HQ above a kebab shop; maybe next time he'd try and pick somewhere close to a gym.

Isabel was sitting next to him on the sofa engrossed in *Frozen* which was playing on the TV. She loved *Frozen* and watched it repeatedly, never seeming to tire of it. That was why Frank had thought it a good idea to invest in the DVD, so she could watch it whenever she came round, even if it meant he had to put up with yet another rendition of that blasted song which he knew he wouldn't be able to get out of his head for the next twenty-four hours. But it was worth it.

He loved seeing his daughter and knew he didn't see her enough, painfully aware that it was his own relentless dedication to his career that lay to blame. He'd let his job destroy his marriage and now his ex-wife, Joanna, had found happiness in another man's arms. In fact, he thought, with a vague unease, they were probably doing exactly that right now – making love in some expensive foreign hotel. Roland – wealthy as he was – had whisked her off on an eight-day romantic break to Cuba, which was the whole reason that Frank was taking care of Isabel. Quite often he wished he'd done things differently in his marriage so it hadn't come to this, with him having to wait to spend time with his daughter, but if he was to be honest with himself, he knew that he was too heavily into his job to have given it up even if he'd tried.

He fondly observed his daughter as she watched the TV. She was dressed in her pyjamas and, technically, being a school night, it was well past her bedtime. Joanna would have made sure she'd gone to bed at least two hours earlier. But Isabel had pleaded with him to stay up and watch *Frozen*, and Frank was a soft touch when it came to anything concerning his daughter. Anyhow, he could see the film was almost drawing to a close; he knew it almost as well as she did by now.

The doorbell rang. He frowned and looked at his watch and wondered who it could be at this time on a Monday evening. It certainly wasn't going to be Joanna. She wasn't due to pick up Isabel until the end of the week.

He sighed. He stood up to go and see who was there.

'Who's at the door?' asked Isabel.

'I'm sure it's nobody important,' he said.

73

The powerful three-litre supercharged V6 engine growled angrily as the Range Rover surged through the night with Bailey craned over the wheel giving it everything she had. Trying to keep her eyes on the road, she frantically rummaged through the glovebox in search of a mobile phone or even a firearm… but no such luck.

She knew the Molloys wouldn't bother chasing after her. She was out in the open and now off their territory and it would be too risky for them to try and do something to her with all the public CCTV and traffic cameras dotted everywhere.

Even so, she made sure to put a decent distance between herself and them before pulling rapidly into a petrol station and demanding to use the phone to make an emergency call to the police.

If the police could get to Frank's house in time to head off Dale, then maybe it would be okay. This would be a grade one emergency call, the most serious type, and the response times for these kinds of calls averaged less than fifteen minutes.

'The address is twenty-seven Knowsley Close,' she gasped down the phone to the 999 operator, as she did her utmost to convey the immense gravity and urgency of the situation.

She would have called Frank directly, but she realised she didn't actually know his telephone number from memory. After all, when the number was saved in your phone, why bother remembering it? And more to the point, she didn't have her phone on her. Dale had her phone.

She jumped back in the car to continue onto Frank's house. She'd be able to coordinate with him and the police once she was there and alert them to Dale's perfidy. All she could do now was just pray that the police reached Frank before Dale did.

Accelerating down the dual carriageway, she reckoned she could get to Frank's house in just under half an hour if she really pushed it. He lived in Enfield and she'd been to his place a few times.

As she drove along, it occurred to her that the Molloys would probably have tried to call Dale to warn him that she'd escaped. But she was certain he wouldn't have his own phone on him as that would potentially place him at the murder scene; and that was the whole reason he was bringing her phone with him – in order to frame her by placing her at the scene instead. But would the Molloys think to call him on her phone? Were they even aware that he'd taken it? At least if they did manage to get through to him, then it might deter him from killing Frank.

The thoughts churned furiously through her mind as she sped through the streets. She wouldn't know for sure until she got there and the tension knotting her guts right now was unbearable.

Glancing at the clock on the dashboard, she saw that it was quarter past nine. She tried to work out what time Dale would have left the restaurant and if he would be at Frank's house yet. There was always the possibility he'd taken some sort of detour first – perhaps to prepare himself for the murder. She could only hope. Any extra minute was vital.

Getting to Frank's part of Enfield, she wrested the car violently through the tranquil suburban streets, the Range Rover skidding to a halt in the small cul-de-sac where his house was.

But she instantly saw that something wasn't right. The cul-de-sac was eerily quiet. Where were the police cars? Where were the blue lights? Why weren't they here? Surely they should have responded by now.

Immediately focusing her gaze on Frank's small semi-detached house, she noticed the dark metallic Tesla parked up on the pavement right outside.

Dale was here.

'Oh God,' she gasped.

She was too late. Or was she?

The neighbourhood appeared sleepy and subdued. A few lights on behind the net curtains. A picture of normality. It didn't seem like a shooting had taken place. Yet. Was there still time to stop him?

But where the hell were the police? She needed them now. Right now.

She looked around wildly, breathing hard.

Then she noticed the street sign.

Knowsley Place.

A nauseous heave of realisation struck her. She'd given the 999 operator the wrong street name. She remembered now how it had always been a bit confusing coming here in the past because there were at least three streets in the area with Knowsley in the name – Knowsley Place, Knowsley Crescent and Knowsley Close. With all that was on her mind right now, she'd gone and mixed up the names... an innocent mistake with potentially fatal consequences.

The police would have gone to Knowsley Close a few streets away, found that nothing was wrong and written it off as a hoax call.

Oh fuck indeed.

What had she done? How could she have screwed up so badly?

Bailey blinked in horror. Had her error cost Frank and his daughter their lives? She'd never be able to forgive herself.

Swallowing hard, she tried to pull herself together. There was no time to call the police now. Even if they did get here within fifteen minutes, that could still be too late. She had to do something immediately and she was on her own.

She pushed open the door of the car, her heart turning over furiously in her chest. Rarely had she ever felt so frightened at what might confront her right now.

She took a deep breath and ran over to Frank's house, slowing down as she entered the driveway, warily observing for any movement from the inside.

As she got closer, she saw that the front door was slightly ajar and she could hear the faint sounds of a movie playing in the living room. It sounded like some kind of kids' film. Treading very softly, and holding her breath, she placed her fingers on the front door and pushed it open very slowly and very carefully.

Something stopped it from opening fully. She squeezed through the gap and the first thing she saw was a pair of legs, the feet, in white socks, pressing against the inside of the door.

Her stomach dropped.

Stepping fully into the hallway, she saw that it was Frank. He was lying on his back at the foot of the stairs with his eyes closed, his beige jumper stained with a huge bloom of dark red blood. It looked like he had been shot in the chest as soon as he'd opened the front door. An acrid whiff of smoke hung in the air. The smell of a gunshot.

'Oh my God, Frank,' she whispered and rushed to kneel down by his side, placing a gentle hand on his shoulder as she examined his injuries. 'I'm so sorry.'

Blood was oozing from his chest, bright, sticky and wet. On closer inspection, it looked like he'd been shot twice. His diaphragm was moving and he was making an unnatural sucking noise as he tried to draw breath. She realised that the bullets must have gone through his lungs, but fortunately not his heart, otherwise he'd be dead. He was still alive, but only just, and he needed medical attention immediately. She needed to find a phone.

But what about Dale?

He was still in here. Somewhere. And he was armed and danger-ous. She glanced around tensely. The narrow hallway stood quiet and empty, the kitchen lying silent at the far end. Directly in front, up the stairs, she could see the top of the landing, but nothing else beyond.

From behind the living room door, to her left, came the sound of singing from the TV.

Where was Isabel? Was she in the living room? Was she dead?

Bailey swallowed nervously, her mouth dry. What should her next move be? To go into the living room or to venture upstairs?

She jumped as she felt something touch her arm. It was Frank's hand, twitching weakly.

His eyes had flickered open, his eyelids fluttering softly. His watery blue eyes met hers with recognition.

'Isabel,' he whispered, and with what seemed like a gargantuan effort, he rolled his eyes upwards to indicate that his daughter was upstairs.

Bailey nodded silently, gave his shoulder the gentlest of squeezes, then stood up.

She peered up the stairs. Maybe it wasn't too late to save Isabel. Maybe.

She started to climb the stairs.

74

Dale crept softly along the carpeted landing of Frank's house holding the gun in front of him, his finger poised to pull the trigger at the slightest movement.

Where the fuck had that little brat got to?

He hadn't been expecting to encounter Frank's daughter when he got here, but when he'd seen her peering over the top of the sofa at him standing over her dad's body, he knew she'd have to go as well. He just could not afford to have any witnesses to his crime. She'd immediately scuttled out of the living room into the kitchen. He'd chased after her, but she'd been too nimble and had looped back through the hallway, past her dad's body and up the stairs.

Bad strategy. She should have gone out of the front door, to a neighbour's house. But now she was trapped upstairs. She was probably hiding under the bed somewhere. Kids were so unimaginative. Thank God he didn't have any himself.

He readjusted his grip on the gun and prowled forward towards what looked like the master bedroom. He had to admit, he felt pretty good whenever he held a gun – it gave him a real rush of power. You could end someone's life just like that, with a tiny squeeze of the trigger. This was the first time he'd used one with a silencer, though, and it made the gun kind of bulky. The silencer wasn't half as quiet as he'd been led to believe either, and certainly nothing like what they made out in the movies. But it was enough to at least take the edge off the bang and make it pass for something else in this suburban environment.

He'd shot Frank twice in the chest as soon as he'd opened the front door. Frank had looked so surprised. No wonder, seeing Dale standing there on his doorstep dressed in his full anti-forensics get-up, pointing a gun at him. The confusion in his eyes had been replaced by realisation as soon as he saw the weapon. But by then it had been too late. He already had two bullets in his chest. Stupid Frank.

The great thing about being in the police, thought Dale, was that it put you in a very advantageous position if you wanted to break the law because you knew exactly what could be deployed against you. Hence his anti-forensics gear. He'd gone to great lengths to ensure that there were no traces of himself at this crime scene, and instead, just evidence that incriminated Bailey. He was wearing a shower hat so as not to drop any hairs from his head, his hands were sheathed in nitrile rubber medical examination gloves, and on his feet he had plastic bags taped over his shoes. To put Bailey squarely in the frame, he was sprinkling strands of her hair here and there, hair that he'd plucked from the hairbrush in her bathroom. Not only that, he was wearing her green cashmere scarf around his neck with the intention of spreading fibres from it here before he planted it back in her flat after he was done. He'd heard her mention that it had gone missing, but she hadn't suspected that it had been him who'd nicked it. Dozy cow. Given all her experience working undercover and the numerous plaudits he'd heard about her, she'd been remarkably easy to deceive, but then he figured she was just like all women – blinded by emotion.

He wanted to laugh at the thought that Bailey had believed he was actually interested in her. Maybe once upon a time, back at Hendon, he might have given her a passing glance, but now, with those unsightly scars, and not to mention her annoyingly stubborn attitude, she did nothing but repulse him.

As he padded along in his plastic-bag-covered shoes, he thought about how it had come down to this, having to murder a young child out of necessity. The thing was, he didn't feel too bad about it. The kid would probably just have grown up into a stupid adult that looked a bit like Frank. And who needed another one of them?

Sure, maybe at one time it might have bothered him. Back when he'd been idealistic. Back when he'd first joined the police. But those days were long gone.

One of the big problems with being in the police, he'd soon realised after signing up, was that the money was shit and it always would be – but then that was the public sector for you. But at the same time he'd also realised that the job itself provided unparalleled opportunities to make cash on the side if you knew how to work it. It was like an illicit bonus scheme.

The only issue was that once you built up a certain kind of lifestyle, you had to be able to maintain it. And he'd developed a taste for it. The cool car. The upscale apartment. The cosmetic surgery. The women... they were the main reason he was doing it. It was amazing the difference a bit of cash made when it came to getting laid. Or at least it did with the types of females that he went for.

It wasn't like he was so ostentatious with his spending that anyone might suspect anything. No, he kept it all skilfully in check. But even so, all those financial commitments he'd built up over the years had ballooned into considerable debts ever since he'd been deprived of his illegal income from the car theft ring. And he didn't like being in debt one bit.

That's why he was so happy about working with the Molloys. Encountering Adrian had been a boon – the chance to get rid of Bailey and the chance to get in with Rick. It had all worked out so well. Better than Dale could ever have expected. A new chapter was beginning. A brand-new influx of cash. Something to pay off his debts. The first thing he'd do would be to help the Molloys shift those guns.

He caught himself. He was getting ahead of himself. First things first. Kill Frank's kid.

He pushed open the door to the master bedroom, flicked the light on and levelled the gun. The room was silent and empty. Sparsely furnished, it contained just a double bed, a wardrobe, a dresser and a small bookcase. Kneeling down, Dale peered beneath the bed.

Nothing but a few shoeboxes.

He stood up and stalked over to the wardrobe. Taking a deep breath, he pulled the door open. It contained two suits on hangers and a number of shirts. Using the silencer, he pushed the garments aside to see if she was hiding behind them. But she wasn't.

He glanced around the rest of the room. There wasn't anywhere else to hide in here. That meant that she had to be in another room.

His bright blue eyes narrowed in a predatory manner and he ran his tongue over his perfect white teeth. Did she seriously think she was smarter than he was? A five-year-old kid? There was no way he was going to let her give him the slip. No way.

He suddenly became aware of Bailey's phone vibrating in his pocket. He'd switched it to silent mode after taking it from her hand-bag, figuring that if it did ring, he might not want it to draw attention to him, like right now for example. But out of curiosity, he pulled it from his pocket. He saw Rick's name flashing up on the small screen. Why was Rick trying to call Bailey when she was already dead? But then he realised that Rick was probably actually trying to call him because, now he thought about it, Rick did know that he'd taken Bailey's phone. But if so, why? He saw then that he'd missed several calls from Rick already since leaving the restaurant. Rick clearly had something to tell him.

His finger hovered uncertainly over the 'answer' button. He was reluctant to answer the phone right now for fear of giving away his position at this crucial moment. But maybe he should answer it. Maybe Rick had something important to say.

Dale was just about to answer the phone when he heard a faint scuffling noise from outside the room.

His head jerked up sharply and he tightened his grip on the gun.

He put the phone back in his pocket. Rick would have to wait for the time being. Dale had business to attend to and the sooner he got it over with, the better.

With the gun pointed in front of him, he stepped back out into the silent hallway and followed in the direction of the noise.

75

Bailey tiptoed up the stairs, her stockinged feet making next to no noise on the carpeted surface. A stair creaked as she stepped on it. She froze, acutely aware that Dale could pop up at any moment and send a bullet smashing through her head. She contemplated going back down to the kitchen and finding a knife or weapon of some sort but immediately nixed the idea – there was no time for that; she had to find Isabel before Dale did.

Her breathing shallow and ragged, she continued upwards. Reaching the top of the stairs, she paused for a moment on the landing, looking to her left, then to her right. No one on the silent landing. Nothing but a table with a lamp, and a mirror on the wall. She caught a glimpse of herself in the mirror. She looked a mess.

Where was Dale? Where was Isabel? She knew the layout of Frank's house from memory, but only vaguely – she hadn't been here for a while. As she recalled, there were only two rooms up here – the master bedroom at the front of the house and a slightly smaller bedroom at the back. Which one should she check first? She knew the wrong move now would be fatal.

She tried to steady her breathing, tried to remain cool, as she stood there by the small table, its lamp giving out a cosy yellow glow that belied the life-and-death stakes that were being played out here in this little suburban semi.

She decided to go with what she knew. Taking a few steps to her right, she pushed open the door to the back bedroom and very quietly flicked the light on. On the floor, she noticed a small bag with some children's clothes spilling out of it. This had to be where Isabel was staying. It was the room that Frank used as a guest bedroom and it had its own en-suite bathroom. Bailey had stayed in it once when Frank had invited her over for dinner a few years ago.

She padded rapidly over to the bed and knelt down to look underneath. There, small and quivering, lay Isabel, curled in a ball, her wide, frightened eyes looking back at Bailey.

A burst of relief went through Bailey. Thank God she was still alive. But they didn't have much time.

'Hey, Isabel,' whispered Bailey, trying to put on a light-hearted smile. 'I'm here to help. I'm a friend of your dad's.'

The eyes stared back at her like mute saucers. At least she wasn't making any noise.

Bailey stretched a hand out under the bed. 'Take my hand,' said Bailey. 'And I'll take you out of here. But we've got to be quick.'

The girl seemed to sense that Bailey meant no harm and to understand the urgency of the situation. Bailey felt the small hand worm into hers, and with a gentle tug, she pulled Isabel out from under the bed.

She was dressed in a pair of pink pyjamas and her red hair was tied up in a ponytail. Giving her a brief once-over, Bailey determined that she didn't appear to have any physical injuries. The important thing was to make sure it stayed that way. She just had to get out of this room, down the stairs and out of the house to safety, probably a neighbour's house. Then she could call for help and come back for Frank.

Hoisting Isabel up in her arms, she turned to leave the bedroom. And just as she did so, Dale appeared in the doorway.

His mouth dropped open in astonishment at the sight of her, his eyes widening as he took in her appearance – her tangled hair... her shoeless feet... He blinked, appearing to have some problem processing the fact that she was standing right here in front of him when she should have been dead and dismembered in a back room in Essex by now.

She in turn digested what she saw – the shower cap on his head, the rubber gloves, the plastic bags on his feet, her missing green cashmere scarf around his neck...

And the black handgun with the silencer attached.

All registered in the space of a fraction of a moment.

Dale shook his head and closed his mouth as he gathered himself.

Bailey had less than one second to react. From memory, she recalled that the doorway to the en-suite bathroom was situated directly behind her.

Dale raised the gun, the long bulky silencer swinging into position, the black mouth of the barrel pointing directly at her.

Clutching Frank's daughter tightly to her shoulder, she launched herself backwards into the en-suite bathroom and pulled the door shut with her other hand.

WHUMPF. A bullet crashed through the wood of the door next to her head and hit the tiles on the wall, shattering them with a sharp crack. Isabel screamed.

With her back against the door, Bailey sank to the floor, pulling Isabel down with her.

WHUMPF. Another shot smashed through the door where her head had been just moments earlier. Splinters of wood tumbled into her hair.

WHUMPF. WHUMPF. WHUMPF.

Three more shots in close succession, stitching a series of jagged holes through the thin wooden panels of the door just above her.

Then silence. Just the sound of her ears ringing, her own sharp breathing and the faster panicked breathing of the little girl she was holding in her arms. The stink of gun smoke wafted through the holes in the door.

Bailey reached up to the small latch lock on the inside of the door and flipped it closed. Better than nothing.

'I don't know how the fuck you managed to escape,' she heard Dale say. 'But this time you're not going to.'

'You're not going to get away with this, Dale,' she shouted back.

'Oh yes I will. I always get away with it. I'm sure I'll work it out somehow. I'm quite creative, you know. Let's see... You came here in a state. I mean... look at you. And then you shot them both. And then shot yourself in a fit of remorse. How about that? Well... it'll have to do.'

'It's over, Dale. You're nicked,' she called out, playing for time.

A brief pause. 'Oh yeah? How are you going to manage that without your warrant card?' She could hear the mocking tone in his voice, and she could imagine the mocking glint in his eyes.

'Consider this a citizen's arrest,' she shouted.

She heard him laugh. 'You really do confound me, Bailey. You just don't know when to give up, do you?'

WHUMPF. Another shot punched through the door, this one lower down, just by her shoulder. She jumped in shock. Isabel yelped. Bailey had to do something. Now.

'Coward!' she yelled.

He laughed contemptuously.

Her mind raced. What was he going to do next? Was he going to force his way into the bathroom? Probably not. Because that would put him too close to her. And he knew she was a jiu-jitsu expert. And he knew she just might get lucky and overpower him.

No, he was just going to keep firing shots through the door until they hit her. After all, it was a small bathroom and the odds were in his favour. As she recalled, the gun held fifteen bullets. He'd used two on Frank. He'd fired a further six at her. That left him with a maximum of seven more. But could she and Isabel both survive seven more shots in this small confined space?

She looked around desperately. There was no window in this en-suite bathroom. It was an internal room. No way out. They were trapped. Fuck.

WHUMPF. Another bullet crashed through the door, whizzing past

Bailey's ear to blow apart a bottle of shampoo standing on the edge of the bath. The bright green liquid splattered across the bathroom, spraying over both of them.

Isabel looked at Bailey, petrified, her hair flecked with globules of shampoo. The little girl appeared to have gone into a state of silent shock.

'Get in the bath and lie down,' whispered Bailey. The bath was made of metal and with luck it would deflect gunshots.

Isabel scampered across the bathroom and got into the bath.

Bailey swallowed and looked around wildly for anything that might help to get them out of this pickle. Keeping low, she clambered over to the cupboard beneath the sink. Wrenching open the door, she started to pull out the contents, tossing them onto the floor next to her. A few bars of soap. A bottle of shower gel. Some scented candles...

She pulled out a hairdryer and held it up to look at it. Could this be of use in some way?

WHUMPF.

The hairdryer literally exploded in her hands as the bullet smashed it out of her grasp, slivers of plastic flying up into her face.

'Oh fuck...!' she gasped, toppling backwards, blinking in shock.

She regained her balance. Glancing at the ruined hairdryer lying on the floor, she suddenly remembered something her father had talked of. As a health and safety inspector, his interest in those matters had inevitably tipped over into domestic life and he was forever lecturing her and her mother about risks in the home. The bathroom was one of his special concerns, in particular, the dangers of electrocution. He'd explained that shaver outlets were deliberately designed to have a very low voltage. But the light socket, on the other hand, was as dangerous as any other light socket and, as he'd explained to her on multiple occasions, that was why you should never change the light bulb in the bathroom while there was still moisture in the air as that would increase your chances of accidentally electrocuting yourself.

She looked up at the light socket. It was her only chance.

Wrapping the hairdryer lead around her right fist, and holding the remains of the hairdryer in her left hand, she yanked the lead with all her might, pulling it right off the appliance. Then she ripped the plug off the other end of the lead. Using her teeth, she bit the rubber coating off both ends to expose the copper wires inside.

WHUMPH.

Bailey jerked convulsively as a bullet slammed through the door and hit the side of the bath with a deafening clang.

'Isabel!' she gasped. She peered into the bath.

Isabel looked up at her with wide eyes. She was okay. The bathtub had stopped the bullet.

Jesus, the neighbours must surely be wondering what was going on in here.

With extra haste, Bailey staggered to her feet. Her fingers trembling, she took one end of the lead and tied the exposed copper wires around the brass door handle on the inside of the bathroom door.

Still holding the lead, she then climbed up onto the edge of the bath, balancing precariously, fully exposed to any further gunshots which might come through the door.

Would the lead be long enough? *Please let it be long enough.*

She pulled it upwards. It stretched taut from the door handle to the light socket. It reached. Just.

Standing almost on her tiptoes on the edge of the bath, she unscrewed the smoked-glass light covering to expose the bare bulb beneath. She let the covering drop. It shattered on the hard surface of the bathroom floor.

'What are you getting up to in there, Bailey?' shouted Dale.

She ignored him.

WHUMPF. Another bullet crashed through the door and smashed into the wall, sending a spray of tile fragments over her and Isabel.

That was close. Too close. That one had passed maybe five centimetres from her right hip.

'Keep your head down, Isabel!' she urged.

How many bullets had he fired now? She was starting to lose count. She desperately tried to recall. Glancing at the door, she frantically started to count the holes. There were ten holes in the door. Ten bullets fired. Plus those two he'd used on Frank. That made twelve he'd fired in total. Which meant he had three left.

As Bailey looked at the door, she realised with concern that sooner or later he'd be able to see through the bullet holes and see what she was doing. She had to get a move on.

With shaking fingers, she unscrewed the light bulb and it dropped to the floor, where it smashed. The bathroom instantly fell into darkness.

'Why have you turned the light off, Bailey?'

WHUMPF. The bullet grazed her left thigh with a searing heat. She gasped in pain, almost toppling off the side of the bath.

'Being in the dark isn't going to protect you,' he shouted.

She stretched upwards, wincing at the pain in her leg. Holding the lead by its rubber coating, she plunged the exposed copper wires into the empty light socket, taking care not to touch either them or the socket with her bare flesh.

And there she held it, stretching it tight from the door handle to the socket, balancing on the edge of the bath, wavering slightly, gritting her teeth against the pain in her leg, and waiting for the next shot to come through the door. She imagined the bullet hitting her square in the guts, shredding her intestines. Or maybe it would hit her in the head and blow half her skull away. Or maybe it would just rip her jaw off. She pushed the horrible thoughts out of her mind.

Silence. Darkness. The smell of gun smoke.

She knew he was wondering if he'd hit either of them and what he should do next. She could see him now, through the bullet holes, peering in. But with the light off, he couldn't see if she was alive or not. He couldn't see her standing on the bath.

She counted the bullets again in her head. She calculated that he was down to two bullets now, if that. He had no choice but to come into the bathroom in order to make sure they were dead and finish them both off if they weren't. He'd want to save those last two bullets for that.

But in order to enter the bathroom he would have to touch the door handle because the door opened outwards and there was no other way to pull it open. He would have to get a good grip on it and wrench it as hard as possible in order to bust the lock.

The big question was whether his thin rubber gloves would protect him from the 240-volt charge that was being conducted from the light socket to the metal door handle.

She was gambling that they wouldn't. She'd seen the special electrician's gloves her father had owned – they were huge, thick, heavy items, nothing like the flimsy little things that Dale was wearing.

She waited. She glanced down at Isabel. The little girl's small round eyes stared up at Bailey, glistening in the dark like those of a diminutive woodland animal.

Bailey tried to smile at her but found that she couldn't.

'I'm going to get you, Bailey,' said Dale in a singsong voice. He sounded like he was very close to the door now.

The door handle suddenly jerked down sharply. Then the door wrenched open with a wooden splintering noise, the lock popping off the door frame, the electrified hairdryer lead jerking away from the door handle and whipping back dangerously inside the room.

Shit. It hadn't worked.

Dale rushed into the bathroom, levelling the gun in front of him. She saw him squinting and realised that his vision hadn't fully adjusted to the darkness.

Taking advantage of his fractional disorientation, Bailey leapt from the bath onto the sink just as he pulled the trigger.

WHUMPF. She felt the bullet nick her left ear.

Without breaking her motion, she catapulted herself off the sink to land on top of him, sending them both crashing sideways onto the floor.

He fell on top of her, writhing to try and turn and face her, pulling the gun around to put that final bullet inside her.

Up close, she could smell him. No longer that pleasant fragrance of cologne and musk, but now the sharp acrid tang of fear.

She realised that she was still clutching the hairdryer lead in her right hand, now no longer attached to either the door handle or the light socket. Grasping the other end of the lead with her left hand, she looped it around his neck and yanked it tight.

He gasped and choked as she started to garrotte him, pulling at the cord with every last ounce of her strength. He kicked and flailed wildly, blindly waving the gun, trying to get the barrel in her face.

She wound the lead around her fists, clenching her teeth as she pulled it tighter.

He dropped the gun with a clunk on the bathroom floor as he brought both hands to bear on the rubber cord biting into his neck, trying in vain to get his fingers beneath it.

Almost there. She could feel him weakening. He was almost done.

Then he suddenly rammed his head backwards into her face, knocking her head back into the hard wall. Stunned, she momentarily lost her hold on the garrotte. He whipped it from his neck, twisted around and punched her hard in the face, the blow slamming the back of her head into the wall a second time. She gasped and blinked. And before she knew it, he had his knee on her chest and had wrapped the hairdryer cord around her neck and suddenly he was garrotting her.

'You stupid fucking whore.' He spat the words into her face with a guttural snarl. 'I'll fucking kill you with my bare hands.'

She gasped and choked, feeling herself going dizzy. She batted at the lead, but it was no good. He was too strong. She knew she only had a few seconds left before she lost consciousness. Her life counting down in seconds. Five, four...

He had won.

Three...

'Get out of here, Isabel!' she tried to cry. But her voice was too weak, coming out as an inaudible slur.

Two...

Blackness coming down. The end.

Then, through her fading vision, she caught a movement behind him. She must have summoned some expression of disbelief, for he glanced over his shoulder.

And froze.

Isabel was standing there, holding the large handgun in both hands, pointing it directly at him.

'You have got to be fucking joking,' he said.

WHUMPF.

Dale's handsome face ruptured apart as the last bullet in the gun punched through his head. A shower of hot wet blood and brains spattered across Bailey.

Yanking the rubber lead away from her neck, Bailey sucked in a deep mouthful of air. She felt the blood rushing back to her brain. Blinking Dale's gore out of her eyes, she looked up at Isabel in amazement.

The little girl lowered the empty smoking gun and smiled at her. 'Can we go downstairs now?' she asked in a small voice.

76

Nancy Molloy sat at the table in the restaurant brooding darkly, whilst the rest of the gang looked on in silence. Before them lay the detritus of their earlier celebration, the appetisers now cold and the beer now flat.

They'd cleaned up the restaurant, removing any traces of the altercation that had occurred just a short while earlier. Archie's body had been rolled up in the plastic sheeting and was already in the process of being disposed of. Apart from the broken paper screen, it would seem that nothing particularly amiss had taken place here.

But that didn't change the fact that the evening had been completely ruined. And it was all thanks to that bloody copper, Bailey Morgan. Nancy's hatred of Bailey had increased several-fold since her escape. Getting one over on Nancy in the first place was bad enough, but Bailey managing to escape like this rubbed salt into the wound in a big way. And what was more, Nancy still hadn't managed to find out who Mister Snigiss was. She was seriously riled.

She glanced over to see Rick studying his phone intently. He looked up at her.

'The Range Rover's got this tracker device installed in case it gets nicked. It comes with this mobile app which lets me see where it's going. It's currently telling me it's in Enfield.'

'Bailey's in Enfield? Wasn't that where our pet plod was heading off to?'

Rick shrugged. 'Haven't been able to get through to him. I've called him at least eight times.'

'Try again,' said Nancy.

Rick sighed and dialled the number for Bailey's undercover phone. The rest of the table watched and waited. He suddenly stiffened and his eyes widened slightly. It appeared that this time someone had answered it.

'Oh yeah?' he rasped.

By the murderous look on his face, Nancy could tell that something was off. She fidgeted impatiently with her lighter, eager for him to tell her what was going on.

'Is that so?' he growled.

He ended the call and stared at his phone in disgust.

'Was that who I think it was?' she said.

He nodded and threw the phone onto the table.

'Yeah. Bailey fucking Morgan. She just informed me that our bent copper's dead. She told me he had his brains blown out by a five-year-old girl.'

Nancy grimaced in anger. With every minute that went by, her loathing of Bailey Morgan seemed to ratchet up yet another notch.

They all lapsed into mute contemplation, filled with toxic thoughts about Bailey.

After a while, Shane broke the silence.

'What do we do with this?' he asked, holding up Bailey's handbag. It had been left in the booth that she and Dale had been occupying.

Nancy afforded it a reluctant sullen glance, as if that was the least of their worries. She flicked her fingers at it dismissively, indicating that Shane should just get rid of it by whatever means necessary.

Then she looked at it again, this time with a sly glimmer in her dark eyes. 'On second thoughts...' she said, and held out her hand.

Shane passed her the handbag. Holding it gingerly between her thumb and forefinger, contaminated as it was by the dirty fingers of the Filth, she upended it, spilling the contents out over the table.

A lipstick. A tampon. A pen. A packet of tissues... The glint of gold caught Nancy's eye. It looked like some kind of small necklace. Nancy peered at it with interest. She picked it up by its thin gold chain. Holding it in front of her, she examined the small green stone pendant.

'What's that?' asked Rick, frowning.

'Looks like a snake to me,' murmured Nancy as she studied the miniature cobra.

The rest of the gang peered at the tiny pendant swinging on the gold chain.

'This has to be something to do with Mister Snigiss,' she said.

Stephen craned his head forward curiously. 'So the snake thing was real after all?'

'Apparently so,' she replied.

'What's she doing with that in her bag then?'

Nancy shrugged, inspecting the pendant in more detail. The stone was slightly translucent, dark green in colour, pitted with age. But there were clear markings inscribed on the back of it. They looked like...

'These are Ancient Egyptian hieroglyphs, if I'm not mistaken.'

'Egyptian what?' said Rick.

'Never mind,' murmured Nancy.

She stared intently at the snake pendant twisting slowly on the gold chain. A curious frown settled on her face.

'Now, when we were chatting one time,' said Nancy, 'Bailey told me that her sister was into the Ancient Egyptians.'

'You mean the missing sister who's actually alive?' said Stephen.

Rick looked perplexed. 'What are you getting at, Mum?'

'Well, on the one hand we've got Mister Snigiss who's into snakes, and on the other hand we've got Bailey's sister who's into the Ancient Egyptians. Put them both together and you've got this,' she said, scrutinising the pendant.

'Are you saying what I think you're saying?' asked Stephen.

Nancy nodded, her eyes narrowing. 'We know that Bailey was

looking for Mister Snigiss because of her sister. We know that Bailey met Mister Snigiss and we know that Bailey's sister is alive. And we know that, for some reason, Bailey was protecting Mister Snigiss. I mean, she was willing to undergo torture rather than reveal Mister Snigiss's identity.'

They all stared at her in silence, awaiting her next pronouncement.

She gazed around the table with her dark close-set eyes. 'Bailey is protecting Mister Snigiss because Mister Snigiss is Bailey's sister,' she announced.

'Wait a minute, I thought Mister Snigiss was a bloke,' said Rick.

Nancy shook her head with a canny smirk. 'Mister Snigiss is just very good at misleading people.' She turned to Stephen. 'Bailey told me that her sister was two years older than her. And assuming she wasn't lying about that, then that would make Mister Snigiss a woman in her thirties, right?'

Stephen nodded slowly.

Nancy continued. 'Didn't you say that one of the people who owned cobras was a woman in her early thirties?'

Stephen nodded, a smile spreading slowly across his face.

'And you know where she lives, right?' said Nancy.

Stephen's smile grew even wider as he nodded again.

Nancy smiled as well now, a dark evil grin descending upon her face. 'I think it's time to break out the power tools.'

77

The woman who'd once been the little girl known as Jennifer Morgan stood in front of the glass vivarium stroking the small white mouse in her hand. It quivered nervously in her palm. She whispered gently in its ear to calm it.

Inside the vivarium – a secure glass climate-controlled tank – was a dark grey cobra lying in a curl of mottled coils. At the sight of her, he began to unwind, lifting his stubby snout, his forked tongue flickering out inquisitively. As always, she was entranced. She loved the way her snakes moved – so smooth and sinuous. She loved their shiny black eyes – like dark gemstones. She loved the geometric tessellations of their scales. And, more than anything, she was enraptured by their lightning-fast deadliness. They were her babies, and on occasion they were also her executioners.

She reached up, lifted the top of the vivarium, and dropped the mouse inside. It landed on the floor of the tank, standing there for a second, motionless, its whiskers twitching. In the same moment, the cobra whipped its head around to pounce on it, sinking its long fangs into the white fur, injecting the mouse full of deadly venom. The mouse didn't even have time to squeak. The cobra gulped its lifeless body down in a single mouthful.

She smiled and moved onto the next vivarium. The room was full of such glass tanks, all of them containing cobras of different species, from all over the world – from Africa, India, South-East Asia. She kept them all here in this particular residence – an old-fashioned high-ceilinged apartment situated in a red-brick mansion block in West Kensington.

The apartment block had been designed to attract the wealthier classes back in the nineteenth century when it had first been built, and it was still populated by those types of people today, the kind of people who kept themselves to themselves, the kind of neighbours who suited someone like her just fine.

The apartment was just one of a number of properties that she owned in London and elsewhere. As an ostensibly law-abiding citizen, this flat was where she mostly resided for the purposes of appearing normal. And looking normal was crucial when it came to conducting business successfully.

If the neighbours ever did speculate about her, they probably thought she was just some well-off, stylishly dressed young woman with a taste for fedora hats who dabbled in the fashion industry or the art world and who happened to be blessed with rich parents who were willing to subsidise her lifestyle and pay for her flat.

And as for the name they knew her by, it was just one of many assumed names that she'd used over the years. A nice normal forget-table name. Like a nom de plume. But, of course, Mister Snigiss was who she really was...

Standing in front of the next vivarium, she leaned in so that her face was just a few centimetres away from the snake on the other side of the glass. His name was Sidney and, out of them all, he was probably her favourite – an Egyptian cobra, copper in colour with a brown mottling down his spine – a magnificent creature, almost two metres long. He began to stir, rearing up, spreading his hood and emitting a long sibilant hiss.

She frowned to herself. They only spread their hoods when they felt threatened, when they wanted to appear more menacing to their enemies. And she wasn't his enemy.

Something was wrong.

She spun around.

A man was standing right behind her. Burly, with olive skin, dressed in a dark suit. He had silently appeared out of nowhere.

A surge of cold panic shot through her. For this stranger to be inside her flat, she knew something somewhere had gone very wrong indeed.

Reacting with animal speed, she hissed like one of her snakes and swiped at his eyes with her long nails. He evaded her with a deft backwards step and settled into a gladiatorial stance, giving her a look which challenged her to try and get past him and out of this room.

She didn't know why he was here or exactly what he wanted, but she had a very strong feeling his intentions weren't good.

Turning swiftly, she flipped the lid off the vivarium behind her and expertly grasped the rearing cobra, holding him just behind the head as she'd done so many times before in a way that ensured he couldn't bite her. She whipped him out of the vivarium and held him, whirling and twisting, in front of her, thrusting his bared fangs at her unwelcome intruder.

'Normally he just kills mice,' she said, 'but today I think I might give him a human being. A special treat. One bite from him and you'll be dead in fifteen minutes.'

The man's eyes widened as he warily regarded the snake.

'Well, if you're going to get all feisty on us...' he said, pulling a small, strange-looking device from the pocket of his suit jacket. She recognised it as a Taser.

She flung the snake at him. With surprising agility, the man ducked to one side, the cobra sailing harmlessly over his shoulder to land on the floor, where it slithered away. At the same time, he pulled the trigger of the Taser. The twin barbed darts whistled into her chest, the electric shock instantly paralysing her. She collapsed to the floor, unable to control the agonising spasms which gripped her body.

As she lay there convulsing in pain, she saw through blurred eyes that another man had entered the room. Very short, dressed in a grey suit and a black polo-neck sweater, he had a strangely smooth and baby-like face... and he appeared to be holding a large roll of silver duct tape.

Smiling unpleasantly, he strode over to her incapacitated form, knelt down next to her, ripped off a big piece of tape and placed it across her mouth.

78

Frank lay in the hospital bed, heavily sedated, his eyes closed, his upper torso extensively bandaged, tubes protruding from his mouth and his chest, a life-support machine bleeping next to him as it ventilated his damaged lungs.

It was now Thursday evening, three days after he'd been shot. After being rushed to hospital, he'd gone straight into surgery, and his condition, although initially critical, was stabilising now that he was being ventilated. Bailey was sitting by his bed in the intensive care unit, watching him intently. She'd been there on and off for the past few days, mounting a vigil of sorts, closely monitoring his progress, desperately praying that he would pull through.

Things were looking positive though. The surgeon had told her that the two bullets had passed through his lungs but had fortunately not damaged either his heart or his spine, and that although the chest trauma was quite severe, the mortality rate for this type of injury was actually relatively low, at around seven per cent, which meant he had a very good chance of recovering, assuming no other complications arose.

She didn't know how she'd be able to live with herself if he did die. Ever since the incident at his house, she'd been beating herself up over her failure to prevent Dale from shooting him. Her only consolation was that at least she'd managed to save Isabel from harm. Thankfully, the little girl didn't seem too traumatised by the whole experience, although Bailey guessed that only time would tell. She was currently staying with her grandmother while Joanna and Roland made their way back from Cuba in all haste.

Once again, Bailey marvelled at how the little girl had managed to operate the handgun. When she'd asked her, she'd got the simple answer 'Daddy showed me' which, funnily enough, didn't surprise Bailey all that much, considering what she knew about Frank.

On top of the black eye she'd got from being punched in the face by Dale, Bailey was utterly exhausted. Once again the job had taken it out of her and the failed outcome of the Molloy operation weighed heavily upon her, even though it wasn't her fault. She had a very strong feeling that Rick would sell those guns one way or another, even if he didn't have Dale there to help him any more. And without knowing where the guns were, there was very little the authorities could do to stop him. The thought of it depressed and angered her.

The Molloys had got away with it. Again. Just like they'd get away with doing what they tried to do to her at the restaurant. When the police had got there, they'd found no signs of the fracas that had taken place and no sign of Archie's body. Bailey knew, with their expertise in evading any kind of criminal blame, trying to pin anything on them would be a long and arduous task.

Since Monday, she'd spent much of the past three days debriefing various teams both on the situation with the Molloys and also on the scope of Dale's misdemeanours. In regard to the latter, she'd spent a long time talking to the Met's anti-corruption unit – the Directorate of Professional Standards – and they were now investigating his affairs in depth. The very thought of him triggered a painful twinge of emotion. She'd let her guard down and she'd trusted him and she'd got burned, badly. She felt like God was trying to tell her something.

She tried to push him out of her mind and think about what she was going to do next. In light of the curtailed Molloy operation and along with what she'd been through generally, she'd been granted some time off. For one thing, she knew there wouldn't be any under-cover work for a while, not with Frank like this, but then maybe she needed a break from it anyhow, some time to get her head back in shape.

One thing she knew she could do now was focus completely on her father, to try and spend as much time with him as possible before he was gone forever. The past few days had been so hectic, what with her coming in here to check on Frank, plus all the follow-ups she'd had to do at work, that she just hadn't had time to go and see him.

Just as she was contemplating the best time to go down to Sydenham the next day to visit him in the hospice, her phone rang. She recognised the ringtone as that of her undercover phone. She'd retrieved it from Dale's body after Rick had called him on it, answering the phone with a certain amount of relish to let him know that Dale was dead. She was still carrying it around with her now on the off-chance that the number might yield some residual value in relation to the aborted Molloy operation.

Taking it out, she saw that it said 'No caller ID'. A premonitory feeling of dread rippled through her. She answered it.

Her heart sank as that familiar husky smoker's voice emanated from the handset.

'Bailey Morgan,' said Nancy, using her real name. 'How are you?'

Bailey didn't answer. She knew Nancy didn't care anyway. By the smug tone in Nancy's voice, Bailey had the nasty feeling this was a prologue to something deeply unpleasant.

Nancy continued, 'I feel like we didn't get a chance to say goodbye properly the last time we met. So I'm giving you a second opportunity.'

A second opportunity? What was she going on about? The specula-tions raced through Bailey's mind. Whatever this was, she knew it wasn't good.

'What are you talking about?' asked Bailey.

'Oh...' said Nancy, affecting a light wistful tone. 'I miss all those little conversations we had. The ones about... your sister for example.'

A vice of anxiety clamped tight across Bailey's chest. Please no...

'Yes...' continued Nancy in that fake airy voice. 'All those things you told me about Jennifer. They were very interesting. And I do have such a memory for detail.'

Bailey swallowed. She said nothing, hoping against everything not to have to hear exactly the thing she was dreading.

Nancy carried on, a spiteful zest in her voice. 'And when I found that necklace in your handbag, I put two and two together.'

Shit. The necklace. Bailey had forgotten all about that.

She realised now, too late, that she'd underestimated just how astute Nancy Molloy really was. It hit her with a crushing horror what a massive mistake she'd made in revealing those supposedly harmless childhood details to someone as cunning and evil as Nancy Molloy.

But wait a minute... maybe it was okay. Even if they did know that Mister Snigiss was Jennifer, it didn't mean they'd actually located her. Yet. Maybe Bailey could somehow get in touch with her sister and warn her.

'I understand now, of course, why you were protecting Mister Snigiss,' said Nancy. 'I would have done the same in your shoes. Sadly, though, it wasn't enough to stop me. Because, as you probably know by now, once I get fixated on something, I just don't give up until I've got my way. And now I've got your sister right where I want her. At my feet. And unless you want me to kill her right now, you'll do exactly what I say.'

Bailey closed her eyes and swallowed. It felt like she was trying to swallow a lump of concrete. She silently tried to work out if Nancy was bluffing or not.

'Cat got your tongue?' said Nancy nastily.

'I don't believe you,' replied Bailey.

'What you're going to do,' said Nancy, 'is you're going to come to our Gravesend building development. Tonight. At ten o'clock. And you're going to come alone. No surveillance. No back-up. No wire. No nothing. We'll be watching closely and if we get the slightest sniff of bacon, we'll kill her immediately.'

Bailey looked at her watch. It was 7.45 p.m. She had just over two hours. That wasn't much time. She took a deep breath.

'I think you're lying,' she said. 'I'll think you're just trying to trick me. And this is just some stupid trap. If you've really got Jennifer, then I want to talk to her. Right now.' Bailey desperately wanted not to believe Nancy, but she had a horribly vexing feeling that she was telling the truth.

'Okay,' said Nancy. 'Suit yourself.'

There was a rustling sound on the other end of the phone. Then some ragged female breathing and a voice came on. A woman's voice. The voice that Bailey did not want to hear.

'Bailey!' panted Jennifer hoarsely. 'Don't come! They'll kill us both. It's a trap. Don't—'

Another sharp rustle as the phone was torn away from her.

Nancy came on the line again.

'Just remember,' she said. 'Come alone. Or else.'

And then the line went dead.

79

A chill wind blew through the huge concrete skeleton of the apartment block in Gravesend. The walls hadn't yet been put in and the whole structure lay open to the elements. When it was finished, it would be a luxury residence, constituting three hundred top-of-the-range apartments, but it was currently little more than a bare shell bristling with exposed girders.

Up on the thirteenth floor of this empty building, bathed in the glare of an industrial lamp, stood Nancy, Rick, Shane, Stephen and a collection of other Molloy associates dressed in black leather jackets, a number of whom were toting sawn-off shotguns. And at their feet, lying on the ground with her wrists and ankles firmly bound with silver duct tape, was Jennifer Morgan.

It was night now and the vast building development was silent and deserted apart from this small gathering of people. Down below, the JCBs and concrete mixer lorries sat inactive amongst the rows of Portakabins, whilst around them, here and there, stood huge cranes, looming immobile over the scene like giant sentinels.

Down to one side was a small jetty, for the development was located right on the edge of the water, the River Thames flowing by in the night, the water black as ink. On the far bank twinkled the distant lights of Tilbury Docks, where even now goods were being unloaded from the giant container ships that had come in from all around the world.

Nancy Molloy huddled a little deeper into the furry collar of her long mink coat and looked down at Jennifer Morgan with a sadistic smile.

'You should really be wearing a hard hat and a hi-viz jacket. Health and safety, you know. All kinds of nasty accidents can happen on a building site.'

Jennifer scowled back at her defiantly, shivering and gritting her teeth against the icy breeze. She was clad in just the thin cotton skirt and blouse she'd been wearing when they'd kidnapped her. Since then, they'd largely been keeping her tied up in the back of the transit van that they'd used to transport her from her apartment to this building site. Apart from briefly putting her on the phone to Bailey, they'd mostly kept her gagged, but now Nancy had ordered the gag to be removed as she wanted the opportunity to talk to Jennifer properly, for that was all part of the fun.

'If you're expecting me to plead for my life,' said Jennifer, 'you've got another think coming.'

'Ooh. Big words,' Nancy replied mockingly. Her face twisted into a cruel sneer. 'Well, you'll soon find out what real pain feels like.'

'You don't scare me, you old hag,' spat Jennifer. 'Nothing you can do scares me, not even death. I've been through way too much for that.'

'Yeah well, we'll see about that when I drill a big fucking hole in your head. It'll be my supreme pleasure to watch you turn into a twitching vegetable right before my very eyes.'

That was the reason Nancy had ordered Jennifer's physical mistreatment be kept to a minimum prior to execution. She didn't want Jennifer to be desensitised in any way that might deprive her of the full horror of what Nancy was planning to inflict on her.

Nancy withdrew a hand from the pocket of her fur coat, taking out the Ancient Egyptian snake pendant. She dropped it on the concrete floor in front of Jennifer's face.

'I believe this belongs to you,' she said. 'Your dumb sister was stupid enough to leave it in her handbag for me to find. And that's how I worked out who you were. That and some other stuff she was careless enough to tell me. So you've really just got her to blame for this predicament you find yourself in.'

Jennifer glanced at the pendant, then up at Nancy with a look of stony hatred. Nancy examined her with interest, a smidgen of admiration in her expression.

'Clever plan with all that blackmail sex video stuff. Getting control of all those powerful men. I respect a woman with ambition. Sadly, though, you made the mistake of murdering my son.'

'From what I've been able to gather, he sounded like a fucking idiot.'

Nancy's eyes flared in fury. 'I carried him for nine months,' she hissed, 'and I loved him for over forty years. And you took it all away. Just like that.' She snapped her fingers with a sharp click. 'He might have had his faults, but you had no right to kill him.'

'I'll kill whoever gets in my way.'

'You're not going to be doing much of anything any more,' said Nancy. She laid a hard kick into Jennifer's stomach with the tip of her black leather boot.

Jennifer gasped, winded.

'Not so tough now, are we, *Mister Snigiss*?' Nancy spat the name sarcastically.

The whole group of them stood over Jennifer, watching her contort on the cold rough concrete as she struggled to regain her breath.

'What are we waiting for?' said Shane. 'Why don't we just kill her now? I've got the drill right here.'

He held up the Black and Decker case he'd been clutching in his right hand.

Nancy shook her head with a nasty grimace. 'Not yet. I'm waiting for Bailey to get here. I want to see the look on her face as that ten-millimetre drill bit makes mincemeat of her sister's brains.'

'Are you really sure she'll come?' asked Rick.

'Of course she will,' said Nancy. 'I know how important family is to her. She might have been lying to us about everything else, but that's one of the few things she was telling the truth about.'

80

Peering ahead determinedly from beneath the brim of her baseball cap, Bailey gunned the BMW M3 down the fast lane of the A2 in the direction of Gravesend. She'd passed through South London and was now heading through the cold dark hinterlands of North Kent.

Tonight she was wearing her undercover outfit – the Hugo Boss jacket, straight-cut blue jeans, white collared man's shirt and leather boots. Somehow it felt appropriate for the impending showdown.

After the call with Nancy had ended, Bailey had seriously contemplated the possibility of acquiring some kind of back-up despite the instructions she'd been given. But the more she'd thought about it, the more she'd realised that it just wasn't going to be viable. Two hours just wasn't enough time to contact the right people, justify the operation, get it signed off, gather the teams together, and brief them appropriately.

And what would she tell them exactly? They'd ask too many questions. She couldn't use Jennifer as justification – someone who didn't even exist as a proper person, who was part of a forbidden investigation. Bailey supposed she could have told them the guns would be there, but the problem there was that she didn't know where exactly the Molloys were holding Jennifer on the building site, and it was likely a big place. The support team would be forced to take a blunt-force approach and storm in, but as soon as they breached the perimeter of the site, and probably before they even got that far, the Molloys would know they were there and then it would be too late for Jennifer.

Bailey knew the Molloys were expert at detecting surveillance and it wouldn't surprise her if they had spotters all over Gravesend on the lookout for anything suspicious. All in all, there was just too much of a risk that they would kill Jennifer prematurely.

No. She had to go it alone. So in the two hours following the call, she'd engaged in what she hoped was a more constructive solution to her problem. She knew, of course, that the Molloys were planning to kill both her and Jennifer. That much was obvious. But she wasn't planning to die tonight. And she wasn't planning on letting Jennifer die either. It was Bailey's fault that Jennifer was in trouble and she was going to do everything within her power to get her sister out of it. Everything.

Her mind felt weirdly clear and focused. She wasn't scared as such. Not any more. The fear that had filled her earlier had now disappeared, to be replaced by a cold determination. She'd committed herself to this course of action and she knew there was no turning back.

It was around a quarter to ten when she reached Gravesend, a place she'd never visited before. All she knew was that it was an old maritime town situated on the south bank of the Thames Estuary. Cruising slowly through the quiet, empty streets, she didn't get the impression it was a particularly wealthy or scenic place. It felt ancient and tough, a personification of all the hard-bitten old seamen who'd passed through it over the centuries.

To her left, as she was driving along, Bailey noticed the River Thames flowing past, black and murky in the night, and on the distant bank, the lights of Tilbury Docks in Essex.

Rick's building development was located on the edge of town, presumably isolated just enough for whatever the gang were planning.

Once again he'd picked an environment that he was in complete control of. She also knew building sites were convenient places to dispose of bodies.

As she drew closer to the development, she slowed the car and killed the headlights, eventually coming to a standstill on a street corner about a hundred metres from the entrance.

She switched off the engine and peered through the windscreen, noting the large hoardings which obscured the building site from public view. Beyond them, she could make out the tall outlines of several cranes and the top of a skeletal, partially constructed apartment block.

Over by the entrance, she saw two of the Molloy thugs in their bulky black leather jackets and beanie hats stamping and blowing into their hands, trying to keep warm on the cold evening. It didn't look like they'd spotted her. So far, so good.

She was supposed to drive through the entrance, where they would take her in to meet her fate. But she knew if she did that, then she would never leave that building development alive and neither would Jennifer.

Taking a crowbar from where it had been lying on the passenger seat beside her, she stealthily slipped out of the car. Immediately, she was hit by the thick, moist chill of the riverine air rolling in off the Thames. Shivering, she looked down at her watch. It was five minutes to ten. She peered back up at the building development and licked her lips nervously.

Up near the top of the huge unfinished apartment block, she saw a sudden small glow – the brief flare of a cigarette being lit. Then it died.

She nodded to herself. So that's where they were.

Clutching the crowbar and keeping to the shadows out of the thugs' view, she glided forwards like a ghost in the night.

81

Nancy Molloy snapped her lighter closed, the illumination from the small flame disappearing, her face once again falling back into shadow. She drew deeply on the cigarette, then blew out a long stream of smoke. She looked at her watch. It was five minutes to ten.

She'd wandered away from the rest of the group, leaving the pool of light cast by the lamp to envelop herself in the darkness at the very edge of the floor. Peering down, she saw, far below, the gaping maw of the huge foundation pit that would form the basis for the second of the two blocks that were being built here. The excavation was so deep that she couldn't even see the bottom of it, just the thrusting tops of the giant steel piles that had been driven into the ground at its base.

This gigantic dark hole was where they'd dispose of the bodies of Bailey and Jennifer, covering them this very evening with a layer of quick-setting concrete. The professional young couples and starter families who would eventually live in these apartments would have no idea that beneath their feet, encased in concrete, deep within the foundations of this place, were the bodies of the two sisters.

Surveying the rest of the building site, Nancy could make out the tiny figures of her men standing over by the entrance to the development. Once Bailey arrived, they would radio Shane to let him know, then they'd take her from her car, check her for a wire and any weapons and bring her up here where the enjoyment would begin. The thought of it sent an anticipatory tingle of pleasure through Nancy.

She finished smoking the cigarette and flicked it over the edge, watching the glowing butt tumble down and disappear into the murk below.

She looked at her watch. It was ten o'clock exactly.

She turned and walked back to the group.

'Where is that fucking bitch?' said Rick, looking at his watch. 'She's late.'

'No, I think you'll find she's exactly on time,' said a voice behind them.

82

They all spun round sharply. Bailey stepped out of the gloom by the top of the bare concrete stairwell to enter the tract of light radiating from the industrial lamp. She stopped and stood with her hands in the pockets of her leather jacket.

Panicked, wary looks flickered between them. This hadn't been part of the plan. Instantly, several of the thugs raised their sawn-off shotguns at her. Among them, Bailey recognised the bald-headed bearded one she'd punched in the restaurant. He was now wearing a large white plaster across his nose. He wasn't taking any chances with her now, his piggy eyes narrowing suspiciously as he levelled the stubby barrels of the shotgun directly at her head.

Rick, standing there looking suave as ever in his black cashmere overcoat, seemed less taken aback. He eyed her coolly, almost looking bemused at her unexpected entrance.

Shane, holding some kind of black plastic suitcase, gave her a dour grimace, while, next to him, Stephen gazed at her with unabashed hostility.

Nancy's initial expression of surprise faded to be replaced by a victorious smirk.

'So you decided to come after all,' she said. 'I knew you would. But then I guess you aren't really all that smart.'

Bailey shrugged. She registered Jennifer, bound with duct tape, lying on the ground at their feet. Jennifer's grey eyes locked onto Bailey's, her face displaying no sign of relief or pleasure at the sight of her sister. But at least she was still alive, and by the looks of it, so far uninjured.

Bailey walked forward slowly, keenly aware of the sawn-off shotguns tracking her every move. But she knew they wouldn't kill her yet. Not until Nancy's say-so, and she knew Nancy would want her to see her sister die first.

Bailey turned to Rick. 'Sorry about your car. I'm afraid it's a bit of a write-off.'

He shrugged, apparently unbothered. 'I was planning to trade up anyway.'

She nodded over at the distant lights of Tilbury Docks. 'I had it in my head that you were going to bring the guns in through the docks to this place.'

'Yeah, I know,' he replied. 'Your bent-copper friend told us all about it. Luckily that was never part of our plan.' He paused reflectively. 'Although it's not a bad idea in theory. I'll have to keep it in mind for future shipments.'

'So where exactly are you bringing the guns in? Or are they already here?'

'I'm due to pick them up tomorrow in fact. They're arriving just as planned, one day before I was due to sell them to you. Not that you're going to be around to do anything about them,' he said with a laugh. 'Considering all the trouble they've caused me, I think I might consider offering them at knock-down rates, just to make sure I really do find a buyer this time.'

Bailey couldn't help but shake her head in disgust at his brazen lack of morals.

'We could spend all evening engaging in small talk,' Nancy interrupted. 'But now that you're here, I think we should really get this show on the road.'

She nodded to Shane. He opened the black plastic suitcase and took out a large drill. He affixed a drill bit to it and then handed the tool to her. Nancy gave the trigger a few squeezes, sending a loud, angry buzz echoing through the night. Brandishing the drill, she smiled sadistically at Bailey, like some kind of malevolent dwarf.

Shane grabbed a handful of Jennifer's hair and pulled her harshly to her knees. With a belligerent sneer, Jennifer twisted her head to look up at Nancy.

'I'll see you in Hell, bitch.'

'I'm already looking forward to it,' grinned Nancy as she depressed the trigger of the drill and lowered it towards Jennifer's temple.

'Not so fast,' said Bailey, withdrawing her right hand from the pocket of her Hugo Boss jacket. She held it up high so they could see what she was clutching in her fist.

83

They all peered at her right hand trying to work out what she was holding. Nancy paused, the drill whirring furiously, its tip poised barely a centimetre from the side of Jennifer's head. After a few long seconds of scrutinising Bailey with her dark close-set eyes, she took her finger off the trigger and the tool lapsed into silence.

Bailey cleared her throat. 'This is an M67 fragmentation grenade,' she said.

Their eyes widened and she saw their fingers tighten on the triggers of their shotguns. Smiling thinly, she withdrew her other hand from her left pocket. She held it up to reveal a small metallic item dangling from her index finger.

'And this is the pin.'

They froze and their eyes grew wider still. They knew that without the pin to hold it in place, the spring-loaded release lever would pop off the grenade, activating a three-second fuse that would detonate the high explosives contained therein... if she released her grip on it.

'This grenade is a bit like a dead man's switch,' she said. 'Sure you could blow my head off with those shotguns, but then I'd drop this grenade and you'd all die.'

The shotguns wavered slightly.

'I looked on the internet just before I came here,' she said, 'and I found out that this particular grenade has a kill radius of five metres, which would make you all dead if I dropped it right now. In addition to that, it'll spread red-hot shrapnel to a radius of fifteen metres... but the shrapnel has been known to travel up to two hundred and twenty metres from the centre of the blast.'

Bailey glanced around at the bare concrete space in which they were gathered.

'There's no cover here. And nowhere for you to run. If I drop this grenade right now, you'll all end up either dead or seriously injured.'

'So will you and your sister,' said Rick.

Bailey shrugged. 'Better that we go out my way rather than your way. And at least I get to take a whole load of you with me as well.'

'She's bullshitting,' said Shane with a sneer.

'Oh yeah?' said Bailey.

With a flick of her left wrist, she tossed the pin out through the open side of the building. It arced into the darkness and tumbled down out of sight below.

'Think I'm bullshitting now?' she said.

'You crazy fucking bitch,' muttered Rick.

Nancy didn't look in the remotest bit scared. 'You'll never escape,' she hissed.

'Put down the drill and untie my sister,' ordered Bailey.

Nancy ground her teeth sullenly, her dark eyes boring into Bailey with unalloyed hatred.

No one made any move.

'I said untie her!' shouted Bailey.

With the greatest reluctance, Nancy gave an infinitesimal nod to Shane. He pulled a folding knife from his pocket, opened it up and sliced the duct tape from Jennifer's wrists and ankles.

Jennifer immediately clambered to her feet and ran over to Bailey, shooting her a look of grudging regard.

'Not bad-going, little sister,' she murmured.

Jennifer turned round to face Nancy, extended one arm and leisurely shot her the finger.

Nancy's jaw clenched furiously. 'You'll never get out of here alive,' she growled in her husky smoker's voice.

'We'll see about that,' muttered Bailey as she began to back away from them, holding the grenade outstretched in front of her.

Together, she and Jennifer edged slowly away from the Molloys, making their way inch by excruciating inch to the concrete stairwell. The shotguns tracked their movements all the way, but no one dared to fire. No one wanted to die.

The two sisters began to descend the stairwell and as soon as the Molloys disappeared from sight, they both turned and rushed down the steps, Bailey leading the way.

Her heart was beating fast now, adrenaline firing through her system, turbo-charging her flight. She knew the Molloys would already be coordinating their pursuit with those outside, hoping to catch them in the middle.

They raced down the rough concrete steps, jumping down two or three at a time, trying not to fall and twist an ankle or break a limb, for that would be truly fatal. Twelve flights later, they reached the bottom of the stairwell.

'This way!' said Bailey breathlessly, pulling Jennifer by the arm, tugging her in the direction of the hoarding through which she'd crowbarred a gap little more than ten minutes earlier.

But with a jolt of dismay, she saw they were too late. Already the Molloy thugs who'd been guarding the entrance were running towards them, cutting them off. And it looked like they were holding guns.

'Shit!' she cursed.

Bailey turned sharply, heading away from them into the centre of the building site, Jennifer close behind. They stumbled over the muddy, uneven ground, their feet catching in the ruts created by the tyres of the huge vehicles now stationary all around them.

Weaving between Portakabins and huge stacks of metal girders, they fled ever deeper into the industrial gloom. All the while, Bailey kept a firm grip on the grenade in her right hand, fully aware that if she loosened her hold on it for even a moment, then she would blow up both herself and her sister.

Behind them, she could hear the Molloys shouting amongst themselves as they spilled out of the apartment block and fanned out across the building site in pursuit.

Bailey crouched down behind a JCB, pulling Jennifer down with her. Panting hard, she peeked over the top of the bonnet. It looked like there were now at least ten armed men searching for them, with Shane leading the way hefting a sawn-off shotgun.

'I can't believe you came for me,' said Jennifer in contemptuous amazement. 'That has to be one of the dumbest things anyone's ever done for me. Why did you even bother? I thought you said I was little more than a common criminal.'

'You might be a criminal, but you're also my sister,' said Bailey. 'And that does still mean something to me.'

A little smile edged onto Jennifer's face. 'You never did know when to quit, Bailey.' She shook her head. 'Like that time you insisted on climbing all the way up that apple tree in the back garden and got stuck at the top.'

Bailey smiled too. 'And we had to call the Fire Brigade to get me down.'

They both suddenly broke into laughter. It was a crazy, nervous laughter, fuelled by the extreme stress of their situation. It was either that or cry.

Jennifer's face straightened. 'How did you get that black eye?'

'A bit of man trouble,' shrugged Bailey. 'Managed to sort it out though.'

Jennifer nodded at the grenade in Bailey's hand. 'So I see I'm not the only one who's au fait with explosive devices.'

Bailey looked down at the small bomb. 'I paid a little visit to the police property storeroom before I came here. It's amazing the things you can find in there.'

'There's only so long you're going to be able to keep holding it.'

'I'll lob it when I have to, but for the time being it's the only protection we've got.'

'There they are!' shouted a man's voice.

A fraction of a second later, a shotgun blast rang out and the windows of the JCB shattered.

'We have to move,' said Bailey.

Wrenching themselves to their feet, they ran onwards, further into the heart of the building site, Bailey hoping somehow to locate an alternative way out.

Ahead of them, she saw three large white cylinders, horizontal tanks positioned side-by-side. Maybe behind those there would be something. Pulling Jennifer after her, she squeezed between the tanks...

... and found that they'd reached the water's edge, the undulating black surface of the river stretching out before them.

It was a dead end.

'Go back,' hissed Bailey.

They turned on their heels and started to retrace their steps when Shane appeared from around the corner of a nearby Portakabin.

His eyes widened when he saw them. 'They're here!' he bellowed. Moments later, a cluster of thugs poured around the corner to join him.

The two sisters ran back behind the cylinders and crouched down. Bailey gritted her teeth in frustration. They were trapped.

'Chuck the grenade,' urged Jennifer.

Bailey looked down at the grenade in her hand. It looked like the time had come to use it. She took a deep breath and pulled her arm back.

She was just about to throw it when she heard Shane shout: 'Shit! They're behind the LPG tanks. Don't shoot at them or you'll blow the tanks and wreck the whole fucking place.'

Bailey froze. She glanced at one of the large tanks. The words 'Liquefied Petroleum Gas' were stencilled in large letters on the side and below that was a warning sticker that said 'Highly Flammable'. She guessed that the fuel in the tanks probably served some purpose related to the construction work going on here.

'Fuck!' she hissed, lowering her arm.

'What?' whispered Jennifer impatiently.

'If I throw this grenade at them, the shrapnel will hit the tanks and blow them up, killing us as well.'

Jennifer looked at the tanks and cursed.

Bailey peeked over the top of the cylinder. She could see the Molloy crew closing in warily. The gas tanks had bought them a fraction more time, but it was running out fast. She looked around desperately.

'Let's jump in the river. Swim to safety.'

Jennifer shook her head. 'We'd be sitting ducks. They'd shoot us to pieces before we got ten feet.'

Bailey knew her sister was right. It looked like all their options had run out. They were truly cornered. Maybe they were both going to die after all.

Then Jennifer's eyes narrowed as if an idea had occurred to her.

'Give me the grenade,' she hissed.

'What are you going to do?' said Bailey.

'Just give me the damn bomb, okay.'

She grabbed Bailey's wrist and, firmly holding down the release lever, started to prise the grenade out of Bailey's hand.

Bailey resisted, clutching the grenade tightly.

'Trust me,' whispered Jennifer, looking deep into Bailey's eyes.

And in that moment Bailey was transported back to their childhood all those years ago when Jennifer would lead her on those fantastical adventures with Mister Snigiss. Her sister had that same look in her eyes right now – that enigmatic certainty that always induced Bailey to follow her.

Bailey sagged and let her take the grenade.

Jennifer smiled at her, then she stood up and poked her head over the top of the gas cylinder.

'What are you waiting for, you pussies!' she shouted.

'Come out and surrender!' shouted Shane.

'We'll never surrender!' shouted Jennifer. 'Never!'

Jennifer ducked back down behind the cylinder and turned to Bailey.

'I never forgot you, Bailey. Through all the pain and the darkness and everything that came after... I never once forgot you.'

Then, with a hard shove, she pushed Bailey backwards into the water.

Bailey plunged into the freezing river, stunned not only by the arctic shock of the water but by the unexpectedness of her sister's actions.

She surfaced, coughing and gasping, the icy current already pulling her downstream, away from the building development.

Moments later, there was a deafening explosion as the three gas tanks erupted into a massive fireball engulfing that whole section of the building development. She felt the scorching heat of the blast on her face as it rolled across the water.

'Jennifer!' she gasped.

No one in the vicinity could have made it out of there alive. Not Shane. Nor any of the thugs. And not her sister either.

Bailey gaped in horror, the emotions tearing her apart inside as she floated away down the river, realising that Jennifer had deliberately detonated the grenade and sacrificed herself in order to save her younger sister.

It had been their final adventure and now Mister Snigiss, invisible for so long, had truly disappeared forever.

84

A morning mist lay across the surface of the Thames. Soon it would burn off for the sun was already bright in the sky. Despite the brisk edge to the air, it was looking like it might turn out to be a very nice day.

The building site was now a massive crime scene, taped off and under investigation. The raging fire which had enveloped the place the previous night had been put out and the blackened aftermath was being picked over by a multitude of police and other emergency personnel.

Even though it was now the next morning, Bailey still hadn't left the scene despite the police telling her she didn't need to be there, and the paramedics telling her she should really have a rest and a change of clothes following her immersion in the freezing river. Brushing aside all of their objections, she had firmly insisted on staying there until she received some news of Jennifer. She was now sitting on the bumper of a large concrete mixer lorry, glumly watching the emergency workers as they poked through the ashes with rakes and shovels in the search for further human remains. So far they'd found the charred corpses of a number of men, but nothing resembling the body of a woman in her early thirties. However, some of the remains they were finding, particularly those close to the epicentre of the explosion where the heat had been most intense, were so badly burnt that proper identification would prove to be extremely difficult, if not impossible.

With no body yet found, was there still hope for Jennifer? Could she still be alive somehow? More than anything, Bailey would have liked to believe so, but she'd seen that inferno with her own eyes and she knew there was no way that Jennifer could have survived.

With a sad sigh, she tried to think what she'd tell her parents. She couldn't even begin to contemplate how she would start to explain it all to them. The more she thought about it, the more she realised that it would be better that they never knew. Sitting there in the morning sun, she made the difficult decision not to tell them. And if her father did ask about Mister Snigiss, as he was wont to do, she would just have to grit her teeth and tell him that her search had so far been fruitless, but that she'd keep on with the quest all the same, even after he passed away. It galled her to have to lie to him like this, but sometimes a lie was the best option when you had someone else's interests at heart.

Bailey's mind turned to the Molloys with a cold rage. Nancy, Rick, Stephen... she was pretty certain that they'd survived the blast, and that they would have evaporated into the night as soon as it became apparent that the explosion would bring the emergency services down on the place. Already their construction company was touting the line that it was an industrial accident caused by trespassers on the development. Bailey knew that whatever she might say to the contrary, trying to prove it would be another thing entirely.

She kicked the heel of her boot morosely at the bumper of the lorry. Rick was going to get away with it again. Just like he would with those guns. She recalled with a rising bile that today was the day he was due to pick them up... wherever they were. She glanced at the date on her watch. It was Friday the eighth of March.

In her mind, she could visualise him there right now, overseeing the delivery of big piles of weapons, gloating in the knowledge that there was fuck all that anyone could do about it...

Staring out despondently at the river, she watched the big container boats chugging slowly to and from the port on the other side. She idly followed one with her gaze, a massive blue freighter with the name 'Sirena' painted in white letters high up on its bow.

She afforded herself a small glum smile. It seemed incongruous that such a big, heavy, masculine thing like that freighter should have such a feminine name, but then it occurred to her that boats were always given female names—

Her breath stopped in her throat as a bolt of insight hit her.

Kaia.

Wendy had talked about Rick meeting someone called Kaia in Torquay. She'd overheard him on the phone. And she'd seen it written in his diary... on Friday the eighth of March.

Bailey looked at her watch again just to double-check.

Today was indeed Friday the eighth of March.

Wendy had assumed Rick was spending a dirty weekend in Torquay with this woman, Kaia. But now that Bailey thought about it, the transaction she'd been planning with him had been due to take place on the ninth of March, the day afterwards... and would Rick really have been conducting the sale of a large quantity of firearms right in the middle of his dirty weekend?

He'd smugly told her that the guns were coming in, as planned, the day before he'd been due to sell them to her.

So as for what Wendy had heard him talking about on the phone, rather than boasting to his mates about a mistress, had he actually been talking business and referring to a boat that was carrying guns? Torquay did have a harbour, after all. And Bailey knew how Rick liked to camouflage his business talk over the phone. It would have been so easy for Wendy to misinterpret...

Bailey's heart beat hard in excitement. She was sure of it now. The guns were coming into the UK today on a boat called Kaia and Torquay was the place where it was going to dock.

She looked at her watch again. It was still early. There might just be time.

Jumping to her feet, she hurriedly went in search of a phone to call her contact at the National Crime Agency.

85

Bailey sat by her father's bedside in the hospice, her hand resting on his, watching his chest gently rise up and down. It was hard to tell if he was asleep or awake, his eyelids fluttering softly as he drifted in and out of consciousness. Her mother sat on the other side of the bed, a Bible in her hand as always, looking down at her dying husband with an expression of wistful affection on her drawn face.

It was Monday morning, just a few days after the events at the building development. Working off Bailey's tip, the NCA had swooped on a fishing trawler called Kaia that had sailed from Dieppe to Torquay. They had arrived at the harbour just in time, armed police in black balaclavas dramatically storming the scene.

On the trawler, they had discovered one hundred and twenty brand-new seven-point-six-two-millimetre CZ 805 BREN assault rifles, one hundred and forty brand-new nine-millimetre K100 pistols, seventy silencers and one hundred and thirty thousand rounds of assorted ammunition. It was exactly the arsenal of weaponry that Rick been planning to sell to her.

With a shipment of this size and importance, the main players often liked to be present and Rick had been no exception in this respect. He had been there to meet the boat. And he had been arrested, along with the crew of the trawler. However, none of the other key members of the Molloy family had been captured with him. Nancy, for one thing, had retired from attending these kinds of meetings. Shane, Bailey was certain, had died in the explosion at the building site, although his body had yet to be formally identified. And as for Stephen, he had either been indisposed for some reason, or just plain lucky not to have been there. Nevertheless, to have netted Rick was still a major result.

He'd been charged with a variety of offences, including the illegal importation of firearms into the UK and being part of a conspiracy to supply firearms, as well as leading and coordinating the activities of a large-scale organised crime group. No lawyer, however expensive, was going to be able to get him off the hook for this one. He'd been caught red-handed and he was looking at a major stretch inside before any chance of parole. It was a significant coup and one that could conceivably spell the end of the Molloy crime family.

Perhaps.

Or perhaps not.

Nancy Molloy was still at liberty, and knowing the vindictive old matriarch as she did, Bailey imagined that she was stewing somewhere plotting her revenge, probably with Stephen's enthusiastic assistance. When it came to reprisals, Bailey was less concerned for herself and more for her parents, her mother in particular. Her father wouldn't be around for too much longer but her mother would still be potentially vulnerable to harm... if Nancy Molloy or her underlings found out a way to get to her. But would they really stoop so low as to harm a 'civilian' like her mother in order to get back at Bailey?

Bailey attempted to push the worrying thoughts from her mind for the time being and focus her attention on her father. All she cared about right now was being with him as much as possible before he left them forever.

She stroked his hand lovingly. His skin had taken on a papery parchment-like feel and he seemed semi-substantial somehow, as if he had already passed halfway into whatever came next.

She knew that he was drawing very close to the end of his life. Maybe today would be the day that he finally passed away. It seemed now that every day could be that day.

After a while, she and her mother stood up to stretch their legs and get a coffee.

'We're just going to get a coffee, Dad,' said Bailey gently, not knowing if he could even hear her.

His eyes opened briefly, and a weak smile flickered across his face, then he closed them once more, lapsing back into whatever oblivion he'd been in. Leaving him like that, they both left the room and walked slowly along the corridor of the hospice in the direction of the café.

The hospice hummed quietly with activity – doctors and nurses trotting back and forth dressed in scrubs, cleaners wheeling trolleys laden with cleaning paraphernalia, patients limping along in their dressing gowns. It all seemed so reassuringly mundane to Bailey. After what she'd been through over the past week or so, she welcomed a bit of normality.

Eventually they reached the café, where Bailey bought coffee for both herself and her mother. They both sat there for a little while, sipping the scalding drinks, Bailey's mother enquiring yet again about her black eye and Bailey yet again trying to avoid going into too much detail as to how it had come about; at least the bruising was starting to go down now.

Physical injuries aside, the past few days had seen Bailey accustoming herself to finding and then losing her sister. She knew it would take some time to come to terms with the whole tumultuous experience, and as she sat there in the café with her mother, it saddened her to be unable to share her feelings about it.

After twenty minutes or so, they ambled slowly back to her father's room.

When they got there, they saw that his eyes were wide open and that he was awake. It was the first time all morning that he'd been properly awake. Looking closer, Bailey saw that he had tears in his eyes.

'What's the matter, Dad?' she said anxiously.

He blinked at them both and swallowed. By the alertness in his gaze, Bailey could tell that he was having a rare moment of lucidity.

'You know, a weird thing happened to me just now,' he said, his voice laboured. 'I had a vision, after you'd gone...'

Bailey and her mother exchanged glances. They both leaned in.

Her father's eyes glowed in an unearthly way and a dreamlike smile came across his face. 'In my vision, Jennifer came into the room. She was all grown up. She was beautiful. A woman. My Jennifer.'

A powerful shiver went through Bailey.

'It must be the drugs,' said her mother. 'Didn't the doctor say that high dosages can make you see funny things?'

He frowned and shook his head. 'It was so real. I can't explain how real it was. But then with this dexamethasone stuff, I don't know if I'm coming or going. They're giving me so much of it these days...'

He smiled up at them with something approaching pure happiness in his eyes.

'She stroked my hand, you know. And then she said goodbye. And she left.'

A tear fell from his eye and rolled down his cheek.

Bailey bit her lip to try and stop emotion from overwhelming her. Had Jennifer somehow survived? She could barely believe it. Surely not. It was impossible. This had to be nothing more than a psychosis brought about by the effects of the dexamethasone.

All the same, a tiny seed of doubt now assailed her...

Either way, she knew she could never tell her father the whole truth of the matter. So instead she squeezed his hand and looked into his eyes.

'Wherever Jennifer is,' she said, 'she loves you.'

86

Wendy Molloy did not particularly enjoy coming to visit the prison where her husband was being held. Sitting there in the noisy visiting hall waiting for him to appear, she observed the other visitors with a certain amount of distaste. They really weren't her kind of people.

However, coming here was something she was duty-bound to do. After all, she was still married to Rick and that being the case, she was determined to stick by him through all of this.

When she'd realised that Kaia wasn't a mistress and that her husband, to her knowledge, hadn't been unfaithful, she'd felt a massive sense of relief, like a weight had been lifted from her shoulders. Not only had she felt bad for ever doubting his fidelity, it had actually served to reinforce her love for him, and she had subsequently discarded the whole idea of a divorce.

So, in a funny way, this whole thing had been good for them. There was, of course, the slight issue of him being here in prison. He was currently being held on remand whilst the Crown Prosecution Service put together a case against him, and from what she understood, it was going to be a big trial.

Whatever the outcome, she was certain he'd get through it. And so would she, although her mother had warned her that she might end up having to move out of the mansion if Rick was found guilty and the authorities decided to confiscate his assets under the Proceeds of Crime Act. But when it came to surviving, Wendy was sure she'd be able to soldier through things one way or another. At the very least, the beauty salon was doing decent enough business to keep some kind of roof over her head.

As she waited there, she tried to anticipate what he'd want to talk about today. He'd want to know about his two dogs and if she was taking proper care of them, that was for sure. And she was hoping he'd notice and comment on her nails. She'd painted them maroon especially for today's visit, because she knew it was one of his favourite colours.

He probably wouldn't want to talk about the court case though, even if she asked him about it, because even now he refrained from telling her anything about his business dealings. So saying, she was curious about how he'd been caught in the end, especially considering how careful she knew he was. Somehow, somewhere, he must have made some kind of slip-up.

Still, what was done was done.

Wendy sighed, her train of thought idly wandering onto other things, such as the importance of having a good friend by her side, especially over the next few months. And with that notion in mind, she suddenly remembered Bailey with a mild perk of interest. Wendy wondered what she was up to these days. She'd seemed like such a nice person. A great person to chat to. Such a good listener...

87

Bailey sat on the sofa in the living room of her Crystal Palace flat and watched as the sudden rainstorm hit, the droplets spattering down on the concrete of the tiny patio outside the window of her basement abode. It had been clear and sunny just a minute ago and now it was raining hard. But then it was the middle of April and the weather could be so changeable during this time of year... a bit like her mood at the moment.

The funeral service for Dennis Morgan had taken place at Beckenham Crematorium two days earlier. His passing had come fairly quickly in the end, and both Bailey and her mother had been present at his bedside when the light had finally gone out of his eyes. Since his 'vision' of Jennifer, he'd been strangely at peace, for not once since then had he mentioned either her or Mister Snigiss again, and Bailey had the reassuring feeling that it was this experience as much as the painkillers that had helped to ease his passing.

All the same, she felt a profound sadness at her father's death which touched the very depths of her soul. One moment she'd be feeling normal and the next she'd be gripped by unbearable pangs of grief. It was a painful process, but one which she knew she had to go through if she was to eventually heal and get over it. On the positive side, it was bringing her closer than ever to her mother as Bailey helped her to sort out her husband's affairs.

Despite all this, Bailey was still considerably occupied on the work front. The week before, she'd attended yet another meeting with the Directorate of Professional Standards to provide more evidence on Dale's corruption. The internal enquiry into the extent of his activities was going to open up a lot of uncomfortable questions, but either way, Bailey was determined to see that he got the posthumous disgrace that he deserved.

And as for Rick Molloy, she'd soon be testifying against him in his upcoming trial, from a position of confidentiality, of course, as an undercover police officer. With the work she'd done to get him captured, it looked certain that Rick would be convicted of the crimes for which he'd been charged. The lawyers from the Crown Prosecution Service were already discussing the likelihood of a thirty-year sentence. Frank would be most pleased about that.

Bailey had been visiting Frank regularly in the hospital since he'd been shot and was both delighted and immensely grateful to see that he was making a slow but steady recovery from his injuries. But it would be a while yet before he was in any state to return to work.

There were a few things still left undone, however. Picking up her purse which was lying next to her on the sofa, Bailey opened it and took out the picture of Mister Snigiss, the one drawn by an eight-year-old Jennifer over twenty-four years ago. She unfolded the fragile piece of paper and examined the stick figures in the crude felt-tip drawing for the last time. Mister Snigiss... His pet snake, Sid... Jennifer... Bailey...

As a physical item, it was so insubstantial, yet it represented so much. But the time had come to finally put it where it belonged. In the past. She stood up, walked into the kitchen, opened the kitchen drawer, took out a box of matches, lit one and put it to the corner of the drawing. Holding the burning picture over the kitchen sink, she watched as the flame consumed it, the felt-tip stick figures curling and wrinkling as the thin dry paper turned rapidly into ash. When the flame reached her fingers, she dropped it into the sink, letting it burn completely and totally into nothing. Turning on the tap, she washed the ashes down the plughole.

She emerged from the kitchen and walked over to the desk in the corner of the living room. Standing on the desk was a laptop lying open with an unsent email on the screen that she'd composed a short while earlier. The email was anonymous and it was addressed to a number of major news organisations. Attached to the email was the MPEG4 file of Tiffany's sex tape featuring Lewis Ballantyne.

Bailey had seen on TV that Ballantyne was streets ahead of the other candidates in the polls and an almost dead cert to win in the London mayoral elections, which were due to take place in just under a month's time in early May. If he got to be Mayor of London, there was every possibility that one day he could end up as Prime Minister of Britain, and already the political pundits were entertaining that very likelihood.

Bailey was ninety-nine per cent sure that Jennifer had died in the blast at the building development in Gravesend. But the element of doubt seeded by her father's dying hallucinations had been increasingly niggling at her. If Jennifer was alive, however minuscule the possibility, Bailey couldn't allow her to be in the position to manipulate the Mayor of London, and potentially the future leader of the UK.

Sending the sex tape to the media would have seismic repercussions and almost certainly destroy Ballantyne's chances of winning the mayoral election and probably end his political career for good. Taking Ballantyne out of the mayoral race would, at least for the time being, neutralise Jennifer's ambitions in that area. The Met's top brass, of course, would be deeply dismayed by the whole thing. But what did they know?

Bailey's finger hovered over the 'send' button as she was hit by a sudden wave of doubt. She wondered if she was being paranoid. Jennifer alive? Of course she wasn't.

But then on the other hand... better safe than sorry.

Bailey clicked the 'send' button on the email, sat back in the chair and waited for the shit to hit the fan.

ACKNOWLEDGMENTS

All of the team at Boldwood Books for their exceptional and meticulous work at all stages of the publication process and their boundless drive and enthusiasm in successfully bringing this novel to market.

Dorie Simmonds, my agent, for her unfailingly good advice, professional acumen and willingness to provide incisive and comprehensive feedback on my writing.

Dr Malcolm Campbell for his invaluable information about the medicine and procedures surrounding cancer treatment and end-of-life care.

Claire, my wife, for her unstinting support, sparkling company and her outstanding and honest appraisal of my work.

I read plenty of non-fiction books as part of my research into this novel. If I were to pick out a few to recommend, then *Good Cop, Bad War* by Neil Woods, *Undercover* by Joe Carter, and *Undercover* by Pete Ashton are all fascinating reads in terms of understanding the mindset and dangers involved in undercover policing, and the books of Wensley Clarkson provide a gripping and informative insight into the landscape and characters of the UK underworld.

MORE FROM CARO SAVAGE

We hope you enjoyed reading *Villain*. If you did, please leave a review.

If you'd like to gift a copy, this book is also available as an ebook, digital audio download and audiobook CD.

Sign up to Caro Savages's mailing list for news, competitions and updates on future books.

http://bit.ly/CaroSavageNewsletter

Jailbird, the first instalment in the Detective Constable Bailey Morgan series, is available to order now.

ABOUT THE AUTHOR

Caro Savage knows all about bestselling thrillers having worked as a Waterstones bookseller for 12 years in a previous life. Now taking up the challenge personally and turning to hard-hitting crime thriller writing.

Follow Caro on social media:

twitter.com/CaroSavageStory

instagram.com/carosavage

bookbub.com/authors/caro-savage

ABOUT BOLDWOOD BOOKS

Boldwood Books is a fiction publishing company seeking out the best stories from around the world.

Find out more at www.boldwoodbooks.com

Sign up to the Book and Tonic newsletter for news, offers and competitions from Boldwood Books!

http://www.bit.ly/bookandtonic

We'd love to hear from you, follow us on social media:

facebook.com/BookandTonic

twitter.com/BoldwoodBooks

instagram.com/BookandTonic

Lightning Source UK Ltd.
Milton Keynes UK
UKHW041126230822
407677UK00003B/447